D1321227

The Archers

THE AMBRIDGE CHRONICLES
PART THREE

Back to the Land

1987-2000

JOANNA TOYE

BBC

For Vanessa, with love and thanks.

This book is published to accompany
the BBC Radio 4 serial entitled *The Archers*.
The Editor of *The Archers* is Vanessa Whitburn.

Published by BBC Worldwide Ltd,
Woodlands, 80 Wood Lane, London W12 0TT

First published 2000

ISBN 0 563 53701 9

Commissioning Editor: Emma Shackleton
Project Editors: Lara Speicher and Erica Jeal
Designed by Tim Higgins
Text set in Adobe Plantin and New Caledonia Semi Bold Italic
by Keystroke, Jacaranda Lodge, Wolverhampton
Printed and bound in Great Britain by Butler & Tanner Ltd,
Frome and London
Jacket printed by Lawrence-Allen Ltd, Weston-super-Mare

Contents

Contents

Acknowledgements

With every successive book, the list of acknowledgements is in danger of getting longer and longer and I apologize unreservedly to anyone I've left out. First of all, I must thank the Editor of *The Archers*, Vanessa Whitburn, for her consistent support throughout the writing of this trilogy, and the stalwart assistance of her production team, chiefly Senior Producer, Keri Davies, and Archivist, Camilla Fisher. At BBC Worldwide, my Project Editor for all three books was Lara Speicher, with additional input latterly from Erica Jeal. The staff of BBC Written Archives at Caversham were a great help in accessing past script material by David Ashton, Tony Bagley, Sam Boardman-Jacobs, Paul Brodrick, Mary Cutler, Adrian Flynn, Simon Frith, Rob Gittins, Caroline Harrington, Graham Harvey, Christopher Hawes, Christine Ingram, Peter Kerry, Christopher Lee, Brendan Martin, Mick Martin, Louise Page, Emily Potts, Janey Preger, Chris Thompson and Sally Wainwright, and I'd like to thank them all for allowing their work to be reproduced in part.

Closer to home, thanks are due to my father, John Skinner: his love and support have been invaluable. Also to John Evans, who wanted to remain anonymous. Sorry. Most of all, though, I'd like to thank my daughter, Livy, who for all of her life has had to share me with my adopted family in Ambridge.

Joanna Toye
July 2000

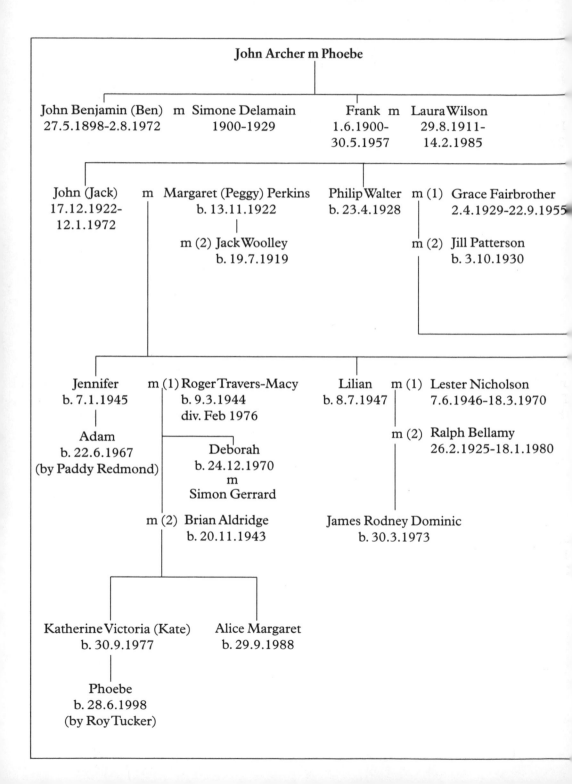

John Archer m Phoebe

John Benjamin (Ben) m Simone Delamain   Frank m Laura Wilson
27.5.1898-2.8.1972   1900-1929   1.6.1900-   29.8.1911-
                                                    30.5.1957   14.2.1985

John (Jack) m Margaret (Peggy) Perkins   Philip Walter m (1) Grace Fairbrother
17.12.1922-   b. 13.11.1922   b. 23.4.1928   2.4.1929-22.9.1955
12.1.1972
                  m (2) Jack Woolley   m (2) Jill Patterson
                        b. 19.7.1919   b. 3.10.1930

Jennifer m (1) Roger Travers-Macy   Lilian m (1) Lester Nicholson
b. 7.1.1945   b. 9.3.1944   b. 8.7.1947   7.6.1946-18.3.1970
                  div. Feb 1976
                                                     m (2) Ralph Bellamy
Adam   26.2.1925-18.1.1980
b. 22.6.1967   Deborah
(by Paddy Redmond) b. 24.12.1970
                        m
                  Simon Gerrard

       m (2) Brian Aldridge   James Rodney Dominic
             b. 20.11.1943   b. 30.3.1973

Katherine Victoria (Kate)   Alice Margaret
    b. 30.9.1977   b. 29.9.1988

    Phoebe
  b. 28.6.1998
  (by Roy Tucker)

amily Tree

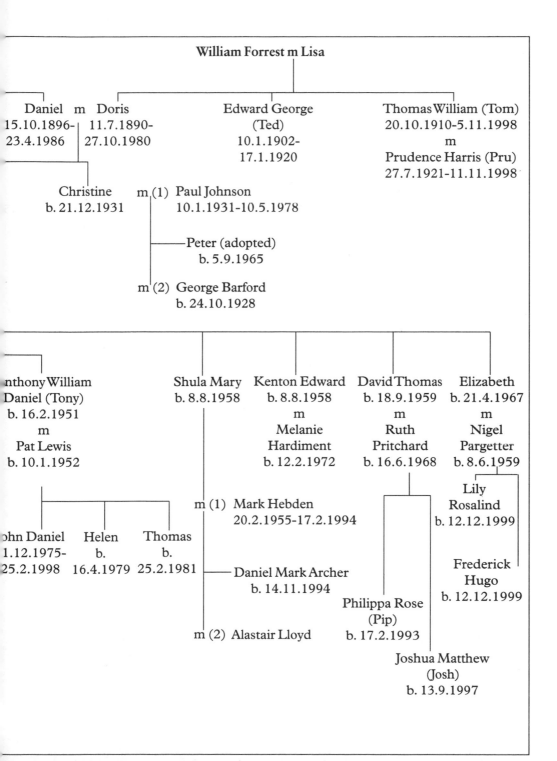

William Forrest m Lisa

Daniel m Doris
15.10.1896-   11.7.1890-
23.4.1986   27.10.1980

Edward George
(Ted)
10.1.1902-
17.1.1920

Thomas William (Tom)
20.10.1910-5.11.1998
m
Prudence Harris (Pru)
27.7.1921-11.11.1998

Christine   m (1) Paul Johnson
b. 21.12.1931   10.1.1931-10.5.1978

———Peter (adopted)
       b. 5.9.1965

m (2) George Barford
       b. 24.10.1928

nthony William   Shula Mary   Kenton Edward   David Thomas   Elizabeth
Daniel (Tony)   b. 8.8.1958   b. 8.8.1958   b. 18.9.1959   b. 21.4.1967
b. 16.2.1951   m   m   m
m   Melanie   Ruth   Nigel
Pat Lewis   Hardiment   Pritchard   Pargetter
b. 10.1.1952   b. 12.2.1972   b. 16.6.1968   b. 8.6.1959

                                                                            Lily
                        m (1) Mark Hebden   Rosalind
                               20.2.1955-17.2.1994   b. 12.12.1999

ohn Daniel   Helen   Thomas
1.12.1975-   b.   b.
25.2.1998   16.4.1979 25.2.1981   Frederick
                        ———— Daniel Mark Archer   Hugo
                               b. 14.11.1994   b. 12.12.1999

                                                      Philippa Rose
                                                      (Pip)
                        m (2) Alastair Lloyd   b. 17.2.1993

                                                      Joshua Matthew
                                                      (Josh)
                                                      b. 13.9.1997

·1·

The Heir Apparent

'Phil, I don't want any arguments. You're staying in bed.'

'But Jill . . .' Her husband glanced fretfully at the clock. 'David'll have finished the milking by now. He's got to look in on the calf that was scouring, there's the cubicles to be mucked out and fodder taken out to the ewes –'

'He's got Graham. And Jethro'll be here in a minute.'

Outside the January rain thudded against the slates of the barn. Jill sighed. Who'd be a farmer?

'Graham's at the dentist this morning,' replied Phil, referring to Brookfield's cowman. 'No, I'll have to get up.'

But the action of lifting himself up in bed made him wince and he dropped back, defeated.

'I did tell you to wait for David before you dealt with that heifer last night,' scolded Jill. 'It's no wonder you've put your back out. I'm going to phone the surgery as soon as it opens.'

Resigned, Phil gave a sigh. 'I think you'll have to. But get David to come up when he's had breakfast, will you?'

'Mum!' David shouted up the stairs. 'Where are the plasters?'

'Oh, Lord,' groaned his father. 'What now?'

'I think there are some in the dresser!' Already on her way, Jill flapped her hand to silence Phil. 'Why, what have you done?'

'Cut my hand on the drain cover,' yelled David over the sound of a dresser drawer being tugged open. 'And there's nothing in the first-aid box.'

Jill went downstairs to find her son churning through the dresser drawers with his left hand while the right one dripped blood.

'I'll find you one,' she said, turning on the tap and taking charge. 'Stick it under here.'

David did as he was told.

'Another day in paradise,' he said morosely, watching the tap water swirl red down the plughole, and tadpoles of rain trail their long tails across the window. 'Ow, it stings. The yard's under eighteen inches of water,' he went on. 'The main drain's blocked and I can't find the rods, the door to the parlour's off its hinges and there's no sign of the milk tanker – or Jethro, for that matter. Honestly, the sooner he retires, the –'

There was a rat-a-tat on the back door. It opened and the gnome-like face of Phil's farm worker, Jethro Larkin, appeared round it.

'Morning, Mrs Archer, Master David.'

'Come in and shut the door, Jethro,' urged Jill. 'It's such a filthy morning.'

'Right you are.'

'Jethro, do you know what time it is?' David interrupted the civilities. 'You said you'd be here early.'

Jethro pulled a face of pantomimic doom.

'That was afore I knew about the wind. My eye! Just like –'

'Never mind the wind,' David broke in, before Jethro could begin the litany of storms he had known. 'Have you seen the water in the yard? What have you done with the drain rods?'

'Oh, we've got a worse problem than the water, Master David,' said Jethro with undisguised relish.

David held out his hand, while Jill tried to decide which was the best way to bandage the cut, which was, of course, in the most awkward place.

'Go on, make my day.'

'The wind's brought down that big old ash by the gate.' There was nothing Jethro liked more than being the bearer of bad news. 'She must have been more'n a hundred years old and now she's laying across the track like . . . like some . . . like some big . . .'

'Tree?' offered Jill.

'Like some big giant.' Jethro was pleased with the comparison, as drinkers in his local, The Bull, would no doubt be able to testify that evening, when he repeated it for the fiftieth time. 'I've had to leave the van and walk up.'

'Oh, brilliant, and I suppose it's brought the fence down with it.' David flexed his hand. 'Mum, I don't think this plaster's going to last five minutes. Anything else, Jethro, while you're at it? Meteorite fallen on the pig unit, perhaps? Spontaneous combustion in the haybarn?'

Jethro gave it some thought.

'Not as I noticed. Mind, it's still pretty dark out there.'

David heaved a hopeless sigh.

'Come on, then, let's make a start.'

'Er . . . not yet, David.' There was never going to be a right time for Jill to deliver her news. 'I'm afraid your father won't be getting up today. His back's gone.'

And it went on like that all day. Who, indeed, would be a farmer, as Jill said to Shula when she called in for a cup of tea that afternoon.

Jill and Phil's twin daughter worked for a local estate agent, Rodway and Watson, and over the years, this had brought many distinct advantages. Shula could often manage to squeeze in five minutes at Brookfield between measuring up a house or meeting prospective purchasers, and now that she was working a couple of days a week as agent for the Estate, which was owned by her cousin Lilian, she was even more available for tea and sympathy.

'The milk tanker couldn't get in because of the tree, so we had to use the emergency tank, and Elizabeth couldn't get her car out to get to work,' Jill explained, cutting Shula a slice of cake. 'It's Jennifer's recipe, the one with the Earl Grey tea,' she added.

'Thanks, Mum.' Shula took the proffered plate. 'No hardship for her, I suppose.' Shula's younger sister had started at the local paper, the *Borchester Echo*, as a tele-ad girl back in the autumn, but she was already writing the odd column and restaurant review.

'No,' agreed Jill, 'she just told them she was researching a story and went back to bed with a magazine.' She cut herself a smaller slice. 'And then Sophie came round and held up David and Jethro when they were trying to put the parlour door back on, and then she held me up worrying about this job she's been offered in London . . .'

'I can't see Sophie in London, can you?' Shula smiled through a sip of tea. David's fiancée was ethereally beautiful and endearingly dippy. 'Imagine her trying to decode the tube map.'

'This fashion company must want her if they've asked her for a second time. Anyway, she's agreed now. She starts on Monday.' Jill poured them both a cup of tea: the Brookfield kettle was rarely off the boil. 'Then the doctor came out to see your father and the minute he'd gone – typical – David cut his hand again, on the chainsaw this time, just picking it up. So I had to drive him into Borchester General to have it stitched.'

'Oh, Mum! What a day!'

Jill nodded wryly.

David was the third generation of the Archer family to farm at Brookfield. When Jill and Phil had married, Phil's parents, Dan and Doris, had been living and working there, and Doris had warned Jill from the start what she was taking on in marrying a farmer. Still, frustrating as it was on days like this, Jill knew deep down that she loved her life. She was proud of the job she'd done over the years supporting Phil on the farm and bringing up their four children.

'Joyous, isn't it?' she reflected. 'And your father's going to be laid up for a while yet, so I can't see David having much time to miss Sophie, can you?'

Sophie, if in Timbuctu rather than Tooting, couldn't have been further from David's thoughts as he stood in the function room of The Bull a couple of weeks later.

The last nine months had been tough ones for Brookfield – the toughest David had known since he'd finished at Agricultural College and had come back to work for his father four years previously. Last April, his grandfather, Dan, had died, and on inheriting the farm, Phil had found himself liable for a huge amount of Capital Gains Tax. He'd come up with several abortive plans to pay it off, but in the end he'd concluded that the only way was to sell off some land. It was the thing that farmers most hated doing, but he had no alternative, and tonight the auction was taking place. If all went as planned, by the end of the evening Brookfield would be reduced by eighty-five acres.

'It's like a funeral,' David muttered to Shula's husband, Mark, who was acting as Brookfield's solicitor. 'With the entire village turning out to see how the chief mourners are taking it.'

'Oh, come on, it's not that bad.'

'It's pure entertainment for most of them,' David protested. 'Joe Grundy! Mike Tucker! They're not going to be bidding, are they?'

'Most of the serious bidders won't show up anyway,' advised Mark. 'They'll have an agent to do it for them.'

David raised a hand in greeting to a friend of his father's from Waterley Cross.

'I'm not enjoying this,' he said. 'I thought when the day came round it'd be a relief, but it feels like the vultures are gathering.'

'Look,' said Mark. 'The auctioneer knows his stuff. You've set a reasonable reserve. OK, it's not the best time to be selling land, but what choice have you got?'

'None whatsoever,' admitted David. He loosened his tie. He didn't know how Mark could bear to wear one to work every day. 'You're right. Let's just hope we get shot of it to someone who knows about farming.' He glanced across the room to where a woman with a piercing voice was trying to persuade the village elders, Mrs Perkins and Walter Gabriel, to move along to make space for herself and her husband. 'One Lynda Snell in this village is more than enough.'

In the end, after all the agonizing, the auction was only a qualified success.

The land had been divided into two lots. One lot of fifty-five acres went for £77,000 to a Mr Burgess from Felpersham, but since he was acting on behalf of the real buyer, no one was any the wiser. It also remained to be seen whether the land would be cultivated or whether it was purely an investment for some sharp-suited city trader who'd prospered under Mrs Thatcher and had turned his eye to the land in case the market in blue-chip stocks suddenly crashed. Worse still, a further thirty acres that Phil had offered for sale failed to reach the reserve, not just by a couple of thousand, but by £12,000, which would have meant a selling price of under £1000 an acre. Shocked and disappointed, Phil had withdrawn them from sale, which meant he still couldn't meet the tax debt and, tainted with failure, the land could linger on the market for ages.

So, when it could have been a positive comfort, had it been done differently, it came as a further blow to the family when, a few days later, David saw one of Home Farm's bulldozers ripping out a hedge on the recently sold land.

'I suppose we should have guessed, really.' Mark, who'd just come in from work, tugged off his tie and threw it down. He didn't really like wearing them any more than David. 'If the Snells weren't the buyers, it had to be Brian.'

Shula nodded. Robert Snell, who was a computer wizard, and his wife Lynda who, appropriately, many felt to be a bit of a witch, had bought Ambridge Hall, which had once belonged to Phil's Aunt Laura, last year. The Snells were part of the growing trend for town-dwellers to move to the countryside, and they were perfect examples of why villagers so hated it. Lynda had hardly unpacked when she'd fallen out with Brian Aldridge about the state of his footpaths and a consequent tear to her immaculate waxed jacket: she then tangled with Eddie Grundy, who'd tried to frighten her with his party trick of producing his favourite ferret from inside his shirt. She'd also, with the typical hypocrisy of the incomer, given Phil a hard time when a building consortium had seemed interested in buying some of the land he'd put up for sale.

Anyway, now they knew. The land hadn't gone for housing, and it hadn't gone to the Snells. It had gone to Brian, who was married to Shula's cousin, Jennifer. Which was keeping it in the family, really.

'What hurts, though,' said Shula, pouring pasta into a pan of water, 'is his being so secretive. It's all very well for Jennifer to say he was just being businesslike, but he could have come along after the auction and told Mum and Dad it was him. I mean, what a way to find out.'

'Hmm.' Mark poured them both a glass of wine. 'And I thought farmers were planting hedges nowadays, not ripping them out.'

'Not Brian,' said Shula, taking her glass. 'It's expand, expand, expand.'

Whereas at Brookfield, she thought, watching their supper bubble, it was contract, contract, contract. With some of the tax bill still left to pay, her father was fretting about spreading the farm overheads over 465 acres instead of 520 – or 435 if they ever got shot of the remaining thirty acres. There was serious talk now about Jethro retiring – not just David's wishful thinking – and even about the cowman, Graham Collard, having to go. It was a tough time altogether to be in farming: under siege from the green lobby on one side and politicians on the other, farmers had probably never felt so vulnerable.

Still, Shula thought, there was one glimmer of hope that her parents didn't yet know about. Nelson Gabriel, wine bar proprietor, antique dealer and entrepreneur, had popped in to see her at Rodway's that afternoon. He had a builder friend, he said, who might be interested in the land – or some of it. Not for a housing development. No, no, he'd assured her, something far more fitting, and in sympathy with the natural environment.

'You're starting to sound like a estate agent,' Shula had observed astutely. 'What are you up to?'

Nelson's face assumed an expression of pained reproach.

'Why is everyone always so suspicious of me?'

'The unsolved Borchester mail-van robbery, for a start,' said Shula crisply. 'Let alone the story that did the rounds a few years ago about the black satin sheets in your flat.'

Nelson waved away her accusations, looking, she thought, rather pleased that his bedwear had made such an impression.

'This project is all fair and above board,' he insisted. 'It would make use of existing buildings at the site.'

'What, the sheds?'

'Barns, Shula, barns. I'm surprised you hadn't spotted their potential yourself.'

'Well, there's some brick there, I suppose,' mused Shula, trying to picture the buildings as she'd last seen them, sprouting nettles and smelling of sheep droppings. 'And an awful lot of corrugated. And an awful lot of fresh air. They're falling down.'

'They're ripe for conversion!' insisted Nelson airily. 'Into luxury homes, with panoramic views over unspoilt countryside – really, I could write the sales particulars myself.'

'And you've got a builder interested?'

'Provided he can get planning permission, which, with a good architect, needn't be a problem . . . We're talking about four or five dwellings, Shula. You don't need me to do the sums. If your father could sell a builder just a couple of acres of the land that didn't sell at auction – well, he might not need to worry about the rest.'

And so, at last, as they pulled out of the long, dreary winter into spring, and the first anniversary of Dan's death approached, it seemed as though Brookfield might at last be turning the corner. Though Phil, ever cautious, was at first reluctant, Nelson's enthusiasm for the barn conversion plan, backed by Shula, persuaded him that it was the best way forward. And it seemed as though the barn conversions might even solve another problem – that of where David and Sophie, who were to be married in October, were to live. The suggestion was that the builder might allow for a smaller house as part of the development, at cost, to be deducted from the purchase price of the land.

'So what d'you think?' David asked her.

It was a Friday in early May and he'd just picked Sophie up from the station. They'd arranged to go to Felpersham Cathedral that afternoon to see the Dean about the wedding. Sophie was looking gorgeous, as usual, in some short trousers, white, like David could remember the cabin boy wearing in *Captain Pugwash*, and a red and white striped T-shirt of her own design, which she told him was borrowed from the style of a Breton fisherman. David couldn't recall any fisherman, Breton or otherwise, ever looking quite so sexy, but Sophie had explained that her top was made of silk jersey, which could partly, he supposed, have made the difference. He shot her a glance as he indicated right by the cattle market. With her red hair scooped up on top of her head, and her skin, which, despite months in the noxious fumes of London, still looked as though she bathed in milk from the bulk tank every morning, she was as lovely as ever. So what was different?

David suddenly realized. She'd hardly said a word since they'd left the station car park. Sophie, who could give Jethro a run for his money when it came to rabbitting on, was completely silent.

'Soph? I asked you a question.'

'Did you?' She dragged her eyes away from a lorryload of hay which was shedding strands in front of them and smiled nervously. 'I'm sorry.'

'The builders could be getting planning permission soon. We've got to make a decision about the house.'

'A decision!'

'Yup. Mum and Dad haven't said a word, and I know they don't want to put any pressure on us, but . . .'

'Oh, David.' Sophie made a web of her fingers. 'I don't know if I want to make any decisions.'

They were at the junction. The lorryload of hay turned right with a moan of gears.

'Sophie,' said David patiently. 'We are now at a crossroads. To the left is Felpersham Cathedral and a series of decisions. To the right is open country where you can be as free as a bird, twitter in the hedgerows and not even think about tomorrow. Now, which is it going to be?'

Sophie looked down at her knitted fingers.

'Left of course,' she said quietly.

'Good,' said David.

Seeing a gap in the traffic, he put the car in gear and nipped out smartly in front of a cattle lorry. He didn't want to follow that all the way through town, with Sophie in tears over the poor little calves being taken away from their mummies. He could see that the afternoon was going to be quite emotional enough already.

Back at Brookfield, Jill, whose maternal antennae had been quivering ever since Sophie had taken the job in London, was thinking much the same thing. Jill's worry mechanism had been triggered, it seemed, when she'd first given birth to Shula and Kenton, and it had never recovered its equilibrium.

'Did David get off all right?'

Phil, who'd been drenching some lambs, washed his hands. Jill expertly knocked back the crust of that night's chicken and leek pie and nodded, but couldn't help showing her concern.

'I thought they'd have been back by now. He only took a sandwich.'

'Come on, Jill, he won't starve.' Jill's response to every event in life manifested itself through food – not that Phil was complaining. 'They do have shops in Felpersham.'

'He ought to eat properly. He's been looking tired.'

Phil considered this as he dried his hands.

'Well, he's been working like a man possessed.'

'Yes,' said Jill. She opened the Aga door and put the pie on a low shelf. 'To take his mind off things.'

'What things?' Phil sat down at the table. 'He's got a lovely girl he's going to marry, the business of where they're going to live is finally sorted out –'

'But is it? She won't make up her mind.'

It was a good job that Graham Collard knocked on the door at that moment with the news that the fuse had gone on the bulk tank because otherwise Jill might have told Phil what she thought. About how, though of course she liked Sophie, the closer they got to the wedding, the less able she was to see her settling down as a farmer's wife – or anyone's wife, come to that.

If love was partly about timing, then David and Sophie's clocks seemed to be totally awry. It was timing, after all, that had sprung him into proposing, when he and Sophie hadn't really been getting along very well, in all the artificial emotion of last year's royal wedding. Now it was timing that had dictated that Sophie take a job in London when there was a wedding to be planned at home, and that kept her away for more and more weekends.

When David did come back that afternoon, he was quiet, very quiet, and Jill was glad that Elizabeth was out. That way she couldn't tease her brother about writing 'HELP' on the soles of his wedding shoes, or wonder aloud if Sophie would achieve the fantastic feat of remembering her own name when it came to the vows.

Of course, Sophie wasn't, as Phil put it, the brightest bulb in the box, but she must have something about her, thought Jill, to have got this job in London. The fashion company seemed to think the world of her, and several of her designs were going into their next collection. No, Jill's worries about her future daughter-in-law had nothing to do with her intellectual shortcomings: it wasn't as if David needed a wife with whom he could sit around in the evenings discussing the finer points of nuclear fission. It was more about Sophie's suitability to life on the farm.

Jill felt almost hypocritical even thinking it, because when she'd married Phil, she'd been a town girl herself. But Jill had always had a strong practical streak. She was much more down to earth than Sophie, for whom the term 'airy-fairy' seemed to have been coined.

If Sophie kept on her job in London, then who, worried Jill, would cook David's supper when he came in from a long day on the combine or in the lambing shed? And, conversely, even if Sophie did give up her job, who, the question still remained, would cook David's supper? When Sophie had last asked Jill if there was anything she could do to help in the kitchen, she'd been astonished to have to show her how to peel a carrot. Sophie had explained that her mother, Tiona, bought everything ready-prepared from Underwoods Food Hall, even, to Jill's amazement, custard.

'So what's happening then?' Jennifer asked Jill a couple of days later, when the reason for David's silence had been explained by his admission that the wedding was postponed because Sophie was in 'a bit of a state'.

'I don't know.' Jill was collecting the eggs from the orchard and could have done without cross-questioning. 'To be honest, their whole relationship's a bit of a mystery to me.'

'It's a mystery to us all.' Elizabeth was perched on the fence with her face raised to the sun. She and Jennifer, who was a long-standing contributor to the *Echo*, seemed to have come to an agreement about freelance work, which involved Elizabeth doing the restaurant reviews under Jennifer's byline. 'Most people go out for a bit and then decide to get married. David and Sophie decide to get married, then they tell us that, after all, they've decided just to go out.'

Jill retrieved an egg strategically placed behind a clump of nettles. In a nearby field some young lambs, delighted to see sunshine at last, noisily held an impromptu skipping race.

'Yes, thank you, Elizabeth, I'm sure they'll sort things out.'

Elizabeth looked at her mother unrepentantly over her sunglasses. She and Jill hadn't been getting on too well lately. The problem was her latest boyfriend, Robin Fairbrother. For a start, he was a lot older than Elizabeth – thirty-four – and, though separated, still technically married. But that wasn't the only difficulty: he was also the half-brother of Phil's first wife, Grace. Jill had thought all her feelings about Grace were tidily filed away, and she'd been surprised by how much she'd resented the past encroaching on their family life again. In the end, it had been wise old Walter Gabriel – Uncle Walter to the Archer family – who'd told her that she had no reason to feel jealous of Grace, ever, and Jill had finally been able to tell Elizabeth that she would, after all, like to meet Robin at some point.

'Well, David and Sophie had better get their act together soon.' Elizabeth returned to her sun-worshipping. 'I'm reviewing the Mont Blanc tonight, aren't I, Jennifer? And I'm not going to skip pudding if there's no bridesmaid's dress to worry about.'

Elizabeth's attitude to things might have been somewhat cavalier, but David had a more serious approach to life, something that he and his sister had frequently – and noisily – disagreed over. Now, what with the uncertainty over his wedding plans and a niggling feeling, which he pushed away, that Sophie might never be ready to marry him and that, actually, that might be a very good thing, David coped in the only way he knew – by throwing himself into work.

It was the middle of June and they were waiting for the next lot of
hay to make. It seemed like a good time, therefore, to trim the trees
beside the track up at Marneys, the part of the farm where, by tradition, the sheep grazed and were handled. The overhanging branches
always caught on the combine, and trimming them was simply part of
the necessary preparation for harvest.

When David and Jethro set off in the Land Rover with the ladder,
the chainsaw and the ropes, there was absolutely nothing to suggest
that it was going to be anything other than a perfectly routine day.
David could remember every detail. How he'd checked it was petrol
not two-stroke in the can for the chainsaw. How, on the way, Jethro
had been rattling on, like he did, about his dog, Gyp, who wouldn't
eat his dinner till he'd had a saucer of tea, and how Clarrie, Jethro's
daughter, who was married to Eddie Grundy, had got to mend his
second-best pair of trousers because he'd torn them on a seat at The
Bull and how Sid Perks ought to do something about it.

Considering that David always thought he never listened to Jethro,
he remembered a lot, really, which was just as well, because he'd had
to go over and over the day for so many people. And then he'd had to
go over and over it again for himself.

He'd had to explain time and again how he'd been up the ladder
with the chainsaw and how Jethro was pulling on the rope. How
David had shouted to him that the branch was coming, how he'd felt
Jethro pull, but . . . Maybe they should have used a longer rope.
Maybe they should never have tried to pull the branch in the first
place. Maybe David should have sent Jethro up the tree and stayed on
the ground himself. Anyway, David had shouted that it was coming,
and told Jethro not to stand too close. But the branch had come away
with a sudden crack when neither of them was expecting it, and
Jethro couldn't get out of the way quickly enough. It had struck
him full in the chest, knocking him flat. He must have hit his head as
he fell because when David had scrambled down, Jethro's face was all
white and clammy.

In his panic David couldn't tell if he was breathing or not. He
called Jethro's name, tried to feel for a pulse, then dashed back to

Brookfield, bursting breathless into the kitchen and jabbering something unintelligible, even to him. Finally, his dad had got the story
out of him and his mum had phoned for an ambulance. Auntie
Christine, his dad's sister, who'd been there, had gone to fetch
Clarrie, but by the time she brought her back to Brookfield it was too
late. Jethro had died there, out in the field, with the skylarks singing
and the sun bright on the barley spears.

And so, ironically, when the recent sale of the broken-down barns as
potential 'executive homes' had relieved Brookfield of the need to
press Jethro to retire, he was gone anyway, and the Health and Safety
Inspector was round asking questions. There were forms to be filled
in and measurements to be taken by the tree and, it seemed to David,
the same questions to be answered over and over again – not that he
felt he had any answers, not ones which satisfied him, anyway.

Swiftly, mercifully, the inquest was opened and adjourned so that
the family could have the funeral. David knew he'd have to attend,
but at the same time, didn't know how he could. He didn't know
what he could possibly say to Clarrie. Everyone kept telling him
it had been an accident, and that there was nothing he could have
done. David didn't believe them. He'd been there, for goodness' sake.
He should have seen it coming. He should have stopped it from
happening.

In the end, Clarrie was wonderful and said she didn't blame David
at all: it had been an accident, pure and simple. Everyone insisted
that when the full inquest was held in August, it wouldn't attach any
blame to him either, but that wasn't the point. It almost didn't matter
whether other people blamed him or not. David blamed himself.

Sophie came back from London for the funeral. She'd always been
fond of Jethro – about the same IQ, Elizabeth had sniped.

Things were strained between David and his fiancée. Since the
postponement of their wedding, she'd been back for a couple of
weekends, and David had been to London to see her, but neither
of them knew how to behave.

They no longer had the impetus of the wedding to work towards and yet, having got that far, it was impossible to revert to the mindless simplicity of a night at the pictures or a pizza in front of the television. They still held hands when they were out together, but more out of politeness than desire, and when David reached for her at the end of the evening she would make a minuscule gesture of reluctance. With relief, he knew she wanted nothing more than a hug.

After the funeral, she stayed several days. They were woefully short-staffed for the hay-making: even David's Auntie Peggy had got her Land Girl breeches out and lent a hand pitching bales. Sophie was no good at any of that, of course, but she managed to make the odd flask of tea and fed the hens for Jill.

'It's all so complicated,' Jill told Christine one afternoon when they were comparing blisters in a break from lugging bales. 'I mean, David and Sophie still seem quite close. Not so close as they were, but – you know – friends.'

'But the wedding's still off?' Chris took a long swig of orange squash and wiped her mouth.

'Yes, that's one thing we do know. Though I'm not honestly sure if it's cancelled or just postponed. It all seems a bit of a muddle.'

Jill couldn't help but worry. David wasn't a person who liked emotion at the best of times – and now, on top of everything, he'd got the guilt and anxiety over Jethro's death to contend with.

'I do wish he and Sophie would sort it out once and for all,' she told Phil as she brushed his best tweed jacket before he and David set off for the Royal Show the following week. 'He's looking so drained.'

'I'm sorry, Jill, but it's not something we can solve for him,' advised Phil. 'Now, have you seen the Show Guide that I pulled out of *Farmer's Weekly*? I'd marked up some of the cattle lines specially.'

But David knew he couldn't go on much longer. It wasn't easy for him because, like so many men of his kind, he hated change, and the way he dealt with it was to stick his head in the sand until it went away or until someone else made a decision. But at the Royal, as they watched the Belgian Blues being judged – the Continental breeds were in fashion – his father asked him tentatively if he and Sophie had made up their minds about the house at the barn conversions, or whether they'd prefer Jethro's old place, Woodbine Cottage. David knew he couldn't fob his parents off any longer, and he didn't really want to. He had to know anyway, for himself. So a couple of days later, he went to London to see Sophie.

There, on a broiling July afternoon, they sat in the airless shade of Hyde Park as the office workers filed miserably back to their desks, and he watched everything that had been between him and Sophie ebb away.

The only comfort was that he wasn't telling her anything she didn't know, and he wasn't feeling anything that she didn't feel herself. They'd only been going on like this for the past few months because neither wanted to be the first to say it.

'I'll always care about you, Soph,' he said, holding her weightless hands. 'But marriage – I just can't see it. We're too different.'

'Oh, David,' she said. Her eyes were starry with tears. 'I'm so sorry.'

'Don't be,' he said, wiping them away for her. 'It'll all be for the best, you'll see.'

But it was all very well being brave and noble about it. He had to admit it: there was an enormous void in both areas of his life that were most important: in his work on the farm without Jethro and in his personal life without Sophie. And then something else got thrown into the mix.

• • •

'What sort of time d'you call this?'

It was six thirty on a fine morning at the end of July. The barley was fit, the combine was greased and ready and David should have been a relatively happy man. That was until his father had told him he'd got to set their new worker on.

She approached across the yard in her ridiculously clean overalls. The first thing that struck him was that she was absolutely tiny: for some reason he'd been expecting a great strapping thing. She didn't look as if she could lift a hay bale, let alone shove a cow into a crush or couple up a trailer. What had his father been thinking of?

When Phil had first proposed taking on a student to replace Jethro, David hadn't been keen, but he'd been too preoccupied with Jethro's accident and about things with Sophie to press the matter. Now he knew he should have sat in on the interviews.

'I've been waiting for you for half an hour,' he snapped. 'We said six o'clock.'

'I'm sorry,' she said. She had a sing-song Northumberland accent. He half expected her to break into verse about a fishy on a little dishy, the only bit of Geordie folklore he was familiar with. 'I'm sure your father told me you don't start milking till half past.'

'We don't. But we have to get the cows in first. They don't have alarm clocks out there.'

She looked at him carefully. He looked straight back.

'You must be David Archer.'

'That's right. And you're Ruth.'

David might not have been too sure about her, but the rest of the village seemed to be bending over backwards to make Ruth feel welcome. Martha Woodford, who ran the village shop, and Marjorie Antrobus, who'd moved into the village with her Afghan hounds, had already, he knew, practically come to blows over where she'd lodge. His dad was doing everything he could to help her settle in, and his mum was very impressed with her two A-levels and the year she'd spent in Israel on a kibbutz.

'Just like you, David,' she said, when Ruth first mentioned it. She'd been invited to stay to supper on the day she started.

'I've never set foot in Israel,' he replied coldly, helping himself to more quiche.

'No, but you went to Holland for that year,' chided Jill. 'Pass Ruth the salad, David, don't hog the bowl all to yourself. It's a good idea to work away from the family farm, isn't it, Ruth?'

'I didn't exactly have much choice,' grinned Ruth, spearing a slice of tomato. 'My family don't farm. In fact, my dad has a factory.'

'Really? Making what?' asked Phil.

'Er, the polite term's paper products. In other words, toilet rolls.'

There really was no answer to that.

Ruth certainly had a lot about her. There was no farming in her background, but she'd known since she was little, she said, that it was all she wanted to do. Now, after spending six months on a friend's smallholding, she'd been accepted by Harper Adams College in Shropshire to do her HND in September of next year – after her gap year at Brookfield.

'She's got no practical experience at all, really,' David grumbled to his father as they helped clear the table that first evening when Ruth had gone.

'She's got to start somewhere,' said Phil in reply.

'I just don't see why it has to be with us. Why should she practise on our cows and our combine?'

'Oh, for heaven's sake, David.' She knew her son had had a hard time lately, but Jill was getting impatient. 'You're not jealous, are you?'

'Jealous? Of what?'

'That she might turn out to be good, perhaps. Have some bright ideas that you haven't thought of.'

'Do me a favour!'

'Well, you'll be working with her,' said Phil with an air of finality. 'She's young and she's keen. After all your moaning about Jethro being so slow, God rest him, I'd have thought you'd be pleased.'

David wasn't quite sure himself what he'd got against Ruth, and he wasn't so pig-headed, despite what Elizabeth maintained, that he didn't give it some thought when he slipped down to The Bull for a pint later that evening. He was always nagging his dad to give him more responsibility, so he should have been thrilled to be supervising a student. Maybe it was just that he wasn't feeling very confident about his abilities as a boss at the moment, after the business with Jethro. Maybe he wasn't feeling very confident, full stop, after the business with Sophie, which had left him feeling sadder than he'd expected.

'You look like you've lost a fiver and found 50p,' observed Sid Perks when he came round collecting the glasses.

Sid should have known about loving and losing: his first wife Polly had been killed in a car accident and he'd brought up their daughter, Lucy, who was now fourteen, on his own. But earlier in the year he'd married Kathy Holland, one of Lucy's teachers, and he'd never looked happier.

'Can't be a ray of sunshine all the time,' said David curtly, and got up to go. 'I'll leave that to Ruth,' he thought, 'since she seems so damn cheerful all the time.'

But gradually – very easily, in fact – he got used to having Ruth around. She was certainly a worker, not a shirker, and she got on well with Graham, and with Neil Carter, who did the pigs. She could probably have got on quite well with David, if he'd given her half a chance, but he gave her her orders and kept his distance, and that was the way he liked it.

He kept his distance from everybody that summer. In August, the inquest, as everyone had predicted, decided that Jethro's death had been an accident, which was an enormous relief, but it wasn't until October, when the date that would have been his wedding day came and went, that David finally felt himself freed from his self-imposed period of mourning both for Jethro and for Sophie.

'Ruth, why don't you go in? You're shivering.'

'No, David. Let's try and finish it tonight.'

It was the end of November and they were in the barn. Outside in the crisp, starry evening, an owl was hunting, wide-eyed over the newly sown fields. Inside, it was scarcely warmer: their breath met between them in a faint fog.

'You didn't think Eddie would get these parts, did you?' She passed him the ring spanner seconds before he needed it.

'These track guides look pretty old,' considered David, who was actually rather pleased with them. 'Look at the rust.'

'He didn't even charge you!'

'I should think not! I've laid out nearly a grand for this digger already. But I'll buy him a pint if it makes you happy.'

David had bought the digger a couple of weeks back at a bankruptcy sale. It needed new tracks and rollers, the drive sprocket was shot to pieces and the idler wasn't great either, but it was his, that was the main thing. With it, he intended doing ditching and clearing work on contract for local farmers: the idea was both to earn a bit extra and to give himself something else to think about. Anything to take his mind off the prospect of a long winter at Brookfield, doing a bit of concreting in the mind-numbing cold or mucking out the cows every day, without even a night out with a girlfriend to look forward to. But then again . . .

He strained at a bolt seized up with years of rust and muck. He'd been surprised when Ruth had offered to stay on and help him, and, he had to admit it, pleased as well. Since he wasn't looking at her, he found himself able to say it.

'I do appreciate it, Ruth. Your helping.'

But before she could reply, the spanner slipped and his knuckle lunged against cold metal.

David dropped the spanner and sucked furiously at his finger.

'Ow! Blast.'

'Count to ten.' Ruth winced for him. She knew how painful they were, these knocks when your hands were half frozen.

'Ow . . .' David hissed in a breath.

'Here.' She produced a bit of grubby tissue from the pocket of her overalls. 'Wipe it with this. No, actually, give it to me, I'll do it.'

He held out his hand, big and rough, and she took it in her small, rough one.

'Careful . . .' he warned as she spat on the tissue and dabbed at the cut.

'Don't be a baby,' she teased. 'It's only a bit of skin gone.'

She was still holding David's hand and smiling at his display of weakness when his father suddenly poked his head round the door.

'Oh! Um . . . Sorry to interrupt!' he said, seeing them standing close.

'Bit of an accident, that's all,' said David, pulling quickly away.

'He'll live,' added Ruth, more composed.

'Good. Anyway, Ruth, it's the telephone for you. A young man.'

'Oh, right. Thanks.' She moved towards the door. 'Won't be a moment.'

His father crunched across the stone floor. David squatted down again by the rusted metal tracks.

'How's it coming along?' asked Phil.

'Oh, not bad.' David busied himself fitting the ring spanner on the reluctant bolt again. 'Um . . . did he say a name?'

'Did who say? Oh, the phone. No, I expect it's a friend.'

'Yeah, probably.' David strained at the spanner. The nut began to turn. 'Got it! At last! And, um . . . did he . . . sound young?'

His father shrugged vaguely.

'Youngish . . .' He rubbed his forehead, a habit of his. 'I wonder . . . maybe Ruth's got a boyfriend and just never mentioned him.'

David gave the spanner a savage twirl.

'Yup. Maybe.'

And just when they'd started to get on.

·2·

The Prodigal Son

'And just when they were starting to get on. It seems such a shame.'

Shula nodded in agreement and let Caroline Bone refill her coffee cup with Grey Gables's special Kenyan blend. Their friend Nigel Pargetter had only been reconciled with his father for a few months. Now Gerald Pargetter had died, and Nigel had inherited what was, in effect, a minor stately home. It looked as though he was going to have to pack a lot of growing up into the next few months.

'I've said I'll help him sort things out,' said Shula through a sip of coffee. 'Lower Loxley's completely gone to rack and ruin.'

Lower Loxley was the Pargetter ancestral home: if the architecture was Jacobean, so were the electrics.

'I can imagine.' Caroline reached for another of the chef, Jean-Paul's, delicious *langues de chat* biscuits. 'Even before he was ill, Gerald Pargetter did nothing but hunt to hounds and write bad-tempered letters to the *Daily Telegraph*.'

That might have been true, but for Shula, the timing of Gerald Pargetter's death was fortuitous.

She wanted to keep busy. Mark had recently taken a job with a large firm of solicitors in Birmingham: he was leaving the house at half seven in the morning and not getting back till half seven at night. Her sister Elizabeth had been going out with Nigel off and on since she was sixteen, but she was away on a working holiday in Australia, so Nigel would be short of female company at Lower Loxley. There was his mother, Julia, of course, but she'd always been a bit of a tippler, and their present problems gave her even more reason to reach for the gin before breakfast.

'Have you had a look at the bumf I gave you?' Shula asked Nigel when she called round to Lower Loxley the next day. He was sitting in what had been his father's study, surrounded by moulting ptarmigans his father had shot in his youth. He put down a crumbling copy of *Treasure Island* – a first edition, for what it was worth – and looked guilty.

'Ah. The Historic Monuments whatsit. Erm, well . . .'

'Oh, Nigel,' Shula chided gently. 'I thought you were turning over a new leaf.'

'Oh, I am. But it turns so far and then . . .' he broke off and looked at her puppyishly. 'Well, then it just flips back again. Do you – do you suppose you could put up with the old leaf for a little bit longer?'

'I suppose I'll have to,' smiled Shula, indulgent. 'Look, I'll explain it, shall I?'

As Nigel pored over the conditions that the Historic Buildings and Monuments Commission would lay down in order for Lower Loxley to qualify for a repair grant, Shula wondered whether he was really up to coping. This was the same Nigel, after all, who'd worried her by arriving back in Ambridge suddenly last summer and telling her he'd been fired from his job in the City.

'Nigel, you're not one of those awful insider dealers, are you?' she'd breathed, glad that Mark was out at cricket practice.

But the reality was rather more mundane and rather more believable. Nigel had got the sack: in truth, no one could understand how he'd lasted as long as he had.

It wasn't long after Jethro's death and Woodbine Cottage had been standing empty. Nigel had moved in and, before long, it was as if he'd never been away. He threw a particularly riotous party on August Bank Holiday weekend, when the Lawson-Hope seat mysteriously disappeared from the Green and was found next day halfway up Lakey Hill. On the same night, old Mrs Potter's garden gnome unaccountably decided to take a dip in the village pond. And for old times' sake, Nigel got hold of his Mr Snowy ice-cream van and served everyone cornets with raspberry sauce at midnight.

But towards the end of the year, Gerald Pargetter, who'd never been able to tolerate Nigel's company for longer than it took him to shout 'You degenerate oaf!' at him, had invited him to lunch, then to go shooting, and he'd told Nigel that he'd got lung cancer and didn't have long to live. Nigel had agreed to buckle down and take an interest in the estate.

It was a pity, thought Shula, that his first attempt at being more responsible had been to swing round on the banister rail of the massive oak staircase and have it come away in his hand. It turned out that the whole staircase had got dry rot but, as Nigel said, it was a blessing in disguise, as it was better to know these things, especially if, as seemed likely, part of the recovery plan for Lower Loxley would be to open the house to the public.

As she drove away from Lower Loxley that evening, Shula felt that at least she'd set Nigel on the right road. It was the end of April and the countryside trembled with promise. The vivid green hedges were alive with birds, and candyfloss blossom billowed in stooping orchards.

On the way back to Ambridge, Shula thought about her own family and their reaction to Nigel's loss. Nigel had never been a favourite of her father's, but Dan's death was still close enough for Phil to remember how painful a bereavement was, and the day Nigel's father had died, he'd gruffly suggested that he and Nigel take a walk together up Lakey Hill, always an Archer totem in times of crisis. Elizabeth had been phoned in Australia and had promised to come home as soon as she could and give Nigel the benefits of her journalistic expertise in writing his promotional brochures. David hadn't really taken much notice: he'd been too busy grumping around and turning the cows out. And at Glebe Cottage, Mark had chosen that night to come home and chuck a load of estate agents' brochures on the sofa and suggest that they spend the next weekend – May Bank Holiday – looking at houses in Birmingham.

Shula hated the idea but she'd said nothing. In two and a half years of marriage, Mark had never asked her for anything, while she'd asked him for lots of things: support during her RICS exams and his agreement, at the beginning of the year, that they should start trying for a baby. So she went along with the idea, and let him arrange the viewings, but as an estate agent herself, it hadn't been difficult to find something wrong with each of the houses they'd looked at. Finally, Mark said, as they walked away down the drive of a dormer bungalow in Sutton Coldfield:

'All right, I give in. I accept it. You'll never leave Ambridge.'

'Mark, I didn't say that!' protested Shula ingenuously.

'I should have known from the start.' Mark unlocked the passenger door and opened it for Shula to get in. 'You'll never leave your family.'

'Are you saying that's a bad thing?'

Mark shut her door – always so polite, even in the middle of a row – moved round the car and let himself in. For once, Shula didn't lean over to unlock his door for him.

'Well?' she demanded. 'Are you?'

Mark opened the sun-roof.

'It doesn't make any difference whether it's good or bad. It's the way it is.'

Maybe he was right. She loved Ambridge. All her friends were there – Caroline, for a start, and Nigel, who needed her at the moment. And she did love her family. She wanted them close and she'd want them even more when she had a baby to look after.

'Oh, it's too hot to argue. And you're too annoying.' Shula wound her window down. 'Please, can we just go home?'

• • •

Ironically, of course, the one member of Shula's family who might have been glad to get away from it all was the very one who couldn't.

At Brookfield, David was still plodding on. He wasn't a person given to huge introspection, but he did find himself wondering occasionally, as he hosed down the parlour or hitched up the mower, quite where life was taking him. He hadn't been meant to marry Sophie, fine, he accepted that now and in his saner moments he could see that it had all been for the best. But a tentative approach he'd made to Ruth back in February had been rebuffed, he thought, when she'd told him they were better off as friends.

'OK, if that's what you want,' he'd said stiffly, before throwing himself into the arms first of a girl called Annette and now someone called Frances, a divorcee with two small daughters. He and Frances got on well and he was learning more about Barbie dolls than he'd ever thought he'd need to know, but he did wonder how long he could carry on romancing one woman and then another, taking them out for the evening or letting them cook him supper. Indefinitely, he supposed. And yet . . . somehow he wouldn't have minded something a bit more settled.

So it was odd when, later in the summer, his brother Kenton, Shula's twin and the epitome of unsettled, should suddenly decide to come home.

'Go on, out you go!'

David slapped the rump of the last cow in the parlour and she stepped daintily into the collecting yard to join the others. David followed her out into the sun. He squeezed past the jigsaw-patterned black and white bellies big with calves to open the gate and let the cows back into the field. His father was hosing down the parlour when he went back in.

'Surprising what a difference an extra pair of hands makes,' offered Phil. 'Thanks.'

'Oh, that's all right,' said David, jumping down into the pit. 'I'd woken up and I can never get back to sleep. Not much point in just lying there.'

'Excited, are you?' asked his father knowingly.

'Excited?'

'Your mother and I have hardly slept at all. Tossing and turning.'

Light dawned.

'Oh, because Kenton's coming home. No, sorry, Dad, I'm afraid I haven't been losing any sleep over Kenton.'

Kenton, the prodigal son, had announced a month ago that he would be home from his job in the merchant navy for his and Shula's thirtieth birthday at the beginning of August. Since Kenton's phone call, there'd been fierce speculation at Brookfield, not least from

Elizabeth, who'd returned from Australia with not much experience in journalism but a lot in sensationalizing a non-story.

'He hasn't been back for over two years!' she mused at breakfast.

'Yes, and he wrecked the fertilizer spinner,' muttered David. He knew it wouldn't be a popular observation: as far as everyone else in the family was concerned, golden boy Kenton could do no wrong.

'Perhaps he's going to surprise us with a dusky native bride,' Elizabeth speculated. 'He's been out East, after all.'

David buttered the last slice of toast.

'Yeah, there's quite a tradition of buying women out there. I can see that's the one way Kenton could get someone to agree to marry him.' He took a bite of his toast and his mother whipped his plate away. 'Hey! I hadn't finished!'

'If all you can do is be snide, I don't want to hear it,' said Jill with unusual prickliness. 'You can take your toast outside.'

Now the big day had rolled around and his mum, Shula and Elizabeth were all trooping off to Birmingham Airport to meet the Boy Wonder. His dad wasn't going, but that was only because it was the middle of harvest, and with the wheat not quite ready to combine, today might be the only chance they got to go through the flock and cull out the ewes they needed to replace before the breeding season started. But even his dad was twitchy, David thought, alert to every vehicle that came down the track, even when it was obviously Ruth on the tractor hauling bales, and continually glancing across towards the house in case they'd managed to sneak in without him seeing.

It was nearly three before they heard the car, but with only twenty more ewes to go, his dad somehow managed to contain his excitement till the job was done. They were just packing up to go back inside when Kenton came out to find them, grinning from ear to ear and looking tanned and relaxed like someone just back off a holiday – which, let's face it, was pretty much what Kenton's life had been so far.

'Kenton!' called Phil, stuffing the spray can with which he'd been marking the ewes in his pocket. 'It's good to see you.'

'It's good to see you, too, Dad.' Kenton swaggered up and gave his dad a slap on the back and a big hug. 'And you, Dave.'

David gritted his teeth. He hated being called Dave. And Kenton knew it.

'Yeah,' he said falsely. 'Welcome home.'

From then on, it was just how David had known it would be. For weeks beforehand, his mother had been in complete overdrive, stuffing the freezer full of Kenton's favourite things and baking for the party she was determined to throw to show him off to the village: never mind his and Shula's joint thirtieth, she didn't need a reason beyond his miraculous return. David went along with the party plans – after all, he'd have Frances there to take his mind off things – but when he found his mother in the loft, looking out the bunting normally used for the fête and cooing over ancient photos of the gruesome twosome – Kenton and Shula as babies – he'd had enough. His father had muttered something about walking the wheat in Lower Parks after supper, but David showered and changed and roared off in his car to see Frances.

'Um, it's a bit awkward, really,' she said when she let him into her terraced house in Borchester. 'I didn't know you were coming.'

'Nor did I.' David put his arms round her and pulled her towards him. 'Shall I nip out and get us a Chinese?'

She pushed him gently away.

'Sorry, we've eaten. And I said the girls could stay up late as a treat and watch a video. How do you feel about *My Little Pony*?'

So she made him an omelette and David had to sit through an hour and a half of some saccharine rubbish about the Ponies saving the Enchanted Forest before the girls finally went to bed.

When Frances came back down, he patted the sofa next to him, but she perched primly at the other end.

'The thing is, David,' she said. 'I like you a lot, I really do . . . but this just isn't working for me. The girls have to come first.'

'Of course. That's fine by me.'

'No, you don't understand. They have to come first. And only.'

He looked round the room at her huge *Beata Beatrix* print on the saffron walls and the stained pine chest which was the girls' toybox.

He thought about her big wrought-iron bed upstairs and the good times they'd had.

'You're giving me the push.'

'I'm sorry. But yes.'

He left then and drove too fast through the quiet streets to the bypass and back to Ambridge. He let himself into the kitchen. His mum had left a plate of sandwiches and a note saying 'Hope you had a good evening'.

The worst of it, thought David miserably, wondering in his gloom how much worse his life could get, was that no one would even care. No one would ask in the morning and there was no point trying to tell his mum, or even Shula: they were far too busy poaching salmon and whipping egg-whites to care about what was happening to him. It was only when his father asked him outright on the night of the party if Frances had been able to get a babysitter that David told him it was all off.

'I know you'd thought it might get complicated, with her having the girls, if we'd ever got it together – well, with the farm and everything.'

'Well, yes,' blustered Phil, still surprised by the news, 'but I'd never have put those sort of worries before your happiness, David. You know I wouldn't.'

David shrugged. He didn't feel too sure about anything any more.

'Well, no cause for alarm now, is there?' he said blithely.

Not when there's a party for Kenton in the offing, he thought bitterly. And not when, since Kenton had declared that he was going to stick around for a bit and work on the farm, the position at Brookfield might not exactly be clear-cut anyway.

'When I started with Mr Highsmith, we used to shift 5000 bales of hay every summer. Just the three of us.' The new worker who was to replace Ruth when she left in September to start her course removed his cap and mopped the back of his neck. Bert Fry had been the foreman on a tenanted farm that had been taken in hand. At fifty-two he'd feared that he'd never work again and he'd jumped at the chance of a job at Brookfield. He, Ruth and Kenton had been carting grain and lugging bales all morning and had stopped, at Kenton's suggestion, for a well-earned rest.

'I'll tell you what,' he continued in his ripe Borsetshire accent, 'you could hold out your hand for your money at the end of the week without a qualm. You'd earned it, see.'

'What the hell is going on?' None of them had heard the Land Rover approach over the beat of the contractor's combine, which was still working the bottom end of the field. David stomped across the stubble towards them. 'The grain pit's empty. Are you all on strike or something?'

Bert speedily replaced his cap.

'I was just on my way in.'

'Good,' said David curtly. 'You haven't got time to sit around chatting, you know. What if the weather breaks?'

'No one's been sitting around,' replied Ruth, stung.

'And you're not back at college yet. We're still paying you, don't forget.'

'What's that supposed to mean?'

'Come on.' Kenton put a hand on David's arm. 'No one's skiving.'

'And you needn't leap to her defence. Ruth knows what's expected round here. And if you're going to stick around, Kenton, it might help if you learned it too.'

They both looked at him coldly, then Ruth turned her back and stalked off towards her tractor.

'What's your problem, Dave?' There was something about Kenton's voice, slightly nasal, slightly wheedling, which always got on David's nerves.

What was the point of even trying to answer? How could David begin to explain to Kenton, if he genuinely didn't know? How could he explain his fury that Kenton, who'd been in the merchant navy since he was sixteen, could swan back half a lifetime later and expect the farm to absorb him – and for the farm and everyone else on it to seem able to do just that? No one else seemed to see it. But, then, they didn't notice either, as David did, that Kenton had a knack of putting his hand up for the easy, or visible, jobs, while it was still David who got up at five for the milking or coped at ten at night with the cow that had decided to calve early out in the field. No one else seemed to care that Phil had bought Kenton a car on the business, and was seriously considering, now that Kenton had come clean and said he was being made redundant, how the farm might support three families in years to come. And above all, no one seemed to care that Kenton appeared to have his eye on Ruth.

'Oh, dear. David's going to be fed up.'

It was later the same afternoon and Jill and Shula were sheltering in Underwoods' doorway from a torrential shower of rain. They'd come into Borchester to liaise with Nelson about the party at The Bull for Uncle Walter's birthday in a week or so's time. He was going to be ninety-two.

'There were a lot of bales still to bring in from that field they were finishing off today,' she went on.

'Oh, no.' Shula shifted her handbag from one shoulder to the other. 'That'll put him in an even worse mood. He was bad enough at the party.'

'I know,' agreed Jill. 'Ever since he split up with Frances.'

'And Kenton came home.' Shula was well aware of the tension between her brothers.

'Kenton helping on the farm does put David in a difficult position,' brooded Jill. 'He can't really treat him like an ordinary worker.'

'And we don't know how long it'll go on, do we?' said Shula. 'I do love my twin but he's not Mr Decisive. All he's said to me is that he's not sure what he wants to do with his life, but farming's on the list.'

'It's such a shame, too, that it's hanging over Ruth's last couple of weeks. David's attitude's really been making her quite jumpy.'

'I don't feel I've ever really got to know Ruth.' Shula peered up at the sky, looking for a glimpse of blue. 'She doesn't give much away, does she?'

'No, she's very private. We've never even found out if that young man who used to ring up for her was her boyfriend or not.'

'Well, we'll probably never know. Look, Mum, I think it's easing off. Shall we make a dash for the car?'

Jill wondered, as Shula drove them home, if she should have a word with Phil again. She'd already suggested that, leaving aside the question of Kenton, the solid work that David had put into Brookfield over the last few years should be reflected by making him a partner.

She hated to see her younger son so miserable. It brought back all those incidents in childhood when Kenton, thirteen months older, had had the edge. And how, when David had shot up and become taller and stronger than his brother, he'd enjoyed getting his own back. David wouldn't have believed it if she'd told him, but he'd always been her favourite, partly for the way he'd coped with coming second all those years, partly for the way he'd turned out the most straightforward and uncomplicated of her children. Except, of course, where his feelings were concerned: look how secretive he'd been about finishing with Frances. You could never get anything personal out of David, so nowadays she didn't even try.

He'd had a lousy day, so David wasn't surprised it was a lousy evening as well. Cricket practice was cancelled because of the rain, and when he went to The Bull for a quiet drink, it was full of Eddie Grundy's mates playing darts and spilling their beer.

David took his pint to the quietest corner he could find and sat down morosely. He'd had a row with his mum before he'd come out about Kenton holding the others up over the baling – but it was no good. As usual, she didn't want to hear any bad about him. He didn't mind falling out with Kenton but he always minded falling out with his mum. And worst of all, he had to admit, he minded falling out with Ruth.

It was only since he'd finished with Frances that he'd had time to think properly about his false start with Ruth back in February. He'd taken her out to dinner on Valentine's Day, cancelling a date with Annette, who was already waiting in the wings, to do so. He'd thought they'd had a good evening and, used to getting his own way with

41

women, had been frankly amazed when Ruth had come out with the 'just good friends' line. To show her how little it mattered to him, he'd immediately taken up with Annette, and then with Frances, while he and Ruth had returned to the guarded politeness that had always been the tenor of their working relationship.

It might have gone on like that until she went to college, he thought as he swigged his beer, but Kenton's return had changed all that, like it had changed so much else around the place. Kenton treated Ruth with the flirtatious ease he used towards all women, and David had stood back smugly, waiting for him to be slapped down. But not only did Ruth put up with it, she actually seemed to like it. David had watched, repelled, as they'd joked their way through harvest, sharing their sandwiches and taking turns on the tractor. Now, with only two weeks of Ruth's time at Brookfield left, he could see that the end of August would get eaten up in the same intimate familiarity.

David couldn't believe he'd been so dense. He'd had Ruth right there under his nose for a whole year. She'd backed off once, and instead of pursuing her, he'd let her, despite the fact that he had more in common with her than any other woman he'd ever met. She was the only woman he knew who could strip down a tractor, and who didn't go all funny when he started talking about dehorning day-old calves. She was worth a hundred of Annette, or of Frances. She was certainly worth better than Kenton.

Clarrie, who worked behind the bar, came and took his glass away. She tried to chat to him but David was too choked to speak. He could have put his head down on the table and wept. He'd had his chance with Ruth and he'd totally blown it. And it was all his own fault.

He stuck it out at the pub for another half hour and another half of bitter, but only because he couldn't think what else to do. He didn't want to go home because Kenton would be there, entertaining his parents with more tales of nautical derring-do. That's if he wasn't out with Ruth. The thought was so awful that it made David want to curl in on himself.

It finally occurred to him that there was one way to find out, and it made him wonder what exactly Ruth did do with her evenings. She'd ended up living at Nightingale Farm. It must be a weird life there with Mrs Antrobus, nice old dear that she was, downstairs on her electric organ playing songs from *South Pacific* with the Afghans yowling an accompaniment.

In all the time Ruth had worked at Brookfield he'd never been round there, not even when they'd been in their 'good friends' phase. They'd worked together for ten months, doing long shifts in the lambing shed, coping with mastitis and milk fever, yet Ruth had never asked him round for a meal, or even a coffee. Maybe she couldn't cook. Maybe she lived on pasties from the shop or slabs of cake provided by Mrs A. Perhaps he should go and see.

'It's funny. I've never been up here before. I've been into Mrs Antrobus's part of the house, but never round to your flat.'

'No reason why you should.' It was later the same evening and Ruth had certainly looked astonished when Mrs A had ushered David up, chuntering coyly on about 'gentlemen callers'. He'd had to give her some tale about needing the receipt for the combine knife blade he'd sent Ruth to fetch the other day.

'Well . . .' David shrugged and looked around.

The flat was bigger than he'd imagined, or perhaps that was just because she hadn't got much stuff. She didn't have any of the usual girlie things his sisters surrounded themselves with – a million photos and flower vases and knick-knacks – to make her feel at home. Quite refreshing, really.

They stood there awkwardly, facing one another.

'Would you like a coffee or something?' she offered.

'No thanks.'

She looked up at him, perplexed.

'I've got some lager if you'd rather.'

'No, it's OK.'

She spread her hands.

'Well, sit down, anyway. You're making me nervous.'

He sat down on the lumpy sofa. It was probably one Mrs A and her late husband had brought back from their travels in the Middle East, stuffed with camel-hair or something. He was feeling pretty nervous himself.

'Ruth.'

'Yeah?'

She'd sat down herself and tucked her legs under her, still looking bemused. No wonder, inviting himself round here out of the blue.

'I've been pretty rotten to you lately, haven't I?' he blurted out.

She bit her lip. Was she trying not to laugh or trying not to cry?

'Yeah,' she grinned. 'You have, if you really want to know.'

David let out a sigh. At least she hadn't totally lost her sense of humour.

'I'm sorry. It's not you, you know that?'

She pushed her hair behind her ear. It was the first time he'd seen it down, instead of scraped back in an elastic band. It was a nice colour – well, lots of colours, really. Shiny, like a Limousin-cross calf.

'I've got a fair idea why,' she said gently. 'It's Kenton, isn't it?'

David couldn't look at her. He glanced away, out of the window. The sun was setting in a sky like streaky bacon.

'I feel such a rat. My own brother.'

Ruth said nothing. He could feel her looking at him. Again he wondered what the hell he'd been doing for the last year, why on earth he'd allowed himself to be distracted and why he'd wasted so much time. He looked at her ruefully. What a fool.

'I wish I wasn't leaving,' she said softly.

What?

'Oh, so do I,' said David urgently.

She looked at him with her honest brown eyes and he couldn't help himself. He leaned over and kissed her.

When, at last, they pulled apart, they gazed at each other as if in shock.

'I thought you'd never do that,' she murmured.

'Did you want me to?' He was still amazed that it had happened at all.

'Of course I did.'

'Oh.' David put his arm round her and pulled her against him. 'I was never sure.'

'You mean you wanted to?'

'I . . . well . . . you could always have asked me.'

'Thanks, leave it all to me!' she retorted, settling into the crook of his arm. 'You were too busy going out with that Frances. And who was it before that? Annette.'

'I thought perhaps you had a bloke,' he protested. 'That guy who used to ring you up.'

'Malcolm?' snorted Ruth. 'Do me a favour. He's just a mate of my cousin's.'

'Oh,' said David inadequately, wishing he'd asked her outright before. 'Anyway,' he rallied, 'I thought you just wanted us to be friends.'

'Oh, David . . .' She turned her head and kissed his hand where it lay on her shoulder. 'I only said that because I thought it might complicate things. And I hate complications.'

'So do I,' said David, heartfelt. 'But, Ruth – why did we wait till now?'

'I've still got a couple of weeks left,' she consoled him.

'Let's make them good ones.'

She manoeuvred her face round so he could kiss her again.

'The best,' she said.

·3·

A Sense of Loss

'Thank goodness that's over.' Jill removed her hat and placed it on the table in front of her. 'Make us a pot of tea, Phil, there's a love.'

Phil moved to the sink and ran the tap. He tutted as water splashed on his suit.

'I could do with one myself. The sherry was certainly flowing.'

Jill smiled briefly.

'It was a good party, wasn't it? Just a pity about the occasion.'

It was four o'clock on a November afternoon. It had been a day of still cloud: now darkness swarmed over the sky. While Phil had been away from the farm, the weaners had been having their tails docked, there'd been a delivery of diesel and the seed merchant had phoned. Soon Graham would be bringing the cows across the yard to the parlour from their winter quarters. The usual routine, because life went on. But without Uncle Walter any more.

His death had come suddenly in the end. Since August, when the gable wall of Honeysuckle Cottage had collapsed, making him homeless, Walter Gabriel had been staying at Mrs Perkins's bungalow in Manorfield Close. When, in the autumn, though the builders were finished, he'd shown a marked reluctance to go home, and had taken to bed at Mrs P's, all his friends had treated it as a joke.

'She's made him too comfortable, if you ask me,' Phil's Uncle Tom had proclaimed. 'Old Walter knows which side his bread's buttered.'

Nelson agreed.

'You must be tougher with him,' he counselled Mrs Perkins. 'I suggest you stop refilling his hot-water bottle and cooking his favourite puddings.'

'It's easy for you to say,' worried Mrs P. 'Me and Mr Forrest have been trying for days to persuade him to get up. We even set a chair up in the garden, sheltered, in the sun. But in the end, he always finds some excuse.'

Soon the nice young doctor, Matthew Thoroughgood, who until recently had been going out with Caroline, was concerned.

'At his age, he ought to be moving around, or there could be complications. If fluid settles on the lungs . . . And we mustn't forget his diabetes.'

But Walter remained unmoved and unmoveable, and before long, Matthew's unhappy predictions were realized. A chest infection developed quickly into pneumonia, and before he could be moved to hospital, Walter died peacefully in the night.

He'd been Dan's contemporary, neighbour and friend, a village fixture. Since anyone could remember, there'd always been Gabriels in Ambridge, but none as memorable as Walter.

'What about when he got hold of those elephants for the village fête?' Phil was reminiscing with Uncle Tom and his wife, Pru, the day after Walter died. 'And that stuffed gorilla that used to stand outside the pet shop he had with Agatha Turvey?'

'No, no, the gorilla was outside the junk shop,' Tom corrected him. 'George, it was called.'

'It's the little things I remember,' added Jill. 'Do you remember, Pru, when he stayed with Mum and Dad years ago, how he scoured all Doris's saucepans, trying to be helpful – except they were non-stick?'

Pru nodded and smiled.

'I remember him at Christmas, on his euphonium.' Phil shook his head. 'That's going back years. And singing. Dad always said his voice sounded like a rusty nail being shoved through the bottom of a cocoa tin.'

'And now we'll never hear it again,' said Tom sadly. 'No more "Hello, me old pals, me old beauties." It doesn't seem possible, really.'

Nelson had said the same thing at the gathering that he'd held after his father's funeral.

'One's never prepared for these things when they actually happen,' he intoned to Jill in his cultured tones, several worlds away from his father's broad accent. 'I just wish – well, I suppose I wish I'd appreciated him more. And been a little kinder to him when he was alive.'

'Oh, Nelson, you've got nothing to feel guilty about.' Jill knew that Nelson was thinking of the anxiety he'd given Walter over the years, with his shady business deals and a lifestyle that kept him – usually – on just the right side of the law. 'Look at those super holidays you took him on. And the fun he had when you opened the antique shop and the wine bar. He was so proud of you. And of Rosemary.'

Nelson pushed an elegant hand through his silver hair. A couple of years before, his illegitimate daughter from a liaison back in the 1960s had arrived in Ambridge and, to everyone's great amusement, given Nelson's known proclivities, had announced that she was training to be a policewoman.

'Maybe,' he acknowledged. 'But he gave so much of himself. I doubt I'll be remembered as fondly.'

'Oh, I don't know, Nelson,' smiled Jill, who'd always had a soft spot for him. 'I think you'll find you have quite a following, too.'

• • •

It was hard, after Uncle Walter's death, to get into the right frame of mind for Ruth and David's wedding, which was only six weeks away. In Ruth's last few weeks at Brookfield they had indeed had the wonderful time they'd promised themselves – but still they'd managed to keep their romance a secret. The ruse had worked. Even Elizabeth, with her journalist's nose for a story, had been convinced that David's smug smile was because it was all back on with Frances, and Ruth's was because she was keen on Kenton. The whole family had therefore been staggered when, after David had inexplicably disappeared off for a couple of weekends – in fact, of course, visiting Ruth at Harper Adams – the pair of them had turned up at Brookfield and announced that they were engaged.

Now, with Kenton as best man – the brothers had been reconciled once David had been made a partner in the farm and had found a partner of another sort too – the wedding was planned for Thursday, 15 December. David had even trusted Kenton to fix their honeymoon: the only remaining problems were how many egg rolls to order for the reception in the village hall and where the happy couple were to live.

The barn conversions had been built and were all sold by now. Brookfield's new worker, Bert Fry, and his redoubtable wife Freda were living in Woodbine Cottage. Phil, however, had another card up his sleeve.

'I've been thinking about it for some time,' he told Ruth and David as they addressed invitations. 'I'm thinking of building a bungalow on the other side of the orchard, with the garden backing on to the river. In time, I suppose, it's where Jill and I will end up – not for a good few years yet, though,' he warned David, who always had his father's retirement at the back, if not the front, of his mind. 'But in the meantime, I thought it would do for you and Ruth.'

David and Ruth looked at each other, astounded.

'It sounds perfect,' Ruth enthused when she found her powers of speech. 'Oh, Mr Archer, thank you.'

'There's just one condition,' Phil smiled. David looked doubtful but his father went on. 'I won't tell you again, Ruth. You've got to start calling me Phil!'

• • •

'Mark actually went and told Matthew! I couldn't believe it!'

Shula's outrage echoed round the yard at Bridge Farm. In her capacity as agent for the Estate, she'd come over to look at a wall that was starting to slip, and to authorize repairs. Pat, who was married to Shula's cousin Tony, had recently persuaded him to diversify into yogurt production on their organic farm. They'd been late with the milking and she was rolling a churn across the icy January yard.

'Just let me drop this down and then –' Pat broke off and stood the churn upright. 'Did I tell you the deli in London that's distributing for us want us to up our production by 50 per cent?'

'That's great.' But Shula wasn't really interested. She was more interested in having a baby. Or, more specifically, why she wasn't having one.

She and Mark had been 'trying', as everyone coyly put it, for a year now, since before he'd taken the job in Birmingham. Shula had been convinced she'd be pregnant by now: when they'd been looking at those horrible houses in commuterland, she especially hadn't wanted to move because of it. But nothing had happened.

And then a couple of weeks ago Mark had gone and mentioned it to Matthew Thoroughgood after one of their sweaty sessions on the squash court. Matthew had immediately started calling it 'sub-fertility' and had suggested that Shula made an appointment to see him so that he could refer her to a 'Well Woman' clinic.

But, as she told Pat when they were indoors with their hands wrapped gratefully round mugs of coffee, she couldn't really be cross with Mark.

'It had been bothering me too,' she mused. 'But I think perhaps I didn't want to go and get checked out because I was worried about what they might tell me. Anyway,' she concluded, 'I went. Last week.'

'And what did they tell you?'

Shula grinned ruefully.

'Everything's fine, apparently. Though they've suggested a laparoscopy just in case.'

'There you are, then.' Pat was listening out for the tanker driver – the winter weather had made him late, too. 'Look, Shula, for what it's worth, all this worrying – well, it could be what's getting in the way. It's only been a year.'

'But Jennifer got pregnant straight away – and she's ancient!' blurted out Shula. 'And now they've got Alice!'

Pat said nothing. Privately she thought Jennifer had been mad to have another baby, just when Kate, at eleven, was practically off her hands and her older children, Adam and Debbie, were totally independent.

But then Jennifer had had to strike some strange bargains with life, and news of her pregnancy, at forty-three, had come suspiciously soon after Brian had developed a strange obsession with Betty Tucker, who'd been working as their cleaner. That had ended, Pat knew, with Jill warning Brian off. Betty had left her job abruptly and the Tuckers had moved out of the Aldridges' farm cottage. They'd set up home at Willow Farm: Mike could run his milk round just as easily from there.

Pat was disappointed in Jennifer. She'd thought that her sister-in-law was brighter than to imagine that having another baby would bind Brian to her. Quite the reverse, in fact: when Jennifer had been in labour, he'd been at the races with Mandy Beesborough, a redhead with a wide smile who ran the local Pony Club.

Shula continued to wallow.

'And there's Ruth and David in the first flush of married bliss and Elizabeth getting her journalism going and Mum and Dad on holiday in Australia – everyone's doing something, or making changes, except me.'

'You are sorry for yourself!' Pat gathered up their mugs and took them over to the sink.

'I know what's going to happen,' Shula agonized. 'They're going to ask me to be godmother. Jennifer said she would.'

'Don't do it, then.' Pat began washing the kids' floating breakfast bowls. 'Take a leaf out of Brian's book. He doesn't do anything he doesn't want to.'

He hadn't come to Pat and Tony's dairy-warming party back in the autumn and Tony had been deeply offended. He'd declared that Brian was too high and mighty and was heading for a fall. But then again, Pat thought, it could have been the drink talking. You could never tell with Tony.

• • •

'So, what can I do for you, Joe, this fine spring day?'

Brian, to everyone's amazement including his own, had been persuaded to stand in the local elections. He would never normally have put himself forward: community service was hardly his strong point, unless you counted, he quipped to himself, hours of selfless devotion to the female population of Borsetshire and, by association, the restaurant and hotel trade. But Sir Sidney Goodman, local bene-factor, ex-mayor and chairman of the canning factory, had had a heart attack and was unable to defend his seat. The local Conservative Association had asked Brian to step into the breach.

As Joe Grundy led him between a reeking dungheap and the pile of rusty corrugated iron that reposed in the middle of the yard at Grange Farm, Brian remembered exactly why it was he had never done anything like this before. It was because it meant dealing with people like Joe.

As tenant, Joe Grundy had seen several Estate owners come and go, and not one had ever been able to persuade him to improve his farm. Instead, Joe preferred, with the willing connivance of his son Eddie, to come up with money-making schemes that involved anything but farming. Now that diversification was the new buzzword – Brian himself had diversified into deer – Joe was in his element.

When canvassing in this, the spring of 1989, Brian had expected to be fielding questions about the poll tax and the government's record, but he hadn't reckoned with Joe's agenda. First he asked Brian's opinion on car-boot sales and open-air concerts – both in flagrant breach of his tenancy agreement – and then demanded to know if there were any subsidies available for growing tulips. Finally, he announced that there was a cow he wanted Brian to have a look at.

'Joe, I'm not a dairy farmer, you know,' Brian protested as Joe led him into a ramshackle cowshed. 'Get the vet if you're not sure.'

Joe led him towards a solitary cow in the furthest pen.

'She won't come into milking. She's lost some condition. And she goes berserk if there's a sudden noise.'

Brian, as he'd said, wasn't a dairyman. But the symptoms Joe described could only point to one thing.

'It's obvious, isn't it?' he replied. 'There's been enough publicity about it lately.'

There was a new disease rife among cattle – bovine spongiform encephalopathy – known, understandably, as BSE for short. No one quite knew how it had started, though the suspicion was that it came from giving them feed containing animal protein. It affected their brains and nervous system. People were calling it 'mad cow' disease.

'Here, I'll show you.' Joe picked up a bucket and approached the cow.

'Joe,' asked Brian uneasily, 'what are you doing?'

The last thing he wanted was a demonstration: the poor beast had a funny enough look in her eye as it was. But Joe started banging on the bucket, right near the cow. She lowered her head and bellowed, then stampeded towards him.

'Out of the way!' cried Brian, leaping forwards. 'She'll have you against that wall! Back, back!'

But in pushing Joe away, Brian put himself directly in front of the cow and with a flick of her strong neck, she butted him, tossing him against the brick wall of the byre. Joe's daughter-in-law, Clarrie, arrived just in time to hear the sickening thud as Brian's head hit the wall, and the lesser one as his body slumped to the floor among the muck and straw.

'Oh Lord!' she gasped. 'Mr Aldridge!'

The injury didn't seem too bad at first: Brian hadn't even wanted to go to hospital. He was certainly *compos mentis* enough to have been his usual prickly self with Matthew Thoroughgood: since his own affair with Caroline, he made it a point of honour to cold-shoulder any of her other boyfriends.

But Matthew insisted on driving Brian to Borchester General himself. He left poor Clarrie to deal with Joe, who'd gone into shock. But that could be remedied with sweet tea and attention and, as Matthew rightly suspected, the full extent of Brian's injuries took some time to emerge.

For Jennifer, it was blow after blow. First Brian had to be operated on for a blood clot to the brain: but he seemed to get through that without any trouble at all. The day after the operation he was sitting up in bed and chatting to the nurses, and Jennifer had never been so glad to see him back to his old self.

But a week later, just when she'd been expecting him to be discharged, an infection set in, one he'd picked up at the time of the original injury. It wasn't surprising, really, as Matthew told her when she went to him for reassurance: farms were not exactly hygienic places, Joe's least of all.

The second operation, for a cerebral abscess, was more complicated and more serious: Brian's recovery from it, as Jennifer had been warned, was slower and more unpredictable.

They finally let him out at the beginning of June, for Alice's postponed christening, but he winced at his baby daughter's screams in the church, and as soon as they all got back to the house, he had to go and lie down.

It was hard for Jennifer, who'd always relied on his strength, to see him so weakened, and it was hard for Brian too. Harder still when, during harvest, he had a fit in a field and was diagnosed with post-traumatic epilepsy.

Jennifer had to go begging to Brookfield again. They'd already helped with the silage and with drafting the lambs and calving the hinds. Now Phil sent David over when he could spare him to cart grain with the contractor and to oversee the straw-burning.

'I suppose we're lucky, really. We've got money we can throw at the problem,' Jennifer told her mother. She was glassy-eyed with tiredness: Alice was a fretful baby and Debbie and Kate weren't being the help she'd hoped for. 'We can buy in help on the farm.'

'It's you I'm worried about, dear.' Peggy had been concerned enough to call out Matthew the other week when Jennifer had come close to fainting in the yard. 'How are you going to cope with it all?'

'Oh, I'll manage,' said Jennifer. 'I get orders from Brian and I pass them on. It's the worry that wears me out, Mum. It's so awful for Brian. And I do feel for him.'

Brian had plenty of time to feel awful: the doctors, it seemed, wanted to stop him from doing anything else with his time. He was on four tablets a day, with the usual proviso. 'May cause drowsiness. If affected, do not drive or operate heavy machinery.' He should be so lucky. Matthew holier-than-thou Thoroughgood had spelt it out: not only was Brian not to drive on public roads for two years, until his so-called 'condition' had settled down, but the good doctor had suggested that the same timescale should apply to the farm. So whenever Brian wanted to see how the men were getting on with the barley or to check on the deer, he had to ask Jenny to drive him around. He couldn't go to Borchester for a spare part or nip a forgotten Thermos out to a tractor driver. And in the middle of harvest!

'How are things down at Brookfield?' Brian asked David one hot, pale-skied August afternoon as they watched lines of flame race across the stubble and thick smoke billow into the air.

'Well . . .' David rubbed his hand over his face.

To tell the truth, things were pretty awful. They were still waiting for planning permission for the bungalow: in the meantime, he and Ruth had been living at Brookfield. Everyone always said it was impossible for two women to share a kitchen, but that wasn't the issue. In fact, the problem was just the opposite.

David loved his mum dearly, but she was a farmer's wife of the old school. At harvest, for example, her role was feeding and watering, fetching and carrying. They couldn't have done without her: if he or his father had had to wait at the house for the dairy supplies rep, instead of leaving a list and relying on her to pass it on, it could have held up combining for the best part of an hour. They might ask her to keep an eye on a cow that looked as though she might calve or to phone about the weaner rations, but that was the extent of it.

Ruth, on the other hand, was far more actively involved: she expected to be out cutting corn, not cutting sandwiches, and David was surprised, especially as Ruth had worked on the farm for over a year, that his mum didn't seem to realize this. Ruth said that Jill was probably just missing her own daughters – Shula married and off her hands, and Elizabeth working all hours at her journalism. But that didn't mean, she insisted, that she had to be turned into Jill's notion of a wife. The final straw had been when Jill had suggested that she and Ruth go into Borchester to look for new bedlinen in the sales on a morning when Ruth had the herd performance figures to go through.

David tried to explain all this to Brian, who looked a bit bemused.

'So Ruth's cooking supper tonight for us all,' David concluded. 'A bit of a peace-offering.'

'Oh, I see,' said Brian. 'Let's hope it works.'

'I shouldn't have used all that chilli. Or maybe it was the paprika.'

David thumped down his glass. He had downed half his pint in one go and still his mouth felt as if Brian had been burning straw in it.

'Honestly, Ruth, it was brilliant, the best curry I've had for years,' he said loyally, putting his arm round her and pulling her against him on the bench in the garden at The Bull.

'But what about your father?' she fretted. 'Your mum's such a brilliant cook.'

'He liked it, Mum liked it, we all liked it! Makes a change from sausages and shepherd's pie.'

Ruth wouldn't be consoled.

'Maybe . . .' she conceded. 'But it's not going to solve anything in the long run. Tomorrow I'll do something to upset your mum and we'll all be back where we started.'

'Evening!' Brian, with a glass of orange juice, came towards them over the grass. 'Phil said you were here, so I got Jenny to drop me off.'

'Come and join us.' David budged up to make room. 'Don't often see you down here in the evenings.'

'You don't often see me anywhere nowadays, do you?' Brian remarked wryly. He sat down and stretched his legs out in front of him, immaculate in cream cotton. 'Not with this half a life I'm having to live.'

Ruth cleared her throat awkwardly. There was a silence before Brian spoke again.

'Still, I've just got to get on with it, I suppose. Get on with what I can do, that is. But there's an awful lot I can't. That's why I've got a proposition for you, David. How would you like to come and be my new foreman?'

'Foreman?' David looked sideways at Ruth, trying to gauge her reaction.

'And from January, Ruth could do her year's practical at Home Farm.' He paused to re-roll the cuff of his striped shirt before adding casually: 'Of course, there'd be a house provided.'

Brian had hardly baited the hook before Ruth was snapping at it.

'Our own house! Oh, David!'

She clutched David's arm, her eyes shining. Cleverly, Brian backed off.

'Think about it,' he said. 'The offer's there.' He drained his glass. 'I'd better be getting back,' he added. 'You know, the funny thing about this epilepsy is that with all the walking and not drinking, I feel fitter than I've ever done in my life.'

Phil didn't feel very good, though, when he was told about the offer, and that David's inclination was to accept.

'He's trying to pension me off, that's what it is! David's using this job at Brian's to try to force me into handing over the farm!'

'It's not quite that simple, is it, dear?' asked Jill, stirring a vast vat of gooseberry jam. 'There's Kenton to think about. David may be a partner, but since Kenton hasn't really found anything else he wants to do –'

'Not that again!' Phil put his head in his hands. 'The whole thing's giving me a headache.'

'There is one thing Kenton's keen on.' Jill squinted at her jam thermometer and hooked it on the side of the bubbling pan. 'Nelson's antique shop. If we were to help him raise the capital to buy it, he really thinks he could make a go of it. And it would sort out the question of who gets Brookfield once and for all.'

Kenton hadn't had a lot of luck since he'd left the navy. He'd had plenty of interviews for jobs, and he'd had a go at a couple of things, commodity broking in London, for instance, but nothing had really suited him.

'OK, so I know nothing about antiques, I admit, but I could learn!' he'd assured his mother when he'd come back from a session in the wine bar with the news that Nelson was selling up the shop. 'And Nelson says he'd always give me advice if I need it. But I can see myself doing it, Mum. I've even thought of the name! "Archer's Antiquities"!'

It took rather more than a name to get a business off the ground in a recession, Jill thought privately, but she'd smiled encouragingly at her son. She knew that Kenton was a bit of a butterfly: he'd only stuck the navy for so long because it had whisked him off to different places the whole time. If he didn't find something locally soon, he'd be off again, Jill knew he would – and just when she'd got used to having him around. With Shula and Mark so wrapped up in each other and David married, there was only Elizabeth at home, and even she was muttering about finding a job in Birmingham.

So Phil found himself doing sums on the back of the telephone bill when the worry kept him awake in the small hours, and a week or so later, he found himself sitting his elder son down for a sensible chat. He explained that he and Jill had talked about it and they were prepared to give Kenton half the purchase price of the shop as an advance on his inheritance – but he'd have to raise the rest with a mortgage.

'Oh, Dad, that's fantastic!' Kenton jumped up and hugged him. 'And you can forget about this mortgage lark. I had a word with Shula and she's persuaded Mark to take some of their millions out of the building society and take a half share with me! So it's all square.'

Phil marvelled at his son's facility for getting people to do what he wanted and for the vacuous ease with which Kenton accepted that things would naturally work out his way. He'd never been more forcibly reminded of his own late brother, Jack, with his monkey-like grin and constant get-rich-quick schemes, which had so plagued his and Peggy's marriage. Or even, given the past rivalry between Kenton and David, of his father's brother, Ben, who'd once made a play for Doris and had emigrated to Canada under a cloud. Phil made a mental note to keep an eye on Kenton when he was in the same room as Ruth in future.

But, as ever, solving one problem at Brookfield created another. When David, who'd by now accepted Brian's offer and was working at Home Farm, heard about Phil's magnanimous gesture, he was incandescent.

'I daresay they thought it would help,' soothed Ruth, placing his supper in front of him in their new house. It was only pork pie and salad, but as she'd warned him all along, she wasn't Jill. She'd been out working all day, too. 'To stop you worrying about Kenton trying to muscle in on the farm.'

'I'm supposed to be a partner, Ruth! And Dad's taking unilateral action with the Brookfield cheque-book!'

'You don't know that –'

David dolloped a spoonful of pickle on his plate.

'He's not going to find that sort of money in his back pocket, is he? Mark's had the wit to get Kenton to pay rent to make up for the building society interest he's losing, but Dad just doles out the cash!'

'It's an advance on Kenton's inheritance, David. It's money that'd be coming to him anyway.'

'Ruth, it's typical, OK? You don't know him.' David hacked savagely at his pie. 'You didn't grow up with him. You didn't have him stealing your bubblegum cards and using all your aftershave.'

Chewing, he got up and went to the fridge. She watched him reach inside and get them a can of lager each. His shirt had come untucked and she could see a triangle of naked brown back. It reminded her just how much she loved him.

'Look at it this way,' she soothed. 'You'd been on edge ever since Kenton came home. Taking this job with Brian at least got you out of Brookfield. Far from favouring Kenton, your dad might even be starting to appreciate what he's lost.'

'Huh! Some hope!' He plonked her lager on the table.

'I don't believe this,' she said with half a smile. 'I really thought when we left Brookfield, we'd be leaving Brookfield. But it's just the same. Your family's still the main topic of conversation.'

'Yeah, the Archers ought to carry a government health warning: Excessive Consumption Can Damage Your Health.'

'Don't get mad about it, David,' she pleaded. 'We're farming and doing what we want, aren't we? Why shouldn't Kenton?'

'Ruth, do I have to spell it out? He –'

She tugged him down towards her. She untucked his shirt all the way round and slid her hands underneath.

'We're in our own home for the first time ever, and for the first time since we got it Brian doesn't want you out on a combine till ten. So if you think I'm spending all evening going over the rights and wrongs of what your dad's done for Kenton, you've got another think coming.'

And for once, David had the good sense to give in.

· · ·

Nelson placed Shula's St Clements on the bar in front of her.

'Drinking alone?' he enquired as he went to the till. 'Or is the lovely Caroline joining you?'

'She's working this evening.' Shula sipped her drink. 'But Mark'll be along in a bit.'

'Oh, excellent.' Nelson lifted a sardonic eyebrow. 'I can look forward to a sharp rise in sales of mineral water.'

Shula smiled thinly. When she'd gone for her laparoscopy in the spring, the gynaecologist, Mr James, had told her that there was bad news and good news. The bad news was that she'd had endometriosis. The good news was that they'd cleared it up and – he said – it shouldn't affect her chances of becoming pregnant at all. Now it was the end of August and, despite a healthy regime of diet, exercise and little or no alcohol for her and for Mark, there was still no sign of a baby.

'By the way.' Nelson poured himself a glass of Rioja and placed a dish of olives in front of her. 'Kenton and I have come to an agreement about a price for the stock.'

'Oh.' Rodway's were handling the sale of the shop, though because of Shula's personal interest, the day-to-day details were being handled by a colleague. 'Good.'

Nelson was clearly in a reflective mood.

'Another rite of passage,' he observed, palming an olive stone gracefully into an ashtray. 'First my move to Honeysuckle Cottage, now the sale of the shop . . .'

'This time last year we were all at the pub for Uncle Walter's birthday party, weren't we?' smiled Shula, thinking back. 'And Sid made him a freeman of The Bull and said all his specials would be on the house. And Uncle Walter said it'd be an expensive present, because . . .'

'Because he was going on for ever.' Nelson cut across her. 'I'm surprised he said that. I found him, you know, just before the party, in the churchyard, by my mother's grave.'

'Did you?'

'He said he just wanted some quiet time. And he reminded me that he'd chosen his epitaph after your grandfather died.'

'What was it? "All the beasts of the forest are mine, and so are the cattle upon a thousand hills",' quoted Shula softly.

'That's right.' Nelson took a slow sip of wine. 'I think, you know, he was ready to go.'

'You must miss him.' Shula knew that whatever she said, it would be inadequate, but Nelson didn't seem to mind.

'I do. I used to complain about digging his bean trench or cleaning out the budgie cage. But now I don't have to do them any more, there's a gap. A huge one.'

Shula knew what he meant. The theory about nature rushing in to fill a vacuum was nonsense. There was a gap in Nelson's life where his father had been and there was a gap in her life where a baby should be. And neither of them would ever be reconciled to it.

·4·

New Departures

Kathy Perks slopped white wine from the bottle on the table into her glass and Pat's.

'Oops, sorry! There you are, Pat! You're on beer, aren't you, Tony?'

'I hope so, if David ever gets back from the bar.'

'Any more for you, Ruth?' Kathy waved the bottle in her face but Ruth covered her glass.

'No, thanks. I wouldn't mind keeping a bit of a clear head.'

'Brian's not making you start work tomorrow, is he?' Tony up-ended the dregs of a packet of dry roasted peanuts into his mouth.

'The day after,' admitted Ruth. 'But I'd like to be able to stand for "Auld Lang Syne".'

With the Brookfield bungalow under construction, and Ruth about to start her year-long placement with Brian, she and David were still happily ensconced in their house at Home Farm.

David's working arrangement with Brian, however, had been short-lived. Finding that the role of foreman involved a lot of being shouted at and ferrying Brian about, he'd secretly been only too pleased when he'd bumped into his father at a ploughing match and Phil had made the first move towards inviting his son back into the fold.

They'd been stretched at Brookfield without David, but Phil had realized it was important for his son to spread his wings. Nonetheless, he missed him. It wasn't so much the farmwork: Graham could cope with the cows and Neil with the pigs. What Phil missed, to his amazement, was talking things over with David: though they'd frequently disagreed in the past, Phil still preferred it to making all the decisions in isolation. At the ploughing match, he'd been keen to ask his son's advice about the wisdom of leasing quota and, a month or so later, Ruth and David had been able to give Phil and Jill their own good tidings: David wanted to go back to work with his dad.

As a result, it had been a lovely Christmas at Brookfield. Ruth and David had volunteered to do the early milking to give Phil a lie-in, and even Elizabeth had behaved herself.

Ruth watched as David came back towards the table with a pint in each hand.

The Bull was heaving. No one could remember quite why Sid had offered to hold a huge New Year's Eve party there, first drink on the house, but no one had forgotten to turn up. With Phil and Jill wanting a quiet night this year, and Brian and Jennifer entertaining her mother Peggy and sister, Lilian, who'd come back from Guernsey for Christmas, the younger Archers anyway had no alternative.

'You've never seen anything like it at the bar.' David squeezed past the beer belly of Eddie Grundy's mate, Baggy, who was talking to Mike Tucker. He put the drinks on the table. 'Dave Barry was actually buying a round.'

'He hasn't bought me a drink yet!' Kathy pouted. 'I'm going to have a word.'

'Don't you think you've had enough?' Pat pulled at the sleeve of Kathy's claret-coloured voile shirt but Kathy had already lurched shakily off.

'Uh-oh. She and Dave Barry used to have a bit of a thing before she was married,' David explained to Ruth.

'She's very low at the moment about this schools amalgamation business,' fretted Pat. 'She could lose her job.' She looked anxiously after her friend. 'She's vulnerable to someone like Dave.'

'Oh, stop worrying. Kathy can look after herself.' Tony raised his glass. 'Well, here's to 1989! And good riddance!'

'Hear, hear!' David clinked his glass against Tony's. 'I shan't be glad to see the back of it.'

'That's a nice way to talk about your first year of marriage!' grinned Ruth, thumping him.

David gave her a silencing kiss.

'You're fantastic. The best thing ever. I was meaning on the farm.'

It had been an awful year for farmers. The spread of BSE and mounting public concern had resulted in a slump in profits in both the beef and dairy industry. Then there'd been a scare about salmonella in eggs, which had led to the resignation of a junior minister and the introduction of new government guidelines for testing, which, it was predicted, could drive many small-scale producers out of business.

'I don't know why you're complaining, though, Tony,' David continued. 'Organics are booming. And you're all set to be the first yogurt millionaire.'

'I'll remember that when I'm pulling leeks by hand with the east wind whipping down my neck,' retorted Tony. Then, interrupting himself: 'Blimey, look who's just walked in.'

'Lilian!' Pat called through the crush to Tony's sister. 'Over here!'

'She must have finished all Brian's gin.' Tony stood up and groped for some change. 'I suppose I'll have to get her a drink. Even if I am just the poor tenant and she's my loaded landlord.'

'Does she come back every Christmas?' asked Ruth, watching how all the male heads swivelled so predictably as Lilian teetered towards the bar in her short velvet skirt and glittery jacket. Ruth's idea of dressing up had been to put on a clean T-shirt with her jeans and wash her hair.

'No, thank goodness,' said Pat, 'or Tony's blood pressure'd be off the scale. He gets in such a tizz about his well-off sisters.'

'I hope she is just back for Christmas,' remarked David. 'I heard her having quite a go at Shula at Auntie Peggy's on Boxing Day. About the Grundys.'

'Oh?' Pat waved to Lilian, who'd been accosted by Eddie. He was always claiming they had a 'special understanding'. Sadly for him, it didn't extend to her waiving his rent.

'And Shula says she's been in and out of the Estate office over the holiday,' David went on. 'Checking up on her. And she's been prowling round the Estate.'

'Not in those shoes, I hope.' Even Ruth couldn't help noticing Lilian's black satin stilettos with diamante heels.

'No, the wellies she wears for swabbing down the deck of her yacht, probably,' grunted David. 'I think she's up to something.'

Ruth snorted with laughter.

'Listen to you! You sound like something out of the Famous Five.'

Pat wrenched her eyes away from the bar, where Dave Barry was dangling a sprig of mistletoe in front of an apparently mesmerized Kathy.

'Fifteen years ago I'd have agreed with you, Ruth,' she said. 'But once you've lived here for a bit, you'll know he's right. There's nowhere like Ambridge for intrigue.'

Barely a month later, Pat was proved right again. Along with all the other tenants, she and Tony received a letter giving them first refusal on buying their farm. The Estate was up for sale.

'And how do we find out about it?' ranted Tony, rattling the letter in Pat's face as she cleared the table after breakfast. 'In the same way as the Grundys! Never mind that it's my sister who's selling, and that my mother and my cousin work in the Estate office.'

Pat couldn't account for Lilian, but then who could?

'You can't blame Shula; she works for Rodway's, not Lilian,' she reasoned.

'And Mum?' Tony glared.

'Perhaps Peggy thought it would be . . . unethical,' she hazarded.

Tony rolled his eyes in disbelief.

'Whose side are you on? Think about it, Pat! Lilian was back here at Christmas, snooping around. She can see what a success we've made of this place. She's just cashing in on our hard labour.'

'You can hardly say that about Grange Farm, though, can you?' Pat put the lid back on the marmalade. 'What I can't understand is why Lilian needs the money.'

'Perhaps she's fallen for some gold-digging toy boy. Perhaps she wants to buy her own distillery.' Tony banged his coffee mug down on the table. 'That's not the point. The point is she and Mum must have plotted this – and neither of them had the decency to say a word.'

Pat sighed inwardly. If she could have had £5 for every time she'd heard Tony rave on about how hard done by he was compared with his sisters, they'd have been able to buy Bridge Farm with money to spare. She took pride in everything they'd achieved on their own, but Tony, it seemed, would have preferred a hand-out every time. He was still chuntering away as Pat went to answer the phone, which had been trilling away in the background.

'Who was that?' he demanded when she came back. He'd already started doing sums in the margin of the letter.

'Kathy,' said Pat glumly.

Pat was worried about things at The Bull. First Sid had asked her if she could have a word with Kathy who, he said, was behaving very distantly with him. He assumed she was depressed about work. Then Kathy had confided in her about a 'friend', supposedly, whose marriage was moribund and who found she was attracted to another man.

'Again?' asked Tony. It was true Kathy had been phoning rather a lot. 'Pass us the calculator.'

'I told you,' said Pat, doing so. 'She's going through a bad patch. So's Sid.'

'Look, Pat, this is all very well, but we've got problems of our own now.' Tony jabbed at the buttons. 'I'm not having this place turned into a cross between a drop-in centre and a women's refuge.'

Pat stacked the breakfast dishes in silence. She knew he was referring not just to Kathy but to Sharon Richards, who'd recently had a baby by the awful Clive Horrobin, who'd promptly deserted her. Sharon's friend Lucy Perks was lobbying for her and baby Kylie to come and live in the caravan at Bridge Farm, and for Pat to give Sharon a job in the dairy. Pat was wavering. Tony had already told her in no uncertain terms that she was crazy even to consider it.

But when Peggy called round later that day, rather bravely Pat thought, Tony was back to his original theme. He berated his mother for not selling The Bull last year when she'd been offered three quarters of a million by a national carvery chain, even though at the time he'd vehemently opposed the idea. Now, though, when he could have found a use for a chunk of the money, his mother had nothing to loan him. She didn't even own her house: Blossom Hill Cottage still belonged to Lilian.

'And she's not selling that from under you, I suppose,' sneered Tony nastily. 'Well, thanks, Mum. Thanks for nothing.'

Poor Peggy. All her life she'd lived for her children, and nothing she did was ever right for them. When Lilian had first told her that she wanted to sell the Estate in order to buy a flat in London that she and her son James could use, Peggy's first thought had been how Tony would take it. Her second had been for herself, wondering if Lilian would ever bother to come to Ambridge once she'd severed her ties there. And her third was to wish that she had someone close with whom she could talk things over – someone who'd understand.

Since her first husband, Jack Archer, had died, Peggy had had her admirers: there'd been Dave Escott all those years ago, though he'd turned out to be something of a con man. More recently, she'd been courted by Godfrey Wendover, a retired naval officer who'd bought one of the barn conversions. For a while he'd brought a nautical touch to Peggy's life: they'd manned the Treasure Island stall at the fête dressed as pirates and he'd played her sea shanties on the pub piano. Tony hadn't liked him, of course: he'd called him, Peggy knew, 'Captain Pugwash' and even – Peggy pursed her lips to think of it – 'Godfrey Legover'.

But Peggy and Godfrey had somehow drifted apart and she'd returned to her oldest confidant – Jack Woolley. It was Jack she told now about Tony's spiteful comments, and he cheered her up, as he always did, by suggesting a walk in the Country Park with his Staffordshire bull terrier, Captain, and inviting her to the masked ball that Caroline was organizing for Valentine's Day.

'Tony either expects me to lend him the money, or wants Lilian to drop the price,' she lamented as they waited while Captain rooted noisily in the sodden leaves by the lake.

'Why should she do that?' enquired Jack. 'I'm sure she's not asking over the odds.'

'Of course not. They'd already be getting the farm at a substantial discount on the price it would fetch on the open market. Lilian's explained all that.'

'Well, then. Come on, Captain!'

Peggy watched as Captain, in his tartan coat, waddled back towards them.

'He could easily get a mortgage,' mused Peggy, 'with the outlook for organics as it is. But I can't see Tony buying the farm. He'd have nothing to moan about then, would he? And he'd rather feel hard done by.'

Peggy felt better for talking to Jack about it, but her children hadn't finished with her.

'He's being rather attentive lately, isn't he?' asked Jennifer coldly, when her mother told her that Jack had asked her to the masked ball.

'We've always been friendly,' shrugged Peggy.

'And that's all it is, is it?' Jennifer lowered an egg into a pan of water for Alice's tea.

Peggy had suddenly had enough.

'I don't know what you mean, Jennifer.' She stood up and retrieved her handbag from the side of her chair. 'But I ought to let you know that I shan't be able to babysit for you on Friday.'

'Oh, Mum –' Jennifer had been intending to go to an NFU function with Brian.

'Jack's asked me out to dinner. Sorry.'

• • •

Time went on: the primroses came out, then the daffodils. Uncle Tom reported that the chiffchaffs were back and building their nests in the brambles down the lane from his cottage: there was the usual village schism over who had allegedly heard the first cuckoo. At the Estate office, Shula hardly had time to glance out of the window, let alone listen to the birds: she was too busy fielding enquiries from prospective purchasers and dealing with tenants anxious about their futures.

Gradually, it became clear that none of the tenants, Tony included, could either raise the money or was willing to take on the repayments required to buy their farms, and one thing emerged as imperative. If the Estate was to be sold, Lilian had to be persuaded to sell it as one lot.

'If it gets split up, the whole character of the village'll change, won't it?' Shula reasoned to her mother.

By now it was early May and she was helping to change the beds for some guests who were due. Jill's diversification into farmhouse bed and breakfast was proving quite a success, which was more than could be said for progress on Ruth and David's bungalow. The builders had gone bust.

'I suppose there are people around with that sort of money.' Jill stuffed a pillow into its case. 'Who'd be able to buy the Estate as a whole.'

'Lots of them. Pop stars, City traders, Arabs, Americans . . .'

'According to Martha Woodford, there was some religious cult interested.' Jill put the pillow in place and smoothed the duvet over it.

'That's a load of rubbish. But I am showing someone round next week. He sounds all right. Scottish, apparently.'

It was one of Pat's least favourite jobs – or, to be accurate, another of them, along with pulling leeks and weeding carrots. With Tony, she was on her knees, scraping the earth away from the potato tubers to see if the shoots were just below the surface. If so, they could safely harrow – for maximum weed control with minimum yield damage.

She'd just been having another go at Tony, trying to persuade him to let Sharon and Kylie have the caravan in return for a bit of field work, when she looked up and saw someone watching them. She wiped a hank of hair off her face with the back of her hand.

'Who's that, Tony? The man on the footpath?'

Tony looked across.

The man was tall and blond, the light wind ruffling his curly hair. He had on a tweed jacket and twill trousers, but even from this distance Pat could see it wasn't a tweed jacket like Tony's tweed jacket, which was from the local chain store and hadn't fitted him properly even when it was new. This stranger's jacket sat beautifully on his shoulders. It was slightly nipped in at the waist, and though it looked from this distance an unremarkable peat brown, Pat knew for sure it would have an overcheck – magenta, perhaps, or a subtle teal green.

'Morning!' he called. He had a Scots accent.

'Good morning!' Pat scrambled to her feet to a look of scorn from Tony.

'I hope I'm not trespassing?'

'I hope you're not either,' muttered Tony, then, louder, 'If you're looking for casual work, you're a bit early.'

Pat gave an inane laugh. Trust Tony!

'Take no notice of my husband,' she apologized. 'He has a strange sense of humour.'

'I'm not after work,' the man conceded. 'But I like to keep up with the latest agricultural trends. So this is organics, is it?'

It was only later in the day when Shula called in for some yogurt and told them that she'd been showing round a prospective purchaser – Scottish, name of Cameron Fraser – that the penny dropped.

'We've already met him,' gasped Pat. 'He came wandering along the footpath this morning.'

'He seems to have put himself about quite a bit.' Shula put the yogurt money on the dresser. 'He had a chat with the vicar about his bees, he cornered Eddie Grundy, and Caroline was practically drooling after she ran into him on the Green.'

'Pat was just the same.' Tony, who'd been washing his hands, dripped his way to the towel. 'Show her a bit of expensive tailoring and her left-wing principles fly straight out of the window.'

'He seems quite keen,' mused Shula. 'In fact . . . I shouldn't really tell you, but he was talking about putting in an offer. What did you think of him, really?'

'Well, we didn't have a chance to get to know him, exactly.' Pat poured them all a cup of tea. 'What did you think, Tony?'

'Not much.' Tony sat down at the table. 'But there was something about him . . .'

'You're telling me.' Pat pushed his cup towards him. 'A heady combination of money and sex appeal.'

'Not that.' Tony reached impatiently for the biscuit tin. 'Something . . . I dunno. Smarmy.'

'You're just jealous,' teased Shula. 'He is very good-looking.'

'Exactly,' mocked Pat, watching her husband cram a chocolate digestive in his mouth. 'Your idea of sophistication's a splash of Old Spice and a foreign lager.'

Tony ignored her jibe. He was used to them.

'So,' he pronounced gloomily. 'We might have met our new land-lord.'

'Oh, cheer up, love,' Pat admonished. 'It could be worse. Last week we thought it was going to be the Moonies.'

Personally she thought Cameron Fraser might be a very interesting addition to the village. Lilian hadn't been the most involved of land-lords, after all. All least this bloke had taken the trouble to walk the farms. She sat forward and sipped her tea.

'Now come on, Shula,' she demanded, 'let's hear the rest of your gossip.'

·5·

Revaluations

Gossip? Shula just wished she had more to tell.

David had slipped easily back into the routine of working with his father and things were chugging along at Brookfield much as they had before. Another firm of builders had taken on the bungalow, but it was doubtful it would be finished by the summer, when Brian had told Ruth and David he needed their house for his new foreman, so they were on the move again. It was a bit of a pain but, to Mrs Antrobus's great delight, they'd finally arranged to rent the flat at Nightingale Farm that Ruth had lived in before she married.

Ruth seemed to be getting along all right at Home Farm and since, thankfully, Brian hadn't suffered any further fits, Jennifer had finally started to relax. Elizabeth had taken a job on a paper in Birmingham, freeing up another bedroom just in time for the summer influx of bed and breakfast guests, and Nigel, who'd had to accept that his long-standing love for Lizzie was at present unrequited, was still busy trying to make Lower Loxley pay by opening the house and grounds.

Kenton seemed to be making a go of the antique shop, though there'd been an upsetting moment when he'd told Mark and Shula about a forthcoming house sale. They'd gone along, thinking they might find a corner cupboard for the dining room, and the Davenport desk that Shula had always wanted. Mark had rocked a carved crib and Shula had found tears rolling down her cheeks because it was empty and because, she was beginning to be convinced, she would never cradle a baby of her own.

Yet again, as summer unfolded its beauty all around, she tried to think about other things. It was a perfect season that year. Pigeons crooned in the trees: two elided notes, one separate. Bees blundered from flower to flower. At Brookfield, they had good weather for the hay-making and for the start of harvest: first the flail mower, then the combine were busy from morning till night.

Shula, too, was busy at work. Cameron Fraser, the handsome Scot, had bought the Estate, and was making changes both to it and the Dower House, which he'd employed an interior designer to renovate. Sharon and Kylie had a less salubrious, but for them equally exciting, new home in the Bridge Farm caravan and Pat told Shula with some amusement that her elder son, John, had developed a teenage crush on Sharon which was manifesting itself in a sudden but useful interest in farmwork. Eddie's idea of improvements at Grange Farm included a maggot-farming scheme and a musical doorbell, which drove Clarrie so wild that she took off on holiday to Jersey by herself with a bit of the money her dad had left her. Caroline's horse, Ivor, died, and she replaced him with a beauty, a nine-year-old called Ippy. She also started seeing Cameron. Shula got herself involved in the village campaign to stop their red phone box being replaced with a plate glass booth, and Kenton ran a book on the raft race at the fete. Dave Barry suddenly announced he was leaving Ambridge for St Albans, where he could keep an eye on his elderly mother: there were rumours, unconfirmed, of an unhappy love affair.

It was all, for Shula, different in the detail and yet exactly the same as all the other summers: waiting and wondering, each month, if this would be the one. It never was.

· · ·

'Auntie Peggy, have you seen the file on the Estate woodlands?'

It was half past two on a bedraggled October afternoon. Shula had got out of bed feeling tired and it had been all she could do to make it through the morning. If she could just sort out the quotes for the felling of some conifers, she really thought she might go home.

'I don't think so . . .' Peggy sifted helplessly through a pile of papers. 'Oh! I'm sorry. I've got it here on my desk.'

'Don't worry,' said Shula, wearily taking it. Auntie Peggy simply wasn't as efficient as she had been. 'As long as it's safe.'

'My mind just isn't on the job at the moment,' confessed Peggy, sinking on to her swivel chair again.

Shula glanced up from the file. Now she looked more closely, her aunt was looking rather peculiar. Sort of excited, but tense.

'What's the problem?' she asked. She hoped Auntie Peggy wasn't going to run off with another Godfrey Wendover. Inefficient or not, she couldn't face any more changes at the Estate this year.

'Well . . .' Peggy looked at her niece conspiratorially. 'You're going to find out soon enough, anyway.'

'Yes?' Now, tired though she was, even Shula was curious. She couldn't imagine what it could be. Nothing ever happened to Auntie Peggy.

Peggy fiddled with her earring and, without success, tried not to look too delighted.

'Jack's asked me to marry him!' she burst out. And having made the confession, she immediately told Shula all the details.

Jack had asked her once before, back in the 1970s, and, fearing another refusal, had been understandably tongue-tied. The poor man had first attempted his latest proposal when they'd been babysitting for Alice, but Brian had burst in at the crucial moment. Then he'd tried to ask her in the kitchen at Grey Gables, but Jennifer, who was helping out because Jean-Paul had thrown one of his tantrums and had left to work for Nelson, kept interrupting with instructions to peel the potatoes and make a ton of pastry. But Jack had finally blurted it out and Peggy, she told a spellbound Shula, had accepted him later that afternoon as they walked under the shimmering beech trees in the Country Park.

'So you were the first to know?' Mark asked Shula that evening as they lay on the sofa listening to some weepy Rachmaninov.

Shula yawned. She was still tired. In fact she felt tired all the time, like at the start of the flu.

'Mmm. And you're not to say anything. Auntie Peggy's got to find the right time to tell Jennifer and Tony. You know what they're like.'

Mark leaned down for his wine glass and took a swig.

'Tony'll be worried about his inheritance and Jennifer'll be worried about losing a free babysitter.'

'Probably,' smiled Shula. 'Though now Kate's been expelled from boarding school, she'll be going to Borchester Green. I suppose Jennifer'll be able to call on her.'

She wondered, not for the first time, who she and Mark would use as a babysitter. Her mum, obviously, would be only too pleased to be asked. Not that Shula could imagine ever wanting to go out again once there was a snuffling little bundle upstairs in the back bedroom, which she'd paint buttercup yellow . . .

'Mark . . .' she began.

He stretched and kissed the top of her head.

'Yes?'

'I've got something else to tell you. Something else that'll be a bit of a surprise.'

'Caroline and Cameron getting hitched?' he speculated. 'Jean-Paul deciding he needs a real change and going to work at the greasy spoon on the bypass?'

Shula took a deep breath.

'I think I could be pregnant,' she said.

And she was. A couple of days later, after a sleepless night, both of them shaking with anticipation and dreading the result not being what they wanted, she and Mark did a test. It was positive. At last, after all the years of waiting, they were going to have a baby.

'Don't let's tell anyone yet,' she begged Mark, when he'd finished hugging her. 'I'll ask Matthew to do a proper test in a week or so to make really sure. Then I might start to believe it.'

'But I want to tell everyone now,' pleaded Mark. 'After all this time, they'll be so thrilled for us.'

'I know, but they won't be any less thrilled if we leave it a week, will they?' She kissed the tip of his nose. 'You are funny. I never thought you'd be this excited.'

'Shula, I'm . . . there aren't the words for how I feel. I'm just . . . oh, never mind. Come here.'

Now Shula didn't mind the tiredness. She didn't mind the times when she felt dizzy – once at the ballet in Birmingham, where Mark had taken her for a belated anniversary treat, and a couple of times when she'd got up suddenly or run up the stairs. She would have put up with anything. She would have been happy to have had to go to bed exhausted at seven, sleep till nine and throw up all day till it was time to go to bed again, just to be pregnant. Then the pains started.

She had the first one when Auntie Peggy had called round, prattling on about how snide Jennifer and Tony had been about her engagement, and how Shula and Kate were the only people who seemed happy for her. Shula tried to hold her breath and contain the pain. She pinned on a smile that made the muscles of her face ache, and she tried to concentrate on that rather than the cramp in her side. By the time Auntie Peggy had gone, so had the pain, but she couldn't hide the fact that something was wrong from Mark. He insisted on taking her over to the surgery, even though it was seven o'clock on a Friday night. Luckily, Matthew was still there.

'I think the best thing for you to do,' he announced cheerfully, when they'd described her symptoms and he'd examined her, 'is to go in and have a scan. So we can see exactly what's going on. And in the meantime, I'm going to do a blood test. The hormone levels in your blood will be able to confirm exactly how pregnant you are.'

'There's nothing to worry about, is there?' asked Shula anxiously. 'I mean, I haven't had any bleeding or anything.'

If she'd been more alert, she might have noticed that Matthew didn't actually answer.

'I suggest you present yourselves at Borchester General as early as possible, eh?' he advised, preparing the syringe. 'Just to be on the safe side.'

'Kenton, you'll have to do more carrots than that. David and Ruth are coming to lunch as well, you know.'

Kenton put down the peeler and flexed his fingers.

'Now you tell me. I'd better go to the store for another sack,' he moaned cheerfully.

Jill bent to the Aga to check on the beef, releasing even more of its delicious sizzle into the kitchen.

'Although at this moment it doesn't look as if anyone's coming to lunch,' she fretted. 'There's your father gone off to Hollowtree, and no sign of Mark and Shula . . .'

'They'll be here,' predicted Kenton. 'We all know how you love having your chicks round you for Sunday lunch.'

Jill sighed as she basted the beef. She hadn't seen much of Shula lately. She and Mark had been keeping themselves tucked away, and Jill always thought that was a bad sign. She hoped Shula wasn't going through another of her bouts of quiet desperation about having a baby. But just as she closed the oven door again, the back door swung open.

'Mark! Thank goodness!' Jill began to untie her apron, then stopped, puzzled. 'Where's Shula?'

Mark crossed the kitchen towards her. He looked drained.

'Now I don't want you to panic, everything's fine,' he began.

'I knew it! Where is she? It's not an accident, is it?'

Jill looked at Kenton, alarmed. He was still sitting, watchful, behind the heaped bright discs of carrot.

'She's in hospital,' said Mark carefully. 'She's had to have a little operation, but she's going to be fine.'

Jill wanted to go to Borchester General straight away, but Mark persuaded her to leave it for a while. Shula, he said, had been sleeping when he left, and anyway, he confessed guiltily, he'd suddenly realized that he was absolutely starving.

'Of course you are,' sympathized Jill, when Mark revealed that he'd been at the hospital all weekend, living on tea and Mars bars. 'But what is it? What's happened?'

Kenton sat Mark down with a beer and he told them everything. He told them about the pregnancy test and then the pains on Friday night. About how they'd gone to the hospital and Shula had had a scan that could find no evidence of a pregnancy. Yet how, at the same time, the blood test Matthew had done and which they'd rushed through analysis had indicated that she was certainly pregnant.

There was only one conclusion: the pregnancy was ectopic. It had developed in Shula's Fallopian tube, which had split under the pressure. It was this internal bleeding that had already caused the dizzy spells and pain she'd experienced. The operation had been to remove the damaged tube and the beginnings of a baby.

As Mark outlined all this for Kenton's benefit, Jill knew already what it meant. Shula, who'd spent nearly three years trying to conceive, had now lost one of her Fallopian tubes which, whatever the doctors said, could only reduce her chances of becoming pregnant again. She looked across the table at poor Mark, who looked so washed out. Jill would do all she could, but he'd shoulder the worst of it, Jill knew, all Shula's disappointment and sense of failure. She hoped they'd both be strong enough to bear it.

They let Shula out of hospital a couple of days later. It was the night of the village bonfire on the green: with the Young Farmers, Ruth and David had been scrounging wood all week, and Ruth was to be a steward.

There was no question of Shula and Mark going, but Jill had popped round to Glebe Cottage beforehand to leave some baked potatoes and a casserole in a low oven. Shula would need to build up her strength and Mark was looking worn out as well.

Shula had always loved Bonfire Night: the smell of cordite and the bright colours falling from the sky. When she'd been small, she'd always loved coming down to the green, wrapped in so many layers of clothing she could hardly move, waving her sparklers with stiff arms. She'd loved making toffee-apples with her mother and burning her mouth on sausages cooked in the fire. She'd never thought it would be possible to be sad on Bonfire Night: now she had ample proof. But she still made Mark pull their bed over to the window so she could see the village green: when he'd seen her mother out, he came upstairs, eased off his shoes and settled down beside her.

'If you want to go down and watch, Mark . . .' she began.

He spread his fingers and locked them with hers.

'I'd rather sit here with you.'

She smiled gratefully and squeezed his hand.

'I'm sorry if I'm not the brightest of company.'

'I don't expect it, not after what you've been through.'

'It hasn't been easy for you, either, has it?' asked Shula softly. It was something she'd been thinking about a lot.

'I'm fine,' said Mark stoutly. 'You know me.'

Shula considered him.

'Well, I think you've been putting on a show. For my benefit,' she added. 'But a show none the less.'

Mark sighed. He rubbed her cheek with their joined hands.

'At this moment,' he said carefully, 'I daren't let go of my feelings. If I did – well, I probably wouldn't be much support to you, would I?'

'I love you,' said Shula, gratefully.

'And I love you.'

'I know,' she said. 'I don't think I could have stood it otherwise.'

She snuggled closer against him and leaned her head on his shoulder.

'Shall I tell you what I was thinking while you were having the operation?' offered Mark.

Shula nodded against his neck.

'All I could think was, please God, please let Shula be all right. I wasn't thinking of the baby. I was just thinking of you.'

Shula moved again so she could see into his eyes.

'When I woke up, I was thinking of you,' she whispered. 'I was thinking, he's going to be so disappointed. I've failed.'

Mark took her face in his hands.

'You never could.'

She looked at him looking at her. She really wanted to believe him. She realized now how blessed she'd been, all those years as a child. Loved and protected by her parents, she'd been shielded from disappointment and safeguarded against failure. Now that she was an adult, however much her parents loved her, she was exposed. Life couldn't be magically neat and satisfying: no one could make it so any more, not even Mark, who loved her so much, and certainly not

Shula herself.

'Will you open the window for me?' she asked impulsively.

'What about the cold?' he frowned.

Dear Mark. Ever practical.

'Please.'

He gave her a look that said 'I'm indulging you' and scrambled across the bed to tug up the sash. The squeals of the rockets and the 'aahs' of the crowd came in on a rush of dark air. They could hear the crackle and spit of the fire and sense the smoky whiff of gunpowder.

'Thank you,' said Shula, as he settled back again and put his arm round her. 'I just wanted to smell the bonfire.'

• • •

'Honestly, you'd think after thirty years in the hotel trade Mr Woolley would have realized that New Year's Day is the worst day of the year to have your wedding,' complained Caroline good-humouredly of her boss. 'What do you think of these?'

Shula chewed thoughtfully on a savoury choux pastry bun filled with porcini mushrooms.

'Not bad. A bit sort of . . . nothing, though.'

'That's what I think. But Jean-Paul and I are determined to come up with something that isn't the dreaded vol-au-vents.'

'Oh, I agree,' said Shula wholeheartedly. 'They seem to turn up at every Ambridge wedding there's ever been. I think they're recycling the same ones.'

'Anyway,' continued Caroline, 'the food's the least of my worries now we've lured Jean-Paul back. At least we can do that in house. It's staffing the thing, and getting fresh flowers that bothers me. And the fact that Nelson's going to be Mr Woolley's best man.'

When Jack and Peggy had announced that they intended getting married on New Year's Day 1991, there'd been a buzz of excitement in the family. Shula, who'd been off work since her ectopic pregnancy, had found herself enlisted as Auntie Peggy's chief handmaiden and had spent many not entirely happy hours helping her hat-hunt in Borchester.

Now, at last, just days before the wedding, everything was in place: Auntie Peggy's cream silk chiffon wedding dress and peach hat, and her going-away suit in blue velvet. A stickler for detail, as Shula had found out to her cost, Auntie Peggy had even contacted the makers of her honeymoon outfit and obtained a piece of matching material with which she'd made a bow-tie for Captain.

In truth, though she'd moaned about Auntie Peggy and their several expeditions to Borchester and beyond, Shula had been glad of the distraction. The closeness that she and Mark had felt in the immediate aftermath of her failed pregnancy had not lasted and Shula knew she was to blame. Confused and despairing about her childlessness, she'd been to see Matthew without telling Mark and had asked him to put her on the pill. Matthew hadn't been keen but eventually she'd persuaded him: she'd rather know that she had no chance of getting pregnant, she said, than to go through the cycle of hope and disappointment which had become such a trial to her.

But Mark had found out. He thought she was behaving perversely and Christmas had been horrible. They'd bought each other thoughtless presents and had opened them resentfully before going to Brookfield, where Elizabeth had been on a high because, according to her, Cameron Fraser had chatted her up in the wine bar and Ruth and David, married two years and at last ensconced in the bungalow, still seemed blissfully happy.

Now, with New Year's Eve and the wedding approaching, Mark and Shula were trapped: they'd had a row, so they were hardly speaking to one another, and they couldn't sort out the row unless they talked.

'Try one of these, Shula. Deep-fried brie with cranberry sauce.' Shula's niece, Kate, who'd been bribed to behave for the duration of her grandmother's wedding, offered her a plate of canapés.

Shula shook her head. The wedding had been lovely, and it was a lovely party, but her head ached and she only wanted to go home. She'd seen Mark deep in conversation with Caroline, and with her mother, and she'd known they were talking about her. But though she knew she could put things right with just a word to Mark, mutinously she wouldn't.

'Doesn't Mum look smashing?' Tony, now apparently reconciled to his mother's choice of husband, materialized at Shula's elbow.

'Lovely,' said Shula warmly. There'd been something very moving about attending the wedding of two older people: something that should have told her that hope never dies, that love could last, and that passion could be rekindled. If only she'd been willing to listen.

'Jack says that when he turned round in church and saw her she quite took his breath away.' Tony, who'd been availing himself of the free-flowing champagne, plumped down beside her. 'Now I can see where our family gets its good looks from.'

'You mean you've never noticed before?' Shula couldn't help smiling.

'You take people for granted, that's all,' said Tony. 'I was proud to walk her down the aisle.'

Shula slowly turned the stem of her glass between her fingers. She looked over at Mark, who was talking to Tony's son, John. She knew she'd taken Mark for granted lately. He'd taken time off work to be with her before Christmas, and she'd repaid him by moaning about the cards he'd chosen and the holly wreath he'd selected. She'd gone out for lunch with Caroline or Auntie Peggy and left him at home sharing sardines on toast with the cats. Finally, and worst of all, she'd abused his love and his trust by not involving him in her decision about the pill, when it affected his life as much as hers.

Suddenly ashamed, she remembered how she'd felt on Bonfire Night. She'd told herself that she was an adult now, not a child sheltered by her parents. Adult things were going to happen to her and she'd have to cope with them. She'd told Mark that she loved him and that she couldn't have endured what she had done without him, yet she was behaving as if she didn't even like him.

To her shame, Shula realized that she'd been behaving like a child, admittedly a child who'd been promised the most marvellous present and then had it snatched away, but a child all the same.

Tony was still chuntering on about his mother and Jack's secret honeymoon destination and chortling about what Higgs, Jack's usually tight-lipped chauffeur, had said to Nelson outside the church. Shula silently got up and walked over to Mark. She tapped him on the arm.

'I think we should go home,' she said.

• • •

'What are these for?' asked Jill.

Shula had just presented her with an enormous bouquet, the biggest she could amass in January – chrysanthemums and carnations, freesias and lilies.

'Can't you guess?'

They were walking back towards the house: Jill had been shutting up her hens for the night.

'Well . . .'

'Oh, come on, Mum, you don't have to be so tactful. I've been absolutely foul, and you know it.'

Jill raised an eyebrow.

'Isn't it Mark you should be showering with flowers?'

'I've done all that,' smiled Shula ruefully. 'I've grovelled and abased myself. And apologized,' she added quickly. 'And I meant it.'

'Good,' said Jill softly.

She knew how hurt Mark had been by Shula's behaviour, and though Jill could understand it emotionally, that didn't make it right.

'I should have taken him with me to see Matthew and discussed it properly.'

'Yes, that would have been better.'

They'd reached the house and they both paused inside the back door to take their boots off.

'That's not all,' said Shula, tugging at her wellingtons. 'When I thought about it, after Auntie Peggy's wedding and everything, and thought about Mark and me getting old together . . . well, I just couldn't imagine it. Not without children, I mean.'

'Right,' said Jill carefully. Automatically, she padded across the kitchen floor and put the kettle on, then began hunting for vases for the flowers.

'I can't face an empty future, Mum.' Shula laid the bouquet in its creaking cellophane on the draining-board. 'I think I was just so scared that if we tried, and I had another ectopic, then that would have been it. I'd have blown my chances for ever. I could never have a baby.'

'But wasn't going on the pill going to do the same?' Jill tenderly separated the flowers and began cutting the stems.

'That's what Mark said, but at least my options would have still been open. I could say I'd chosen not to have a baby, instead of having failed to have one. Do you see?'

Jill held out a frond of lilies for Shula to smell.

'I suppose so. But you do complicate things for yourself, darling.'

'Mark said that too. But I was just so mixed up: all this going on the pill was me wanting to stay in control of my own destiny and yet not doing what I really wanted.'

'But you're sure now.'

'Absolutely certain. I want a baby. And I'm sorry for being such a pain.'

'Don't be silly.' Jill hugged her daughter tight. 'I'm just so glad that you and Mark have sorted things out. Now, your Gran's cut-glass vase for the freesias, don't you think?'

·6·

Affairs of the Heart

Jill watched the rich mixture turn under the spoon. Doris Archer's Christmas pudding recipe, handed down through generations of her family, was dark and delicious, dotted with bright chunks of cherry and chopped mixed peel.

'Phil!' she called. It was the last Sunday of November – Stir-Up Sunday, the traditional day for mixing the Christmas cake and pudding. While Jill was busy in the kitchen, Phil had promised to sort out the teetering pile of *Pig Breeder* magazines in the office. 'Phil! Are you coming to make a wish?'

It wasn't hard to guess what Phil would have wished for – or David for that matter. The BSE outbreak, which had affected beef sales, had had an even more lasting effect on the dairy industry, whose cull cows went for the pies and beefburgers that were thought to be the culprits in a human strain of the disease which had begun to emerge. Although the milk cheque, thankfully, kept coming, the market in dairy cows and calves had plummeted, and just when they'd become reconciled to a bit of belt-tightening, there'd been a scare that blue ear disease might strike the pigs. Add to that the rare Montagu's Harrier that had decided to nest in the barley in the early summer, and Phil's hip twinges, which had got so bad that he was to have a hip replacement operation before Christmas, and Jill didn't need a crystal ball to guess that Phil would be wishing for an easier time of it next year. As he clearly hadn't heard her calling him, immersed, no doubt, in a gripping article about tail biting in weaners, Jill gave the pudding mixture another turn and wished for him.

Wishing on behalf of the rest of the family wasn't so difficult either. It was just over a year since Shula's ectopic. She and Mark were outwardly cheerful: Shula had thrown herself into her work at the Estate and Mark had decided to make the break from the Birmingham law firm where he worked when it was taken over. Shula had been thrilled when, fed up with the commuting, he'd set up his own practice in Borchester with a female partner, Usha Gupta.

Elizabeth was back from Birmingham, too: she'd left the newspaper where she'd been working in the spring, when she'd come home with a dose of glandular fever. She was now freelancing for the *Echo* and other papers, and, slightly to Jill's alarm, going out with Cameron Fraser.

Ruth had finished her final year at Harper Adams, having passed her exams with a credit, and although they'd had to make Graham Collard redundant to make room for her on the farm, Graham had luckily got settled straight away with a job at Hollerton.

Kenton, meanwhile, was still toiling away at Archer's Antiquities in partnership with Nelson and under the watchful eye of Mark, who was now on the spot to monitor his investment.

And so, for the first time for many years, all Jill's 'chicks', as Phil called them, were close to the roost.

She smiled a satisfied smile. Her arm was beginning to ache and the handle of the wooden spoon was hot in her palm. Closing her eyes, she wished in quick succession. For Mark and Shula: a baby. For Elizabeth: a proper job. For Kenton: a wife, perhaps? And for Ruth? Jill sighed. Would it be uncharitable to wish, for David's sake, that she would learn to cook?

In kitchens all across Ambridge, where old traditions die hard, this was the scene that November afternoon, with the sky heavy outside and a wicked wind whistling through ill-fitting window frames and rattling the slates on the barns.

At Grange Farm, the wind's whistling was loudest of all and Clarrie Grundy stirred her puddings to the sound of Eddie crooning to his guitar. Her father-in-law Joe snored and snorted by the

Rayburn, and the boys, William and Edward Junior, raced their bikes round the yard, frightening the turkeys who, though they didn't know it, were having the time of their short lives, eating their heads off in the old poultry shed.

At Bridge Farm, Pat, whose interest in cooking was limited these days to experiments with the newly launched Bridge Farm Organic Ice Cream, was debating, as she spooned her mixture into basins, the merits or otherwise of Christmas Pudding ice cream.

And at Home Farm, where Jennifer was making a traditional Christmas pudding and a vegetarian version for the ever-more-difficult Kate, she was reflecting, like Jill, on another eventful year.

Brian had decided that diversification was the only way forward: and not just into alternative livestock enterprises, such as the deer, or new crop varieties, such as linseed. Typical Brian, he was, he said, looking at 'the bigger picture'. Leisure, according to him, was the answer: the new middle-management class who spent the week fiddling their expense accounts and burbling on their mobile phones wanted, he said, something to do at weekends that fitted in with their 'aspirational values'. (Jennifer had to forgive him: he'd read an awful lot of consultancy documents on the subject, and if he occasionally lapsed into their language, it was only to be expected.) Anyway, he'd considered and dismissed a golf course, before settling for an off-the-road riding scheme and a fishing lake, both of which were now under construction and which would open in the spring.

Brian was well pleased. It was the way farming was going, he said. Farmers had got to get down off their high horses and be a bit more accessible to the public, albeit a public that was able to fork out a hefty sum for a fishing permit or a day at the riding course. And what with the land he still had in set-aside, and the EEC subsidy on the vast acreage of arable crops he grew, he'd assured Jenny, as she staggered back from Underwoods with quails' eggs and out-of-season strawberries for a dinner party, they certainly wouldn't starve.

Yes, thought Jennifer, she'd had much to be thankful for this year. Though, sadly, her grandmother, Mrs Perkins, had died in the spring, at least Brian's epilepsy had finally stabilized. Alice was growing up: she'd been three in September. Kate was a worry, of course, but she was fourteen, and as all the articles Jennifer read about adolescence – and she never missed one – always told her, it 'went with the territory'. Adam was still working on an irrigation project in Africa, happily it seemed, but the best news of all for Jennifer in the past year was that Debbie had come home.

Admittedly, the circumstances had been worrying at first, especially when she'd announced that she intended taking a year off from her degree course at Exeter. Despite Jennifer's probings, Debbie wasn't giving away any details, and it was only gradually that they emerged. She'd had an unhappy love affair. Jennifer was sorry for her daughter, but had thought that was the end of it: these things happened. Debbie took a part-time job in The Bull while she sorted herself out, and Jennifer began to enjoy having her around again.

Then the man in question had turned up in the village. To Jennifer's horror, he wasn't another student, as she'd assumed, but a Canadian, Simon Gerrard, a visiting lecturer and twice Debbie's age. As far as he was concerned, Jennifer later found out, the affair was far from over and he'd even tried to persuade Debbie to run off to Canada with him. Brian had come across them one night at Home Farm when Simon had been – literally, according to Brian – trying to twist Debbie's arm, and he had without ceremony shown Simon the door. Jennifer had been beside herself, fearful of what Brian's strong-arm tactics might achieve, and she'd been proved right when Debbie had disappeared without a word.

But a few days later she was back again, pale and red-eyed. It appeared that she'd said a final goodbye to Simon: the difference in their ages and lifestyles was, she said, too great for anything between them to work at the moment.

Her breath taken away by her daughter's maturity and wisdom, Jennifer had hugged her close and, unable to help herself, had burst into tears.

'Oh, Debbie,' she snuffled, 'I'm so grateful to have you back. You don't know what it means to me. It may not seem like it now, but I know you've made the right decision.'

Debbie had pulled away impatiently.

'Mum,' she said crossly. 'This is my crisis, not yours. Save the tears, will you? I know they're not for me.'

Maturity and wisdom, Jennifer had thought, wiping her eyes with the tissue Debbie had fetched her, well beyond her years.

● ● ●

It was a month later: Christmas Eve. The puddings that had been so carefully prepared were in larders all across Ambridge, tightly cuffed in greaseproof paper, ready for tomorrow's steaming. The cakes had been iced and decorated according to taste and the number of small helpers: they bore massive robins that loomed like velociraptors over miniature plastic Santas (the Grundys) or a sprig of holly and a tasteful green ribbon (Home Farm, despite Alice's pleas). Presents had been bought, trees decorated, mistletoe hung. But for Debbie, there was another celebration before tomorrow's could even be thought about: her twenty-first birthday lunch at Grey Gables.

She wasn't sure that she had much to celebrate, really: the year had been a mess. Ever since Simon Gerrard, who was on a teacher exchange from Quebec, had been appointed as her tutor in her subsidiary subject, French Canadian literature, her university work had been forgotten. Within days of their first meeting, he'd started taking her out for crab sandwiches in clifftop pubs instead of discussing contextual reality or form and content. In the wild winter weather, they'd walked the moors or lurked indoors with tea and buttered crumpets: the very things, he claimed, he'd come to England for. He talked to her about anything and everything: Wittgenstein and the Appalachian Mountains, Billie Holiday and the culture of the American roadside diner. Soon they were lovers. After the clumsy advances of her fellow students, Debbie was as enraptured by Simon's dextrous tenderness as she was by his conversation, and for six months she lived in a state of grace, the perfect romantic idyll. Spring passed and summer came, and she had exams to take, which frightened her rather because she couldn't put down Simon's thoughts on North American Indians when she was supposed to be answering questions about Dickens or Molière. Simon said he'd help her with her revision, but every time they met, they ended up opening a bottle of wine and taking it to bed with them, until Debbie had to ban him from seeing her until the exams were over. He didn't like it, but he made a grand, if tongue-in-cheek, speech about how he'd miss her and save himself for her, and told her he'd call her in ten days – if he didn't die of lovesickness before then.

The very next afternoon, Debbie took her books to a far-flung corner of the university campus to revise – revise! Read for the first time, more like. She found herself a spot where she could have her head in the shade and her legs in the sun. She spread herself out and picked up *Daniel Deronda*. And there, under the shade of a copper beech, she saw Simon with Sylvie Norton, a teaching colleague, in what could only be called a compromising position.

It was a mistake, he pleaded when she confronted him.

'What, a mistake two-timing me, or a mistake getting caught?' Debbie had shouted, beating him with her fists. She'd never known passion like that she'd shared with Simon, and she'd never known such betrayal either.

She'd taken the rest of her exams in a trance, writing little more than her name at the top of the sheet, and, still feeling as though she were sleepwalking, had crawled home to Ambridge, refusing to take Simon's calls. By the time he'd turned up in the village, though, she'd begun to feel rather differently about him: the numbness had worn off and the wistful memories had seeped through the pain.

Simon had told her that it was all over with Sylvie, and that he desperately wanted her back. She desperately wanted to go back, but she wouldn't let herself admit it. She tried to tell him to leave, but he was persistent. He almost wore her down. Even now, she didn't like to think what might have happened if Brian hadn't come in when Simon was once again trying to persuade her. But it had all got too awful and complicated: Debbie had gone away for a few days to think things through, and had ended up telling Simon stonily that she didn't want to see him again.

But she hadn't found it easy to break off with Simon, and even now she didn't know why she'd done it. It wasn't to please her mum or Brian, that much she knew: it was more about doing what she wanted, even if she had to finish with him to find out what that was – and even if she'd missed her chance with Simon in the process.

But all that had been nearly six months ago, thought Debbie, as she waited at Grey Gables reception with the birthday CD that Jack had said they could play for her over the speakers in the restaurant, where the family were finishing lunch.

She hadn't thought she'd get over Simon. She hadn't even much wanted to. But Brian had begun to web her into the farm, offering her the job of running the off-road riding scheme when it was set up, and though her mum was still wittering on about her taking up her degree course again, Debbie knew in her heart of hearts that she wouldn't go back. Though she'd never before considered a career in agriculture – with the rather more artistic leanings of her mother and her natural father, why would she? – Debbie had begun to wonder if her future, as much as her distant past – those Archer genes – might after all lie on the land.

'Hello, Deborah.'

Debbie whipped round. That voice, so familiar after all this time. He stood in front of her, so close she could have touched him.

'What are you doing here?' she mouthed, frozen, thinking only of her mum and Brian and Kate and Alice in the restaurant fifty yards away, and that any one of them might come out at any moment.

Roger Travers-Macy shrugged and smiled. He was still so good-looking. Dark-haired, like Debbie. And his eyes crinkled up at the corners in a way that Debbie knew was exactly the same as hers.

'I just wanted to wish my daughter Happy Birthday.'

She should never have agreed to it. And, having agreed, she should never have tried to keep it a secret, especially not from her mother, who was pathologically incapable of letting Debbie live her own life. But she still agreed to meet Roger in Nelson's wine bar in Borchester on the Friday after Christmas and, when her mother overheard her confirming the arrangement on the phone, though she couldn't possibly have suspected, Debbie found herself telling her that she was meeting Lucy Perks.

But even knowing her mother as she did, Debbie couldn't have imagined that Jennifer's mind was already working overtime, fearing that Simon was back on the scene, and that she'd ring Lucy to check up on her. Or that when Debbie arrived in Nelson's that Friday, she'd find her mother already there, sitting with her ex-husband at a table in the corner and looking sheepish, as well she might.

'I thought you were meeting Simon,' her mother explained lamely when Roger, who seemed more amused than abashed by the situation, had gone to get Debbie a drink. 'So I came to – I don't know . . . Put him off.'

'Well, thanks a lot. Thanks for trusting me,' replied Debbie.

'Trust you? Then why didn't you tell me you were meeting Roger?'

'Because I knew you'd react like this, I suppose.' Debbie rubbed at a watermark on the table-top.

'Oh, Debbie –'

'Look, Mum, Roger's not going to come pushing his way into my life again except on my terms. I just want to see that he doesn't want something from me.'

'Of course he wants something from you,' snapped her mother, agitated. Though not so agitated she hadn't had the presence of mind to whip out a mirror from her handbag to check her appearance the minute Roger had gone to the bar, Debbie noted. 'Look what he got from me.'

'Here we are,' Roger smoothed his way between the pinstriped suits and tweed jackets with Debbie's Coke and a brandy, which he placed in front of Jennifer.

'I said I didn't want anything,' she said stiffly.

'I'm sorry.' He slid easily on to the bench seat beside her. 'I thought you could do with it.'

'I can do without your brandy and I can do without you!' Jennifer scrambled to her feet and Roger automatically stood up as well. Debbie watched, fascinated. She hadn't seen her parents together since she was a child. 'And I've no doubt that when our daughter knows what you're like, she'll think the same.' Shaking, Jennifer tugged on her long camel coat with its fur collar.

'I'll see you later, Mum,' said Debbie quietly.

Jennifer looped the strap of her handbag over her shoulder and gave her daughter a tortured look.

'When the two of you have sorted out your relationship, perhaps you'll let me know where I stand.'

• • •

'Mmm. I could lie here for ever.'

'Me too.' Roger stroked a strand of Jennifer's hair off her face. She moved her head minutely and kissed his shoulder, breathing in the particular smell of his skin. 'No guilt?' he asked gently.

Jennifer exhaled.

'No. Isn't that awful?'

'It's not good or bad. Just how it is.' Roger shifted in the bed and Jennifer moulded herself to him again. He looked straight into her eyes and smiled at her. 'Perhaps it just means we're right for each other.'

She smiled back, feeling as though she might implode with happiness.

'Could do.'

The hotel was just outside Leamington, where Jennifer had come, supposedly, to look over a riding course similar to Brian's. Roger, who dealt in antiquarian books, had been on business in Warwick.

They'd arranged to meet for lunch but both of them had known as soon as they'd met downstairs by the fierce log fire that they'd be going straight up to Roger's room. They'd known because, even at their first disastrous, ill-timed and mismanaged meeting in Nelson's, the physical attraction that had flung them together years before was still there, as strong as, if not stronger than, ever.

It was the end of January. Already the light was leaching out of the sky beyond the skeletal trees. Jennifer sighed. She knew she couldn't stay long: she had to get back and collect Alice.

Well, it had happened now. She'd been unfaithful – and with her ex-husband. Did that make it worse, or better?

Jennifer had done a lot of thinking – inevitably – since Roger's return. There was nothing she liked more than analysing things – especially when they involved her – and the situation she now found herself in was rich with resonance.

She'd thought back to when she'd first parted from Roger: how wounded she'd been by his growing indifference to her, and how hurt she'd been on Debbie's behalf that she, like Adam, would grow up with an absent father. She couldn't help but blame herself: even in the middle of her grief, she couldn't help but perceive a pattern. The circumstances of Adam's birth had been entirely different, of course, but she'd still asked herself over and over again what it was in her that drove these men away. And however much she'd tried to tell herself that she'd been unlucky, and that the problem was their emotional immaturity, rather than anything to do with her, she still didn't quite believe it.

When Brian had come to the village, apparently such a knight in shining armour, her family had started plotting to marry them off before she'd even been divorced from Roger, and perhaps that was the problem. Her growing feelings for Brian had overlaid the feelings she still had for Roger, so a line had never been drawn under their relationship. It had never felt finished. And now it had started up again.

Jennifer knew she should have felt guilty. In so many ways she had everything – more than everything – that most women would want. She was married to the wealthiest farmer in the district, and if that weren't enough, Brian was intelligent, witty and handsome. Though hardly over-involved, he wasn't a bad father to Kate and Alice, and he'd been a wonderful father to Adam and Debbie when they were growing up.

But as a husband? Leaving aside the affairs she knew about, with Caroline Bone and Mandy Beesborough, Brian was a charmer. He adored women and his ego required them to adore him – and to show it. Which was fine, but adoration wasn't something Jennifer could keep up on a daily basis – no wife could. Not when she was scraping fish pie off the tablecloth, taking a call from the feed merchant and coping with a sickly lamb in the Aga. Normal life got in the way.

Over the years, however, Jennifer and Brian had evolved a working relationship: they were a good team. He humoured her and, other responsibilities permitting, she indulged him. Well, maybe it was time to indulge herself for a change.

She shifted her head slightly. Roger's chest rose and fell rhythmically under her fingers and she could see that his eyes were closed. It didn't matter. She didn't want to talk to him. They'd said all they needed to say: he, that he should never have left her and that he'd regretted it instantly, and she that she should never have let him go.

Roger stirred, twitched his nose and opened his eyes. He looked down to find her looking at him and bent his head to kiss her.

'It's starting to get dark out there. Shall I draw the curtains?'

'No, no, don't,' she said quickly. 'I like looking at it. It doesn't seem real somehow. It helps me.'

'Would you like anything from room service?' he asked. 'Drink? Sandwich?'

'No,' she smiled. 'Nothing.' She pulled him towards her. He was quite enough.

'Shall I tell you what bothers me?' she asked when she was getting dressed.

'If you want to.' He was lying back against the pillows with his arms folded behind his head, watching her.

Jennifer buttoned her skirt.

'If you and I have always belonged together, what have I been doing with Brian all these years?'

He sat forward and looked at her pleadingly.

'Jenny. I thought you said no guilt?'

'It's not guilt. It just makes me sad, that's all.'

It was half past four when Jennifer left: much later than she'd intended. In the car park of the hotel she unlocked the Range Rover and looked up at Roger's window. He was standing there between the parted curtains and it wrenched her heart to leave him. What sort of life did he lead, shuttling between one hotel and another, eating bar meals with pub bores, going to auctions in draughty country houses, driving alone for miles? She could feel herself getting tearful so she gave him a reluctant wave, clambered in and slammed the door.

Instantly, though she didn't want to be, she was Jennifer Aldridge again. There were Alice's nursery rhyme tapes on the back seat, along with Brian's second-best Barbour and a litter of crisp crumbs. As she started the engine and let off the handbrake, she caught sight of the packet of antibiotics she'd picked up from the vet that morning for a sickly calf and that she'd promised Brian he'd have by mid-afternoon.

With a heavy sigh, she negotiated the winding drive and turned on to the main road. Before long, she was in the rush-hour traffic, looking fretfully at the dashboard clock and rehearsing her excuses. But there were none, really. Debbie had made it plain that she found Roger's reappearance too unsettling. She'd told him that, though she'd keep in touch, she didn't particularly want to see him. It was Jennifer who wanted to see him. But what was she doing, getting involved again with her ex-husband? Where on earth did she think it was leading?

'Dad? I brought you a cup of tea.'

Brian looked over the barrier of straw bales with which the lambing shed was divided and saw Debbie approaching with Alice.

'Oh, thanks. I could do with it.' He took the mug Debbie was holding out to him, while Alice scampered off to see if Sammy Whipple, the shepherd, had got any toffees in his pocket. 'What's Alice doing here?'

'You don't mind me bringing her over to see the lambs, do you? We were making a collage but she got bored.'

'You're not still minding her, are you?' Brian asked between swigs. 'Where's your mother got to, for God's sake?'

'I don't know.'

'I'd have gone and got that calf's antibiotic myself if I'd thought she was going to be this long. It's gone five o'clock. She can't be looking over a riding course in the dark.'

Debbie bit her lip. She had her suspicions – more than suspicions. In fact, ever since she'd seen her parents together in Nelson's, she'd known. She'd known because she could sense the same electricity between them, even when they were arguing, that there'd been between herself and Simon. Maybe, she thought wryly, that was the real reason she'd told Roger that she didn't want to see him. In a fairytale way, she'd thought that when her long-lost father came back, he'd come back to love her, but she knew from what she'd seen, from Roger's seductiveness and her mother's discomposure, that he'd simply fallen for Jennifer all over again and she for him.

'I don't know.' Brian rested his empty mug on the bales and went back to the sheep. 'She hasn't been the same since Roger appeared back on the scene. She's gone all distracted and . . . silly.'

'What are you doing?' Debbie asked abruptly. She didn't even want to think about her mother and Roger.

'Hm? Oh, I'm trying to persuade this ewe to take on this little chap here. She's lost her lamb and he's lost his mum.'

He dragged the lamb across to the ewe and let her sniff him. Four or five times he tried, and each time the ewe butted the lamb away.

'One more time.' Brian lifted the lamb back again and pulled the ewe's muzzle down into his skimpy coat. 'Come on, old girl, you don't want him to starve, do you?'

This time the ewe didn't butt the lamb away. Instead she started to sniff and nuzzle him, and when she did push him with her head, it was in the direction of her udder. Brian gave Debbie a thumbs-up sign and squatted back on his haunches. The lamb, tottering on its spindly legs, lurched a few steps, then ducked its head under the ewe's belly, searching for a teat. The ewe turned her head around, as if in encouragement, then, as the lamb began to suck, slowly turned her head away again and started pulling at some hay.

Brian and Debbie smiled at each other complicitly.

'One less to bottle feed, anyway,' said Brian with satisfaction. 'Look at him, sucking away. Quite happy.'

'He's getting all he needs from that ewe, isn't he?' said Debbie.

'That's what counts.'

Suddenly they weren't talking about sheep any more.

'This is getting deep,' said Brian, keeping things light. 'Are you trying to tell me something?'

'Only that I love you,' replied Debbie simply. 'Look, Dad, I don't want this to sound hurtful, but –'

'Go on.'

'Well, all my life – I couldn't help it – I'd wondered what it would be like to have had my real father around. I'm sorry – but that's how it was.'

'No, it's all right. I understand.' The ewe and lamb were established now, and Brian got up and came over to her. 'So what are you trying to tell me, Debbie?'

'That when Roger came back, I realized I was being stupid. I did have a real dad. I had you.'

• • •

'Again? But I thought you'd already been to this riding place in Leamington?'

Peggy dipped her paintbrush in the water and wiped it dry. As Shrove Tuesday was approaching, she was busy with her entry for the WI competition: 'A Painted Egg'.

Jennifer laughed nonchalantly. Her mother had come to tea, bringing all her painting accoutrements with her and remarking tartly that it was nice to be invited to Home Farm for her company for a change, rather than to look after Alice.

'I have, but you must remember, Mum, it was a filthy day last time. Knee deep in mud. I couldn't really bring back very much useful information.'

'I don't seem to remember the weather being that bad here. Alice and I had a walk. We looked for catkins.'

'Well, it was horrid in Leamington,' asserted Jennifer, spooning tea into the pot. 'Teeming with rain. It must have been very localized, that's all.'

It was the day she'd spent with Roger, of course. So she'd have to go again, for real this time, but if she set off early and made the riding course people whizz her round, she could still meet him in the afternoon . . .

Peggy applied herself to the fleur-de-lis she was painting on her egg.

'I really can't keep on having Alice like this, Jennifer. I've got things to do.'

Jennifer swallowed the urge to scream and tried to look suitably grateful.

'I know it's asking a lot of you, Mum. And I know you've been having Alice more than usual lately. But I am keen to help Brian out with this riding scheme.'

'It might help him,' said Peggy tartly, 'if you stayed at home more!'

And Jennifer couldn't argue with that. But then Peggy didn't know what she was leaving home for: to hear Roger say over and over that he should never have left her, to hear him say he'd so nearly come back and how he'd thought about her so much. But how his pride had stopped him, and that, anyway, there was someone else by then, but how much he'd learnt from his mistakes and how different their lives could have been.

And to hear him say that he loved her. Always had. Always would. And to have him make love to her as if he really meant it.

'I am helping Brian, Mum.' Jennifer poured water from the kettle and stirred the pot. 'I'm helping with the publicity for the riding course. There's advertisements to be placed, artwork for the hand-outs, seeing the printers . . . and you have to stand over them the whole time, you can't just hand it over and let them get on with it.'

'I thought Debbie had been doing most of that.'

Irritatingly, Peggy wouldn't let it drop.

'She's been helping, of course. But she's got her job at The Bull and –'

'And she's been looking after Alice nearly as much as I have.' Peggy lifted her brush and considered the effect. 'What do you think?'

Jennifer stared mulishly at her. 'What?'

'My egg. What do you think?'

'Oh, very nice.'

'I think so.' Peggy went back to her painting. 'And what about Roger?' she asked casually.

'Roger?'

'You haven't seen him?'

Jennifer could feel her throat constricting, almost choking her. To cover her unease, she went to the larder and started opening tins.

'No, of course not. You know what we agreed. He can see Debbie when he wants to. Or when she wants to. But we decided it was best if he didn't come here.' She turned and smiled falsely at her mother. 'The children have eaten all the cake. We'll have to settle for biscuits, I'm afraid.'

One day at the beginning of March, Roger suggested that they meet in Woodstock. He'd got some calls to make in Oxford, then, he said, he'd book them a room at The Bear. They might even get a four-poster. Jennifer agreed eagerly. She wasn't sure what excuse she'd use because she'd supposedly visited every printer and riding course in the Midlands by now, but she told him she'd think of something.

Telling Brian she'd be away for the day was easy. Busy spraying his emerging barley, he hardly even seemed to register the conversation, but when Jennifer asked Peggy to have Alice, her mother simply refused. No excuses, no 'previous engagement' – just a straight no.

The sensible thing would have been to cancel, but Jennifer was being anything but sensible – that much she knew. So she took Alice with her, humming down the A34 in the spring sunshine, and it was only when she got there and saw Roger waiting, lounging against the golden stone of the hotel doorway, that she realized how foolish she'd been.

Unwrapping yet another lollipop for Alice – she'd never sleep tonight – Jennifer left her in the Range Rover and bolted across to see him. Gabbling, she explained what had happened and he couldn't have been more understanding, suggesting a walk in the grounds of Blenheim Palace and a pub lunch.

'I can't, don't you see?' she said urgently. 'She might say something to Brian, or the girls. Anyway, having her here with us – it makes it feel wrong. Dirty, somehow.'

'Jennifer, for God's sake, we were married!' Roger exclaimed.

She'd known he wouldn't like the slightly hysterical tone in her voice: he never had.

'Were,' she said sadly. 'Precisely.'

And then she'd driven home, with Alice kicking her feet against the back of the driving seat in time to 'The Farmer Wants a Wife' and demanding to know why Jennifer wasn't singing along.

Other things were stacking up too. One day Jennifer came home – from a genuine errand this time – to find Brian and Debbie conspiratorial in the kitchen, their heads bent over a farming magazine and roaring with laughter.

'What's the joke?' she asked.

'Oh, nothing,' Brian guffawed, wiping away tears of mirth.

'We just had this thing with the auger . . .' Debbie began kindly, and Brian burst out laughing again. 'And Dad said . . .' she started to giggle. 'Oh, it's nothing, Mum, you wouldn't understand.'

Jennifer nodded quietly and went to fill the kettle. She supposed it was fair, really. If she had her secrets, Brian and Debbie were surely entitled to theirs.

But the next day, Uncle Tom stopped her outside the shop.

'It's nothing short of a disgrace!' he began.

Momentarily paralysed – had someone seen her and Roger together? – Jennifer couldn't reply.

'If you'd been there on Sunday, you'd have seen for yourself!' he ranted. 'It's not as if we're asking for much – there's no flowers needed in Lent! All the more reason for the brasses to have had a good polish, I'd have thought!'

Jennifer clapped her hand to her mouth. The church rota! It had been her turn!

Suddenly she felt stripped and exposed. Forgetting her place on the church rota, of all things. She might as well have been branded an adulteress and stoned out of the village.

'I'm so sorry, Uncle Tom,' she apologized. 'I'll see to them this afternoon.'

'There's no need,' said Uncle Tom huffily. 'My Pru's done them for you, and a very nice job she's made of it, too. But she shouldn't have had to.'

'Absolutely not!' gushed Jennifer. 'I'll buy her a little something to make up for it. Chocolates?'

'My Pru don't want chocolates!' snapped Uncle Tom, his deer-stalker quivering with indignation. 'It's the principle. I don't know what you were thinking of!'

Jennifer knew just what she'd been thinking of – the stolen afternoons in Roger's arms and the feel of his fingers on her skin. Three months ago she would have added the huge feeling of peace and pleasure it gave her, but she felt that less often now. Instead she felt harassed all the time, rushed and guilty, deceitful and – the word she'd used to him in Woodstock – dirty.

She loved Roger, of course she did, but – as she'd asked herself at the outset – where was all this leading? They couldn't put the clock back, and anyway, however much they loved each other, they'd split up once. Who was to say, if she gave up everything she had, that it wouldn't happen again?

She chose the Botanical Gardens in Felpersham. There was a mynah bird there called Monty whom Alice loved. Before Roger arrived, Jennifer went and stood in front of Monty's cage and he chortled and cheeked her.

'Hello, darling.'

Jennifer turned and smiled. How lightly the words were used. Monty had just been saying the very same thing.

'Hello.' She let him give her a quick kiss, then linked her arm in his. 'Shall we have a stroll?'

She didn't want to stand around the caged birds. She felt too sorry for them.

'Are we staying here?' he asked, surprised. 'I'd got visions of my nice warm hotel room.'

'Oh, Roger,' said Jennifer sadly.

It was certainly a dreary day. In the centre of the swooping lawn, a cedar tree dripped gloom. Even the wild birds seemed hunched in the trees. But he walked with her uncomplainingly along the gravel paths, until they were alone in an avenue of pleached limes. From a branch beside them a determined blackbird chirped a cheery workman's whistle. Roger stopped abruptly.

'I've missed you,' he said. 'Come here.'

But she backed away.

'No! I'm sorry. But . . . Roger, this isn't easy. It's best if we don't.'

'I see. Do I?' he queried, looking hurt.

'I really can't handle this any more,' she blurted out. 'I've tried but I can't.'

'You said you could.'

'It's the atmosphere at home. Debbie. And Brian. They just close ranks whenever I'm there. And Mum's being funny about having Alice.'

There was a minute pause.

'Brian doesn't know, does he?' asked Roger sharply.

She shook her head, registering a tiny disappointment, the feeling that he was asking out of concern for his position, not hers.

'I don't think so. But I'm sorry, Roger, we'll have to stop this.'

He seized both her hands in his.

'Just like that?'

'What choice do I have?'

He squeezed her hands even tighter.

'Jennifer, for God's sake, don't do this. You said you could handle it!'

Gently she pulled away.

'I thought I could. But I can't. I feel too guilty.'

It was a fortnight later, the beginning of April. The riding course was nearly finished and by the end of the month the fishing lake would be stocked. The baby weeping willows around it were trailing green fronds in the water. Beneath them, despite the digging and disruption, the primroses and wild daffodils had come back.

Uncle Tom had started lobbying for the job of manager, but Brian said he was only interested in the little hut that went with it as a peaceful retreat where he could read his *Shooting Times* undisturbed. There'd been an unfortunate misprint in one of the leaflets – Jennifer couldn't think how she'd transposed 'trot' for 'trout' – but Brian had merely raised an eyebrow and remarked that he'd never thought she'd had her mind entirely on the job.

Roger phoned, saying he regarded their parting as no more than a trial separation: he could see that she needed to concentrate on her family till things calmed down. Jennifer gently replaced the receiver in the middle of his anguished pleas. She didn't know how she was finding it in herself to be so strong when she wanted the comfort he could give her more than ever.

But at least Brian was being quite nice to her – why else would he have brought her to the Apple Tree for lunch in the middle of the week when they were busy with the spring cultivations and turning the lambs out?

'Well, I'm ready to order. How about you?' he said, snapping shut his menu.

'Um . . .' Jennifer hadn't been thinking about ordering at all. She'd been thinking about the illicit lunchtime picnics she and Roger had shared in bed.

'Is this one of the places you used to come to?' Brian casually sipped his orange juice.

'Sorry?'

'With Roger,' said Brian.

Jennifer's heart clenched. She swallowed hard.

'I know you've been seeing him,' he went on. 'But it's over now, isn't it?'

It wasn't really a question, more Brian pointing out to her how clever he was, but automatically, Jennifer nodded. Brian nodded too, rather smugly.

'I thought so. I could tell.'

Jennifer found her voice.

'Brian, the thing is . . . I want you to know . . .'

He held up his hand fastidiously.

'Oh, please, spare me the details. As far as I'm concerned you were just talking over old times.'

Jennifer stared at her husband over the table. He looked like someone she'd never seen before. A waiter came to take their order but with a minuscule gesture, Brian sent him away.

'Well? Isn't that about right?'

Still she said nothing. All that time, the months she'd been seeing Roger, and Brian had known all along. He'd let her go on deceiving him. It should have made her feel less guilty because it was as if he'd condoned it, but it made her feel worse.

Brian wrinkled his nose and nodded understandingly.

'No, perhaps you're right, old girl. There's really no more to say on the subject.' He topped up her glass with the white Burgundy he'd ordered. She wasn't even aware she'd been drinking it. 'Now,' he went on smoothly, 'have you chosen?'

'Melon,' said Jennifer flatly. 'And lamb.' She said the first thing that came into her head. She didn't even know if they were on the menu. They must be. They were on every menu.

Brian pulled a face.

'Not very exciting. Still, if that's what you want.'

'Yes,' said Jennifer. 'Not very exciting, maybe. But that's what I want.'

·7·

A Fallen Woman

'So you're not seeing him any more?'

Debbie lifted the fork to check on the state of the bread she and Elizabeth were toasting over the open fire in the sitting room at Brookfield. The April afternoon had turned out rainy – too wet for the walk they'd originally planned. She turned the bread over and held the fork towards the flames again.

'Roger?' she answered. 'No.'

Elizabeth, who was lying prone on the sofa, pulled a puzzled face.

'But when he came back, you seemed so excited . . . that he'd come to find you after all these years . . .'

Debbie inched the fork nearer to the crackling apple logs. Making toast this way always took such a tantalizingly long time. She pondered momentarily whether to tell Elizabeth what had been going on – her well-founded suspicions, which she knew Brian shared, about her mother and Roger. It was fleetingly tempting, but she didn't give in to it. She was sure that it had stopped now, anyway, so what would be the point?

'Well, I was wrong,' she said dismissively. 'I thought he'd come back for my sake, but really he only came back for his. To make himself feel less guilty or something. Here, have a piece of toast.'

Elizabeth waved the proffered fork away.

'You have the first one. I'm not really hungry.'

'Pass me the butter, then. Thanks.' Debbie reached across as Elizabeth did so. 'Loss of appetite, is that one of your symptoms?'

Elizabeth had been complaining for the past couple of weeks about feeling unwell.

'I'm OK in the evening,' she explained wanly, 'but the rest of the day I feel sick.'

'Are you ever sick?' Debbie bit deliciously into her toast.

'Sometimes,' admitted Elizabeth, looking on with revulsion as Debbie licked her buttery fingers. 'Most spectacularly at a meeting with Nigel and some designers.'

She had just started a new job as Nigel's marketing manager at Lower Loxley: it looked as though his plans to open the Hall to the public and to run conferences there would finally come to fruition.

'And actually,' she added, 'I was sick this morning as well.'

Debbie picked a toast crumb off her jeans.

'So you start off feeling terrible, and you're sick, and then you gradually feel better as the day wears on.'

Elizabeth nodded glumly.

'That's about it.'

Debbie speared another piece of Jill's granary bread.

'Well,' she declared, holding it out to the fire. 'You're obviously pregnant.'

And to Elizabeth's – what? Amazement? Horror? Shock? She was. She and Debbie scuttled off to a backstreet chemist in Borchester, bought a kit and did the test in the bathroom at Home Farm. It was pink. Positively pink.

'Oh, Cameron,' wailed Elizabeth, sinking down on the side of the bath, 'where are you when I need you?'

Cameron, whom she'd been seeing for six months now, was out of the country on business.

'He'll be back on Thursday,' soothed Debbie, gathering together the empty test box and phials. She didn't want her mother finding them in the bin and jumping to the wrong conclusion. 'You'll feel better when you've told him.'

'Will I?' Elizabeth was ashen, and it wasn't just because she'd been sick again that morning.

'Well, it's not just your problem, is it?' asked Debbie reasonably.

'I don't know. I can't think straight.' Elizabeth counted on her

fingers. 'I'll have to see the doctor and everything. It'll be due in –
what, November? And I've only just started working for Nigel!'

'Elizabeth! Stop it! One thing at a time.'

'And then there's Mum and Dad. They don't even like Cameron
very much. And Dad and David are trying to do this deal with him on
the land at Red House Farm . . .'

'Elizabeth, I won't tell you again. It's all irrelevant. What matters is
that you're having a baby. Cameron's the father and he's got to be
told. Then you can work out what's best.'

'Yes, yes, you're right.' Elizabeth turned a tragic face to her cousin.
'Debbie, thank you. You're brilliant at this sort of thing. So sensible.
How do you know what to do?'

Debbie smiled and shook her head. She didn't tell Elizabeth that it
was years of practice in dealing with her mother.

Elizabeth had had years of practice in dealing with her own
mother, too, and she knew that Jill already had her suspicions. After
all, Elizabeth conceded, there was enough evidence. As well as all the
times over the past fortnight that Nigel had had to bring her home
from work, she'd been going to bed at nine o'clock every night, and
had refused even to appear in the kitchen until she was sure that her
father's greasy breakfast plate was well and truly in the dishwasher.
No wonder her mother had been giving her funny looks.

The only thing she could hope to do, Elizabeth reasoned, until
Cameron came back and she could tell him about the baby, was to try
to avoid Brookfield as much as possible: not easy when all she wanted
was the sanctuary of her room and a cool pillow under her head. But
in the end, even lurking in her room wasn't the answer: her mother
simply sought her out.

'I'm waiting, Elizabeth.'

Jill stood there with a pile of towels she'd brought up to the airing
cupboard. Her tone was exactly the same as the one she'd used when
Elizabeth was a child and had broken a treasured ornament, or had
been late for tea.

'This is silly, Mum.' Elizabeth forced herself to swing her legs off the bed and sit up. The room spun and she closed her eyes. 'You're making me feel like a prisoner in my own room, giving me the third degree like this.'

Jill looked stern. It was because she was worried, Elizabeth knew, but it was still scary.

'You're not well, you don't want to see a doctor, yet you're not getting better,' said Jill. 'What are we supposed to think? You must have something you're keeping from us.'

Elizabeth bit her lip. The temptation to fling herself into her mother's arms and sob among the scattered towels was almost too much to bear.

Jill spoke again, gentler this time.

'If it's too hard to say, Elizabeth, I could say it for you. You see, I think I know.'

The silence between them reverberated. Outside, Jill's hens clucked peaceably in the orchard. Elizabeth heard someone revving the engine of the quad bike: David, probably, off to check on the sheep. Everything at Brookfield was carrying on as normal. With one big difference.

'Oh, Elizabeth.' Jill put down her bundle of towels, sat beside her on the bed and reached out for her daughter's hands. 'Are you pregnant?'

The moment Elizabeth had dreaded was over, and it was such a relief, she wondered why she'd ever put it off. But her mother had made it easy for her, and telling her father, Elizabeth knew, would be a different matter. Jill knew it too, and when she offered to tell him, Elizabeth accepted eagerly.

Jill set the stage for the unsuspecting Phil with cherry cake and Doris's best teacups and Elizabeth was fortunately spared the vehemence of her father's initial outburst. By the time he spoke to her, Phil had calmed down and it was genuinely more in sorrow than in anger that he told her she didn't have to marry Cameron if she didn't want to: the family would rally round and support her, emotionally and financially, and that they'd find her somewhere to live.

'But I do want to marry Cameron!'

The more Elizabeth had thought about it, the more it seemed the perfect solution. She was sure Cameron would have proposed to her anyway, in time: he said he loved her and she knew she loved him. They were compatible together on every level. All the pregnancy had done was to precipitate things.

'That's for you to decide,' Phil replied circumspectly. Leaving aside the conditions Cameron was attaching to the sale of the Red House Farm land – he wanted it all signed and sealed in a fortnight, if you please – he was still far from convinced about Cameron Fraser as a person, still less a son-in-law.

'Dad, I know you don't like him, but he's really not as bad as you think.'

Phil tutted.

'Whether I like him or not isn't important.'

'Of course it is. It's important to me.'

Phil sighed. Elizabeth had always been the most headstrong of the children – spoilt rotten, really, since she'd been born with that heart defect, and didn't it show! She'd had the best education – or chance of it – of any of them. She'd had every opportunity. They'd indulged her passions for ponies, for wildlife, for journalism – and now look at her. Everything thrown away and pregnant by a man who, if his business dealings were anything to judge by, had the morals of a wild mink and a sexual appetite to match. But Elizabeth was clearly obsessed with Fraser, and convinced he'd do the decent thing. Phil smiled feebly, feeling weak and inadequate.

'If you really feel your future lies with Cameron, then I'll back you all the way.'

He knew as he said it that this wasn't true, and Elizabeth knew it as well. She knew her family felt that she was a sorry disappointment to them – a fact that David had articulated only too clearly when he and Ruth had been told about the baby at a family supper. As her brother blustered and swore, it fell to Ruth to say a quiet 'congratulations' and for Phil to point out tactfully that David's expostulations about 'stupidity' weren't exactly helpful.

Elizabeth knew, though, that David couldn't say anything she hadn't already said to herself a million times. And there were still two enormous hurdles to get over: not just telling Cameron, but telling Shula, poor uptight Shula, with her strict views on the correct order in which you did things and the horribly empty cot in Glebe Cottage's back bedroom.

When Elizabeth finally nerved herself to tell Nigel, she thought he'd be disappointed in her too, just like her family were, and disappointed for himself, which he'd have every right to be. He'd loved her for years and he'd picked her up after so many failed romances. But he didn't like Cameron and Cameron didn't like him.

It was clear enough that Nigel was jealous of his place in Lizzie's affections, but Elizabeth took it to be jealousy on Cameron's side too, for all the things that she and Nigel had shared in the past. She read it as a good sign – an indication of how serious Cameron was about her. She didn't bother to look a little further and see that Cameron might feel threatened by Nigel on a far deeper level – because Nigel was all the things that Cameron wasn't but aspired to be: well-born, well-connected and well-brought up. And sweet, kind and considerate to boot.

She didn't even want to think about the feelings Nigel had had for her all these years, and how she'd deserted him whenever she got a better offer, so she concentrated on how she was letting him down at work: she would, after all, be abandoning the job he'd created, she was sure, with her in mind. She expected him to want her to go straight away: after all, she hadn't been the most reliable of employees, what with feeling sick and worn out all the time. She'd have quite understood if he'd preferred her to leave so that he could get someone committed to take on the job. But instead, when she'd offered to resign, he'd hugged her tight, right there in the office with the fax chattering and a pile of mailshots to be sent out.

'I'll always be here, Lizzie,' was all he'd said. 'No matter what. You can depend on that.'

By the time Elizabeth got round to telling Cameron, after all she'd been through with her family and friends, it felt almost like an anticlimax. She wished she'd been stronger, or her emotions less transparent, so that he could have been the first to hear that he was going to be a father. Instead, she had to set off for the Dower House on the day of his return under the knowing eye of her mother, who felt it was incumbent upon her to provide dry toast and weak tea, and her father and David, who were mending a hose on the sprayer.

'We'll see you later, Elizabeth,' called her father cheerily.

'Yeah, good luck, sis,' added David, who'd obviously been given a going-over by Ruth and had apologized to Elizabeth for his outburst.

Feeling sick – no change there, then – Elizabeth had driven to the Dower House and crunched the car up the gravel drive. The wisteria on the front of the house was just coming out, its elegant, grape-like clusters drooping from the branches, just showing mauve. Elizabeth got out and slammed the car door. A magpie started up from the grass, cackling. Superstitiously, Elizabeth looked for its mate, but it was nowhere to be seen. She shrugged and moved towards the front door. Just because she was a fallen woman, she didn't have to start behaving like a Thomas Hardy heroine. Next she'd be reading something into the fact that the doorbell wasn't working. Impatiently she rapped on the worn oak of the door. After what seemed like for ever, she heard footsteps coming towards her down the hall. She braced herself for her first view in a week of the man she was going to marry.

Her first impression was that he looked tired. But he kissed her with longing and led her into the sitting room, where the French windows were open in the faint spring sunshine.

'I'm fine,' he insisted when she quizzed him about his trip, anxious he'd been working too hard. 'Anyway, you're the one who's been feeling poorly.'

She'd told him on the phone how ill she'd been. But that was all she'd told him.

'Well . . .' she said, feeling her heart flutter. 'That's what I wanted to talk about. You see, Cameron . . .' she went on, the words coming out in a rush, 'I haven't been ill at all.'

She paused long enough to look at him and register the puzzlement on his face, his raised eyebrows almost hidden in his curly blond hair. It needed cutting. Perhaps she'd cut it for him in future. That would be intimate. She bit her lip at the thought.

She met his eyes, which were the palest blue. The blue of Scottish lochs, he'd joked, which, when Elizabeth, in the first throes of passion, had repeated it at Brookfield, had caused David to choke on his coffee.

'I'm pregnant, Cameron.'

There was a long pause, longer than Elizabeth liked. Surely this was the point at which he would bound across to her, wrap her in his arms and murmur tender things into her hair? That was what had always happened when she'd run the scene in her head, as she'd done about twenty times a day since she'd found out.

Cameron's eyebrows slowly settled back to their usual position. He let out a sigh. He opened his mouth to speak. Elizabeth held her breath. Now, surely –

'Are you quite sure?'

This wasn't what she'd been expecting at all. Even while she'd been waiting for his response, she'd been rewriting the script in her head, and her new version had him speechless with delight and disbelief. Now here he was, asking her questions. What did he want, details of her menstrual cycle?

Maybe she was being hard on him. After all, she'd been stunned at first: she hadn't known whether she was delighted or disgusted by the idea. And he'd only just flown in. It must have come as a terrible shock.

'Yes,' she smiled reassuringly. 'I did a test and it was positive. And I've been getting morning sickness.'

'I see.' He looked at her, she thought, distastefully. She had a sudden, unhelpful vision of him faced with a dirty nappy. 'And I presume –?'

'There's nobody else, Cameron!' she said indignantly.

He nodded in acknowledgement.

'Have you seen a doctor?' he asked.

More questions!

'No, I wanted to tell you first. But you've been away and I couldn't tell you on the phone –'

'Does anyone else know?'

There he was again.

'Only Mum, she guessed. And she told Dad, and –'

He interrupted her.

'That's a pity.'

'I'm sorry, I couldn't help it,' flashed Lizzie before she could stop herself.

What were they doing, practically having an argument when they should have been celebrating? Cameron had got up and was pacing backwards and forwards in front of the fireplace.

'What's the matter?' asked Elizabeth tentatively. 'All right, I know it wasn't planned, but now that it's happened –'

Cameron wheeled round.

'We'd better not waste any more time,' he said, suddenly decisive. 'We'll have to do something about it.' Seeing the look on her face, he held up his hand. 'It's all right, you can leave it to me. I'll find you the best place, book you straight in –'

Elizabeth blinked. She wondered if it was true what they said about the pregnancy hormones making it harder to concentrate because she must have missed something here. He couldn't be suggesting . . .

'I'm offering to pay for you to have an abortion,' he said impatiently, seeing her struggle to comprehend. 'So long as we do something now, it's just . . .' His shoulders moved almost imperceptibly under his impeccable shirt. 'Just an inconvenience.'

'I must be really stupid,' Elizabeth mourned sadly to Debbie later that day.

She'd gone to find her at the fishing lake. She didn't dare tell her parents what Cameron had said: her dad and David between them would have hounded him out of the village.

'All the times I imagined telling him,' she went on, 'it worked out differently, but only in the detail. Like: we'd get married quickly, before the baby started to show, or I'd have it first, then we'd have a Christmas wedding, or which room would be the nursery at the Dower House . . .'

Her voice squeaked to a stop and she started to cry. Debbie tutted gently and put an arm round her shoulders.

'I don't know what to say,' she admitted. 'Except that if that's really how he thinks, you're better off without him.'

'But I'm not!' wailed Elizabeth. 'I love him! And even if I were better off without him, which I can't believe, what about the baby?'

A mother moorhen herded her chicks anxiously away from the noise on the bank, with much splashing and flapping of wings. Debbie, who knew all about absent and so-called fathers, said nothing, just hugged her friend tighter.

'It could be that you just caught him by surprise,' she improvised. 'Maybe when he's thought about it, he'll come round to the idea.'

'He's got to!' cried Elizabeth. She broke away and rubbed at her tears. 'I love him! And I need him!'

If Elizabeth had been able to step outside herself and distance herself from her own predicament for one moment – not something she'd ever been good at – she might have found something to understand in Cameron's attitude. Not to condone, not to agree with, but to understand.

Shula, even, who worked alongside him at the Estate office, could have explained to her the pressure he seemed to be under, not to do with the Estate as such, but to do with his investment business in Scotland. Lately, both she and Susan Carter, Neil's wife, who was employed as Cameron's personal assistant, had spent hours every day fielding calls from people who insisted that Mr Fraser had promised that their cheque would be in the post, or that their case would be receiving his personal attention. One woman had even broken down in tears on the phone and Susan had taken a call from a very abusive man calling Cameron all the names under the sun.

But when Shula spoke to Cameron about it, he insisted it was just a hiccup, a tiny cashflow problem, and that small investors simply didn't realize that moving money around the markets wasn't like drawing out two and sixpence from your Post Office account.

Shula's relations with him were strained enough. In a hideous irony, given Elizabeth's agonizings and knowing nothing of Shula's own past history, Cameron had talked openly to Shula about the baby, assuming she knew. Devastated, Shula had taken Elizabeth to task for being too cowardly to tell her, but then she'd had a long talk with Mark, and with her mother. As a result, she'd decided that she must add this load to the cross she already bore. She told Elizabeth that she'd look on the baby as a Brookfield baby and love it for all she was worth.

'Shula, thank you! I don't deserve you.'

When Shula had told her, tears had sprung to Elizabeth's eyes: she cried at everything, these days.

She hadn't seen Cameron since their encounter at the Dower House: her assumption now was that she would be left to bring up his child on her own. It didn't stop her hoping that he might, by some miracle, change his mind.

She hadn't dared, nor would she ever, she felt sure, to tell Shula that Cameron's first reaction had been to get rid of the baby. She'd finally had to tell her parents what he'd suggested and that had been bad enough: though Elizabeth had no idea, Phil had been to see Cameron and had told him exactly what he thought of him. But abortion was something Elizabeth knew her sister really would find unforgivable.

April had passed in its usual unpredictable way, with impossible sunshine and insolent rain. Phil and David grumbled about the weather and the milk price and the cost of seed potatoes. Jill cleaned and cooked and sewed, and spent her spare time planning to turn Rickyard Cottage into a home for Elizabeth and the baby: Shula even gave her some rolls of wallpaper that she'd bought for the nursery before her ectopic pregnancy. Kenton sold antiques, though not very successfully, Nelson dispensed drinks, and Nigel, with Elizabeth's help, carried on with his plans to market Lower Loxley as a conference venue. Elizabeth's twenty-fifth birthday approached, at the end of the month, and, to her surprise, Cameron got in touch.

He didn't beat about the bush.

'I'm sorry,' he said, taking her hands. She'd gone round to see him at home because he'd asked her, without telling her parents. 'I've behaved appallingly. I was so bogged down in the business, I couldn't think straight. I want you to forgive me.'

'Forgive you?' echoed Elizabeth stupidly, though she already had.

If she'd been waiting for him to mention the abortion and tell her to forget all about it, she would have been disappointed, but for Elizabeth, just the thought of having him back was enough. He kissed her fingertips, taking them one by one into his mouth, and her stomach tied itself into a knot.

'I've been crass and insensitive, to say the least.' He certainly sounded contrite. 'I'm sorry, Elizabeth.'

If she'd listened hard enough, she'd have realized that he hadn't even said that he wanted them to be together. In fact, he'd said nothing at all. But it was all Elizabeth needed.

'Oh, Cameron!' She flung her arms round his neck. 'Oh! That's all I ever wanted you to say! Oh, darling Cameron! Don't worry about it!'

Smiling, Cameron took her in his arms. He wasn't really sure what he was doing, getting involved with Elizabeth again in this way, but then nothing was certain at the moment.

In the kitchen bin – he'd brought them away from the Estate office in case Shula and Susan had taken to going through his wastebasket – were half a dozen letters from angry creditors, one from the Office of Fair Trading, and three from solicitors acting on behalf of clients. There was also a letter from the court, warning him that if certain debts were not paid in full within seven days, he could expect a notice to be served on him by the bailiffs.

Just now, he needed Elizabeth. About the baby, he was less sure, but – well, there was still plenty of time to do something about it. Elizabeth was nibbling his ear. He stood up and pulled her up against him.

'Come on,' he said. 'Let's go to bed. Let's see if I can kiss it better.'

'You're going away? With Cameron?'

'Well, of course with Cameron. Debbie, will you stop doing disgusting things to that sheep and listen to me.'

'Just a minute.'

Debbie released the ewe whose feet she'd been trimming and it ran off, bleating, to join the others that Sammy Whipple was penning in a corner of the yard. Debbie nudged the bits of hoof trimming into a pile with her boot and turned to Elizabeth. 'All right, I'm listening.'

Elizabeth was glowing. Maybe it was the fact that she'd stopped being sick, maybe it was the fact that she was back on speaking terms with Cameron, but she hadn't looked – or felt – this well for weeks.

'You know he called me and asked me round the other day? Well, he said then that work's just been ridiculous. He's been working like stink and he needs a break.'

'As in a holiday?'

'Well, I don't think we're running away to Gretna Green. Even I'm not that gullible.'

'You're going abroad?'

Elizabeth beamed. She wrapped her arms round her still-flat stomach.

'Yup. Somewhere hot and heavenly. I know Nigel'll give me the time off.'

'And what about the baby? Has he changed his mind about you having it?'

Elizabeth pulled at a bit of sheep's wool that had caught on the hinge of the gate.

'Not exactly,' she admitted. 'He hasn't mentioned it and neither have I. But he's obviously coming round to the idea, or he wouldn't have started seeing me again, would he?'

'Well –' Debbie started to say what she really thought, which was that she wouldn't have trusted Cameron as far as she could throw him, and Debbie had a powerful throw. But she could tell that Elizabeth wouldn't want to hear it, and wouldn't have listened if Debbie had tried.

'And I just know,' Elizabeth continued passionately, 'that when we're on our own, away from my family and his work –'

'He'll go down on one knee and say "Darling, will you marry me?".'

Elizabeth put her head on one side.

'Yes,' she said. 'Yes, I think he will.'

They left on Friday, 1 May. Everyone was looking forward to a long weekend: the following Monday would be a bank holiday. Even at Brookfield, where, as Phil always liked to remark, no one told the cows he was entitled to a lie-in, there was something of a festive atmosphere: the weather seemed settled, for a few days at least, the hawthorn was out, and so were the apple blossom and the bluebells. The cows in calf were plump and glossy, the lambs were gaining weight and the crops were emerging.

The tension over Cameron and the baby, which had been at a rolling boil since Elizabeth had broken the news, had subsided to a simmer. As far as the family were concerned, Cameron was a cad and a bounder. They would have been happier if he'd been driven out of the village by a mob waving pitchforks, though David said that that was too good for him and Phil privately agreed.

But even Phil had had to accept that he was not a paterfamilias in a Victorian novel: this was the twentieth century, these things happened, and his and Jill's role now was to help Elizabeth to cope in the best way she could. If not exactly thrilled by the idea of his daughter as a single parent, Phil had had to concede that it was probably preferable to her being married to the loathsome Cameron.

To all intents and purposes, he reassured himself, Elizabeth seemed reconciled to the situation, too: she'd had no contact with Cameron that they knew of, and she intended to carry on her job with Nigel until the birth, after which time she'd move into Rickyard Cottage, which Jill had been using for her B&B guests. That was about as far as anyone was prepared to plan.

'Honestly, it was like a French farce.'

Elizabeth smiled as she adjusted the seat in Cameron's Jaguar. He still hadn't told her where they were going, except that they were flying from Heathrow, so it was presumably long haul. Elizabeth hadn't packed much. She reasoned that she could always buy sun lotion and a bikini when they got there.

'The first time I tried to sneak down the stairs with my bag, Mum suddenly came out of the kitchen. And the second time, David barged in from the office . . .'

Cameron changed down to overtake a truck, then looked at her quizzically.

'Sneak out?' he queried. 'They do know where you are, don't they?'

'No.'

'You mean you haven't told them?'

'They'd only have made a fuss,' shrugged Elizabeth. 'I'll phone them when we get to the airport.'

'Make sure you do,' said Cameron sternly. 'We don't want the Borsetshire Constabulary on our tail.'

Lizzie laughed. 'You are funny, Cameron.'

She looked at him lovingly. With his blond curls and fresh face, he looked like an angel who'd fallen from heaven.

'You do understand, don't you, why I couldn't tell them?' she probed. But he was busy flashing his headlights at an unfortunate Toyota that was impeding his progress in the fast lane, so she carried on. 'They'd have stopped me coming. Mum and Dad seem to think that you're never going to make an honest woman of me, and I'd be better off without you.'

'That's your decision,' he said, shooting the Toyota driver a poisonous look as it pulled over and they zoomed past.

'I know,' confirmed Elizabeth. 'And I've decided. I definitely wouldn't be better off without you. In fact, I'd be thoroughly miserable. And you'd be miserable without me, wouldn't you?'

She looked to him for a reply, but he was fiddling about with the CD player. It was then that she realized she was ravenous. She must be making up for all those weeks of feeling sick.

'Cameron?' she asked. He'd found the track he wanted now. It was the Eagles – *Hotel California*. 'Could we stop for a bite to eat?'

'There are no services on this motorway.' The M40 hadn't been open long.

'Well, could we turn off then?' she pleaded. 'Have we got time? I'm absolutely starving.'

He took his eyes off the road momentarily and looked at her. Elizabeth found his look slightly unnerving. It was as if he'd just discovered she was in the car.

'You want to stop somewhere?' he asked.

'Well, yes, if that's all right . . .'

'Sure.' He smiled at her indulgently and she felt instantly reassured. 'No problem.'

·8·

Secrets and Lies

Debbie clattered her coffee cup back on to its saucer in disbelief.

'You mean Cameron just left you? Dumped you in a motorway service station car park?'

'Actually, it was a pub off the motorway.'

'It's still a car park!'

Elizabeth bit her lip.

'I thought he was going to the loo,' she began, her voice wobbling. 'He was ages. After a bit, I asked the waiter to go in and look for him. I thought he might have been taken ill or something.' She swallowed hard but she couldn't stop herself from starting to cry again. 'And he . . .' She dabbed at her eyes with a scrap of tissue. 'He told me he'd seen Cameron get into the car and drive off.'

Debbie leaned across, plucked another handful of tissues from the box and gave them to her.

'Thanks.' Elizabeth blew her nose. 'Oh, Debbie. I've been so stupid. Didn't he realize what it'd do to me?'

Debbie rubbed her hands over her face. The whole thing with Cameron had, it seemed to her, got way out of hand. She'd always been dubious about this 'holiday' idea he'd suddenly come up with. Elizabeth had never even seen a ticket – supposedly they'd been going to pick them up at the airport. Privately, Debbie wondered if he'd ever intended to take Elizabeth with him – but why encourage her hopes? And as for dumping her in the middle of nowhere, pregnant with his child, and letting her hitch back –

In answer to Elizabeth's question, thought Debbie cynically, he knew all right.

'What are you going to do now?' she asked gently.

Elizabeth gathered up the damp balls of tissue and took them to the bin.

'I don't know,' she answered. 'Wait for him to get in touch, I suppose. I've tried his mobile and it's not switched on.'

'Well, there's a surprise.' Debbie shook her head. 'But he'd better not try showing his face in this village again, that's for sure. I don't think he'd get a very warm welcome.'

As Elizabeth drove slowly home in the brilliant perfection of a May evening, the beauty of the countryside around her seemed to mock her own despair.

Apart from Debbie, there was no one she could talk to, and she'd never been good at drawing on her own resources.

She couldn't turn to her parents for support over Cameron: their opinion of him was low enough already. Shula, though doing her best to be supportive about the baby, had been moaning for ages about how distracted he'd seemed at the Estate office: now she'd have to manage without him entirely.

As far as Lizzie knew, he hadn't warned anyone he was taking time off: the way he'd put it to her, work had got on top of him and he needed to get away from it all. This was why she reproached herself. This was where she'd been so stupid. She knew, for all that she'd accepted Debbie's sympathy, that his leaving her had been nothing but her own fault.

All the way down the motorway, she recalled to her remorse, she'd been prattling on about the baby and their future together, married or not. All she'd wanted was to hear him agree. He hadn't, of course; he'd just been non-committal, but still she'd droned on and on, even when she knew he was utterly bogged down in something that had gone wrong with his wretched investment business in Crieff, and which he'd mentioned a couple of times when she'd let him get a word in.

She'd been so stupid! She could see it now. She'd been so thrilled when he'd taken up with her again that she'd thrown herself at him, and had tried to pen him in, when she should have known that that was exactly the way to frighten him off. So stupid! It was all very well to wonder if Cameron had realized what he'd been doing. She should have realized what she'd been doing herself.

Despite what she'd said to Debbie, and what she hoped for every aching minute, Elizabeth had no idea if she'd ever hear from Cameron again. Now, as she pulled up in the yard at Brookfield, she knew she had to face the horrible truth: her last memory of the father of her child might quite possibly always be his false words of reassurance and his departing back in the tatty bar. And she didn't know what to do about it.

The days dragged on. Shula fulminated about Cameron to Mark: in the office, she and Susan were still having to fob off a stream of irate callers. Phil fumed about the deal on the land at Red House Farm, which was stalled in Cameron's absence. David asked what else he'd expected, dealing with a toad like Fraser, and whenever Elizabeth came into the room, everyone stopped talking and changed the subject.

She had never felt more like an exile in her own family. There didn't seem to be anywhere she could go where anyone would understand. She couldn't bring herself to tell her parents the humiliation Cameron had put her through: they hadn't even known she'd been planning to go away with him, and to add his callous and public abandonment of her to his heinous list of crimes would hardly have helped the situation. As the days crept by, she waited for the call from him that would explain everything and, even now, turn the muddle into magic. It never came.

A whole week passed. It was a Friday – an afternoon of sparkling sunshine. Elizabeth came into the kitchen – she'd been counting buttercups in the orchard – to find her mother and Shula in a huddle. She knew at once it was something serious: her mother hadn't even bothered to make the customary pot of tea. Jill looked at Shula and Shula looked at Jill, and Elizabeth looked at them both.

'What is it?' Every nerve ending in her body had sprung to attention.

Shula looked at her hopelessly.

'I'm sorry, Elizabeth,' she said. 'There's been some rather bad news about Cameron.'

Elizabeth sat down abruptly and clutched the edge of the table. Of course. He'd had an accident. That's why he hadn't phoned. He'd had an accident on the way to the airport and he'd just come out of a coma. No. No, the police would have been in touch before now. An accident abroad, then. Diving! A fall! Or he'd overturned the Jeep he'd hired! Every possibility telegraphed itself to her tired brain until the images were almost superimposed. Jill stretched out a hand to her but she shook it away.

'What, tell me!'

So Shula told her. It was nothing like she'd been expecting.

'The Fraud Squad are looking for him,' Shula explained. 'He's been doing some dodgy share dealing.'

'No!'

'A lot of it,' Shula continued sadly, 'with money belonging to old people or people who've been made redundant.'

'I know Cameron!' blustered Elizabeth, defending him even now. 'He wouldn't!'

'The bank have called in all his assets, including the Estate.'

'No!'

Shula went into a lot of detail, but what it boiled down to was that he'd apparently been robbing little old ladies of their life savings, telling them he was putting them in safe government stocks. In fact, he'd invested in high-risk shares, and for some time he'd made good profits – profits with which he'd bought the Estate. Then things had started to go wrong. The shares had fallen, and when his investors had wanted their money out, it wasn't there to be given back to them. He had debts, Shula said, of millions of pounds. That was why the bank had called in his assets, the Fraud Squad were after him, and the Official Receiver wouldn't be far behind.

Elizabeth felt sick, sicker than she'd felt in her entire pregnancy, and that was saying something. She saw her mother and Shula exchange looks.

'Elizabeth,' said Shula kindly, 'you weren't to know.'

'He can't love me very much if he wanted to keep this from me,' she whispered.

'Perhaps that's why he kept it from you,' suggested Shula.

Elizabeth shook her head. She'd deceived herself enough over Cameron. It was about time she stopped.

'No,' she said sadly. 'He just thought I was a child. And that I'd believe anything he said. And he was right, wasn't he? He's fooled me all the way down the line, just the way he's fooled everybody else.'

It was a terrible weekend at Brookfield. It was the time of year when Phil and Jill took their annual walk round the farm, just as Dan and Doris had always done. They'd remark on the changes in the fields and hedgerows, the state of the sheep and cattle, and generally congratulate themselves on coming through another winter unscathed. Not this year. They walked around in glum silence, knowing that Elizabeth was shut up in her room, Shula was at the Estate office trying to make sense of the files, and David was banging around the bungalow in a filthy mood because the Red House Farm deal, which would have given them the land he wanted for expansion, was off.

Everyone was relieved when Monday rolled around and Bert turned up for work, as cheery as ever with tales of his cat, Pickle's, latest antics and a batch of tooth-rotting fudge that his wife Freda had made.

Elizabeth left the house early while Phil was milking and Jill was still upstairs, and it wasn't until Nigel phoned, late in the afternoon, that Jill suspected anything was amiss.

'I was wondering,' he asked, 'if she'll be well enough to come in tomorrow.'

'Tomorrow?' repeated Jill foolishly.

'I do realize,' Nigel went on, 'this news about Cameron must have upset her and I've managed today without her but – well, I do have a very busy week. I am sympathetic, truly I am,' he added. 'But she is supposed to be my marketing manager and –'

'Of course she is,' said Jill, trying to think straight. 'Look, Nigel, I'll get her to ring you.'

She'd just put the phone down when Phil came in with the surprising news that he'd seen Elizabeth getting out of a taxi at the end of the lane.

'Why on earth,' he wondered, popping a piece of fudge into his mouth, 'is she taking taxis to work?'

'She hasn't been at work,' said Jill, amazed at Phil's powers to eat whatever was in front of him. 'I thought she'd run away –'

The back door opened and Elizabeth came in, looking wan.

'Elizabeth,' started Jill at once. 'Where have you been?'

Her first – unthinkable – thought was that Elizabeth might have had a message from Cameron and had sneaked off to see him.

'I've been to Felpersham,' said Elizabeth bleakly. 'That's where the clinic is.'

'Clinic?' puzzled Jill. 'Is there something wrong with the baby?'

'No,' replied Elizabeth. 'Not any more.'

'Elizabeth, darling,' pleaded Jill. 'Whatever's happened to you?'

Elizabeth looked at her mother, standing there in the familiar kitchen, at the frayed tea towel on the rail of the Aga and the plastic box of fudge on the table. How could she say it? How could she even speak the word?

'I went to –' she began. 'I decided to – I've had an abortion.'

'What!' mouthed her father.

Jill put her hands to her cheeks.

'Oh, Elizabeth, no!'

'I'm sorry, Mum,' said Elizabeth brokenly. 'I thought about it so much – so much. You don't know how hard it was. But I couldn't have the baby. I just couldn't.'

'Oh, Elizabeth.'

She saw her mother reach out a hand and her father grasp it.

'It was so hard. And I feel so empty. But – I had to do it. Say I did the right thing. Please.'

Jill couldn't. They'd put aside their doubts about Cameron. They'd given her so much support. Yet still, without talking to anyone about it, Elizabeth had nonetheless gone ahead and killed their grandchild.

Of course she'd been in turmoil: the whole village was, as the catalogue of Cameron's crimes became longer by the day. He'd invested money for Caroline Bone, it emerged, and Marjorie Antrobus, quite large sums that they'd be lucky ever to see again. Shula was wearing herself thin with reports for the sequestrators and someone called the Interim Trustee: the fact that Cameron's company had been registered in Scotland made it all the more complicated. But the financial losses paled into insignificance against all that Elizabeth had lost with Cameron's disappearance: even so, why, Jill wailed to Phil late at night, had she acted alone, and so impulsively? Why hadn't she trusted them to help her make the decision? Who was she to decide?

'Well, if she can't decide, I don't know who can,' reasoned Ruth to David when the shocking news filtered from Brookfield to the bungalow. 'I must say, in her position I'd probably have been tempted to do the same.'

'Would you?' David sounded surprised. 'I don't know. I suppose I never really saw Elizabeth as a single mother, somehow. It's just not what she's cut out for. But this –'

'If only your mum could accept it. It must have been a difficult enough decision for Elizabeth to make without feeling your parents are holding it against her.'

'They can't help it,' replied David. 'You know how excited they were about the thought of a grandchild.'

'Yes,' said Ruth quietly. 'I do know.'

Jill was devastated. Never before had she been unable to reach out and comfort one of her children when they needed it – but none of them had ever done anything with which she disagreed so strongly.

'I don't know how to help her.' She and Phil were sitting over their untasted breakfast a couple of days after Elizabeth had broken the news. 'I don't know what to say.'

Phil squeezed her hand.

'I know just how you feel,' he said. 'It's something I never imagined ever having to face. Never thought about it at all. I don't know what my response should be. I don't know what it is. I feel sorry for her, sorry in my heart –'

'But the baby, Phil!' cried Jill. 'Elizabeth's killed her baby!'

If Jill found Elizabeth's decision difficult to accept, Shula found it impossible. After the clumsy way in which Shula had found out about her pregnancy, Elizabeth was determined that the same thing wouldn't happen again. Drawing on reserves she didn't know she had, she'd sought Shula out and had told her the worst thing, she knew, she would ever have to say to her sister. As she'd expected, Shula's shock and grief were unspeakable, but Elizabeth didn't know a fraction of what had been going through Shula's mind. For, as she told Nigel when he called round one evening, she and Mark had even dared to hope that they might adopt the baby and bring it up as their own – if Elizabeth had agreed.

'You'd have had to fight me for it,' smiled Nigel wryly. Mark had gone off to fetch him a glass of wine.

Shula looked puzzled. 'What?'

'I was nursing this little fantasy,' confessed Nigel. 'I thought perhaps Lizzie would accept me on the rebound . . . I'd have married her, Shula, and adopted the baby as my own.'

'There you go, Nigel,' said Mark, coming in with a glass. 'It's New Zealand, by the way.'

Shula looked at her husband resentfully. He'd already told her, in his pedantic, lawyerish way, that the decision had had to rest with Elizabeth and it had been her right to choose.

'Her right?' Shula had cried. 'What about the child's rights?'

'I don't think she thought of it as a child. It was just a foetus, an embryo . . .'

'Well, I did,' Shula replied. 'I thought of it as a child. And now it's dead.'

It was at times like this, when everything in your private life was awful, thought Shula, that people told you to concentrate on your work and get through it that way. But her work was bound up with Cameron, and every time she had to think about him, she thought about Elizabeth, and about the baby – the baby that could have been hers and Mark's, and now didn't even exist any more.

She didn't think things could get any worse, until one Friday in the middle of June, when David asked her and Mark to The Bull for a lunchtime drink. Shula would have cried off: she didn't feel much like being sociable, but David wouldn't take no for an answer, and even brushed aside Shula's enquiries about the hay-making.

'The hay can keep,' he said airily. 'It's not going to go away.'

'The weather might change,' Shula pointed out.

David waved away her concerns.

'Look, just be there. Half past twelve, OK? Stop finding problems.'

When Shula got there, the first thing she saw was a bottle of champagne. The second thing she saw was that Ruth was drinking orange juice and she knew at once. Of course. David and Ruth had been married for over three years. They'd got used to married life, moved into the bungalow – what was the next thing on most young couples' agenda?

'Congratulations,' she said warmly when Ruth, quite unnecessarily, told her. 'I'm so pleased for you both!'

And she looked straight across at Elizabeth, sitting stock still on the other side of the table. She'd hardly spoken to her sister since Elizabeth had told her about the abortion: what Shula felt about it was better left unsaid. David had whispered that he and Ruth hadn't known how to break the news about their baby and had decided, in the end, to do it *en masse*. They didn't want to seem insensitive but it was good news, and Elizabeth would have to be told some time.

Shula felt bitterly sorry for her sister. Goodness knew, it was costing her something to sit there and smile, but she was more practised than Elizabeth in disappointment. She'd had to congratulate old school-friends and work colleagues, sign their leaving cards, contribute to the collection and buy them gifts. Elizabeth was still such a child herself. Her pregnancy was the first grown-up thing that had ever happened to her, and it had been ghastly from its beginning to its abrupt and unnatural end. Beneath the resentment that Shula still couldn't help feeling for what Elizabeth had done, she felt a tiny flicker of admiration. Elizabeth had coped. It wasn't the outcome Shula would have wished for, but at least she'd taken a decision. Maybe she should be given credit for that.

· · ·

Surely nothing else could go wrong, Jill had thought after all the business of Cameron's bankruptcy, the enforced sale of the Estate and the terrible outcome of Elizabeth's pregnancy. She had cried with sheer happiness when David and Ruth had told them about the baby – some good news at last! But even as she was congratulating them, she'd known how hard it would be for both Shula and Elizabeth and, as the summer progressed, the atmosphere at Brookfield was still strained.

It was almost a relief when harvest started, with the usual niggles about bushel weights and lost moisture meters. Then their pigman, Neil Carter, announced that he was leaving for a salesman's job with the local feed company, Borchester Mills, and there was yet more talk about the reform of the Common Agricultural Policy to keep Phil and David occupied.

It was to be a busy summer in the village, too. A new vicar, Robin Stokes, had arrived and one of the first things he'd had to contend with was a building programme at the church, during the course of which Anglo-Saxon timbers had been unearthed. It wouldn't have been so bad, but Ambridge was in the National Gardens Scheme that year and there was much anxiety about whether the resulting excavation would be tidied up in time for the big day.

It was also the summer when Eddie and Clarrie had a serious falling-out. There was a bid to twin Ambridge with the French village of Meyruelle, and Clarrie had developed an enthusiasm for all things French, and the singer Roch Voisine in particular. It all got very complicated and very personal, and ended up with Eddie throwing a punch at Grey Gables's French chef, Jean-Paul, whom he thought had been writing Clarrie love poems, when all he'd been doing was translating song lyrics for her. Clarrie was mortified and meted out to Eddie the only punishment she could: the camp bed in the attic. Eddie, unabashed, decided to woo Clarrie back by pursuing her on a WI trip to the Norfolk lavender fields. There, they re-plighted their love, only for the coach to break down on the return journey, with the result that the Ambridge village fête had to be run by the men – a very successful innovation.

Among the family, Pat and Tony's organic ice cream enjoyed another profitable season and they started planning a farm shop. But at Home Farm there were more problems, this time with Kate, who was generally running wild and leading Brenda Tucker and William Grundy astray with her.

'What a year,' sighed Jill, when Phil brought her out a mid-morning cup of coffee to the rose garden, where she was trying to repair the damage wreaked by one of Lynda Snell's escaped goats.

'Quite,' replied Phil tersely. It was the beginning of August, perfect harvesting weather, and Brian had just phoned to say that there'd been a fault with their shared combine. Could he keep it till mid-afternoon to finish off a field? The only comfort was that David wasn't around to say 'I told you so.' He'd never wanted to share with Brian in the first place.

'I've been on to the Ministry place again about my bees,' said Jill guiltily. With everything that had been going on, she knew she'd been neglecting her hives. 'You know, I think they have got varroa, Phil.'

'So it's a fumigation job, is it?'

Jill hacked back an 'Ena Harkness' rose.

'Special strips, apparently. I've got to send off some samples for testing first, though.'

Phil sipped his coffee.

'You sometimes wonder what else can go wrong, don't you?'

'That's exactly what I was thinking before you arrived.' Jill pulled off her gardening gloves and came to sit beside him on the bench.

'Do you think Shula and Elizabeth will ever make it up?'

'I'm sure they will. Eventually.'

'I don't feel I've been much help. I was hard enough on Elizabeth myself.'

Jill had gone through much soul-searching in the past few months. She knew she'd never agree with what Elizabeth had done, but she'd had to accept it. She couldn't change it, after all, and her initial fear, that it would change Elizabeth, had proved groundless, at least in the sense she'd expected. She'd thought it might make her hard and cynical but, if anything, she seemed softer now, more willing to see another person's point of view, less sure of herself and rather nicer for it. Shula was more of a concern: the ceaseless stress at the Estate office and the pain she'd been through over Elizabeth's pregnancy, and now Ruth's, had made her develop a brittleness that Jill was uneasy about.

The sun came out from behind a puffball cloud and one of the farm cats swaggered out from under a laurel to flop down in it.

'I don't know, Phil. I understand now about children. I understand why Doris always used to say that you never stop worrying about them.'

'She was right, wasn't she? But then Mum was right about a lot of things, bless her.'

Jill smiled suddenly.

'She didn't like me at first, do you remember? I think she thought I was a fast piece. And that it was too soon after Grace.'

'I said she was right about a lot of things, love. I didn't say about everything.' Phil shifted slightly to look at her. 'If it weren't for you, Jill, I wouldn't have any of this. Yes, I know –' he held up his hand as she started to speak. 'None of the worries with the children. But none of the good bits either. And don't pretend we haven't had a few of those.'

'Well . . .' smiled Jill. 'If you say so.'

'Thirty-five years in November,' Phil reminded her. 'So we must be doing something right.'

'Dad!' David's voice bellowed from the direction of the yard. Phil got up reluctantly.

'I'd better go and face the music,' he conceded. 'Tell him the bad news about the combine. You know, I can remember when I was the one telling him off.'

'Don't tell me,' smiled Jill. 'It seems like only yesterday!'

'Dad!' David yelled again.

Phil turned to leave, then turned back.

'Elizabeth and Shula will be fine, you know, love. They'll get through this and come out the other side.'

'I hope so,' said Jill. 'It won't feel like our family otherwise.'

·9·

No Return

'Oh, Ruth, she's lovely.' Shula straightened her new niece's fingers and examined them. 'Those tiny, tiny nails,' she marvelled. 'Just perfect.'

Ruth smiled wearily from the sofa. She and Pip – Philippa Rose to give her her full name – had only been home a day and a half, and already Ruth was missing the comforting routine of the hospital. She missed the capable nurses who'd always been on hand to help with breastfeeding. She missed the meals that had arrived at regular intervals and the high bed and firm chairs that were more comfortable for her stitches.

Pip had been as good as gold at Borchester General, but back at the bungalow she didn't seem able to settle. They were in the middle of lambing at Brookfield, and David was out all day and, often, some of the night: the last thing he needed when he got in was to be presented with the squalling ball of dampness that was his daughter. And Ruth just knew that if she admitted how tired and fed up she felt, Jill would take over at the bungalow and force-feed them casseroles and she and David would be lucky if they saw Pip again before she went to university.

She leant forward to put the lid back on a jar of nappy cream. She ought to be grateful for Shula's visit: at least she wasn't demanding like Lynda Snell, who'd picked last night to come round and talk about the refit she was masterminding of the village hall kitchen. Shula, on the other hand, had come during her lunch hour, had made them both a sandwich and had even done last night's washing-up.

Even more than that, Ruth was grateful for Shula's generosity:

139

there was still no sign of a baby for her and Mark, yet she'd been one of the first to visit Ruth in hospital, presenting Pip with a silver christening mug, which she admitted she'd bought for the baby she and Mark had lost. Elizabeth, on the other hand, had had to be coerced into coming, and when she did, Ruth knew it was only because Shula had told her she must. She'd brought a bottle of champagne for them to drink and nothing for Pip. She'd hardly glanced at the baby, then, perched on the bed with her back to the cot, drinking her champagne out of a plastic beaker, had regaled Ruth and David with tales of Nigel's mother, Julia, who'd returned from her winter in Barbados with the Peacock Throne crowd, and was being squired around Borsetshire by Nelson Gabriel. Why, Ruth had wondered as she tentatively sipped her own champagne – if it went straight to the milk it was sure to give Pip wind – why was life always so complicated in the Archer family?

The back door of the bungalow slammed and the new father came in from outside.

'Hiya!'

They heard David ease off his boots, wash his hands and loot the biscuit tin. He came through to them, munching.

'How's things?' he asked as he bent to kiss Ruth. 'How's little Pipsqueak?'

'There hasn't been a peep out of her since Shula arrived,' admitted Ruth, slightly jealous. 'How are things in the lambing shed?'

David threw himself down on the sofa and a pile of nappies slid to the floor.

'Lost another ewe,' he admitted.

'How?'

'My own fault.' He swallowed and wiped a crumb from his mouth. 'I could see she was in trouble when I went in first thing.'

'So why didn't you do something?'

'I had to get on with the milking.'

Ruth gave a heavy sigh. On top of her feelings of inadequacy with the baby, who seemed blissfully content with everyone but her, she was agitated about work on the farm. She knew David and Phil were stretched without her, and she knew they'd cut corners, especially in the parlour, which was Ruth's particular area of responsibility.

In one of the brief respites when Pip had been asleep, she'd already had a look at the figures and had seen that the milk yields were still going down. They'd started to slide when she'd given up doing the milking in the latter stages of her pregnancy. David had maintained they'd hit a bad batch of silage – too wet or something – but he claimed he'd overcome it by feeding more cake. The fact that the latest yield figures were still low pointed to something else – like his being impatient with the cows and not settling them down properly before they were milked. Ruth knew she'd have to tackle him about it but when, she wondered, would there ever be time – a time when they were both awake enough and Pip wasn't yelling?

'She seems to have gone off,' Shula whispered. 'I suppose I'd better put her down. I ought to get back.'

'Fantastic,' said David gratefully, sliding down on the sofa. 'I'm just going to shut my eyes for ten minutes, Ruth, OK?'

'Budge up,' she replied. 'I think I might join you.'

'They both seem absolutely exhausted, poor things,' Shula reported to Mark later. They'd gone to The Bull for a quiet drink, only to find a darts match in progress.

'That's the bit no one tells you, isn't it?' Mark watched as Neil Carter threw his final dart – not one that his team was pleased with, judging by the groans and catcalls.

'No. But Mark –'

Shula had deliberately suggested coming out tonight so that she could put what she had to say to him on neutral territory. She'd hoped for a rather more conducive atmosphere than The Bull versus The Griffin's Head annual derby, but it couldn't be helped. They were here now.

'Yes?'

'When I gave Pip that christening mug . . .'

Mark shook his head.

'I knew it.'

'What did you know?'

Mark straightened his beermat on the table, lining it up with the ashtray. He touched her fingers briefly.

'That you were being a bit ambitious, thinking you could just . . . sail through it. Without feeling . . . bereft.'

Shula looked at him lovingly. He cared about her so much.

'I think I did it on purpose,' she said evenly. 'I wanted to know what I really felt about losing the baby. To test myself.'

'Why?' Mark puzzled. 'Why torture yourself?'

Shula sighed. It was so difficult to explain, even to him.

'I just wanted to know what my gut told me, not my nice, rational, well-ordered brain.'

'And what did it tell you?'

He looked at her, waiting for her to answer. A cheer went up from the Bull team as Mike Tucker hit double top.

'That having a baby,' replied Shula simply, 'is the most important thing in my life.'

'Darling, look –'

Shula put a hand on his arm.

'No, Mark, it isn't up for discussion any more. I know I shouldn't be like this about it, but I'll do anything it takes to have a baby, anything at all.' She saw him open his mouth to interrupt her, to calm her down, but she carried on. It had taken her long enough to come to the realization. She didn't want him to try to dissuade her now. 'And I don't mean just going on trying,' she insisted. 'There are all sorts of medical techniques for people like me. IVF and everything. I want us to really go for it, Mark.'

Having made the momentous decision, and having got Mark to agree, the person Shula was most nervous about telling was her father. There was a bit of her that thought the upright, pillar-of-the-community, JP and church-organist side of Phil might consider that what she and Mark were proposing to do was meddling with nature. But in the end, both he and David took the same pragmatic line.

'Well, it's happening on the farm all the time, isn't it?' David pronounced after hugging Shula and wishing her all the luck in the world. 'Artificial insemination and everything. No point in having these scientific advances if you don't make use of them.'

'Well, thanks,' grinned Shula. 'Likening it to the AI man! I'll tell Mark you said that.'

'It's brilliant, Shula.' Ruth handed Pip to David so that she could hug her, too. 'You're just made to be a mum. No doubt about it.'

But Shula had already had her first consultation with Richard Locke, the new young doctor, and she knew that there was no guarantee of her becoming a mum, ever.

'I'm trying not to get my hopes up,' she acknowledged, stroking Pip's peachy cheek. 'There's only a one in five chance of getting pregnant – and a one in ten chance of the baby going full term. But it's got to be worth a try.'

She took Caroline into her confidence, too, a couple of weeks later, when the date for her first appointment with the fertility clinic in Birmingham came through. Richard was sending her along for tests and then a special sort of X-ray that would give them a better idea of what was happening – or not – inside her. But Caroline had some good news of her own to report.

'It's a secret,' she began, obviously excited.

It was early evening and they'd come out for one of their favourite rides along the banks of the Am. It was always beautiful along there, but especially so at this time of year, with the willows a luminous green and the wild violets glimmering beneath them.

'Go on,' said Shula, mystified.

'It has to be a secret because Robin has to speak to the Bishop and he can't see him till next week.'

'What?'

Shula knew what she hoped it was but she didn't dare say. Caroline had been going out with Robin Stokes, the vicar, for some time.

'We're engaged,' Caroline blurted out, thrilled. 'Last Friday.'

'Caroline!'

' I know, I know.' Caroline's whole being radiated happiness. 'I'm up here somewhere,' – she waved a hand in the air above her head – 'and I'm going mad not telling anyone. So, I've told you now.'

'Oh, well done!' cried Shula, frustrated that she couldn't give her a big hug. 'Congratulations. I mean, we all knew it was on the cards, but –'

'But it's done now,' concurred Caroline with satisfaction. 'It's said and it's agreed.'

Behind them, from the church tower, the ringers began their weekly practice session. Shula should have been there too, but she'd let her one-time interest lapse while she was concentrating on making babies.

'Just think,' she said mischievously. 'You – as the vicar's wife. With your wicked past.'

'Don't,' winced Caroline. 'It sounds like a book by Joanna Trollope.'

They wheeled their horses round into the wind. The peals rang out from the church, up and down, and up and down, filling the air and flooding over the river.

'Grandsire Doubles,' nodded Shula. 'With Uncle Tom leading.'

'They'll be ringing out for me and Robin one day soon,' mused Caroline. 'Oooh. It's made me go all shivery.'

Shula looked fondly at her friend. Caroline had waited a long time for the right man. She'd been out with some absolute so-and-sos, such as Brian and the odious Cameron Fraser – men who'd taken far more than they'd given in love and trust. Now she had gentle, understanding Robin, part-time vet and part-time vicar, and would be stepmother to his two boys, Sam and Oliver, who lived with their mother in Kent, but who came to Ambridge for holidays.

'And they'll be ringing out for you too, Shula.' Caroline looked suddenly serious. 'At the christening. I know they will.'

Shula tried to concentrate on other things, but it was hard when she had a panicky, fluttery feeling all the time. At last, after all these years of waiting, something might actually happen.

But this was not the time to let things slip at work. Nine months after Cameron's bankruptcy, and after the usual wild rumours in the village, a serious buyer for the Estate had emerged in the shape of Guy Pemberton, a farmer in his early sixties who was moving from Suffolk. Back in February, he'd made a sensible offer that the Trustees had accepted, and in early April had moved to Ambridge, staying at Grey Gables while the worst excrescences of Cameron's rather flashy taste – the dolphin-shaped taps and the corner baths – were excised from the Dower House.

It fell to Shula to take him around the village and introduce him to the tenants. The fact that she was still waiting anxiously for her X-ray appointment, which had to be done at a particular point in her cycle, was something that she would have to hide under her heaviest coat of professionalism.

'He seems very nice,' said Pat when Tony had taken Guy off for a walk around the cabbages. 'And very supportive of our farm shop idea.'

Pat and Tony were hoping to expand the shop that sold their organic veg and dairy products, but they'd run into a surprising amount of opposition from the Borsetshire Environment Trust, whipped up into a frenzy, Tony suspected, by the ever-zealous Lynda Snell, who'd found out that he needed to rip out part of a hedge in order to widen the approach.

'He is very nice,' agreed Shula. 'It'll be good for the Estate to have someone in charge who's been a hands-on farmer.'

'Even if he hasn't got experience of dairying.' Pat handed Shula her coffee and sat down at the table opposite her. She began to split and butter the scones which had been cooling on a rack ready for the men's return. 'Are we going to see much of this son of his?'

'Simon?' Shula took a sip. 'I don't think so. He's got a business in Leamington, apparently. Irrigation equipment or something. He's abroad a lot.'

Pat pulled a face.

'Perhaps they don't get on.'

'What makes you say that?'

Pat laughed and shook her head.

'Good point. Nothing at all.' She gave a wry smile. 'Except perhaps – what do they call it? Projection.'

'And which of your sons are you not getting on with?' queried Shula.

'Need you ask?' Pat pushed the plate of scones across. 'Try one of these. They've got yogurt in. And dried apricots. Makes them taste a bit different.'

'John?' Shula queried, taking one. 'Thanks.'

Pat stirred her coffee thoughtfully.

'Yes, John, of course. I mean, apart from burning the candle at both ends with his conservation-grade weaners and these discos he does, you've heard he's been seeing Sharon?'

'Er, well . . .'

Of course Shula had heard. Along with the farm shop, it was the talk of The Bull, the WI and the Over Sixties. Sharon Richards, Pat's dairy worker, twenty-two-year-old single mother, and young John Archer . . .

'At first we thought she was just using him, for lifts and things. But then a couple of weeks ago Tony went down to her house in the middle of the day to check on something for me, and caught John there with his shirt off.'

Shula winced. Sharon had moved a little while back into one of the council houses on The Green and she and John were obviously relishing the privacy.

'Oops. How embarrassing. For both of them.'

'John didn't seem very embarrassed. He seemed quite proud of it, really. But he's so young, Shula,' worried Pat. 'I'd like him to get some A-levels, go on to university. He's bright enough.'

'University? You mean you want to get him away from Sharon,' said Shula astutely.

'Is it that obvious?' sighed Pat. 'I suppose it'll be obvious to John, then.'

But at that moment, the men came back, with much stamping of boots and blowing on chilled fingers, and Pat put the kettle on to boil again, while Shula had to listen to Tony going on about the flame weeder he'd bought for his carrots. But at least some of the time she could let her mind wander to the only thing she really wanted to think about – the baby that might very soon be a reality.

• • •

It was a week later – the end of April – the 22nd, to be exact. Next day would be St George's day, Shakespeare's birthday, and Phil's, of course – his sixty-fifth.

Jennifer had already taken his present round: as it was the school holidays, she had to do these things when she had the time. Things were busy at Home Farm: she'd got her mother and Jack coming for supper that night and Brian had particularly wanted her to make her special trout mousse with some of his rainbow trout from the fishing lake. The next day, a Friday, she'd thought she might take Alice and Kate to Stratford for the Shakespeare birthday celebrations. Kate would pour scorn on the idea, of course, but then she seemed to hold everything Jennifer said or did in contempt these days. She'd already been in trouble with the police for taking and driving away a car with a young lad, Warren, and an educational psychologist had been recommended.

But, to Jennifer's horror, Kate seemed to find a more sympathetic counsellor in Lynda Snell, something that Lynda, of course, had encouraged, publishing Kate's tortured adolescent poems in the parish magazine under the headline 'Young People – Is Anyone Listening?'

'She wouldn't be so keen to listen if she had to put up with that deafening music of Kate's like we do,' Brian had sneered.

But Jennifer had retrieved the parish magazine from the log basket where he'd thrown it and had read again Kate's lines about 'black duvets of blankness' and 'faceless friends' and had wondered where, as a parent, she'd gone wrong.

At least Debbie was all right, she consoled herself as she laid the table for supper, involved on the farm and the riding course and, maybe, fingers crossed, starting to see that nice new young doctor, who was renting one of Jennifer's holiday cottages until his house in

Manchester was sold and he could buy a place in Ambridge. This evening, believe it or not, Debbie and Kate had even gone for a walk together, though Jennifer suspected that this was only because Kate had some salacious gossip about John and Sharon that she just couldn't share in the confines of the house.

'No, everything's going pretty well on the whole,' she could hear Brian assuring her mother as he mixed the gin and tonics. 'The beet's germinating evenly. The linseed's coming up well.'

'Darling,' she chided. 'Mum doesn't want to talk about the farm.' She stooped to the Aga and checked the casserole: prune and pheasant. 'Where has Jack got to?'

Her mother looked at her watch, concerned. The plan had been for Jack's chauffeur, Higgs, who'd already dropped Peggy off, to take Jack to the village shop, which he owned, to collect the takings. Jack would then be returned to Home Farm and Higgs would carry on to Borchester and deposit the money in the night safe.

'Perhaps Jack's decided to go with Higgs,' speculated Jennifer.

'I wouldn't put it past him.' Peggy accepted her drink from Brian, adding, half fond and half frustrated, 'He's supposed to be retired!'

At that moment, the phone rang. Brian, in an unusually sunny mood, said he'd get it. Meanwhile, Jennifer and Peggy chatted about the weather, which had improved, and the house-martins having returned to build their mud nests under the eaves and poor Clarrie Grundy's Q fever, which she'd caught through drying off premature lambs in the house. And then, suddenly, simultaneously, they were both aware that the phone call was in some way significant.

'Debbie?' Brian was sounding concerned. 'Hang on . . . Hang on! More slowly. Start again.'

'Brian? Is something the matter?' asked Jennifer.

Brian waved his hand at her to shut up.

'Shhh! . . . Oh, my God! Are you all right?'

'What's happened? Brian?'

Jennifer went over to the phone. Her mother was still seated at the kitchen table, clutching her fizzing glass.

'Jack?' said Brian into the phone. 'And he's –'

'Brian!'

Jennifer stood in front of her husband. What was going on? What could have happened to the girls? And what had Jack got to do with it?

Brian still wouldn't let her interrupt and she and an agitated Peggy had to listen to more worrying snippets of the one-sided conversation, involving ever more alarming words like 'police' and 'hospital'. Finally, with many reassurances, Brian put down the receiver.

'Well?' Jennifer demanded.

Brian gave a deep sigh, then led her back to the table. He made her sit down, then he told them.

'I'm afraid,' he began, 'there's been a raid on the shop. Jack was in there. And the girls. It was two lads. And they had a shotgun.'

·10·

Family Feelings

It was the story the *Borchester Echo* had been waiting for. Surveys had revealed that so-called urban crimes and social problems were now being visited on the countryside, and here was the proof on Ambridge's own doorstep.

As the older residents of the village reasonably pointed out, in fact, Ambridge had always had its fair share of violence, both home-grown and imported: what about the manslaughter charge that had put Tom Forrest in prison all those years ago, or the time the post bus had been hijacked, or Walter Gabriel beaten up by teddy boys and left unconscious? Jack Woolley himself had been the victim of armed raiders before, at Grey Gables: Peggy had found him bound and gagged beside the empty safe. But that had been twenty years ago, when Jack had been a younger and fitter man. He was over seventy now, with a pacemaker, and everyone knew that the shock of his ordeal in the village shop could have killed him.

In truth, any or all of them who had been in the shop at the time – Jack, Debbie, Kate and Betty Tucker, who ran it, could have been killed. And all because two lads, armed with a shotgun but amateurish and probably scared witless themselves, had decided that a tiny village post office was worth raiding for a couple of hundred pounds and all the cigarettes they could carry.

As the village went into shock and, belatedly, people began padlocking their garden sheds and locking the back door when they went out, the victims of the raid had to cope in their own way.

A fragile Jack was released from hospital, having aged ten years in ten days. Betty, supported by Mike, had to face the fact that her livelihood depended on being able to steel herself to go near the shop again, and to stay there by herself during the day. Kate fell to pieces, blaming herself for wanting a can of Coke and so having got herself and Debbie involved in the first place, and Debbie went to work. She got up early and came in late, striding round the riding course, pacing the fishing lake. And Jennifer, unsurprisingly, went into maternal overdrive.

Even then, the raid might, in time, have been assimilated into village history like the teddy boys and the attack on the post bus: but this time, there was a difference. The shop raiders weren't, in fact, urban delinquents who'd stolen a car and driven out into the country in search of rich pickings. They were locals. They couldn't have been more local.

Though the raiders were masked, Betty and Debbie had suspected it at the time, as soon as they'd heard the voice. The raid had been carried out by Clive Horrobin and an accomplice. Clive was Sharon's ex-boyfriend, Kylie's father and Susan Carter's brother. Not wily enough to evade arrest for long, he was quickly picked up and placed on remand, to Betty's enormous relief and Susan's undying shame.

The aftermath of the raid, appalling as it was, touched Shula least of all. Following the investigative tests, she and Mark had been accepted for IVF treatment and she was was obsessed with her body. The treatment she was undergoing would suppress her own hormone production so that, when the clinic decided the time was right, her hormones could receive an artificial boost which would give an implanted embryo the best chance of survival. She was using a nasal spray and there would be daily hormone injections to come. Shula didn't care. By now, she would have done anything to conceive.

At work, she was grateful that Guy Pemberton didn't seem to need her advice on a day-to-day basis. He involved himself in the Estate with just the right degree of tact, and in the village with just the right degree of reserve that his position demanded. After Lilian's nonchalant absenteeism and the brash *arriviste* Cameron Fraser, it felt as though Ambridge had returned to having something approaching a squire, and the inhabitants felt nothing but relief.

In an unguarded moment with Shula, though, Guy revealed that he hadn't left Suffolk merely because he fancied a change. His elder son, he told her, who'd managed his farm there, had been killed in a car accident and shortly afterwards Guy's wife had died of cancer. Simon, the younger son, had always made it plain that he was not interested in the farm and Guy hadn't had the heart to carry it on. The way he spoke about Simon hinted at unresolved tensions between father and son, but Shula paid little attention. The only son she was interested in was the one she might soon be carrying for Mark.

At Brookfield, they were as busy as ever. David had been on a farm walk and had come back with the idea of creating wildlife habitats along the field margins simply by fencing them off with a strip of barbed wire. His intention wasn't all philanthropic. He'd calculated that Brookfield wasted over half a ton of fertilizer a year at the edge of the fields, which was just the sort of argument that weighed heavily with Phil, especially with the imminent demise of the Milk Marketing Board and the arrival of a free market for milk producers. Little Pip was blooming, round and rosy, and much happier now she'd started on solids. Bert had been found to have a winning way with her, and though David mocked that he bored her to sleep with his rhyming couplets, both he and Ruth were glad of the respite. They'd fixed a date for Pip's christening – Sunday, 4 July – and had asked Shula to be godmother.

Elizabeth was still chilly about the baby, and things were still awkward between her and Shula, and between her and Ruth, but Jill had told her in no uncertain terms that she would be expected at the christening, and that she would be expected to smile – however difficult she found it. For herself, Shula was hoping that she would have her own pregnancy to smile about by then.

In the end, she had to face another bitter disappointment. In late June, on the same day that Caroline and Robin announced their engagement to the village, Shula was able to tell her mother that she was again pregnant. Jill, who'd been icing Pip's christening cake, had dropped the sugar flower she'd been about to position and had folded her daughter in her arms.

'Oh, love! At last! Oh, I'm so thrilled!'

Caroline had been there too, helping Jill to shape the icing sugar flowers round cocktail sticks and she and Shula had looked at each other, both remembering their ride back in the spring and their different hopes for happiness in the year to come.

But Shula's, at least, would be short-lived. Just three days later, when Caroline had called at Glebe Cottage to show them her engagement ring and was admiring Mark's efforts with the herbaceous border, Shula came out of the house to join them. They were sitting in deck-chairs on the lawn.

'Mmm, this is heavenly,' Shula heard Caroline murmur as she approached. 'The evening sun, the scent of the flowers . . .'

'Mark . . .' said Shula, her throat tight.

'Darling, what is it?' Mark got to his feet.

'It's gone wrong.'

'What?'

'It's gone wrong.'

'Oh, no!' breathed Caroline.

Mark came and took Shula's arm, leading her to his chair.

'Sit down, darling,' he urged, dragging another chair across. 'Come on, put your feet up. It might just be . . .' He was trying so hard to help. 'They said there could be a bit of . . .'

Shula shook her head sadly and his words tailed off. All the sitting down in the world would make no difference, she knew.

'No, Mark,' she said. 'There's no doubt, I'm afraid. I've lost the baby.'

Just over a week later, it was Pip's christening. A nervous David – poor thing, how he hated all this emotion, all these complications – had come to see Shula to ask if she could still go through with being godmother.

'Of course,' she assured him, only crying when he'd gone, only privately wondering how on earth she was going to stand at the font, holding her niece and vowing to act as her guardian on earth, when she had to face the possibility that she might never hold her own baby in her arms.

Not that they'd said that at the clinic, of course. Instead they'd reminded her of the known failure rates, and had suggested, kindly, that she give her body a rest. They wouldn't, they said, be prepared to consider another implant until the autumn. They advised her and Mark to take a holiday, to carry on as normal and to come back then.

Shula wore daffodil yellow for the christening, and Elizabeth a short dress in hot pink, both of them defying the ghosts of their own lost children. Pip behaved beautifully, and even the sheep getting out on to the road and taking Phil, Bert and David away from the party for the best part of an hour couldn't spoil everyone else's day.

But for Shula it was torture. She endured it for as long as she could, making small talk with Ruth's relatives, then fled to the sanctuary of the Brookfield rose garden to think her own thoughts. She wasn't the only one who'd had the same idea. Elizabeth was there too.

'I thought I'd escape from the adoring hordes,' confessed Shula, sitting down on the sunwarmed bench beside her sister.

'Me too.' Elizabeth shot her a quick glance. 'Are you all right?' she asked tentatively.

'I was fine,' admitted Shula, 'until one of Ruth's cousins asked me when Mark and I were going to start a family.'

'Oh, Shula –' Elizabeth grimaced. 'It was probably the same cousin who asked me when I was going to settle down.'

'Probably,' replied Shula shortly.

Elizabeth twisted on the bench, exposing even more tanned thigh.

'Look, I know I've not always been the most sensitive person in the world but I do think you and Mark . . .' she trailed off, then tried again. 'I really want the IVF to work, Shula. I didn't know what to pray for in church, so I prayed for that, though why on earth God should listen to me I don't know –'

'Of course he'll listen to you!'

Shula had to smile. Typical Elizabeth, clumsily trying to put things right for someone else and managing to switch the focus back on to herself.

'Shula? Elizabeth?' Jill approached across the lawn. 'I came to tell you tea was nearly ready.'

'You mean we're going to taste that cake of yours at last?' Elizabeth made a brave effort to break the mood. The thought of Jill's orange and Cointreau christening cake had been tantalizing the family for weeks.

'But before we do . . .' Jill inserted herself on the bench between her two daughters and put her arms round them. 'I just wanted to say how proud I am, of both of you. I know it can't have been easy for you today, with all the fuss that's being made about Pip.'

'Oh, Mum.' Shula laid her head on her mother's shoulder. She so wanted, and yet didn't want, to cry. 'Don't say any more.'

'No,' said Elizabeth thickly. 'You don't want both your daughters with mascara all down their cheeks.'

Jill just squeezed them tighter and they sat there in the unrelenting sun until they felt able to go inside. It had not been the easiest day of Shula's life but at least, she felt, at last, something had been aired between herself and Elizabeth that might begin to bury the pain of the abortion for good.

• • •

It was October. It was about the time, Shula had thought, that they might have another attempt at IVF: if it was successful, the baby would be born in July and could lie in its pram underneath the apple tree at Glebe Cottage, and Shula could wheel it down to Brookfield along the sleepy, late summer lanes.

But she'd been so wrapped up in her own life and her own concerns that she hadn't been paying attention to what was happening around her. She hadn't really noticed that Susan, with whom she worked at the Estate office, had looked pale and drawn. She hadn't really registered that, a couple of times, the phone had been put down when Shula had answered it or that Susan had seemed jumpy when

Shula returned unexpectedly from lunch. Then one morning, very early, when she and Mark were about to have breakfast, the phone rang at Glebe Cottage.

'Shula, something dreadful's happened.'

'Susan?' She sounded terrible. 'Are you all right?'

'I don't know how to tell you.' Susan's voice was nearly breaking.

'Take a deep breath and take it slowly,' soothed Shula, wondering what on earth it could be. An accident, perhaps? Neil? One of the children?

'Oh, Shula, I'm so sorry.'

'What for?'

'Is she all right?' mouthed Mark, getting out the marmalade.

'All the trouble I'm causing,' Susan went on brokenly. She gulped a breath. 'I've been arrested.'

'Arrested?' repeated Shula, stunned.

'Susan Carter?' Mark sounded incredulous.

'Be quiet, Mark,' hissed Shula.

'Actually, it's Mark that I need to speak to,' replied Susan. 'I need a solicitor.'

Mark was always scrupulous about not discussing clients' business with Shula: she found it quite frustrating sometimes when she later read in the paper about a case he'd handled and understood why he'd been so tetchy or had over-reacted to some innocuous thing she'd said that had reminded him of work.

But they both knew Susan: Shula had known her all her life, growing up in the council house with her four brothers and her younger sister, and her father, Bert, a lengthman for the council, and her mother, Ivy, who cleaned for various people in the village. Another brother, as well as Clive, had been in trouble with the police, but Susan had always been determined not to be tarred with the Horrobin brush. In marrying Neil and making what Susan would have called 'a nice home' for him and the children, she'd hoped that she'd put her family behind her, not a sentiment with which Clive would have agreed.

When Mark got back that evening from his interview with Susan at the police station he looked worn and weary. Shula poured them each a glass of wine and put something gentle and classical on the stereo. Mark sipped his drink thoughtfully.

'This is when I feel worst about my job,' he said, sliding his arm round her on the sofa. 'There I am dealing with these poor unfortunates all day – especially when it's someone I know, like Susan – and I walk away from the interview room or the court and come home to my wife and my supper cooked and my savings in the bank. What have they got?'

'What's happened about Susan?' probed Shula. 'You'll have to tell me. I need to know something, anyway,' she added, 'because of the Estate office. I'll have to explain to Mr Pemberton.'

So, for once, Mark told her all the details. The beginning of it, Shula already knew. Last month, on his way to a hearing to have his remand term extended, Clive had escaped from a prison van and had gone on the run. Lots of people had been nervous about his turning up in Ambridge – Debbie, Kate, and Betty for a start – but, it appeared, when he had shown up, he'd gone to his family.

He'd surprised Susan one day by arriving at her house, demanding food, money and a place to sleep for a few hours. Over the following weeks, he'd lain low around the area, landing on Susan at regular intervals. He'd made her get a key cut for him. He'd made her buy him new clothes with money she'd put aside for the children. Worst of all, a detail so devastating that it made Shula feel quite sick, he'd made her help him dye his hair in the bathroom of her house.

And when, despite everything, the police had caught up with him again, he'd done as he'd threatened all along, that he'd 'take Susan down with him', and had told the police about her involvement. She'd been arrested, therefore, on a charge of attempting to pervert the course of justice – by aiding and abetting Clive to avoid recapture.

Mark had, he told Shula, spent the best part of the morning trying to persuade Susan that while the right to silence still existed, she should take advantage of it. All the police had, after all, was Clive's word against hers and the circumstantial evidence of the remains of a bottle of hair dye which probably wouldn't have any fingerprints on it because she'd handled it wearing rubber gloves. He felt the police case was weak: it probably wouldn't even come to a prosecution. But Susan's guilt and shame were overwhelming.

As he drained his glass, Mark told Shula that Susan had insisted on confessing, in the naive assumption that if she told the police everything, they might in some obscure way think more of her and be sympathetic. It was beyond Mark's powers to explain to her that that was not how the law worked: now they faced weeks of waiting to find out if the CPS would prosecute and, if they did, a possible Crown Court trial.

'Oh, Mark!' Shula stroked his cheek sympathetically. 'What a mess!'

'I know,' he sighed. 'Poor Neil looked as if he'd been sandbagged. And Susan says she can never hold her head up in the village again. Clive threatened her, you know. And the children. If it comes to court, we'll just have to make the most we can of that.'

Shula got up. She'd have to go and put the supper on, or they'd never eat.

'Come with me,' she said to Mark. 'Come and talk to me in the kitchen.'

So Mark followed her and she told him about bits of her day, but she could tell he was preoccupied with Susan. And she knew then that they wouldn't be going for IVF that autumn. She knew that, after last time, she'd be even more jumpy, and would demand even more of his time. It wouldn't be fair on Mark while he had all this to think about. The baby would have to wait.

Shula couldn't go to court for the whole day. It was 23 December – the last full day in the Estate office before the Christmas break, and Mr Pemberton wouldn't be in himself: he'd been called by Susan's barrister, Jane Fellows, as a character witness.

But all morning, as she laboured over spreadsheets and typed the final letters for the post, Shula thought about Susan in the dock alongside Clive. The CPS had decided to prosecute, and the case had gone to Felpersham Crown Court.

When Susan and Mark had attended court for the pleas and directions hearing at the beginning of December, he hadn't expected a trial date to be set so soon, but the fact that Clive had been on remand for practically six months in total had quickened the pace. It was hardly a consolation, but the result was that Susan wouldn't have the threat of the trial hanging over her at Christmas after all.

Mark had told her that she was likely to receive a community service order, given the picture that he and Jane, with Guy's help, were going to paint of her. They intended to present her as a concerned wife and mother, who'd acted foolishly but out of fear for her family, in the face of her violent brother's threats. He told her that he felt they had a good case.

Shula thumped her fist down on the Christmas stamps on the envelopes. She thought about poor Neil watching from the gallery, and Mark from the solicitor's benches, as the prosecution and the defence gave their final summings-up and sentence was pronounced. Suddenly she couldn't sit there waiting and wondering any longer. She switched off the computer and locked the office. She'd take an hour or so out to go to court: she could always make up the time over the holiday.

She arrived in court just in time to hear Jane Fellows's concluding speech.

'Your Honour,' she was saying, 'you must remember that my client knew her brother to be a dangerous man. A man who can get hold of one gun could easily get hold of another, particularly in the countryside. My client's fear of what her brother might do to her was, therefore, entirely justified.'

Shula slid into a seat in the public gallery, hoping she could catch Mark's eye.

'In front of you, Your Honour,' Jane continued, 'is a woman who was torn between loyalty to her husband and children and loyalty to her brother. What tipped the scales in her brother's favour, in such a tragic way, was the emotional blackmail and the veiled threats he used to persuade her to take the fatal decision to help him. She believes that, in the end, she had no choice.'

Shula hadn't intended to stay long. She still had so much to do at the office, and she had things to do at home – mince pies to make, the holly wreath to put up, and last-minute Christmas cards to deliver. But now she was here, she felt that she couldn't leave. She couldn't desert Susan, and she couldn't desert Mark.

It was getting dark by the time the judge was ready to pronounce sentence. Outside, Shula knew, the crowds of shoppers would be jostling on the pavements, and if she strained her ears, she could hear the handbell ringers outside the new shopping centre, playing Christmas carols. Inside the courtroom, the fluorescent lights buzzed and the radiator gurgled contentedly to itself.

The judge dealt summarily and wearily with Clive: he dealt with incompetent petty criminals like him every day of his life. He sentenced him to six years for the armed robbery, with a further year for the charge of escaping from custody, to run concurrently. Then he turned his attention to Susan, and it was obvious from the start that her involvement in the case was the element that interested him. And one, Shula realized with foreboding, where he perhaps saw that he could make a bit of a name for himself: a mention in the local paper, or maybe in the law columns of the nationals. More than that, it could enhance his reputation on the circuit and beyond. Who knew what exalted position he had his eye on?

'I recognize,' he opined, 'that Mrs Carter is of good character. I have listened to the many good things that Mr Pemberton has said about her. But I cannot ignore what she did. The due administration of our system of justice is the core of a civilized and democratic people,' he continued. Now Shula was really beginning to worry. 'It is becoming increasingly common for people who do not want to see others justly punished to try and undermine this. I sadly hear from other courts about jury interference and witness intimidation. Any attempt to undermine the judicial system is a serious criminal act, and I would be failing in my duty to the public and to the victims if

I did not impose a custodial sentence today. Therefore, Susan Carter, I have no alternative but to send you to prison for six months.'

The court gasped. Shula saw Mark lean forward to confer with Jane and Susan sway in the dock. The policewoman beside her took her arm and guided her to hold on to the rail in front of her. The judge sat back in his chair.

'Take her down,' he said.

'All this talk about appeals.' Mark's hand beat the air in frustration. 'People just don't understand.'

It was Christmas Eve and they'd all gathered at Brookfield for supper. Phil nodded his head sympathetically, drawing on his years of experience on the magistrates' bench.

'If I'm right,' he said, 'for an appeal to succeed you'd have to prove that the sentence was wrong in principle, not just tough. Isn't that it?'

Mark nodded as he sipped his punch.

'Exactly. The sentence was severe, but it wasn't over the top. I've been looking into it all day.'

'But isn't it worth a try?' asked Nigel. He'd never given up hope in his pursuit of Elizabeth, and in the summer, to the family's delight, they'd started going out again. They'd had some stupid row earlier in the week over the usual subject – his mother, her drinking and her interference in the running of Lower Loxley – but they seemed to have kissed and made up. Poor Nigel did so hate it when they quarrelled.

'You see, Nigel,' Mark explained, 'We'd have to get leave from the single judge first. Because of Christmas and the New Year, it could be well into January before he even looked at the papers, and I don't think he'd give bail pending an appeal. Even if he granted leave to appeal, we'd be into March before we got in front of the court and Susan would be finishing her sentence by then.'

'I still think it's terrible,' sighed Shula. She looked at the tall Christmas tree, which Elizabeth had covered in tartan ribbons, at the bowls of nuts and satsumas and the snapping log fire. There'd be none of this for Susan.

'So do I,' agreed Mark. 'Community service would have been the obvious thing in my opinion. And the thing is . . .' He turned to Phil again. 'I feel so helpless. There's nothing I can do.'

It seemed there was nothing any of them could do. Shula had offered to help with the children, but Clarrie had already offered, as had a friend of Susan's, Maureen Travis. Susan, it emerged, had been taken off to a prison near Bristol, where Mark had told Shula she'd spend Christmas Day eating a turkey dinner with plastic cutlery (a precaution against fights and self-harm) and trying to hang on to her place in the queue for the phone.

Shula decided to leave the men to it, and went to find her mother in the kitchen. Jill was lifting an enormous clove-bedecked ham on to a serving dish.

'Where's Elizabeth?' Shula asked, holding the dish steady.

'Thanks, love.' Jill manoeuvred her heavy burden into the centre of the dish and stood back. 'She's taken a present for Pip over to the bungalow.'

'That's nice.'

Jill took the ham saucepan back to the Aga.

'They'll be over in a minute. David was a bit unhappy about one of the cows at milking, so he had to pen her up on her own.'

'Like poor Susan. I just can't stop thinking about her, Mum.'

'I know.'

Jill came back to the table and Shula watched as she arranged watercress sprigs and orange segments round the ham.

'It makes me realize how lucky I am – well, we all are. I'd hoped to be pregnant by this Christmas. Elizabeth's baby would have been a year old. But what have we got to be miserable about, really? Susan's got two children – poor little Christopher's only five – and she can't be with them at all.'

As much as she could, Shula felt contented that Christmas. Elizabeth had Nigel and it seemed as though, this time, they might really make a go of it. Ruth and David had little Pip, and her parents had got the grandchild they'd been waiting for. And Shula? Shula had Mark.

Her feelings about her childlessness had moved from frustration and disappointment through anger and despair to a more resigned acceptance. A couple of weeks ago, before the trial, when they'd been writing their Christmas cards, once again signing them merely 'Mark and Shula', she'd talked to Mark about another IVF attempt. She'd told him she wanted it to be their last.

'I think what I've realized,' she'd said, 'is that if the next one fails and yet I go on and on having treatments, I've got more to lose, Mark, than I have to gain. Because I can see it coming between us. I can see it being a big block that we won't be able to get round. And I don't want that. You're too important to me.'

Mark had got up wordlessly and had come and held her.

'I'm so glad you said that,' he said at last. 'I never thought you would. I thought I was going to have to and it'd mean rows and you'd say I didn't understand and I was holding you back.' He hugged her and sighed. 'I think you're absolutely right.'

'Good,' said Shula simply. 'I'm glad we understand each other.'

For they did. Baby or no baby, Shula was convinced of one thing: she had the best husband in the world.

·11·

A Kind of Immortality

Shula checked the table one last time. Napkins, wine glasses, water glasses, bread, butter, the pearl-handled butter knife that had belonged to her grandmother . . .

From the sitting room, she could hear Elizabeth's whoops of triumph as her horse romped home: as after-dinner entertainment for Caroline's hen party, she and Nigel had brought along a horse-racing video that they used for their corporate events and they hadn't been able to resist trying it out.

In the dining room at Glebe Cottage, the salmon mousse and the puddings were laid out on the sideboard: in the other room, the dips were ready in their cling-filmed bowls. Shula had spent all the previous evening cooking and had been up at eight blending cream cheese and chives and making the salad dressing. Mark had come down, complaining good-naturedly about getting no supper last night and now, he supposed, no breakfast either.

Shula had planned Caroline's surprise send-off down to the last detail. Mark had agreed to be the waiter for the evening, in his DJ, while Nigel was going to be 'Honest Nige', high-class bookie and the working girl's friend. Debbie had been enlisted as decoy to take the bride-to-be off for a ride. Then the plan was that, at around half past six, she'd bring Caroline to Shula's, purportedly to collect her so that they could all have a quick drink at The Bull. That was when Caroline would see the food, the drinks, the balloons and the banner Shula had laboured over all lunchtime with a selection of the Estate office's felt-tipped pens. 'Good Luck, Caroline' it read.

A Kind of Immortality

Shula rearranged the posy of snowdrops that she'd picked from the garden. It wasn't the most exciting centrepiece but it was all she could find in the middle of February. She hadn't had time to go into Borchester to buy flowers. It had been a busy week and it was about to get busier: Caroline and Robin had chosen the first Saturday of his boys' half-term as their wedding day and Shula was to be matron-of-honour. Robin had had his stag night on Tuesday: a pancake race on the Malverns, of all things, organized by his so-called friend, the doctor, Richard Locke. Today, Thursday, was Pip's first birthday, but as David and Ruth had taken her up to Prudhoe to see Ruth's parents, her party in Ambridge had been the day before. And then on Sunday, assuming they all still had the energy, there would be Mark's birthday to celebrate. He would be thirty-nine.

Mark turned the demister up a setting and swabbed at the wind-screen with the back of his hand. It was a murky night, with a drizzle that couldn't make up its mind whether it wanted to grow up and be rain. He'd just phoned Shula on his mobile, telling her that he wouldn't be late: if he was going to keep his promise, he'd have to put his foot down.

It was a relief to turn off the Borchester bypass and on to the lanes: now he could have his headlights on full and not be dazzled by the beams of cars coming in the other direction. He sighed inwardly. He'd got to get home, shower and change and be ready to serve drinks and be charming by half past six: all after the day from hell. Which reminded him: he really ought to call Alan, the social worker assigned to the injunction case he'd been dealing with, and tell him how things had gone.

Debbie was feeling pleased with herself. She'd casually dropped the idea of inviting Shula for a drink to Caroline, and though she'd said she really needed to have another go at the seating plan, Caroline had agreed. They'd had a good ride, too, that afternoon: out over Heydon Berrow in some tenuous sunshine, then back through Leader's Wood as the sky darkened, with the tree creepers and dunnocks busy in the undergrowth and the magpies discussing weighty matters in loud voices in the treetops. Even Caroline's horse, Dandy, borrowed from Christine because her own horse, Ippy, had been stolen, had calmed down: he'd been flighty to start with and Caroline had had trouble controlling him.

Now they were back on the lanes, with the occasional car passing in the drizzle as commuters drove home from Borchester, clip clopping along in single file with Caroline in front, conversation impossible. Tired but contented from the fresh air and the exercise, Debbie felt the confident movements of her horse, Tolly, beneath her, and looked forward to supper cooked by Shula. All in all, life seemed a pretty good place to be.

'We were lucky with this one, the judge saw us at half two.' Mark had got through to Alan on the mobile. He was, shamingly, still at the office, whereas Mark had sloped off early. 'You can never tell, can you? Sometimes you can end up sitting there all day.' Mark flinched as the lights of a car that had suddenly come up behind him flashed in his mirror. Then, with a roar of the engine and a squeal of tyres, the car accelerated and overtook him. Mark cursed. They were coming up to a bend. Anything could have been coming in the other direction. They were lucky there hadn't been an accident.

It all happened so fast. One minute they were trotting down the lane, the next, there was a car coming round the bend in the middle of the road, practically straight at them.

'Look out!' shouted Debbie. 'Caroline!'

But Dandy, terrified, reared and shied: there was nothing even a horsewoman as experienced as Caroline could have done. As the car sped past them, Debbie saw her flung into the road, to land with a scream and then a ghastly thud. And that was when another car came round the corner towards them.

There was nothing else that needed doing: all that was needed now were the guests – and Mark, of course. Shula wandered back into the other room. Nigel and Elizabeth were squabbling over the remote control: Nigel was saying that she wouldn't be allowed to bet on the first race as she'd already seen it run and Elizabeth was asking if he was sure the horses had been drug tested.

Shula thought how close and happy they looked. Jill had guessed, but no one else knew: Elizabeth and Nigel were secretly engaged. He'd proposed at the end of January in typical Nigel style, on bended knee with candlelight and champagne in the Lower Loxley ballroom. But Julia Pargetter was still being a pain. She'd finally acknowledged her drink problem and had checked into an addiction clinic, but Lizzie and Nigel had decided they couldn't go public on the announcement until she'd been told, and she was in too fragile a state for that at the moment.

'This isn't how it should be,' Nigel had told Lizzie, anguished, after she'd accepted his proposal and declared that she would wear the ring he'd given her on a chain round her neck for the time being. 'We should be able to blaze our love from the rooftops.'

'We know how we feel,' Lizzie had assured him. 'That's the only thing that matters.'

Ignorant of all this, Shula merely smiled indulgently at her little sister and her own ex-boyfriend and looked at the clock. It was six twenty-five. Mark had phoned from the car just after half five to say he was on his way home: he wouldn't be late, as he'd warned her he might be, and Nigel wouldn't have to substitute for him as butler and toastmaster.

Shula and Mark had a secret as well: they'd been back to the clinic. After their first IVF attempt, the remaining embryos had been frozen and at the weekend, the three that had survived the freezing process had been implanted.

Shula hadn't told anyone, not even her mum. After last time, and the very public disappointment, she wanted to wait and see what happened. She was glad of all the activity this week. At least it stopped her from spending every waking moment wondering if, this time, the pregnancy would succeed.

She glanced at the clock again, her grandfather's carriage clock, which had mysteriously stopped working after his death, but which had started again the following Christmas. Six thirty. Where on earth was Mark? Even at this time of night, the journey from Borchester shouldn't take more than half an hour.

The door bell shrilled and Shula jumped.

'It's them!' Elizabeth jumped up. 'Are we ready?'

'I think so, though I don't know where Mark's got to.' Shula moved towards the front door. 'I can't wait to see Caroline's face.'

'Debbie's done a splendid job,' added Nigel. He was standing by, ready to open the champagne.

And that was the last thing Shula could remember: Nigel winding the gold foil off the champagne bottle, before she opened the door and saw the policeman and policewoman standing there.

'They reckon he wouldn't have felt anything.' It was early the next morning and, with her parents, Shula was seated at the kitchen table at Brookfield. 'The sergeant said he was probably unconscious the second it hit the tree.'

'Yes.'

It was what Jill so wanted to believe: she couldn't bear to think of Mark having died in pain, not when the pain Shula was feeling was so tangible.

'It's funny.' Shula's voice was compressed, as if she'd folded in on herself. 'There was hardly a scratch on his face. You couldn't even see the injury. It must have been the way they put his head.'

'Oh, Shula.'

Jill felt Phil reach out and take her hand. Her other arm was already round her daughter.

'I didn't think I was going to be able to look.' Shula's voice trembled. 'All the way along the corridor, I was thinking, "I can't go through with this".'

Phil had offered to go and identify the body for her, but Shula wouldn't hear of it. It broke Jill's heart to think of what she must have been through, walking down that hospital corridor with the cushioned floor and the peculiar smell, that Jill knew so well from her

WRVS work. All the way along that corridor, following the signs that said 'Mortuary'.

'And the funny thing is,' Shula went on, unable to stop now she'd started, 'it wasn't Mark at all. Not the real Mark, I mean. It was . . . it was . . .' She began to weep.

'Yes . . . I know.'

Jill felt helpless. For once there was nothing in her great store of wisdom that could offer the slightest comfort to her daughter when she needed it most.

'Oh, Mum . . .'

'That's it,' said Jill fiercely. 'You cry, my darling.'

Phil watched silently, squeezing Jill's hand. His father and his sister, Christine, had been seated round this same table nearly forty years ago when he'd had to come in and tell them that his first wife, Grace, had died, also in a tragic accident. He could remember Christine bursting into tears and Dan comforting her, or trying to, the way Jill was doing with Shula now. But nothing and no one had been able to console Phil himself, and he knew that was how it would be with Shula.

The police were still trying to piece together what had happened but gradually the facts were beginning to emerge. It seemed that Mark had been coming in one direction, Caroline and Debbie on horseback in the other. Some lunatic, apparently, had overtaken Mark on a blind bend, startling Caroline's horse which had reared and thrown her. It had then sped off into the darkness.

The scene must have been chaos: the rainy night, the horse careering about, Debbie trying to catch it, and a body lying in the road. At which point Mark had driven round the corner.

From the measurements they'd taken, the police said, they were pretty sure what had happened: to avoid Caroline's body, he'd put his car into a skid and and it had hit a tree. He'd died instantaneously.

Shula was wiping her eyes on the sleeve of Phil's summer dressing-gown which she'd borrowed and whose sleeves almost hid her hands.

'Perhaps I'll have a bath,' she whispered.

'Whatever you want, dear.' Jill made a superlative effort to control herself. If Shula could do it, she had to. 'There are plenty of clean towels in the airing cupboard.'

'OK,' said Shula tautly, getting up and pressing her mother's shoulder. 'Thanks.'

She closed the door behind her and they could hear her feet going slowly up the stairs. Phil knew, because he could remember, how heavy her body must feel and what a pointless burden life was.

'Oh, Phil.' Jill turned into his arms. 'I just want to hold her. And take all the pain away. Like when she was a little girl.'

'I know.'

Jill let out a shuddering breath.

'I really don't think I can bear it, Phil. Seeing her hurting so much.'

'We have to bear it,' he told her. 'We mustn't let her down. She's going to need us.'

The village couldn't believe it: they didn't want to believe it, but the evidence was there in the lane – a twisted strip of rubber, the tyre marks, the smashed glass. And, very soon, that same morning, bunches of flowers laid over the crushed winter aconites: cellophane and paper-wrapped, children's posies and proper bouquets alongside the police notice appealing for witnesses. Not that there'd be any.

At Home Farm, Debbie reproached herself.

'How could I be so stupid? I keep asking myself that over and over again.'

'You mustn't blame yourself. It wasn't your fault,' said Jennifer, ineffectually she knew, but she had to say something.

She was looking for Debbie's gloves in the dresser drawer. Debbie insisted on going out to check on the ewes: she said she wanted to keep busy.

'I talked Caroline into going for that ride. I arranged for her to borrow the horse.' Jennifer found the gloves and held them out to her. Debbie took them roughly.

'And the car.' She was determined to punish herself. 'I couldn't even do that right, could I? I couldn't even tell the police the colour of the car. Let alone the number plate.'

It was no good Jennifer saying that it had been dark, or that it had all happened in a matter of seconds. Like Jill, she would have to come to terms with the fact that whatever she said would be useless, whatever she did would be of no comfort, and that, for once, there was nothing she could do.

It didn't mean she wouldn't try, and get it wrong, and probably be shouted at for her trouble, but sadly she had to acknowledge that something very grown-up had happened to one of her children. It was something she could not have foreseen, or in any way have protected Debbie from, something she could not justify, explain or make better.

When Richard Locke called at Brookfield later, he'd been at the hospital, and he brought them news of Caroline. She was in intensive care, he reported, with a hairline skull fracture, a broken arm and other minor injuries. The CAT scan, though, had been encouraging – her neural function was all right and there was no bleeding into the brain. Nonetheless, she still hadn't regained consciousness and all the hospital would say was that it could take time.

Robin was at her bedside: Marjorie Antrobus, his right-hand woman in church matters, had been given the dreadful job of ringing round the wedding guests and supervising the arrangements – or rather, the un-arrangements.

'I'm sorry, I can't go and see her. Not yet,' said Shula abruptly. She was alone with Richard in the sitting room. She'd had her bath and had got dressed in some clothes that her father had fetched from the cottage. It was just jeans and a jumper – was that very disrespectful to Mark?

'No one expects you to.'

Richard was preparing the syringe for her injection. That was why he'd come: she'd been having daily hormone injections to encourage her womb to hold on to the implanted embryos. Richard had told her he wanted to continue with them and she didn't have the fight in her to argue. What did it matter?

'I want her to be OK, I really do,' said Shula dully. 'But . . .'

Richard came over to her. He had nice eyes. Green. Grey. Both. Shula had noticed them before.

'You're thinking why Mark and not her? Is that it?' he asked.

Shula undid her jeans and rolled them down. He rubbed the top of her leg with a little cold pad. He was very gentle, he always was, but she flinched more than usual as the needle went in. It must be because she was hurting so much already.

'Perhaps,' she replied. 'Oh, not really. I just want someone to tell me why, that's all.'

He indicated that she could get dressed again.

'That's something I can't do, I'm afraid.'

He was so kind, and he'd been a good friend to Mark. They'd played cricket together. Together they'd taken poor Robin on his forced route march on the Malverns and had made him cook pancakes on a Primus stove and eat the rubbery results. Three days ago, that's all.

'Time you went back on a refresher course then,' said Shula lightly.

'Useless, aren't I?' he smiled. He was clattering his things back into his bag. 'But look, I'm going to keep a regular check on you for quite a long time and if there's anything I can do, Shula . . . You've only got to ask. Anything.'

That was what everyone said. All the people who, over the next few days, phoned or wrote said the same thing, but it was hopeless. They knew it when they said it and Shula knew when she heard it that it was no good. There probably were things, little things, they could have done for her, but she was incapable of organizing her thoughts enough to ask them.

Anyway, she wanted to do things herself: to tidy up Glebe Cottage, to throw away all the uneaten food from Caroline's hen night, to fold up the silly 'Good Luck' banner and put it in a drawer, and to put away the cricket bat she'd bought Mark for his birthday and which he'd never now try out. She wanted to get everything right for the funeral: it seemed the only way she could pay tribute to Mark and show him how much he'd mattered to her. But the thing she most wanted, and which no one could do for her, was to bring him back.

She'd spent the first night, that awful sleepless, too-shocked-to-cry night, at Brookfield. In the middle of it, Elizabeth, hearing her moving around, had come and got into bed with her in her old room and they'd hugged each other and at last had cried together. But after that, Shula wanted to be back at Glebe. It was her home, after all, and she felt closer to Mark there.

That was where Nigel found her, the weekend after it happened. She'd been sitting with Tibby, the more peaceable of the cats, on her knee, slowly stroking his ears and feeling him start to purr.

She'd sat there all afternoon. It had been light at first: she'd watched the blue tits flitting in and out of the nest box that Mark had put up on the willow tree and flapping hopefully round the empty bird table. She'd never believed they could – or should – encourage birds into the garden with the cats, but Mark had convinced her. It seemed harsh, he'd said, but the laws of nature meant that, despite the size of the broods, birds only ever expected to replace themselves. If one fledgling survived the year, in the place of a parent that had died, well, that was success.

When the bell rang, she tipped Tibby gently off her knee and went to answer it. Every time she did, now, it took her back to the dreadful moment when she'd opened the door to the police. But it was only Nigel.

She let him in. He was carrying a mass of freesias, to add to the millions of flowers people had already sent her.

'I don't know why I brought these,' he apologized. 'I can see you've run out of vases. But I just love the smell of them.'

'I love it too.'

He put them down awkwardly on a side table and looked at her.

'I had to come, Shula. I've just dropped Lizzie back at Brookfield. I took her out to try to cheer her up. I didn't know if you'd be there or . . .'

'No, I wanted to be back here. Mum's staying with me, though. She's had to go home to see to Dad's supper and stuff. She'll be back down in a bit.'

'Good,' said Nigel. 'Good. As long as you're not on your own.'

Shula looked at him levelly.

'But I am on my own,' she said. 'And I always will be, now.'

It was almost a week later, a Friday, 25 February. That was what the calendar on Richard's desk said, anyway: that was the only reason Shula knew. She simply stepped, or, if she was lucky, slept, from one day to another. Time had no meaning for her.

She knew she'd seen Robin a couple of times about the funeral, when the poor thing was chasing between all his other duties and the hospital, and that he'd been deferential to her wishes, and kind and quiet, and that they'd prayed together, for Mark and for Caroline. There was some good news: Caroline had finally come round. She was still very confused, with little or no memory of the accident, but it was the sign everyone had been waiting for. Village impresario Lynda Snell, who'd suspended rehearsals for her pantomime, tactfully reinstated them in a low-key way, and she'd been to ask Shula if she would mind if the pantomime was staged in memory of Mark. Shula couldn't have cared less: people did react in funny ways. It was as if they were all reflecting Mark's death through a prism of their own concerns, and Shula had her own.

'Shula? Shula, are you listening to me?'

'Sorry?'

Richard gently put his hand on her arm.

'Look, Shula. Look at the test. It's positive.'

Shula looked stupidly at the little glass phial.

'No.'

'It is. Look.'

'It can't be.'

'It is.'

'I really am pregnant?'

'Yes, you are.'

'I'm going to have a baby?'

'It's wonderful, isn't it?'

Shula held the implication of what Richard was telling her inside her for a minute. She waited to feel something. Both times before when she'd learnt she was pregnant she'd felt an overwhelming rush of delight and disbelief and she'd turned to Mark and hugged him and he'd hugged her right back. She didn't feel disbelief this time – how could she? – Richard was a good enough doctor.

She didn't feel anything, really. Not pleasure, not excitement, not relief. It was impossible for anything, however joyous, to dent the sadness that surrounded her.

'Mark always said we could do it,' she whispered.

'That's right,' Richard reassured her. 'So you hang on to it, for him.'

·12·

Stresses and Strains

A cold rain was falling when they emerged from the Coroner's Court. Nigel, who'd taken the time off from Lower Loxley especially to support Shula, put up his umbrella and they huddled beneath it, feeling that something should be said, but no one quite knowing what.

'I must say,' said Phil finally, 'I was expecting a verdict of accidental death.'

'An open verdict somehow implies unfinished business, doesn't it?' Jill buttoned her jacket. It had been bright and sunny when they'd set off from Ambridge an hour ago.

'Oh, no, Mum.' Shula had been resolute in court, listening intently to the evidence. 'I don't feel that. The registrar's issued the death certificate and that's it. The file's closed.'

In the end, Phil supposed, the coroner had gone for an open verdict because, if the driver of the other car could be traced, there might be a case for death by reckless driving – but the car wasn't going to be traced now, surely, over a month since the accident. Still, if Shula was happy with the verdict, that was all that mattered.

She'd been through so much in the past month. After the first few days of stunned pain, there'd been Mark's funeral to arrange and to get through: all the family gathered at the grave in the frigid March wind, and Bunty, Mark's mother, beyond herself with grief. Shula had wanted everything to be right for the funeral: it was the only way, she said, that she could show Mark how much she cared.

'I hope he knew,' she'd whispered, as the bell had tolled from the church tower. 'I hope he knew how much I loved him.'

And then there were the pleasantries to be got through and the sad, swollen faces of the villagers who'd come to pay their respects. There were also Robin's feelings to be observed; his fiancée, Caroline, was still described only as 'comfortable' by the hospital, and he looked half like a dead man himself. But the day had passed and then, suddenly, there was nothing to work towards any more, just the spring beckoning fraudulently with its blatant sunshine and sudden, nervy showers of rain.

Then, for Shula, had begun the vast task of sorting things out. She'd had to deal with all the tedious administrative things – cancelling Mark's credit cards and writing those crucifying official letters to the bank and the building society informing them of his death. Jill had helped her to pack up his clothes, but more than that, Shula had had to pack up his life, and their life together, and tidy it all away: and all the time in the knowledge, the happy and heartbreaking knowledge, that she was, at last, carrying Mark's child and that he would never know.

'Are you all right, darling?' Jill was asking her now. 'Are you going to come back to Brookfield?'

'Oh, um, I don't know.' Shula looked appealingly at Nigel. She seemed to find his presence an enormous comfort, and Jill was grateful that he seemed to be able to take time away from Lower Loxley to support her. When Jill had asked if Elizabeth minded, Nigel had merely joked that she always said she got things done faster without him: she hoped it was true. 'I think I'd rather go home, actually. Why don't you come and have tea at Glebe?'

Phil demurred.

'I really ought to be getting back.' As Jill shot him a reproachful look he added, 'I want to talk to David about that TB test.'

Just that morning, carrying out the routine TB tests on the herd, Robin had found a possible reactor. As a result, he'd had to slap a restriction order on the farm, which meant that Phil couldn't move any stock without a licence. And there were five bullocks due to go to market next week.

Shula said that she understood, and Nigel was only too happy to drive her home. Promising that she'd take care of herself, Shula kissed her parents and linked her arm through Nigel's.

'You keep the brolly, Mr Archer,' Nigel insisted. 'We'll make a dash for it.'

Jill watched them go, skirting the puddles, then she turned on Phil. 'Oh, Phil, how could you?'

'What? What have I done?'

Not for the first time in his life, Phil was oblivious to his crime.

'How can you think about your blessed cows at a time like this?'

'Jill,' protested Phil, stung by the unexpected savagery. 'We may have TB in the herd.'

'A remote chance,' retorted Jill. 'Robin said it was very doubtful.'

'Even so.' Phil handed her the umbrella and patted his pockets in search of the car keys. 'It's potentially extremely serious.'

'Phil,' said Jill firmly, as he found them, 'we have just attended the inquest on your son-in-law's death. What could possibly be more serious than that?'

Well, quite a lot of things, as it emerged over the next few months: if not exactly more serious, then just as serious to those going through them.

All round the village, it seemed, people were battling their own personal crises. Many of them were, in fact, linked in some way to Mark's death: it was as if that random accident had somehow unpicked a stitch that had been holding together a whole mesh of things: as a result, it was not just the immediate Archer family who felt as though their lives were unravelling.

At Number One, The Green, Susan Carter's release from prison was hardly the joyous homecoming Neil had imagined. She'd served an extra ten days on her sentence: not for going absent without leave to attend Mark's funeral, which she'd felt compelled to do, but for fighting with another inmate who'd torn up a picture of the children. Poor, bemused Neil, already shocked by some of the language and attitudes Susan had picked up during her time inside, had been devastated when she'd announced that she didn't want him to visit during her extended sentence: it was her punishment, she told him, and she wanted to see it out as such.

On her return home, she was withdrawn and reluctant to mix, convinced everyone would see her as a jailbird, a fear compounded by the apparent coolness of her former friend, Maureen Travis, who didn't seem to want to know the Carters any more. Neil knew the truth: Maureen ('Call me Mo – all my friends do') had propositioned him and he'd rebuffed her. Mo's chilly reaction was not to Susan but to him.

It took Susan months to readjust to village life and to re-establish her relationship with Neil: months after her release she told Shula she still had nightmares about Clive escaping from prison and coming to seek her out.

Caroline's recovery also took longer than anyone had imagined. Even when she'd regained consciousness, her memory was hazy, and Robin had the awful task of telling her not once but twice that in the same accident in which she'd been injured, Mark had been killed. Caroline had been both disbelieving and guilt-stricken: when, after Mark's funeral, Shula had come to see her, she'd been terrified her best friend would hate her.

'Why?' pleaded Shula. 'Do you think I'd want you dead, too?'

Caroline lay there, all tubes and bandages, and silently wept.

'I just lie here,' she gulped, 'trying to make some sense of it.'

But there was no sense to be made of a pointless accident. All Shula could do to console her was to tell her gently that she was going to need all the friends she could get: she was pregnant, after all, and her child had already lost its father.

Robin had rather less success in reaching Caroline. She had never been a churchgoer. When they'd fallen in love and planned to marry, she and Robin had started attending marriage preparation classes designed for the clergy, and Caroline had found some of the questions they raised about faith and spirituality disturbing. Now, after all that had happened, she was confronted by what she saw as Robin's smugness in his belief in a benign God, and all her doubts returned. As she became physically stronger, her mental attitude towards him hardened and, by May, she had to tell him that she didn't think she could go through with their wedding.

The other wedding planned for that year was almost cancelled, too. Their engagement was still not public and Elizabeth wasn't as blithe about the time Nigel was lavishing on Shula as she pretended.

'But what can I say?' she wailed to Debbie, whom she'd had to let in on the secret. She felt too mean-spirited to talk to her mother about it, and she certainly couldn't talk to Shula. 'She's my sister for good-ness' sake, she's lost Mark and she's having a baby. Of course she needs someone. But does it have to be Nigel?'

Debbie had said all the right things: that it was only temporary, and that while Nigel might love Shula in a brotherly way, it was Elizabeth he was in love with and whom he wanted to marry.

But Elizabeth didn't feel sure. Nigel and Shula had a history together. They'd drunk champagne and danced the conga around Grey Gables while Elizabeth was still at school: it was for Shula that Nigel had first beaten his chest in his gorilla suit while Elizabeth was only fifteen and in her 'Save the Planet' phase, intent on saving real gorillas and the hump-backed whale. Now Nigel was busy cutting Shula's lawn and taking her to the supermarket, playing the fool and miaowing in the catfood aisle while Elizabeth slogged on at Lower Loxley with the Borsetshire Building Federation and the absurd breeze-block pyramid they wanted to construct near Uncle Cedric's folly for the duration of their conference.

It came to a head one afternoon in late April, all birdsong and brilliance. The atmosphere was already strained between Elizabeth and Nigel: he'd taken Shula out for dinner on the night of Elizabeth's birthday, and the note of explanation he'd left her had gone astray. Then he'd invited Shula over to help set up a medieval banquet: while Shula and Nigel had fooled around and reminisced about medieval banquets they had known, Elizabeth felt she'd ended up doing all the work. Now he had plans for clearing out the conservatory and making it a sort of Palm Court. Inevitably, he'd asked Shula over for her opinion.

'Oh, yes,' Shula had breathed when Nigel had explained his plans for camellias and palms and wicker furniture. 'There's such atmosphere.'

'I knew you'd see it,' declared Nigel in triumph. Elizabeth wasn't keen on the plan: Lower Loxley ate money as it was.

'Well, let's go for it, then,' she said in a brittle tone. 'Never mind if it bankrupts the entire enterprise.'

'Do try and be a bit positive, Lizzie,' Nigel reproached her.

Elizabeth erupted.

'Don't worry about me!' she exploded. 'What does it matter what I think if you're both convinced it's such a brilliant idea!'

There was an awkward silence, then Shula made some excuse about not realizing the time and needing to get away, and slunk out of the side door. Nigel immediately turned on Elizabeth, demanding to know what the matter was. Aggrieved that he'd had to ask when she wanted him just to know, Elizabeth spelt out how jealous she was. And then she said what she'd really hoped she wouldn't have to say.

'It wasn't you who finished it last time you and Shula went out, was it?' she speculated sadly. 'So what would have happened if Mark hadn't come along? Maybe you'd have ended up together.'

'I don't know!' Nigel lifted his shoulders in frustration. 'No, we wouldn't!'

It was pointless talking about it, really. It was like wondering if the driver of the car that had overtaken Mark would ever be traced. It would simply always be there, a question mark.

'Well, I don't think we should go on with it,' said Lizzie gravely. 'Not while we're both so unsure about our feelings.' She felt for the clasp of the chain on which she wore her engagement ring – the beautiful emerald and diamond ring that had been left to Nigel's future bride in his grandmother's will. 'So perhaps you'd better have this back.'

There. Now it was said, and if she'd hoped that getting things out into the open would make her feel better, it hadn't worked.

'Lizzie!' exclaimed Nigel in anguish.

'I'm sorry,' said Elizabeth, trying not to cry. 'I've thought about this a lot. I'm sure it's the best thing. Bye, Nigel.'

Distraught now, she forced the ring into his hand and blundered her way to the door.

As she slammed it behind her, she could hear Nigel calling her name, but she didn't turn round. She got in her car and drove dangerously fast all the way to Brookfield with tears streaming down her cheeks.

Way up in the sky, a skylark was wheeling round and round for no other reason, it seemed, than the sheer pleasure of being alive. Elizabeth let out a long sigh and snuggled into Nigel's shoulder. After laying siege to Brookfield for a week, and finally taking Jill into his confidence, he'd lured Lizzie to Lakey Hill, Ambridge's traditional trysting place.

'I thought I was losing you, Lizzie. It was awful,' he whispered.

'Oh, Nigel. That's how I felt too. It just seemed as if you didn't care about me at all.'

'I'm so sorry. It's only because I felt so secure about us. It seemed we were so lucky. Everything we had going for us. I suppose I wanted to give something of it back to Shula.'

Elizabeth looked upwards and saw fleecy clouds on vivid blue, a picture-book sky. Life at Brookfield had been anything but picture-book lately: as well as Shula's troubles, and Elizabeth's own, there was the ongoing worry about the retest for TB, due in a week, and the implications for the Brookfield herd should the same cow react again, or if the disease had spread. Her father, Ruth and David spent the whole time telling each other not to worry, while their faces revealed that no one was finding it possible to take the other's sensible advice. Elizabeth blinked. There was the skylark again, swooping lower now, singing.

'I used to come up here with Grandad,' she murmured dreamily, 'and watch the skylarks.'

He'd used to carry her on his shoulders, and tell her that if she looked far enough into the distance, she'd be able to see the Taj Mahal. She never could, though, not even, though she strained her eyes, the Taj Mahal restaurant in Borchester, which had fascinated her as a small girl with its flashing neon sign depicting a steaming bowl of curry.

'It's a good spot,' Nigel confirmed. 'That's why I brought you here.'

'The final showdown?' she smiled.

'No.' He turned and took her in his arms. 'Not that.'

After they'd lain there for some time, they'd gone back down to Brookfield and this time Nigel had asked Phil for Elizabeth's hand, because, being Nigel, he insisted on doing things properly, and because, he said, that way she wouldn't be able to wriggle out of it again. And Jill had cried and put the kettle on and now the only problem was telling Nigel's mother, who was still in the clinic but was due to come out at the end of May.

But as Elizabeth's fears for her future eased, the worries at Brookfield intensified. At the mid-May retest, the suspect cow was classed as a definite TB reactor. She would have to be valued and slaughtered, the whole herd would have to be tested and no bovine stock could be moved on or off the farm. The cow in question – wasn't it always the way? – was one of their very best milkers. What's more, she was in calf to a special bull they'd paid a fortune for.

As soon as he told her about the May reactor, in the kitchen with the coffee on and lunchtime smells wafting from the oven, Jill knew what Phil would be thinking. It had been before she'd come to Ambridge, but she knew that there'd been an outbreak of foot-and-mouth at Brookfield in the 1950s. Every cloven-footed beast on the farm had had to be slaughtered and Dan had had to come to terms with the loss of his life's work. He'd been compensated, just as Phil would be now, though at only 75 per cent of the animals' value, but that was not the point. It was months before Dan had eventually found the heart to replace the stock, and Jill knew from Phil that it had nearly broken him. Though the situation was not the same – not yet anyway – Jill knew that Phil would go through just the same cycle of emotion: the worry of the financial loss, the self-reproach – as if his husbandry skills were in some way to blame – and the guilt and shame of bringing a notifiable disease into the district.

Until the next test, at the beginning of June, they all busied themselves with the usual round of jobs: there were still a hundred-odd cows to be milked, the pigs to be seen to, and the silage and hay to be cut. They tried to tell themselves that the reactor had just been an isolated case, something that could have happened to anyone.

But the tests went on with monotonous regularity throughout the summer, with ever-increasing numbers of reactors, until, at the beginning of August, there were eleven: nearly 10 per cent of the dairy herd, and all of them in calf. Jill had heard David and Phil discuss the possibility often enough to know that such a high proportion, and the fact that taking out the reactors didn't seem to be stemming the infection, could mean that they had to face the worst possibility of all: they might be looking at slaughtering the whole herd.

'I've been trying to steel myself for this moment,' Phil told Jill when she finally ventured out into the yard that August afternoon. From the kitchen, she'd been watching the cows led in and out of the crush as she moved between the sink and the table and the Aga – she was making Shula's birthday cake, though what sort of birthday she'd have this year was anyone's guess.

'That's only natural,' Jill replied. 'It makes sense to expect the worst.'

'But part of me,' Phil admitted, 'clung on to the hope that everything was going to be all right. And now the worst's happened,' – he looked beseechingly at Jill – 'I don't know what I'm going to do.'

What they had to do, as they always did, as Shula had done after Mark's death at the beginning of the year, was somehow to carry on. Nigel and Elizabeth had set a date for the wedding, after all – 29 September – and it would be unfair to let the TB outbreak overshadow that. Jill knew that the day would already be traumatic enough for Shula, who would be eight months pregnant, added to which the volatile Julia was capable of throwing a whole bagful of spanners into the works.

When Nigel had nerved himself to tell her about the engagement, she'd made it plain that a 'yeoman farmer's daughter' was not the daughter-in-law she'd had in mind: then she and Jill had nearly come to blows over Julia's assumption that Lower Loxley would be the venue for the wedding reception. It was only when they'd met in the florist's, each about to order table decorations, that a whole raft of duplicated arrangements had been uncovered, but, in the end, Jill's plans – a marquee at Brookfield – had, quite properly, won the day. Lizzie had chosen her bridesmaids (Debbie, Kate and Alice) and Nigel had chosen Richard Locke as his best man. In a stroke of genius, and to reconcile Julia to the event, Nigel had also secretly arranged for her sister, Ellen, to fly over from her home on the Costa Blanca for the wedding. TB aside, everything seemed to be set fair.

Jill suspected, of course, from the moment she walked into the church. Ellen had been invited partly so that Julia didn't have to sit out a lonely vigil while they waited for the bride, yet there they were, the sisters, sitting in different pews. And when Elizabeth, so pretty in antique lace, and Nigel, so nervous, yet so proud, had said their vows and all the photos had been taken and the confetti had been thrown, and they piled back to Brookfield for the buffet, the reason for their estrangement emerged.

'Finishing school? Us two?' chortled Ellen, who possessed a laugh that could have been used to cut the cake. 'Good Lord, no. Our father was a greengrocer in Lewisham!'

And that was the least of it. Plied with champagne by fascinated guests, while Julia sulked behind a pillar with an orange juice, Ellen revealed the truth about Julia's stage career, her meeting with Gerald Pargetter while she was playing Bridlington and he was stationed nearby with his regiment, and, most devastating of all, the fact that her real name was Joan. Only by forcibly wrestling the bottle from her hands did Nelson stop Julia from turning to drink again.

When Nigel and Lizzie finally escaped, and had stopped in the lane to remove the tin cans that Richard had attached to the bumper, Nigel slumped wearily in his seat.

'I think it's all been too much for me!' he joked feebly. 'All that chasing round trying to make sure Mummy didn't get drunk. Auntie Ellen's interminable stories. I'm exhausted!'

'I know how you feel.' Lizzie reached over and kissed him. His cheeks were pink. 'But it's all over. It's just us now. Just you and me.'

Nigel gave a happy sigh.

'I know. I can't believe I could be so happy. That you'd agree to marry me.'

'I didn't just agree,' laughed Elizabeth. 'I went ahead and did it!'

Nigel turned to her, serious for a moment. It wasn't even a conscious thought, but suddenly an image of Shula had slipped into his head. She'd found Elizabeth's hen party, coming so close to what should have been her own wedding anniversary, horribly difficult, he knew. And though she'd smiled bravely for the photos and throughout the reception, nothing could alter the fact that tonight she'd be going back to Glebe Cottage on her own.

'You won't ever leave me, will you, Lizzie?' he asked urgently, holding her tight.

'No,' said Elizabeth, moved by the vulnerability of his appeal. 'Never.'

·13·

Motherly Love

'Another glass of Chardonnay, ladies?'

Nelson, clearing their lunch plates, hovered hopefully. Pat looked at Jennifer. Jennifer looked at Pat.

'Take it from me,' Nelson urged them, 'It's the coming thing. Soon Entre Deux Mers and even Californian Sauvignon will be no more than a dim and distant memory.'

Pat drained her glass.

'It is rather delicious.'

'I don't think so, Nelson, thanks all the same,' Jennifer butted in regretfully. 'In fact, we'd better have a couple of coffees. We don't want to go breathing fumes all over the baby.'

'Let me guess.' Nelson's hand executed a world-weary arc as he summoned the coffees from his pert assistant, Shane. 'This must be Shula's miracle baby, as the tabloid press would have it.'

Daniel Mark Archer Hebden had been born the day before, Thursday, 14 November. According to the proud grandparents, he'd weighed seven pounds and twelve ounces at birth, had a shock of black hair and blue eyes, just like his father's.

'Well,' conceded Pat. 'He is rather special.'

'Yes,' agreed Jennifer. 'But then they all are, aren't they, to us mothers?'

She got up and reached for her handbag.

'I'll just nip to the loo, Pat, then we'll have our coffee and be on our way. Visiting starts at two thirty.'

Pat sat back contentedly. Unlike Jennifer, it wasn't often that she could justify taking a couple of hours out in the middle of the day, but the birth of Shula's baby was one of the best reasons she could think of.

It was time Brookfield had something to celebrate: after the awfulness of Mark's death, they'd spent all summer battling the TB outbreak. Although that finally seemed to be on the wane – only one reactor at the last test – Phil and David still faced the problem of not being able to move stock off the farm. There were fifty extra calves, for a start, which Phil had told Tony would cost them up to £7000 in extra feed and labour over the winter, and which had had to be housed in an old shed.

Phil had been embarrassed, Pat knew, when Tony's stock, and Brian's deer, whose grazing pastures bordered Brookfield, had had to be tested for TB as a result of the outbreak. Fortunately, the results had been negative, but Brookfield was still frustrated by the Ministry's inability to trace the source of the disease. After much deliberation, their Badger Panel had finally decided against culling the badgers on Lakey Hill. Phil wasn't convinced that badgers were the culprits either, but it still left the burning question: where had the TB infection come from? Increasingly, Phil was having to accept that he simply might never know, but he didn't like a loose end any more than the next person, and Pat knew that he would always be fretting away at it, testing the limits of his endurance and trying to tie it neatly in.

Jennifer came back to the table and sat down again.

'You were miles away!' she teased. Their coffees had arrived and she poured a dribble of cream into her cup.

'Just thinking about Brookfield, and what a heavy year they've had,' Pat replied. 'Still, things seem to be looking up. What with Daniel, and Nigel and Elizabeth married.'

'Even if she has taken on the mother-in-law from hell.' Jennifer lowered her voice. Nelson was being kept busy as escort to both Julia Pargetter and her sister Ellen, who'd stayed on longer than expected after the wedding. The rumour was that there seemed to be some rivalry for his affections. 'Although Brian says Elizabeth can always come to him for some tips on dealing with the in-laws.'

'That's a bit unfair.' Pat had found her own mother-in-law irritating enough in the past, but just at the moment she was feeling rather guilty towards her. As ever, the cause of the problem was her elder son.

It had been Peggy's seventieth birthday recently, and last weekend Jack had organized a big family party at Grey Gables. Pat had duly accepted for herself and Tony, and had primed John, Helen and Tommy to be there and to be on their best behaviour. They'd all agreed – albeit reluctantly – at least until John had decided differently. He'd suddenly disappeared for the weekend, and the way he'd chosen to mark his grandmother's birthday was with a reverse charge phone call. Peggy hadn't seemed to mind, saying it was thoughtful of him to have bothered, but for Pat it was the last straw.

She'd been to Brookfield on Monday morning to have it out with him – he was working there now, on his sandwich year from college – but he'd been rude and insolent, refusing to explain where he'd been and telling her brusquely that David was waiting for him at the pig unit. Pat had had no alternative but to let him go, knowing that she'd thrown away yet another chance to get through to him: the story of their relationship since he'd left home a month before. She still winced when she thought about how that had come about and how she'd mishandled things, effectively driving him out.

It was one of those stupid things that happen in families. Things are said which, at another time, wouldn't even strike home. But all along, Pat now recognized, she'd misjudged the depth of John's feelings for his girlfriend, Sharon: she'd still been thinking of him as her baby, not as a young man of eighteen with adult, and adult male, emotions.

'Where will it end?' she'd raged to Tony. 'He's absolutely besotted with her. If she says jump, his only question is how high.'

Tony had merely shrugged and fetched a can of lager from the fridge. He'd had a hard day drilling barley, and the last thing he wanted was an ear-bending from Pat. She'd gone off like this about Sharon before, once when she'd cut and gelled John's hair for the play the village had put on for the town twinning ceremony with Meyruelle and, most famously, in the summer, when Sharon's knickers had fallen out of a duvet cover Pat was putting through the wash. He'd tried to calm her down on both occasions, pointing out that when he'd been John's age, he'd had hair down to his shoulders and an eye for the girls. And could she honestly, in all conscience, not remember a youthful indiscretion or two of her own? But the only thing that appeased her was Tony's insistence that it would all burn itself out in time.

But then something had happened that Pat really could not let rest. Sharon had been moaning for ages about learning to drive. John had started teaching her in his van and she'd promptly crashed it into Peggy's car.

'How irresponsible can you be?' she'd stormed to John. 'You can't just go round smashing into people's cars and expecting to get away with it.'

'I haven't got away with it,' John had snapped. 'I'm the one who's going to be forking out a couple of hundred quid, aren't I?'

'Precisely!' rapped Pat. 'When it was Sharon's fault. She's the one who should be paying.'

'Oh yeah? On the pittance you pay her for slaving away over your yogurt pots?'

That had hurt Pat, throwing it back at her as if it were her fault. She was the one person in the village who'd supported Sharon when no one else had had a good word to say for her, giving her the caravan to live in before she got the council house on The Green. Sharon was on the standard agricultural basic, and it wasn't even as if she was a very good worker, always sloping off for a fag break and often late because Kylie had missed the school bus and she'd had to beg a lift to Penny Hassett.

'I've had enough, John,' she'd retorted. 'I don't want you seeing her any more. No more Sharon.'

He'd looked at her levelly, then turned to leave the room.

'I shan't want any supper,' he said. 'I'll be too busy packing my stuff.'

The next day he'd moved out to live with Sharon.

At eighteen, moving in with Sharon achieved everything John wanted. Not only could they be together, it would show his parents that he wasn't a kid any more. Even better, now he wasn't living under their roof, he wouldn't have to put up with any more of his mum's lectures.

But pleased though she was to have him there, Sharon was wiser in the ways of the world: she was concerned less about grand gestures than what they were going to live on. John was earning only £70 a week as a student at Brookfield, and she'd given up her job at Bridge Farm when he'd moved out, knowing she could no longer work alongside Pat.

'We'll be fine,' John had assured her, touchingly handing over his wage packet. 'Just give me back, say, twenty, for drinks and stuff – you can have the rest.'

'You want the three of us to live on £50 a week?' Sharon had asked, incredulous. Didn't he know how much fruit cost, and toilet rolls, and chicken nuggets for Kylie?

'It's OK,' John replied. 'Auntie Jill's given me a hundredweight sack of potatoes. And a boxful of apples.'

'And you reckon we can live on those?'

'We don't need food, do we?' he'd asked, pulling her towards him. 'I know I don't.'

Sharon shook her head ruefully but she let herself be held. As a boyfriend, John was terrific, but as a provider – well, he hadn't got a clue. And when she challenged him on it, he came up with a neat solution: they should get married.

'Are you serious?' she asked him.

''Course I'm serious.'

He lifted her long red hair and nibbled at her neck.

'You really want to marry me?'

She pulled back and looked at him, and for a moment, despite all her education in the school of hard knocks, she let herself believe in happy endings. Then he'd blown it.

'It'd show my family, wouldn't it?' he'd said. 'Put their noses right out of joint.'

That was when Sharon had regretfully decided it could never, ever work between them. He was just too young.

She didn't say anything to John. Instead, a couple of days later, she told him she was taking Kylie to her mum's in Borchester for half-term. He hadn't wanted her to go, and she'd teased him about being scared of being left on his own in the house.

'It's not that,' he'd insisted. 'It's just . . . don't leave me, Sharon.'

It was as if he knew, just as Sharon had known when she'd closed the door that October afternoon. She'd known she could never come back.

A week later, out of the blue, Pat had received a form from a staff agency. Sharon had given her name as a referee, and it was asking about her suitability for a mother's help position in Leeds. Even leaving aside Sharon's dubious mothering qualities, it put Pat in a quandary. John had told her nothing about Sharon leaving. Asking questions round the village, she found out about Sharon's supposed week away, and that she'd been in touch with Susan Carter, her sister-out-of-law, as it were, asking for a few of Kylie's things.

With Tony, late at night, Pat deliberated. Should she give Sharon a glowing reference, thus getting her out of John's life for good? Or should she tell the agency the truth about her 'reliability and cheerfulness'?

All Pat knew was that Sharon had gone. She didn't know any of the background, and relations between her and John were so soured that she knew he wouldn't tell her if she asked. But when she saw her son at the village bonfire on Guy Fawkes night, she was shocked by how dreadful he looked. She'd tried to talk to him, and he'd finally let her get close enough to give him a hug and for him to blurt out that he loved Sharon and that she'd broken his heart. It was enough to break Pat's, but there was no more she could do.

Now their temporary moment of closeness at the bonfire had been lost in the tirade she'd given him about the phone call to Peggy. John had been in Leeds, of course, she now knew, trying to persuade Sharon to come back to him. He obviously hadn't succeeded, and then, when he'd been so low, Pat had shouted at him as well.

'Are we ready, Pat?'

While Pat had been re-running the saga of her problems with John, Jennifer had been interrogating Shane about his artichoke soup.

Pat turned to her sister-in-law: she'd scribbled the soup recipe on a napkin and was tucking it in her bag. Poor Jennifer. Even if John had left home, at least he was still in Ambridge, whereas no one had any idea where Kate was.

The village had been raising its collective eyebrows for years over Jennifer's middle daughter, who could most kindly be described as something of a wild child. In fact, she'd been running amok in Ambridge since she was thirteen, lording it over a gang of acolytes, including William Grundy and Brenda Tucker, and her unfortunate involvement in the raid on the shop had done nothing to stabilize her. This past summer Kate had taken her GCSEs, but even while she was supposedly on study leave, she'd gone to an apparently innocuous folk festival and craft fair at Lower Loxley and had attached herself to some of the rather 'alternative' characters manning the stalls of silver jewellery and Peruvian blankets. With her parents' reluctant consent – as Kate was quick to point out, she was sixteen, so she didn't need it, anyway – she started going to festivals with them.

When her results came through in August, they were as bad as Kate herself had predicted. Jennifer threw herself into a spin – Brian was too busy harvesting to be any help, of course – and spent days persuading her to enrol at Borchester Tech to resit them, with inducements of upping her allowance and buying her a car as soon as she passed her driving test.

Although she let herself be persuaded, Kate obviously had other plans. With a cynicism that, Jennifer would have said, was characteristic of his attitude towards Kate, Brian declared that he should have known something was up when she offered to make herself useful for once and man the riding course on the Friday before August Bank Holiday. At the end of the day, she disappeared with the takings.

Even so, the hope and belief in the Aldridge household was that she'd decamped to some festival for the weekend, and would be back when the money ran out. It didn't happen. Kate didn't come home for her birthday and she didn't come home in time to be Elizabeth's bridesmaid. Jennifer and Brian had to involve the local paper and then, as time went on and Kate's disappearance took on a more serious aspect, the National Missing Persons' Helpline.

Poor Jennifer, thought Pat again. She'd often mocked her, with her literary pretensions and knack of self-dramatization. Tony was no kinder towards his sister. She must be worried about Kate, he'd said: his mum had told him that Jennifer hadn't even bothered to go to Underwoods for her exclusive preview of the autumn collections ('By Invitation Only. Complimentary Glass of Champagne on Arrival'). But Pat, at least, ached for her.

Throughout September and October, there'd been weeks of unsatisfactory contact with various New Age types through a friend of Kate's called Spike. She was sighted in Somerset, supposedly, but when Brian and Jennifer hared down there, they were told she'd decamped to Wales. Then a woman called Zoe had turned up at Home Farm, claiming to be in contact with Kate, who, she said, didn't want to get in touch in person. Although Brian was sceptical, Jennifer had allowed Zoe the run of the house, clinging to her as her only link with her daughter. But Brian had finally been proved right when Zoe disappeared overnight, just as Kate had done.

Now poor Jennifer had nothing to hang on to except, as she'd told Pat earlier, the prospect of looking for Kate at King's Cross when she and Debbie went up to Smithfield with Brian next month.

Pat shivered. What a place to have to look for your child. Kate was alive, that was for sure. There'd been positive sightings, which was why the police weren't more concerned. But how heartless of her not even to get in touch.

Kate heartless, John broken-hearted. Jennifer had finished her coffee and was pulling on her coat. Pat reached for her battered Barbour. A fine pair they were, she thought, to visit Shula and dispense worldly wisdom about motherhood. It didn't seem five minutes to her since

John had been born: she was sure Jennifer must feel the same about Kate.

'Give Shula my regards,' intoned Nelson from the bar as they made their way to the door. 'I'm sure she'll understand if I don't visit. I've never felt I'd be entirely comfortable in a maternity ward.'

'How's Rosemary, Nelson?' Pat asked curiously. Nelson's long-lost daughter Rosemary had been a police cadet at Hendon when she'd re-established contact with her father, to the amusement of everyone in Ambridge who knew about Nelson's nefarious past. Nelson twitched an eyebrow and signalled Pat over.

'She's a store detective at John Lewis,' he hissed. 'But I'd be grateful if you didn't pass it on.'

Jennifer was waiting for her, poised in the doorway, where the weak November sunshine fell on the bleached wood floor.

'Come on, Pat,' she urged. 'I can't wait to see this beautiful baby I've heard so much about.'

If only they could stay babies, thought Pat. How simple life would be.

·14·

Belonging

'It's perfectly simple, Caroline.' Brown eyes are usually described as warm, but Simon Pemberton's lowered the temperature in Caroline's office by ten degrees. 'All I ask is to be kept informed of my father's progress – or not.'

Caroline counted to twenty before replying. At the end of January, Guy Pemberton had come off his horse, Moonlight, on Brian's riding course. He'd broken his pelvis and had knocked himself about a bit, and Caroline, who'd been seeing quite a lot of Guy since the New Year, had appointed herself chief carer. Simon had already made it plain that he'd have preferred an agency nurse, but Guy's wishes had prevailed. Then, the other day, Guy, who was still on crutches, had slipped on a polished floor at the Dower House. He'd brushed it off as a trivial tumble but now, it seemed, Simon had found out about it.

'He's told you?' she asked at last.

'He hasn't, not in as many words. I heard from Mrs Antrobus.'

Of course. Marjorie Antrobus, whose nose was ever so slightly out of joint since Caroline and Guy had become a couple, and who was constantly fussing around Guy, offering to change his library books and bringing him cake.

'I'm surprised you didn't ring me.' Simon's tone managed to combine the hurt of the dutiful son and the disbelief of the thwarted dictator.

'Simon,' sighed Caroline, not wanting to get into a row. 'What have you come to say?'

Simon glanced at his watch: as usual, Caroline felt she was wasting his valuable time.

'I appreciate what you're doing for my father,' he replied carefully. He always gave the impression that he calibrated his words before he spoke. 'But I think the time has come for me to insist on more sensible domestic arrangements being put in place.'

'His domestic arrangements are sensible,' objected Caroline. She knew only too well what it was like, recuperating from an accident. You didn't want a stranger looking after you: only certain people would do. 'And they're what Guy wants.'

'He's not exactly in the best position to judge,' countered Simon. 'As I said in the beginning, he needs a professional, not this gaggle of . . . of well-meaning amateurs.'

Caroline opened her mouth to protest but Simon drew their conversation to a close by standing and buttoning the jacket of his expensive Italian suit. Caroline stood up too. Inside she was fuming. She dealt with difficult guests every day, she'd been dealing with Jean-Paul's tantrums for years, but Simon rendered her speechless every time.

She'd have liked to have told him exactly what she thought of someone who for years had maintained no contact with his father, and now was trying to bully him when he was vulnerable. In private, she raged to Shula about it, but in front of Simon, she had to keep her cool. She desperately didn't want to say anything that Simon would be able to take out on Guy.

'I intend to make sure things are done properly from now on,' Simon concluded, just to remove any last shreds of doubt. 'At least while I'm running my father's affairs.'

He went out, closing the door behind him with a smug click, and at lunchtime, it took Caroline twenty minutes on the treadmill at the leisure centre to tease out the great knot of tension he'd knitted into her spine.

'He's impossible!' she ranted to Shula that night.

It was the end of February, and the anniversary of Mark's death, coming so close to his birthday, had been hard for Shula. Although she had Daniel, with whom she was besotted, and who gave a purpose to her life, he could never be a replacement for the husband she'd loved. She leaned forward and topped up Caroline's glass.

'What does Guy say?'

Caroline hesitated. She'd spoken to Guy that afternoon. In order to buy Simon off on the vexed question of a professional carer, Guy had had to agree to something that would affect Shula directly when she went back to work at the end of her maternity leave.

'To keep him quiet, Guy's agreed to Simon running the Estate until he's better.'

That should have been the end of it: Simon had got what he wanted, or at least some of what he wanted. But once he'd got his feet under the desk at the Estate office, he seemed to regard it as an opportunity to run things in his own inimitable style.

'He's had a terrible row with Geoff Williams,' Susan told Shula when they met outside the shop.

'But Geoff's the nicest bloke; he's impossible to row with.'

Shula had worked alongside Geoff, who managed the Estate dairy herd, for years and had never known him to raise his voice.

Susan shrugged.

'And I heard Simon on the phone to his dad giving him a right earful. Saying how his dad had this muddle-headed approach to business, and he was just being taken advantage of.'

'Honestly, Simon shouldn't judge everyone by his own standards!'

Shula had reason to be incensed. Any criticism of Geoff, or indeed of Guy, was a criticism of Rodway's advice on the Estate, and thus of her.

'I can't wait for you to come back to work, I really can't.' Susan sounded heartfelt. 'Simon Pemberton just makes me nervous and Graham Ryder's so . . . smarmy.'

Graham, known at Rodway's as 'The Grim Creeper', had been put in place to cover Shula's maternity leave: she could well imagine how he might be ingratiating himself with Simon. She smiled weakly. Given what Susan had told her about the office, she could hardly wait to return.

All round the village, it seemed, Simon was putting people's backs up. At The Bull, where Guy and Sid had been partners since Peggy had sold up the previous year, and a new up-market restaurant was under construction, he was outraged when he found out Kathy was pregnant, believing that the business should come first. He was still muttering, according to Caroline, about Guy's refusal to sue Brian over the accident and he'd offended her by offering to pay her for taking care of Guy's horse. He sent all the tenants a curt letter giving them a year's notice of a rent rise. And then he picked another fight with Geoff Williams and Geoff resigned.

'Trust Simon,' fumed Caroline to Shula. 'He's put in charge of running the Estate, he alienates all the staff and then what does he do? Pretends it's all worked out to his advantage. He's ordered a review of the entire management of the Estate which that toady Graham Ryder is running about doing. And poor Guy just has to sit back and watch it happen.'

There was no respite even when Shula went round to Brookfield: David had heard the rumours about the Estate and was wondering if Simon would consider letting some land if, as seemed likely, the Estate got out of dairying.

'It'd be perfect, Shula,' he pleaded. 'We could upgrade our tackle. We could justify having our own combine again, instead of having to share Brian's, which is a nightmare every summer. You know Ruth and I are desperate to expand.'

Shula could see that nothing she said would make any difference. Even when Simon told him he had no intention of letting, but wanted the surplus land contract-farmed, David persuaded Phil to put in a tender. Although Simon would have preferred a larger company to take it on, Guy put his foot down and the contract was duly awarded to another father and son – Phil and David. It would run for three years.

It was with much trepidation that Shula returned to work in May. Simon had had such a universally bad press, not just from Susan and Caroline, but from the whole village, that she was expecting the worst, but with Shula, though formal, he was never less than polite. And there was one memorable occasion, not long after she'd started back to work, when she really warmed to him.

Her mum and dad had snatched a rare week away on a coach trip to Meyruelle and she'd left Daniel with Nigel and Elizabeth. But there was a crisis at Lower Loxley and Shula had no alternative but to take Daniel to the office with her for the afternoon. Daniel was such a placid baby, content to flex his toes and try to catch sunbeams from the comfort of his carry-chair, that she should have got away with it – had Simon not staged an unexpected visit.

'I thought your sister was supposed to be looking after him,' he queried, peering down dubiously at the baby. Daniel beamed back, showing off his one jutting tooth.

'She was,' admitted Shula. 'I'd have got Ruth to have him but she and David are in the middle of shearing.'

'So you thought you'd bring him in here.' Simon moved gingerly to one side as Daniel lunged at his trouser leg.

'He's not disturbing me,' said Shula evenly, though Daniel was beginning to whimper. It was time for his tea. 'Bringing him in this afternoon was an exception. It won't happen again.'

Simon looked at her. The phone began to ring. Daniel whimpered again. With a sigh, Shula reached for it, but Simon intercepted her.

'I'll get it,' he offered. 'I think he needs his mum.'

Caroline couldn't believe it when Shula told her, still less that Simon had picked Daniel up and played 'This Little Piggy' with his toes.

'I'd have thought if you asked Simon how he liked children he'd have answered "fried or boiled",' she said tartly. 'Perhaps you bring out the best in him, Shula.'

Or perhaps Daniel did. Shula didn't know, but as the weeks progressed, she found herself siding with Simon more and more – against her father, her brother and her own best friend.

At the end of May, Caroline and Guy got engaged. They'd been away for the weekend to Southwold and had come back grinning soppily:

Shula was the only one to be told, but an ecstatic Caroline said that before too long they wanted all Ambridge to share their happiness. So the following month, Guy threw a party: a combined engagement celebration and a thank you to everyone who'd helped him out after his fall.

'Since horses brought us together, we're hoping for a stable relationship,' joked Guy in his little speech, and Shula saw Simon cringe: Guy had only braced himself to tell his son the news about half an hour before the party started.

Shula could have wept for him, and she could have wept for Guy: what on earth had gone on between father and son that made them consistently and, it seemed, wilfully hurt each other? There had to be more to it than the death of Simon's brother, who, it was acknowledged, had been the favourite son.

'It's all about when Simon was setting up in business,' Caroline told Shula, as she turned her fabulous aquamarine and diamond engagement ring in a shaft of sunlight. It was Saturday morning, and when Caroline had arrived, Shula had been trimming back some shrivelled heads of lilac while Daniel kicked on the garden rug. Now they were seated in the sun, drinking ginger beer. 'Guy was disappointed that Simon went for engineering not agriculture. He asked for a loan to get him started – and Guy refused. Guy regrets it now, of course, but Simon's never forgiven him.'

Shula nodded slowly. She could well imagine the patrician, public-school side of Guy making it impossible for him to reach out and ask forgiveness from Simon. And even if he had, she could well imagine Simon turning his back rather than the other cheek.

Whatever the rights and wrongs of it, Shula found herself more and more taking Simon's part. When David complained about the fact that Simon now wanted the Estate farmed using fewer pesticides and fertilizers, which would make the terms he'd agreed less profitable for Brookfield, Shula told him firmly that it was a case of *caveat emptor*. When Caroline worried to Shula that Simon would do something to ruin her wedding day – set for 11 September – Shula told her crisply that Simon was a grown man, not a child. And when

Guy approached Shula, asking her to accompany Simon to the wedding, Shula knew what was really being said. She was being asked to be his minder. And she minded – for Simon's sake.

Caroline's wedding day was perfect in every detail, and after so many disappointments with so many hopeless suitors, Shula was thrilled for her. Slim and elegant in a designer suit and a Philip Treacy hat, Caroline was shaking with emotion as Guy slid the wedding ring on to her finger during the civil ceremony at Lower Loxley. Then relatives and friends would move through for lunch in the neo-classical drawing room before the church blessing at St Stephen's in mid-afternoon. In the evening, Jack Woolley was throwing a party at Grey Gables, his wedding present to Caroline, whom he'd always regarded as a surrogate daughter.

'And Simon's behaved beautifully, hasn't he?' remarked Shula when she caught up with Caroline after the cake had been cut.

'Apart from one snide remark about the flowers, yes,' Caroline acknowledged. 'What could he find to object to in a simple arrangement of lilies?'

Shula knew the answer: rigid with indignation, Simon had told her when he'd dragged her out on to the terrace before lunch. White lilies had been his late mother's favourite.

Shula had felt torn. Caroline had chosen the flowers: she wouldn't have known. There was no slight intended. But she also knew that though it seemed petty and trivial, it wasn't. Not when you'd lost someone. She'd experienced something like it herself recently, with Simon.

He'd called round to see her one evening after work. It was about some woodland that badly needed thinning out: he said he'd meant to discuss it with her that afternoon. Shula smiled to herself as she uncorked a bottle of wine and tipped some pistachios into a bowl: if he wanted to play his little games, then who was she to stop him? She rather suspected that, instead of battling it out in the rush hour on the M40 on the way back to Leamington, where he'd presumably remove the sleeve and pierce the film on some microwaveable delicacy, he'd rather linger at Shula's, where he might even, if he was lucky, be asked to stay to supper.

But when she went back into the sitting room, he was standing in the window, where the evening sun came in. He was holding Daniel above his head, and Daniel was kicking his little booted feet and squealing. Shula put the wineglasses and the dish of nuts down silently.

It wasn't Simon's fault – just as it wasn't Caroline's fault about the flowers. She hadn't meant any disrespect by them, but Shula knew exactly what Simon had meant when he'd told her that it was as if his mother had never existed. Shula had felt the same when she'd seen him holding Daniel. It shouldn't have been Simon holding Daniel. It should have been Mark.

But still something drew her towards Simon. Caroline and Guy went off on their honeymoon, and Simon had to watch her things being moved into the Dower House. Trying to effect a thaw in relations, he called round when they came back, only, he complained to Shula, to find them kissing on the doorstep.

'They've only just got married,' Shula reasoned. 'Please, Simon, just try to understand.'

He wasn't around in Ambridge much for the next couple of weeks: they'd got the auditors in at Leamington. Then, one Friday in October, he turned up unexpectedly at the Estate office just as Shula was packing up for the day. Susan had already gone home.

'I thought I'd come in person,' he said, 'to show you I'm serious. I couldn't have got through the last few months without you to talk to, Shula. I really do owe you a lot.'

Shula could feel herself blushing.

'Are you trying to embarrass me?' she said lightly.

'No, I'm trying to ask you out,' he replied. 'Have dinner with me. Tonight. Botticelli's at eight o'clock.'

Shula was dumbfounded. Hadn't he noticed that it was five past five already? And that she'd got a baby to think about?

'But – tonight?' she faltered. 'What about Daniel?'

'Don't give me that,' he laughed. 'You've got a family that's a cross between *Little Women* and *The Waltons*. I can't believe there isn't someone who'll babysit.'

Amazed by his easy assumption, but flattered at the same time, Shula left the office promising to see what she could do. She wasn't very hopeful: her mum and dad were going to a concert, and Elizabeth and Nigel had a big corporate do on. Ruth and David maybe?

In the end, Ruth was happy to babysit, saying it would make a change to sit in a house that didn't smell of slurry. Simon collected Shula promptly at half past seven and ushered her to the car.

'You look lovely,' he said as they drove away.

She'd decided on the sapphire blue silk dress she'd worn to Caroline's wedding: he was in the same dark suit he'd been wearing at the office but he'd changed his shirt and tie and had obviously shaved. He smelt of some deep-noted aftershave that tickled Shula's throat and made her spine tingle. The leather headrest yielded slightly as she leant her head back. She smiled to herself.

In the restaurant, he was at his best. He made her laugh by telling her about the vagaries of the irrigation business and some of his more demanding customers: he told her about his love of rock climbing and about his favourite holiday ever, on a tall ship in the Caribbean. Shula told him about growing up in Ambridge. He couldn't believe that she'd never wanted to leave. She told him indignantly that she'd been round the world when she was twenty, and how she'd been to Hong Kong to visit Mark.

'I'm not a complete country bumpkin, you know.'

'It never crossed my mind,' he said silkily, refilling her glass.

When they got back, she ushered Ruth out, ignoring her curious looks, and went to check on Daniel. He was sleeping in his usual position of rapturous abandon, arms flung above his head. Shula hung the duvet, which he'd kicked off, over the end of the cot and looked at her sleeping son. Then she went back downstairs.

Simon had put some Nina Simone on the stereo. He was sitting on the sofa, his arm stretched along the back of it, perfectly relaxed. Shula made for the armchair but he patted the place beside him.

'Come and sit down beside me,' he suggested.

Shula sat.

'He looks so like Mark when he's sleeping,' she said suddenly.

She didn't know where the words had come from and she cursed herself. She'd had a lovely evening with Simon and all she could do was to go on about the past.

'But it's not the same,' he said gently.

'No,' said Shula, looking straight ahead, her hands clenched in her lap. 'He can't put his arms round me and give me a cuddle.'

There was a fractional pause, then Simon shifted his arm from the back of the sofa to rest on her shoulders.

'I can,' he said. And then: 'Is that nice?'

Shula nodded. She wanted nothing more than to relax against him, but she didn't dare.

'Come on,' he said, easing her towards him. 'It's what you need.'

'Simon . . .' she began, worried. There'd been no one since Mark, and she hadn't wanted anyone. Yet she did need it, desperately. She could either go on fighting it, or she could take the risk.

Shula had spent her life in Ambridge but she'd spent the past eighteen months not belonging. She'd had enough of always being the odd one out at family gatherings, of going to sleep and waking up alone in the bed she'd once shared with Mark and she knew she simply couldn't bear it any more. She wanted to love someone beyond Daniel and her family, and she wanted someone to love her out of choice, not through a sense of obligation.

And then, quite unexpectedly, Simon had arrived, another oddity, just as she was. He stood outside the life of the village for a different reason, but Shula felt for him in his isolation. Surely, if she could do something to make him feel included, he might be able to do something to rehabilitate her?

Simon bent his head to kiss her. 'And I'll tell you what else you need,' he said.

·15·

A Friend in Need

'Did I do something terribly wrong when he was a baby, I wonder?' mused Guy, helping himself to marmalade. 'Or was it when he was older?'

'Yes, you should obviously have sent him up more chimneys.' It was a restless day at the end of March. Outside the windows of the dining room at the Dower House the trees wriggled in the wind. Caroline refilled her husband's coffee cup and passed it to him. 'Come on, Guy, you know as well as I do when all the trouble between you and Simon started.'

Guy chewed his toast thoughtfully.

'I refused him a loan ten years ago, and he's holding it against me? Cause and effect?' He added milk to his coffee and took a sip. 'No, Caroline, it has to go back further than that. I've been a bad father somewhere along the line.'

'Oh, Guy, please –'

Every conversation about Simon these days seemed to end up with Guy coming to the same conclusion.

'Or maybe just not enough of a father, busy working when the boys were small, then sending them away to school. I never had a conversation with Simon when he was growing up. And now I don't dare talk to him about anything.'

Caroline reached across and covered Guy's hand with her own. She hated to see him torturing himself like this. And it was worse this time because she'd been the one who'd started him off on this topic – by insisting that he tackle Simon properly about what was going on.

Back in January, Guy had overheard Simon talking affectionately on the phone to someone called Harriet. As Simon and Shula were now officially a couple, Guy had, quite reasonably, asked Simon about it and had received short shrift. The woman in question was, he'd finally admitted, Harriet Williams, an old flame of his who'd eventually married someone else. Now, Simon told Guy, her marriage was in trouble and she'd turned to him as a shoulder to cry on. He'd insisted it was nothing more than that and he'd made it clear to Guy that any further questions would be not just unwelcome but intrusive.

Guy appeared convinced by Simon's assurances, but Caroline was sceptical. There was something about Simon that she'd never trusted, but when she'd tried to voice her concerns to Shula, even before this Harriet woman had resurfaced, Shula had seemed puzzled – and rather hurt.

'You don't know him, Caroline,' she'd insisted. 'At least not like I do. I see a different side to him from everyone else. He's really not as bad as you say. And I wish you wouldn't say it.'

Caroline was worried about her friend. Lord knew, she'd been out with a few unsuitable men herself. She knew how tempting it was to believe that this was the one, and how seductive it was after months – years – on your own to have a new boyfriend. She knew how Shula had suffered since Mark's death, and she recognized that deep down Shula's need to be part of a couple was greater than her own. But Shula and Simon together? She really couldn't see it, long or short term, and she knew that Jill was having difficulty too.

'I'd like to be wrong, I really would,' Jill had worried when she'd bumped into Caroline on the green. 'But I can't see him making her happy. And more grief is the last thing she needs.'

Caroline agreed. She knew from Guy that the phone calls were continuing, and although Simon continued to maintain that he and Harriet were no more than old friends, she was on the alert through-out the winter. When she saw Simon at the station with a redhead, she didn't say anything, but she was interested to learn that Simon had told Shula he was in back-to-back meetings all day and couldn't meet her for lunch. When he let Shula down on Valentine's Day, Caroline was tactfully sympathetic, but not surprised: if Shula felt that Simon's offer to provide the wine for the new vicar, Janet Fisher's, welcome party was compensation enough, who was she to argue?

But a month later, when she went to call on Shula at the Estate office and found Simon simpering down the phone to Harriet, she'd had enough. This relationship wasn't in the past, it clearly had a present and quite possibly a future. Caroline couldn't have cared less who Simon went out with: in fact, she'd have preferred it to be anyone but Shula. But she wouldn't stand for him two-timing her best friend. That was when she'd told Guy that it was up to him to get Simon to tell him the truth about Harriet. And if Guy didn't, she said, then she would.

She should have known, she told herself later, that she was asking too much. She'd observed in the past how an encounter with Simon could leave Guy. Simon was still running the Estate, and if a discussion with him about fodder crops or new business units was enough to leave Guy drained then she should have realized that a challenge about his personal life would be sure to make Simon lash out.

She didn't need Guy to tell her the detail of the conversation: Caroline knew when she came in from Grey Gables and found him sitting quietly with a whisky at a quarter past five that things had been said that went deeper than some superficial questioning about an old flame.

'We both made our feelings known,' Guy said sadly when Caroline had taken off her coat and was sitting at his feet by the fire. 'And on more than just Harriet.'

Caroline reached for his glass and took a sip herself: she was sure her name would have come up. If she didn't approve of Simon for Shula, it was nothing compared to Simon's feelings about her. He'd made it clear from the time of the engagement that he thought Caroline was a gold-digger who was after Guy's considerable wealth. Caroline hadn't mentioned the family trusts that gave her an annuity in addition to her salary from Grey Gables, and that when her uncle, Lord Netherbourne, died, she'd be inheriting an embarrassing amount from him. She'd kept her dignity and let Simon think what he wanted: she would simply bide her time and prove him wrong and the best way she could do that was to be the loving wife she wanted to be. She picked up Guy's hand and kissed the palm.

'I'm sorry,' she said gently. 'I should never have asked you to do it. I should have spoken to Simon. He loathes me anyway – what have I got to lose?'

Guy shook his head.

'No,' he said wryly. 'I'm his father, after all. Not that Simon thinks I've ever been one to him.'

'Is that what he said?'

'Yes,' replied Guy. 'And not even in as many words. That's exactly what he said.'

The following Saturday, when Caroline still felt that Guy looked tired and washed out, they'd promised to put in an appearance at the Grand Grange Farm Car Boot Sale. For once, this wasn't one of Joe and Eddie's scams, but a bona fide event to raise money for the play-ground that was to be built in the village to mark what would have been Dan Archer's hundredth birthday in October. Ragged posters had been going up around the village for weeks, advising 'booters' to book their spaces early, and Caroline had sorted out boxes of frayed tablecloths and faded pot-pourri from Grey Gables. Guy had suggested that they take a stall to get rid of their own unwanted wedding presents from his East Anglian relatives, but Caroline had drawn the line at standing in a freezing field all day flogging off egg coddlers.

'We'll go for an hour,' she told him, as he searched for his scarf. 'We'll spend some money and then leave. It's salmon with sesame and pak choi for lunch, then we're going to do the crossword together. How does that sound?'

'Perfect,' Guy had agreed with a smile.

'And,' said Caroline firmly. 'We're not answering the door. Or the phone for that matter.'

By the time they got there, it was gone eleven and, Joe Grundy told them delightedly, people had been queuing in the lane since half past seven.

'All the best stuff's gone,' he warned them. 'Though if you want a nice drop o'cider, come up to the house after and I'll do you a good price.'

'Morning!' Shula approached them across the uneven grass, her cheeks pink. She explained that she'd been there for hours and had a vast haul of picture books and Duplo for Daniel stowed in the Brookfield Land Rover.

'It's a pity about Simon, isn't it?' she said brightly. 'These business trips seem to keep cropping up at the moment.'

'Where's he gone this time?' enquired Guy, rather too nonchalantly.

'I don't know,' shrugged Shula. 'But it's going to take all weekend. He – Guy?'

Guy had lurched forwards, grabbing at his chest. Both Shula and Caroline tried to catch him but he fell between them to his knees, his chest heaving, his head back as he gasped for air.

'Eddie!' shrieked Shula. 'Get Richard!'

Richard Locke was there, luckily, running a stall with Usha, Mark's former business partner, with whom he now lived at Blossom Hill Cottage.

Caroline was kneeling on the muddy grass, loosening Guy's collar and murmuring his name. Eddie came tearing back with Richard, and Shula took his jacket to make a pillow for Guy's head. She patted Caroline on the shoulder in a helpless, automatic sort of way.

'It'll be all right, Caroline,' she said. 'He'll be all right.'

'You'll be all right, Guy,' Caroline repeated. 'Everything's going to be all right.'

'Ambulance is on its way.' Joe Grundy loomed up again, thankfully with a hip-flask of brandy provided by Mrs Antrobus rather than a flagon of his killer cider. Shula fumbled the top off and passed it to Caroline, who tried to wet Guy's lips. Joe shook his head gravely. In a whisper which could have been heard in Borchester, he pulled Shula to one side.

'He don't look too good, does he?'

It was a heart attack, inevitably: at Borchester General they said it was lucky Richard had been on hand. They told Caroline that the next forty-eight hours were critical: if Guy could get through those without having another attack, there would be reason for optimism. Caroline didn't leave his side, and when Monday came and there was no sign of a repeat attack, she began, just slightly, to relax.

But the doctors warned her that Guy, though by no means an old man, was at a dangerous age: he should take things very quietly and there were to be no shocks and no stress.

'And that means no Simon,' she told Shula categorically, pulling her into the corridor after Shula had been to visit. 'Shula, you've got to help me. Just keep him away!'

Shula sighed. She'd already had Simon raging at her, furious that Caroline had practically barred his way from seeing Guy in the hospital.

'She all but blamed me for causing the attack,' he'd complained. 'I wasn't even there!'

But Caroline had told Shula about the row Guy and Simon had had just a couple of days before: there was no doubt in her mind that the two events were directly connected.

Shula felt torn. She knew how worried Caroline was about Guy: she knew the depth of her love for him and how precious it was to her for coming late in both their lives. Caroline was Shula's best friend: they'd cared about each other for years. But Shula cared for Simon too: Guy was his father. Even though they'd been estranged in the past, maybe this was a chance for them to build some bridges. And if they'd had a row just before Guy's attack, surely that was even more reason for Simon to be given the chance to put things right?

But Guy's attack had happened at a bad time for Simon: negotiations on a big contract for his irrigation business were at a crucial stage and he was having to spend a lot of time in Leamington. The woman he was dealing with, he'd told Shula, was called Harriet Williams, and she certainly seemed to be on the phone a lot.

'Is there anything I can do to keep her off your back?' Shula asked. 'If you talk me through it, I'm sure I could –'

'That's very sweet of you, Shula.' Simon looked up from some spreadsheets he was checking. 'But it won't be necessary. I think it's better if I deal with Harriet Williams myself.'

Caroline's birthday fell on 3 April. She was forty-one. Shula gave her some bath oils in blue apothecary bottles from a new herbal beauty place in Borchester: as Easter was the following weekend, Caroline retaliated with a present of her own: a chocolate dinosaur for Daniel.

'And don't you go eating all of it!' she warned Shula. 'I know you!'

'As if I would,' said Shula indignantly, eyeing up the biscuits Caroline was putting out to go with their coffee. A bit of comfort eating would have been forgivable: she'd hardly seen Simon for the past few days, and he'd just rung to tell her that next week would be complicated too.

Caroline took their coffee through so that they could have it with Guy: he was sitting in the beautifully panelled morning room, which Caroline had filled with daffodils.

'How are you?' asked Shula. 'Everyone's asking about you.'

Caroline had been strict on the 'no visitors' rule to make the fact that Simon wasn't allowed to visit less obvious a slight.

'I'm fed up of being a decrepit old nuisance,' grumbled Guy. 'As soon as I get the all-clear from the doctors, I'm taking Caroline off on a hang-gliding holiday.'

'Well, you'll be going on your own,' retorted Caroline. 'I want to live, even if you don't.'

'I do,' said Guy simply. 'Very much, now I've got you.'

But just a week later, when Shula was putting Daniel to bed, the phone rang at Glebe Cottage. It was Caroline, so distressed that she could hardly speak.

'Oh, Shula,' she said brokenly. 'It's Guy.'

'What is it?' asked Shula. 'They haven't taken him back into hospital?'

She could hear Caroline gulping for control at the other end of the phone.

'It's not that,' she sobbed. 'Oh, Shula. He's dead.'

And that, for Shula, though she couldn't know it at the time, was when everything began to fall apart.

Guy had persuaded Caroline that she didn't need to be with him twenty-four hours a day and had convinced her to go back to work. She'd been reluctant but he'd assured her that he would be all right: after all, she was only a phone call away. On the day that he died, it seemed, he'd phoned her, just for a chat, but during the conversation, he'd become short of breath and collapsed. This time, although Richard had got there almost as quickly as before, the attack had been more serious. There had been nothing anyone could do.

Caroline was beside herself with grief but Simon reacted in the only way he knew: by taking control. On hearing that Caroline had contacted the undertaker and had arranged a cremation, he informed her curtly that there was a family plot in Suffolk: it had always been the intention that Guy should be buried there, beside his first wife. Numb, Caroline concurred, and a miserable party of villagers duly made their way over there for the funeral.

All Guy's relatives and friends were polite to her, but Shula could see how isolated Caroline felt. The vicar's address was about Guy the public man: his years of work for the Parish Council and the Country Landowners Association, his work as a JP. There was nothing, as Caroline told Shula later, about the funny, kind, sensitive man she'd known and loved.

'It's no good,' she said. 'They've taken him away from me. It's as if his time in Ambridge and his time with me didn't exist. It's as if he was just there on holiday. And now they've taken him back home.'

'We've got to do something,' Shula told Janet Fisher, when she went to bell-ringing practice the following week. 'Caroline's not a believer but that service was so wrong for her. And so untrue of what she knew of Guy.'

'She's not alone,' observed Janet. She hadn't been universally welcomed when she'd been appointed as vicar of Ambridge: Bert had been dubious, and Peggy had taken to worshipping in Borchester. But those who'd stuck with St Stephen's had found Janet to be an excellent minister, combining a wry detachment with a highly practical strain of Christianity. As Shula gave her an enquiring look, she went on: 'Lots of people have said they feel rather cheated that they haven't had a chance to pay their respects. I was wondering about a memorial service.'

Shula thought it was a brilliant idea, and volunteered to broach it with Caroline. She knew how many painful memories the loss of Guy must have exhumed for her. When Mark had been killed, Caroline had railed against a God who allowed such random tragedies to happen, and it had been a huge factor in the breakdown of her relationship with Robin. Now she was having to face another seemingly indiscriminate loss.

She found Caroline walking by the lake at Grey Gables. Jack Woolley had urged Shula to go down there and find her: he was worried about her, he said, and when she saw her, Shula was worried too. Caroline was pale and thin: she couldn't afford to lose the weight that had dropped off her since Guy's death and she was rigid with a tension borne of suppressed sorrow and fury. They sat on a bench in the shifting sunshine and Shula explained about the memorial service.

'Oh, do what you like,' Caroline said. 'I'll come, I suppose, but please don't expect me to get involved in organizing it.'

'Oh, Caroline, thank you! I hope it'll help you, I really do.'

Caroline turned and looked at Shula coldly.

'The thing that would help me most – not that you'll see it because you always take his side – is if Simon would admit the part he played in causing his father's death. I don't know how he can live with himself.'

Shula sighed. Caroline had already accused Simon to his face of killing his father, and Simon, shocked, had told Shula about it. Shula thought her friend was being unreasonable: Simon was already staggering under a huge burden of guilt. Guy, it transpired, had written Simon a letter apologizing for his deficiencies as a father, which Simon had received only after his death: in addition, Guy had left him the Estate, leaving to Caroline the Dower House and his share in The Bull.

'Simon's not a monster,' Shula pleaded. Behind them, in the beech trees, she could hear a wood warbler tuning up with a run of low notes before his silvery song. A brimstone butterfly flew erratically past, testing its wings. 'You're being so unfair! He really cared about Guy. His death has come as a terrible shock. Simon's grief is just as real as yours.'

Caroline snorted.

'I don't believe that man's capable of any sincere emotions.'

'I wish you'd believe me,' begged Shula. 'You just don't know him as well as I do.'

Caroline looked at Shula in a way that seemed to marry pity and scorn.

'Know him?' she sneered. 'You don't know him at all.'

'What do you mean? Of course I do.'

There was a long pause. Caroline wrapped her arms across her chest and looked around her, but Shula knew she wasn't taking in any of the budding beauty of the woods, or if she was, she was hating it for the new life it represented when the only life she cared about had come to an end. Shula had felt just the same after Mark died: and she'd been carrying a new life of her own.

'Shula,' said Caroline finally, her tone less harsh. 'There's no way I can say this without hurting you. But I've got to say it.'

'What?'

'Harriet Williams,' said Caroline. 'Simon's so-called business contact.'

'What about her?' Shula was perplexed.

'It's not a business relationship. They've been having an affair.'

Shula felt as if her windpipe had been severed. There was a thud in her chest as her heart stopped, then started again.

'No,' she mouthed.

'I'm sorry,' said Caroline flatly, 'but it's true.'

·16·

The Truth Always Hurts

Shula felt sick. She'd felt sick since Caroline had first spoken those words in the spring sunshine at Arkwright Lake, and now, hours later, when she was safe at home, she still felt the same.

Daniel had been at nursery in Borchester all day and he was tired. When she'd fed and bathed him and admired for the hundredth time the crayoned scribble that he insisted was a tractor, they were both as glad as each other when she could lay him in his cot. Exhausted, she read him one story, then another, then closed the book firmly. She twirled his mobile for him, the little felt clowns with their heads made of ping-pong balls. They dipped and bobbed, and Daniel, watching them, began to drift off. Shula tiptoed towards the door.

'Mummy staaay!' cried Daniel and, defeated, Shula crept back. She sat on the floor by the cot and held his hand through the bars. What did it matter? It wasn't as if there was anyone waiting for her downstairs.

'Mummy's here,' she reassured him. 'I won't leave you.'

When she promised Daniel something like that she meant it. All her life Shula had been brought up to be a truthful person and it had always been repaid in kind. She'd never been on the receiving end of deception or deliberate hurt, and she couldn't believe that she had been now.

Right, she thought to herself, shifting her weight from one side to the other as she tried to get comfy on Daniel's corded carpet. Let's take things one at a time.

Caroline had told her straight out that Simon had been unfaithful. When Shula had protested, she'd detailed a whole catalogue of deceptions that Simon had perpetrated, going right back to the beginning of the year and culminating in a conversation with this Harriet woman, which Caroline had overheard. Harriet was, apparently, an old girlfriend whose marriage was on the rocks.

'Think about it!' Caroline had cried, as Shula had shaken her head in disbelief. 'All the phone calls. The business meetings – the weekend trips. He's been meeting her behind your back!'

'How can you know?' Shula had demanded wildly. 'You've got no proof.'

'I saw them together at the station,' replied Caroline, exasperated. 'He told me he wasn't even there. He lied to me, Shula. He lied to Guy as well, to everybody. But Guy knew what was going on. He tried to stop it. Look at me!' Shula had turned away to hide her humiliated tears. 'Simon's been deceiving you! It's been going on for months!'

Shula hadn't wanted to look at Caroline, and not just because of what she was telling her. There was something in Caroline's manner, almost a satisfaction in having been proved right, that Shula didn't like and didn't recognize in her friend. It was the way in which Caroline was telling her, as much as what she was telling her, that repelled Shula, and which made what she was saying about Simon even harder to believe. If, indeed, she could believe it at all.

Shula knew only too well what grief could do to you, and how it could distort your perception of reality. What if that was what had happened to Caroline? She hated Simon, and she wanted everyone else to hate him too. Maybe, thought Shula, she was hurting so badly that she wanted to hurt someone else, to see if it made her pain more bearable, or to see, perhaps, if it might make it go away altogether.

It was the longest weekend of Shula's life, and when she realized it was a bank holiday and she wouldn't see Simon at the office to confront him about it till Tuesday, she thought she'd explode with frustration. But on Monday morning, just as she was buttoning

Daniel into his little cardigan with the pigs round the bottom that her mother had knitted him, Simon arrived at Glebe.

It was, as always, a shock to see him out of his suit and tie. He was wearing jeans and a polo shirt. He looked relaxed and he'd caught the sun: he'd been climbing in Derbyshire, he told her, the day before.

'That was nice for you,' said Shula sourly, thinking of the day she'd had making Daniel a den out of cardboard boxes and doing the washing. She'd wished she could take her brain out and wash it too, to get rid of the muddiness and muddle.

'It was,' he agreed. If, of course, he had been climbing . . .

Daniel had got his farm animals out and was pressing a cow into Simon's hand.

'Cow say moo!' he announced.

'That's right!' said Simon, detecting Shula's reserve. He spotted Daniel's crayons on a chair, ready to take to Brookfield, where Shula was due for lunch. 'Tell you what, Daniel, why don't you draw me a nice picture of the cows in your grandad's field?'

Shula watched as Simon helped Daniel assemble the paper and crayons he needed, and how he brought him a cushion so that he could kneel up to the table. He didn't seem like someone who despised her so much that he thought he could deceive her with another woman. She'd always thought she was a good judge of character. Surely she couldn't have been so wrong?

With Daniel settled, she led Simon into the kitchen and made them both a cup of coffee. She let him chat on about his climbing trip: if he hadn't been there, he'd certainly done his research. She laced her fingers round her mug and looked out at the garden. The blue tits were back: they'd taken the nest box on another long let. Only the other day, she'd heard the babies cheeping. Simon had fallen silent and she could feel him watching her.

'I saw Caroline on Friday,' she said, turning casually from the window. 'She told me you're having an affair with Harriet Williams.'

'What?' Shula had never actually seen the colour drain from someone's face before: Simon went white. He put his coffee mug down. 'Oh, God, Shula, I'm sorry. I hoped you'd be spared this.'

What was he saying? Was it true?

'Look,' he asked pleadingly, pushing his hands through his hair. 'Can I explain?'

'I don't know,' replied Shula. 'Can you?'

The way Simon told it equated with at least some of what Caroline had outlined: the old girlfriend bit and the marriage in trouble bit. But Simon claimed that the persistent phone calls were as far as it went. He'd provided a listening ear, that was all. He admitted, though, that Guy had challenged him about it and that he'd been terse with him in reply.

'It all comes back to that, doesn't it?' he asked rhetorically. 'If we'd talked to each other more, he might have trusted me when I said there was nothing going on.'

'But why did you lie to me?' puzzled Shula. 'Why did you say Harriet was a client?'

Simon pulled a regretful face.

'I'm sorry; that was stupid. But I just didn't see the need for you to get involved. I didn't think it would go on this long. She's just – she's more needy than you are, Shula. She's not as strong.'

He went to take her hand but she wouldn't let him. He flinched back, looking hurt.

'You're upset, I can understand that. But if you want the truth – well, the truth is that Caroline, for all sorts of perfectly understandable reasons, has got this totally out of proportion. She's already accused me of patricide, so infidelity is a relatively minor crime, don't you think?'

She didn't know what to think, and she'd told him so. All day at Brookfield she was quiet, not really taking in what her mother was telling her about plans for the village's Midsummer Festival and Eddie's attempts to sell Jack a personalized number plate for his Bentley.

Her father made them take a walk round the farm. It was his annual ritual with Jill, and this year he'd decided Shula and Daniel should come too, but she couldn't take any pleasure in the blackthorn blossom or the blue-green corn. Churning inside, she just wanted to see Simon again to tell him what she thought.

When they finally – finally – got back to the farmhouse, she asked her mum if she could hang on to Daniel for a bit. She didn't explain where she was going: from the thin answers she'd already given to her mother's questions about Simon, she assumed they'd work it out. She knew her parents were anxious about her but she couldn't reassure them: not till she'd sorted things out with him once and for all.

He was on the phone when she got to the Estate office – she could see him through the window – but he looked up when he heard the car and brought his call to an end. He came to the door to meet her.

'I wasn't expecting to see you again today,' he admitted. 'If ever.'

Shula hadn't been sure herself. There'd been times over the past few days when she'd thought her resignation on his desk would be the only way out.

'I've decided,' she began.

He looked wary and she smiled despite herself.

'It's OK,' she said. 'I believe you, Simon. I know why Caroline's like she is, but you're right. She's got a massive complex about you and it's – well, it's clouding her judgement.'

Simon let out a huge breath of relief.

'Oh, Shula,' he said. 'I'm so glad. I thought . . . this morning . . .'

'I know,' said Shula. 'I'm sorry.'

He reached out for her and she moved into his arms. She let him hold her tight and as she felt the solidity of him, the final traces of doubt seemed to melt away. He bent his head and kissed her.

'She's wrong about you, Simon,' Shula whispered as she snuggled back against him. 'That much I do know.'

Shula hated being at odds with anyone: more than anything she wanted to make her peace with Caroline. She'd been hurt by what Caroline had said and by what seemed the wilfully destructive way she'd said it, but she had to allow for the fact that Caroline simply wasn't herself. Although she was the wronged party, Shula was stronger than Caroline at present: she should be the one to conciliate.

Her chance came two days later, at Guy's memorial service. Caroline had been dignified and gracious with everyone who'd come to pay their respects, and had told Janet she was grateful to her for organizing it, but afterwards, at The Bull, where refreshments had been laid on, Shula found her in floods of tears in the Ladies'.

She took her back to Glebe Cottage and insisted she stay the night. Then, after supper, when they were finishing off a bottle of wine, Shula knew that she'd have to broach the subject of Simon.

She wanted Caroline to know that she was still seeing him, and why. And although she didn't want to say that Caroline had been lying, she must make her see that she'd given Shula a version of events distorted by her own perception of him and her bitterness over the loss she'd suffered.

'Look,' she began. 'When you told me last week about Simon, you know how upset you were . . .'

'Oh, Shula,' said Caroline wearily. Her tears had wrung her out. 'I'd love to be able to tell you it's all in my mind because in spite of it all, I know how Simon makes you feel. But the fact is —'

'Think about it logically,' Shula interrupted. 'It's a question of a few phone calls.'

'More than a few,' corrected Caroline. 'And it's not just that. I saw them at the station together. I've seen a photograph of her, Shula. It was taken a few years ago but she still looks the same. Still the same red hair.'

Something flickered inside Shula. A horrible darting feeling that seemed to squeeze her heart.

'Red hair?' she echoed.

'That's right. Shula . . . ?'

Suddenly it all made sense. Nightmarish sense, but sense.

'I've been so blind,' she whispered. 'Caroline, if that's Harriet, she was there. At the service this afternoon.'

Caroline wouldn't have noticed, she'd been concentrating too much on not breaking down. But Shula had seen the woman arrive. She had the most fabulous red hair that curled on her shoulders, almost in ringlets, and the fine porcelain skin that went with the colouring. She'd slipped into the back of the church after the service had started and Shula had actually pointed her out to Simon. She had to hand it to him – he'd seemed unperturbed. He'd whispered that she was a distant cousin whom he'd half expected: she'd been unable to come to the funeral in Suffolk and he'd mentioned this as an alternative. Shula hadn't thought any more of it, but now . . .

She'd seen her leave. That is, as she'd been walking over to The Bull with her parents, she'd seen Simon with her at the car. And now it came back to her, a frozen moment. Simon had kissed her goodbye and the woman had put her hand on Simon's arm: not an overly personal display but one that now hit Shula with its full proprietorial force. Harriet didn't need to be any more overt: it was the casual understatedness of the gesture that underlined the intimacy of their relationship.

The next day at the Estate office she told Simon that they were finished for good. She didn't want any more excuses: she wasn't going to be fooled by him a second time.

'It's Caroline! She's turned you against me!' he scowled.

'I'm not listening to you any more,' she said coldly. 'I have an appointment. We'll obviously have to go on working together, but I'd appreciate it if you didn't call me at home for the time being.'

'Shula!' He grabbed her arm but she shook him off. 'What about us?'

'There isn't an "us" any more, Simon,' she snapped. 'There hasn't been an "us" for quite some time as far as you've been concerned, so I don't know why you're suddenly so surprised.'

She left him then: she didn't see why she should justify herself to him any more. But all day long, as she showed prospective purchasers around and chased up mortgage applications, she could see him standing there in the office and the look of outrage on his face. She'd trusted Simon with her feelings. She'd introduced him to Daniel and had let them get close. She'd allowed herself to feel close to him as well. It wasn't something she'd be doing with anyone else in a hurry.

But Simon wasn't the sort of man to let anyone else have the last word. Shula had just got Daniel into bed when the doorbell rang. When she opened the front door, Simon promptly put his foot in the gap.

'We can either have this conversation on the doorstep,' he began, 'or you can let me in. But as half the village seems to be out taking the evening air, you might prefer the latter course.'

Resignedly, Shula let him in: she knew from his business dealings how determined he could be. But she wouldn't let him further than the hall.

'Well?' she demanded.

He'd changed tack now. Now he was claiming that it was all over between him and Harriet – that he'd finished with her and she'd only come to the memorial service to try to change his mind.

'Is that the best you can do?' asked Shula, incredulous.

'You don't understand,' he begged her. 'This thing with Harriet was out of my control.'

'Hang on,' said Shula. 'If it was out of your control, whose was it in? Mine? You betrayed me with another woman, for goodness' sake!'

'You're twisting what I say,' he objected sulkily. Suddenly Shula saw the petulant side of him, which was all Caroline knew. 'And anyway, I don't see it as a betrayal. It's not even as if you and I were sleeping together. Maybe if we had been, I wouldn't have gone and slept with Harriet.'

Shula gasped with indignation. One of the things she'd most liked about Simon was that he hadn't forced himself on her. He'd kissed her fondly, sometimes forcefully, and he'd held her close, but he'd seemed to respect her need for things to proceed slowly. He'd never complained. How dare he try to fling this thing with Harriet back at her as if it were her fault?

She moved towards the door. She'd thought that at the very least he'd come to apologize. Instead, he seemed to think his behaviour was justified.

'I think it's time you left,' she told him coldly.

She reached past him to open the door but he grabbed her hand and forced it back.

'I haven't finished,' he snapped, holding her wrist. 'Why won't you listen?'

'Please!' repeated Shula. 'Just go!'

She didn't like the proximity. She didn't like the way he was gripping her wrist. In this small space he seemed taller than she'd remembered and she felt uneasy.

She tried to pull away but he grasped her harder. Then, as she struggled, he abruptly let go and, to her horror, she saw his arm go back and his hand come swinging towards her. It all happened in seconds. She ducked but he still caught her a flailing blow on the cheek, which made her cry out.

'I'm sorry,' said Simon at once. The sound of the slap still rang in the small hallway. Shula didn't think she'd ever forget it. 'Please, I didn't mean . . .'

'Just go.' Shula felt sick with shock. 'Go!'

She didn't know what she'd do if he resisted. He was taller and stronger than she was: he could do anything to her and there was no one she could call to for help. But it seemed as though his action had shocked Simon too.

'I'm so sorry,' he whispered. 'Let me . . .'

'No!' She pressed herself back against the wall, not wanting him anywhere near her. She was shaking all over.

'Shula . . .' He opened the door, but turned on the step.

'Get out,' she told him, managing to sound more in control than she was. 'Now.'

·17·

Déjà Vu

'A conditional discharge? And £200 compensation? Simon Pemberton can spend that on an evening out.'

Shula pulled Debbie with her along the corridor of Borchester Magistrates Court. An usher was calling for a Mrs Harrison: a solicitor's clerk with an armful of folders dodged past them.

'Come on,' she urged her. 'Let's get out of this place.'

With a last look over her shoulder in case Simon was following them, Debbie complied. Together they went out into the bold sunshine of early June and along to the new coffee shop that had opened on Bell Street.

'I can't believe it,' Debbie said as she sifted chocolate over her cappuccino. 'They didn't even bring your evidence into consideration. That must really hurt.'

Shula unwrapped the little ratafia biscuit that had come with her coffee. She wasn't sure how she felt. Part of her wanted to let the whole world know what Simon Pemberton was really like, while another part of her just wanted to keep everything quiet. It had taken her long enough to go to the police, after all – and then the CPS had obviously decided that as Simon's violence to her had been over a year ago, and there was no medical evidence to present, it was not worth bringing into the equation. Shula hadn't wanted justice for herself: she'd only reported it to strengthen Debbie's case against him.

Simon had apologized to Shula after that dreadful night in the hallway of the cottage. He'd insisted that it had been a momentary loss of self-control, and, wanting only to put it – and him – behind

229

her, Shula had let him think she believed him. She still had to work alongside him at the Estate office, after all – all she wanted was to re-establish their relationship as a formal, business-like arrangement.

But she'd worried from the moment she'd found out that he'd begun to see Debbie. She'd wanted to say something, to warn her off, but the moment had never arisen. And then, after only a couple of months, he'd hit Debbie too.

Sipping her coffee, safe with Shula, it seemed incredible to Debbie that it had happened at all. Any of the other customers in the coffee shop would have assumed that they were two perfectly nice young women – friends, cousins, whatever – who'd bumped into each other and had popped in for a chat. They might have imagined that they'd be talking about holidays, mutual friends, plans for the weekend.

Certainly, no one would have believed that what had brought them both there was a violent ex-boyfriend who'd just walked away from court with a self-satisfied smile after his solicitor had put in some self-serving mitigation about the stress of running the Estate after his father's death and his voluntary registration on a course to modify aggressive behaviour. Talk about getting off scot-free!

Debbie's relationship with Simon had been totally different from Shula's. For a start, she'd never had Shula's mission to make him more tractable or to help him to fit into the village. When they'd started seeing each other, back in March, she hadn't even been sure that she liked him very much. But when they were alone together, there was an electricity between them you could have channelled through a socket, and when the physical side was so fantastic, perhaps it didn't matter if he wasn't the easiest person in the world to talk to.

But, over the weeks, as she'd got to know him, Debbie had found that they did have some things in common. Since Guy's death, Simon's learning curve about farming had been practically vertical, and Debbie was impressed by the knowledge he'd amassed. She'd thought Brian was a sharp operator when it came to subsidies and set-aside opportunities, but Simon had crop plans that included things even Brian had never thought of – flax, for instance.

But he was never going to be popular in the village. He was trying to get the Grundys out of Grange Farm, claiming that a serious fire there had been caused by their own negligence. David, who was still contract-farming for Simon, had bravely refused to testify against the Grundys at the ensuing tribunal, and Simon responded by terminating his contract. Shula testified for them, and he threatened her with everything, only to find that she'd already resigned from Rodway's and was going to spend her time helping her Auntie Chris at the stables.

When the tribunal found in the Grundys' favour, Simon was incandescent, and when Debbie tried to calm him down, he accused her of being as sentimental and soft-hearted as the rest of the village.

The thing about Simon, Debbie had fast discovered, was that he was incredibly wearing. He proceeded on the supposition that if you weren't for him, you were against him, and Debbie, who would have walked a mile in the other direction rather than get into a row, found it just too tiring. She'd tried to tell Simon this one evening at Home Farm and he turned on her savagely.

'It's this place,' he ranted. 'Can't you see what it does to people? What it did to my father? You're going to get stuck in the same pathetic rut as the rest of them. People with small minds who think Lakey Hill's the end of the universe. You're worth more than that.'

Debbie increasingly disliked the way Simon was behaving. He'd offered Brian the opportunity to contract-farm the Estate in Brookfield's place but she wasn't sure she was keen even to work for Simon, let alone be involved with him any more. Not wanting to start an argument, she'd asked him to leave, but he'd suddenly erupted, shouting at her and demanding that she listen to him. When she answered him back, he slapped her hard in the face. And when Debbie, reeling, had slapped him too, a sheer reflex action, he'd really laid into her, pummelling her with his fists.

Again, as with Shula, the loss of control had been momentary, and almost before Debbie had time to realize what was happening, he'd stood up, straightening his tie, apologizing profusely and blaming the stress of the tribunal.

Brian and Jennifer were out and Debbie knew they wouldn't be back till late. When Simon had gone, she dragged herself upstairs to the bathroom. There, through an eye that was rapidly closing up, she dared to look at her battered face. A livid bruise was already spreading over her right cheek. Shaking, she ran the tap and bathed away the blood that had poured from her split lip and which was daubed all down her shirt. All she could think of was that no one must ever know.

The next day, she tried to tell her mum and dad that she'd come off her horse, but the more she lied, the more she kept reliving the terrifying reality of what had happened, and before long, she'd had to confess everything. Brian, beside himself, pursued Simon to Leamington, but Simon calmly announced that he was leaving the country. Brian wouldn't be able to touch him and, anyway, it was his word against Debbie's.

Still hurting, still shocked, and deeply humiliated by it all, Debbie hadn't known what to do. It was Shula, hearing what had happened, who'd eventually persuaded her to go to the police, and Simon had come back to England for the court case. In the meantime, though, he'd obviously decided he'd had enough of Ambridge and had put the Estate up for sale.

Since Squire Lawson-Hope had been forced through debts to sell off the Estate in 1954, it had had only five owners, but it had changed hands three times in the last seven years and, counting the hand-over from Guy to Simon, twice in the last four. Add to that the fact that Cameron Fraser had gone bankrupt and Guy had died so prematurely and it was no wonder that the talk in the tap room of The Cat and Fiddle, after several pints of scrumpy had been consumed, began to turn to the notion of the Estate being jinxed.

'That's ridiculous!' Phil exclaimed when Jill heard this as gossip in the shop. 'For goodness' sake, Charles Grenville had a car accident and Lilian's Ralph had a heart attack – are people saying those were the Estate's fault too?'

'Ralph did have to retire through ill health; that's why he and Lilian moved to Guernsey,' Jill pointed out, stowing away several pounds of sugar. She'd made her strawberry and raspberry jam already, but the blackcurrants would be ripe soon, and the gooseberries.

'It's just nonsense!' Phil scrabbled his *Farmer's Weekly* from its polythene wrapping and headed for the office. 'I'm going to look at some figures if anyone wants me.'

Jill put away the rest of the shopping thoughtfully. Of course it was absurd to say that the Estate was cursed, but she couldn't help being uneasy – as uneasy as Phil was – about Ruth and David's eagerness to put in an offer for the in-hand land, namely the land that the Estate ran for itself and that Brookfield had been farming on contract. David's logic was that the machinery they'd bought to fulfil the contract was now costing them money: they could either sell it at a loss or they could expand to spread their overheads over a bigger acreage.

It wasn't the first expansion idea Ruth and David had come up with lately, Jill reflected, as she went out into the garden to pick some beans for lunch. At the beginning of the year, Ruth had mooted some ideas to expand the herd by twenty cows, buy a mixer wagon and move to complete diet feeding. Phil had stalled her, but Jill had the feeling that Ruth wouldn't let it drop, even though the baby she was expecting in September would surely slow her down. What with the slump in the milk price and cereal prices not looking good either, Jill seriously doubted the wisdom of any sort of expansion. But where Phil muttered about 'good money after bad', Ruth and David talked about having to speculate to accumulate. Dropping beans tinnily into the colander, though, Jill felt sure that any involvement with the Estate land wasn't the way forward for them. You didn't have to be superstitious, she thought, to remember that Elizabeth had nearly come to grief over Cameron, and Shula over Simon Pemberton. Maybe the less that Brookfield had to do with the new owner of the Estate, the better.

It was early July, and at Brookfield it was the storm before the storm. Every year it was the same on the farms throughout Ambridge. It was one endless rush to get everything ready for harvest: the tractor tyres checked and the combine greased, the grain store swept out and enough sacking ordered for the laterals in the drier should harvest turn out to be wet.

'You and Bert take the top field,' Phil told Ruth one morning. They were taking a swift second cut of silage before the barley was fit. 'I'll sort out the rest with David when he gets back from Hollowtree.'

'Right you are,' grinned Ruth. She could still squeeze behind the wheel of a tractor – just. 'I should warn you he's not in the best of tempers.'

'Oh, dear,' sighed Phil. 'Is this about Brian?'

'Can you blame him?' The baby was kicking and Ruth put her hand to her stomach. 'I'm pretty mad about it myself. Aren't you?'

After all the speculation about the Estate's future owner, there was some virtue, of course, in the devil you know, but it was true that Phil hadn't been very pleased to find out that Brian was the buyer of the in-hand land. First, because David had had a go at his father for procrastinating over the decision and thus making Brookfield miss the boat, and second, because Brian had been so devious about it. They'd only found out at all because David, suspicious of something Brian had said, had wheedled it out of Susan Carter at the Estate office. But then, as Jill had pointed out, there was a precedent for Brian's behaviour.

'What about when Dad died and we had to sell off some land?' she'd reminded Phil when, stinging from David's attack, he'd come and found her in the orchard. She was feeding the hens. 'He bought those fifty-five acres at Willow Farm on the quiet, then claimed he was trying to be tactful. I bet he does the same now.'

And sure enough, Brian did. He came to see Phil that same morning on his way to a meeting, all smiles and Savile Row tweeds.

According to Brian, he couldn't say very much until the deal was finalized, but he wasn't acting alone in buying the in-hand land. He was in a consortium for which he would provide the farming expertise: he was bound by the confidentiality of the boardroom.

'It just doesn't feel very friendly, that's all,' Phil had pointed out mildly as they stood in the yard drinking the coffee Jill had provided.

'I know.' Brian sounded contrite. 'And I'm sorry about that. I'd hate this to jeopardize any future working relationship we might have.'

'Working relationship?' repeated Phil.

'It's possible we've bitten off more than we can chew in buying this land,' confessed Brian. 'I'm pointing out a business opportunity, Phil. I shall be looking for help in farming it.'

He was cunning, Phil reflected when Brian had roared off in his spanking new Mercedes. He'd pipped them at the post to buy the land, and now he wanted Brookfield to do all the work. He wasn't even offering them the chance to contract-farm it in the same way they'd been doing for Pemberton. All he was talking about was offering them odd bits of work at busy times.

It wasn't the outcome that David had wanted, and Phil could imagine his likely reaction: it was exactly how he'd have reacted thirty years ago. But now he saw things differently. It would at least deal with the problem of the surplus tackle and keep down their unit production costs by spreading the depreciation over a bigger area. With the state of farming as it was, Phil thought as he collected Brian's coffee mug from the wall, they might not have any choice. David would just have to swallow his pride.

Brian couldn't help smiling to himself as he pointed the car in the direction of Felpersham for a meeting with his co-directors at Borchester Land. Phil was a nice enough chap but he simply couldn't cut it in business in this day and age. David had the right idea, but he didn't have the wherewithal to proceed without Phil's backing, and since by temperament Phil was a plodder, David wouldn't get anywhere.

Brian, on the other hand, had acted swiftly the moment he'd heard the Estate was up for sale. He'd promptly bought for Home Farm the eighty acres of grassland that he already rented from the Estate, but that wasn't enough for him. The price of land was astonishingly low at present, and he knew that the in-hand Estate land was too good an opportunity to miss.

Farming was bumping along the bottom, had been for years, but there was a new Labour government in power now. Brian hadn't voted them in, of course, but the rest of the country seemed convinced that things could, indeed, only get better. In which case optimism would return, the pound would strengthen, land prices would rise and the Estate would turn out to be a spectacularly good investment for all concerned, especially with the capital gains tax-break on land for farming use. He didn't have that sort of money himself, of course, not with all the capital he'd got tied up in Home Farm. That was why Brian had offered his services to a consortium of City businessmen. That was why they'd had to get in quick, in case this Labour lot changed the rules.

Pulling out on to the dual carriageway and accelerating past the envious – or possibly murderous – glances of two yokels in a pick-up truck, Brian further reflected that it was not finished yet. There was still the issue of the let land, the tenanted farms occupied by Pat and Tony, the Grundys, and others. Simon Pemberton had, in his wisdom, decided to sell those off separately from the in-hand land, and the tenants had all been given the option to buy. It was out of the question for the Grundys, but Pat and Tony, Brian knew, had given it serious thought.

Unusually, it had been Pat who'd been unwilling to take on the burden of a mortgage: they were in the process of expanding the dairy again and she felt that they were stretched enough. Tony had, typically, caved in.

Although Brian had remained aloof from the agonizings at Bridge Farm, which had permeated the entire family, he wondered if perhaps he should have tipped Tony the wink. Still, there was no sentiment in business – not the way Brian conducted it, anyway. The directors of the consortium, Borchester Land, were meeting today to draft the wording of the announcement. By the end of the month, Tony would know that his brother-in-law was part of the consortium that was to buy both the in-hand and the tenanted land:

Brian would be his new landlord. Till then, the news had to remain a secret.

With all this backstage activity going on, thought Brian as he drove, he could have done without the Wildlife Open Day he was having to host at Home Farm a few days later – not that it wasn't a good bit of PR, picking up an award from Borchester Mills as the most conservation-conscious farmer in the district.

But anyway, he reasoned to himself, Debbie was now his official deputy. With her beetle banks and her unsprayed headlands, she'd persuaded him to enter in the first place, so it was only fair that she should run around organizing the display boards and finalizing the route of the farm walk. With any luck, Brian concluded, his sole involvement on the day would be standing up and making a speech.

In all his calculations, though, Brian had reckoned without one thing: his troublesome daughter, Kate. She'd returned, finally, unscathed and unrepentant, from her time on the road with the New Age travellers, but if anyone believed that she'd got her teenage rebellion out of her system, they'd have been wrong.

Brian sometimes thought that his elder daughter had been visited on him as a punishment for crimes he'd committed in a previous life – for, of course, he felt he led a blameless existence in this one. But even if he'd been Jack the Ripper or Attila the Hun, he didn't feel he'd have deserved a scourge like Kate.

Kate's view of the situation was, inevitably, rather different. Ambridge was everything she abhorred. When she'd come back from six months on the road, taking part in road-widening protests and living in hippy camps, Jennifer had tried to suck her straight back into the village and had urged her to enrol at college. Kate had done so, in the end, but thanks not to her mother but to Roy Tucker, Mike and Betty's son, whom she'd started going out with. Roy had had problems of his own at the time: he'd got mixed up with a racist gang who'd targeted Usha Gupta but, though she herself was at the opposite end of the political spectrum, Kate had stood by him. Then he'd stood by her when they'd split up briefly last New Year and she'd stupidly mixed whisky with some pills that one of her friends had given her.

Now they were back together, even taking the parts of two of the lovers in Lynda Snell's latest production – *A Midsummer Night's Dream*. Kate's cousin John and his girlfriend Hayley were playing the other pair. Kate liked Hayley, a Birmingham girl who said what she thought. She was just right for John: she didn't let him get away with anything, and she was even prepared to put up with his pigs. Pat and Tony liked Hayley, too. Partly, Kate knew, it was because she wasn't Sharon, but they also weren't such snobs as her own parents. While her mother acknowledged that it was only thanks to Roy that Kate hadn't taken off again, in her heart of hearts Kate knew she thought he was 'not our class' and not good enough for her daughter. Whereas Brian, thought Kate bitterly, had such a low opinion of her that he probably thought Roy was too good.

Now, on the Open Day, a muggy Friday in early July, she stood at the back of the crowd and listened to her father's self-satisfied acceptance speech. He was going on about how important it was for farmers to put something back into the countryside – after all, they were only its custodians. Kate shook her head. How many times had she heard that from people like him who were only too happy to take grants to rip out hedges one year and subsidies to put them back the next? The urge to heckle was almost too strong to resist, but, though Brian would have laughed at the idea, Kate had matured. She'd tackle him later; despite her father believing that Kate's head was full of rebirthing rituals and eco-causes, she had a brain she was prepared to use.

As soon as Debbie had told her on the quiet that Brian and a consortium had bought the in-hand land, and then she'd heard that another business consortium had bought the tenanted land, her mind had been ticking. Her experience in fighting developers had taught her something about the way business operated. Two consortiums at the same time interested in land in Ambridge? It would never happen. It simply didn't add up.

She watched as the crowd applauded and then began to disperse for tea. Her father stood there beaming, still clutching his award from Borchester Mills. (There was another hypocrisy: Borchester Mills, whose feed was stuffed with antibiotics and additives, giving a conservation award.) Kate strolled over, smiling.

'I don't know how you have the nerve,' she began. 'You stand there,' she continued, 'and present yourself as a friend of the country-side and a pillar of the community and all the while you're selling everybody out under their noses.'

'What are you talking about?' Brian broke off to shake a local worthy by the hand and receive another slap on the back.

'You've bought the in-hand land,' Kate went on when the little display was over, 'with some consortium. Debbie told me, so don't bother trying to deny it.'

'She shouldn't have.' Brian didn't want details leaking out when there was a planned statement being prepared for release in a couple of weeks' time. 'It's confidential. No one knows – well, only Phil, I had to tell him because of Brookfield's interest in the in-hand land.'

'And you had to tell Debbie because Ruth told her, assuming she'd know. And Debs wasn't very pleased, was she, at being kept in the dark?'

'Debbie understands that there are some decisions about which I can't consult her. She understands the need for it to be confidential.'

'Not as confidential,' smirked Kate triumphantly – she could see he was rattled now – 'as you being one of the consortium that's plan-ning to buy the *tenanted* land. That is, there's only one consortium and they're buying the lot. Go on,' she goaded him, 'try me. See if you can tell me a lie to my face.'

It was wonderful to see him squirm throughout the rest of the afternoon, terrified that she was going to blow his cover in front of the family and the local press. But Kate held back. She'd made her point and it would be more advantageous to her to use her silence as a weapon against her father in some subtle way later, when she wanted something, perhaps. She didn't need to capitalize on it now.

If Brian had thought that the afternoon of the Open Day was awkward, the following weekend was worse. With Phil and David still sore about the in-hand land, and Tony fretting about the mystery consortium, Brian thought he'd better lie low at the farm, but with neither Kate nor Debbie speaking to him, the barbecue that Jennifer had organized by the pool for Sunday lunch was a rather sticky affair. The result was that he now had his wife on his back, demanding to know what he'd done to the girls. Although he tried to claim that he'd had a falling out with Debbie over something to do with harvest, and that he and Kate had never needed an excuse to row, Jennifer wasn't convinced.

'It's more than that,' she argued on Monday morning. 'But how can I understand when no one will tell me what's going on? I don't like being made to feel a stranger in my own home.'

Brian tried to fob her off, but she kept going on and on, and eventually he had to promise to meet her in Borchester for lunch and put her in the picture.

It was just unfortunate that the negotiations on the tenanted land hit a stumbling block, and a meeting with Borchester Land, which should have occupied the morning, now looked set to last all day and to continue over dinner with their lawyers in Birmingham.

'I'm sorry, darling, but we've simply got to get our business finished.' He'd slipped out to meet her in the bar of The Feathers, where his meeting was taking place in one of the conference rooms.

'Do you think I'm completely stupid?' Jennifer demanded. She'd had her hair done for the occasion, Brian noted. He didn't comment. Women always thought that this was because men didn't notice, but that wasn't the reason. Brian just didn't want to stick his head above the parapet till he was sure that Jennifer herself was pleased with the result.

'Of course not,' he said wearily.

'Everyone else does,' retorted Jennifer. 'But it's difficult to appear intelligent when you're continually kept in the dark.'

'You're not kept in the dark.' She *would* pick this moment to go into melodrama overdrive. He grabbed a handful of peanuts from a bowl on the bar. They'd been ordering sandwiches for a working lunch when he'd left: at this rate there'd only be parsley and tomato roses left by the time he got back.

'Oh, yes I am. I don't know why you and David had words about the Estate but it makes me look a fool when I'm talking to him, my daughters won't tell me why they're rowing with you –'

'They don't want to bother you.' Brian signalled to the barman. He could do with a drink.

'Or –' Jennifer's expression changed, 'they're trying to keep something from me. And I've just realized what it is.'

'Have you?' Brian fancied a double Scotch but ordered a double orange juice. He'd need a clear head this afternoon.

'Everyone's right,' said Jennifer, wonderingly. 'I am a fool. It's obvious. You're having an affair.'

That was rich! Brian covered his mouth to hide a smile. The one time in his life when he wasn't, and Jennifer was accusing him of two-timing her. There was nothing for it. He'd have to tell her now. But he'd have to make sure that she didn't go blabbing to Jill, to her mother and particularly to Tony, until all the details were sorted out and the contract signed.

'Of course!' she went on, convincing herself by the second. 'You're seeing her tonight!'

'I'm seeing the consortium tonight,' Brian explained. 'As I have been all day. We're taking over the Estate. All of it. And I'm one of them.'

'What?' Jennifer gaped.

'There you are,' said Brian. 'Now you know. Satisfied?'

He stayed long enough to drink his orange juice, then got up to leave. Jennifer was still wittering about how she'd ever face Tony, who'd assume she'd known all along.

'Don't worry about it, old girl,' said Brian smoothly. 'Look, as you're here, why don't you trot along to Underwoods and see what they've got in the sale?'

'Well . . .' Jennifer had already been in that morning and had been trying to justify the purchase of a beautiful silk jersey dress cut on the bias, which even at its reduced price was a ridiculous indulgence.

'Why not treat yourself?' suggested Brian. 'Since your horrid husband's been giving you such a hard time.'

'Oh, Brian.' Jennifer put a beseeching hand on his arm. 'I just wish you'd confide in me, that's all.'

'I'm sorry darling. It's all been happening rather fast. And as I'm not the only one involved, it makes it rather more complicated.'

'I understand.' Jennifer slipped off her bar stool and smoothed out her skirt. 'Perhaps I will go and have a peep in Underwoods.'

'Good idea,' affirmed Brian, standing up too and pecking her on the cheek. 'Look, I haven't a clue what time I'll be back. Don't wait up.'

'Bye, darling. Don't work too hard.'

'I won't. And Jenny – all this stuff about me having an affair. Be realistic, darling. When would I have the time?'

'I know. I'm sorry, Brian. That was silly of me.'

Jennifer kissed him back and Brian watched her go, marvelling at how contented she was with so little. Opening his wallet to pay for the drinks, he pulled out the business card he'd been given that morning by the girl who was doing the PR for the consortium. Tara Haig. Based in Felpersham. Attractive woman. Perhaps he'd give her a call next week and ask her out to lunch. They'd be talking business, naturally.

·18·

Out of Control

Stripped to the waist under the August sun, John Archer bent to move the plastic irrigation pipes on a field of cabbages. He was working at Bridge Farm full time now, raising his own organic pigs in his so-called 'spare' time – which was severely limited since he'd agreed to play Demetrius in Lynda Snell's *Midsummer Night's Dream* at Lower Loxley.

John wasn't sure how he'd been talked into it, really. He supposed he'd thought it would be a laugh: all his mates were in it. His girlfriend Hayley was cast as Hermia, Demetrius's girlfriend, though in the end Demetrius got off with this other bird, Helena, who'd fancied him all along. Hermia ended up with a bloke called Lysander, who was played by John's mate and Kate's real-life boyfriend, Roy. In fact, Kate was the biggest problem: she was playing the part of Helena and she'd gone and decamped to some festival, seriously messing up rehearsals. Lynda was threatening to recast, and John was with her on that one: anything to stop Lynda herself standing in as Helena, especially in the snogging scenes. He heaved the pipes over to a particularly thin patch of soil just as Hayley's unmissable tones floated over to him.

'Ooh, look at the state of you!'

'What?'

John straightened as she picked her way between the cabbage plants in her platform sandals.

'It's the sight of you,' she breathed, 'with the sweat glistening on your deltoids . . .'

'Oh, yeah?' Now she had his attention.

'I just want to wrestle you to the ground, rip off the rest of your clothes . . .'

John grinned.

'Well, what are you waiting for?'

Hayley sighed. She reached out and traced a finger along his collarbone.

'I promised Helen I wouldn't be long.'

Pat and Tony were in Florida, and John's sister Helen, on holiday from Reaseheath where she was studying dairy management, was minding the dairy and the shop. She'd also agreed to keep an eye on Becky, the little girl Hayley looked after in her job as a nanny – but only for ten minutes.

'I bumped into Roy this morning,' Hayley explained. 'Kate's back. Well, she's not actually back yet. But she said she'd definitely be here at the weekend. She really doesn't want to be chucked out of the play.'

John snorted. Kate had been the keenest of them all for Lynda's amateur dramatics, but she had a funny way of showing it, disappearing off like that. John didn't know how Roy stood her.

'I wouldn't put up with it if you went swanning off for weeks on end,' he told Hayley. 'I'd come after you. Drag you back home by your hair.'

'Would you really?' Interested, Hayley put her head on one side and looked up at him from under her eyelashes.

'Either that,' declared John. 'Or I'd go down The Cat and Fiddle and – what's the name of that new girl they've got there?'

'You wouldn't!' Hayley thumped him on the arm.

'No, don't hit me!' John raised his other arm to defend himself.

'You scumbag!'

But she was laughing as he held her off, pinning her arms and pulling her against his chest.

'I don't know why I bother with you,' she said, when he'd finished kissing her. 'You don't appreciate me one little bit.'

'Oh, but I do,' he said.

Even if he didn't, everyone else did. He strongly suspected his kid brother Tommy had a sad adolescent crush on her, and his mum and dad thought Hayley was great. They were always telling him how good she was to put up with him and help him with his pigs. Even his gran liked her. John had been nervous about telling her that he and Hayley were going to live together in April Cottage, which had become vacant when Martha Woodford had died, but she'd been fine about it. She'd even persuaded Jack, who owned the cottage, to give them some cash to redecorate.

'I do appreciate you,' he repeated. He kissed her again to prove it.

'Mmm,' said Hayley languorously. 'You're all sweaty. Come here.'

It would have been good to have been wrestled to the ground among the cabbages, but Hayley said she'd had about nine of her ten minutes already, so he arranged to meet her at The Bull later, which was convenient because she'd be there till half seven anyway, babysitting Jamie Perks, Sid and Kathy's two-year-old.

After that, the afternoon zoomed by, what with hoeing the carrots and checking on the barley, which they'd be harvesting next week. John had to rush to get the cows in for milking and by the time that was finished and he'd taken them back out to the field, it was half past six. He still had his pigs to see to. He wondered if Hayley would object if he didn't change: she hadn't seemed to mind his being all sweaty earlier. Like the guy in the Levi's advert, she'd said. Or the one on his Diet Coke break.

As he crossed the yard from the parlour, he thought he could see someone moving about in the shop. He yelled for Helen. He didn't want to get involved with serving some old biddy and carrying her shopping to her car.

'It's all right.' A young woman emerged from the doorway. 'I'm not a customer. Hello, John.'

John stopped dead.

'Sharon!' he exclaimed. 'What are you doing here?'

'Come to see you,' she smiled. 'What do you think?'

She hadn't changed, though she said he had. 'Filled out,' she called it, which, embarrassed even though he had his shirt back on, he said wasn't surprising when you were heaving sacks of pig nuts about the place. She still had the same red hair that she sort of shook about a lot, always fiddling with it and twisting it round her fingers. John could still remember how it had used to feel against his chest, soft and ticklish. She still had the same Borsetshire accent, untouched by her time in Leeds, and the way she said his name, lengthening the vowel sound to 'Jahrn' made his stomach flip right over. He knew it was crazy. He was meeting Hayley – Hayley, his girlfriend, remember – in less than an hour. But he still felt he had to do it.

'Look, um . . .' He shrugged and smiled. 'Do you fancy coming in for a cup of tea?'

Sharon smiled back, that wide curving smile of hers. She had the most fantastic mouth. She reached out and touched his collarbone – just like Hayley had done.

'Thought you'd never ask.'

She told him she was back for good: she was staying with her mate Donna in Penny Hassett. Donna had a little girl the same age as Kylie, who, incredibly, was nearly eight. Sharon told him she'd need a job, but that she was finished with Leeds – things hadn't worked out there, she said vaguely. She didn't go into any detail, just looked into her cup as she swished the dregs around.

'That was a rotten trick I pulled, wasn't it?' she asked abruptly. 'Walking out on you like that.'

John shrugged. That was putting it mildly.

'Leaving you all alone in that little house of mine,' continued Sharon.

'I camped out there for weeks,' he confessed. 'Hoping you'd come back.'

'I know, me mum said.' Sharon sighed. 'I didn't expect you to be still here. I thought you'd have moved on. Got a place of your own. Either that or got married.'

Now was the time to mention April Cottage – and Hayley.

'Married? Me?' he bluffed.

'You're not married?' she persisted.

'No.' He shook his head so hard his hair flopped into his eyes. 'No, of course not.'

That was all it took. One cup of tea in the kitchen at Bridge Farm and all the feelings he'd ever had for her came rushing right back, perhaps because they'd never gone away.

There was nothing wrong with his relationship with Hayley. In fact, there was an awful lot that was right with it, but once Sharon was back on the scene, Hayley didn't get a look-in. It was easier for John to tell himself that Hayley was getting on his nerves than to look a bit deeper and admit that he was finding fault with her because he was stressed, tired and guilty all at the same time.

It was no wonder. He was constantly getting calls from Sharon on his mobile, pressing him to meet her. She'd ring him constantly at home, and he'd have to pretend to Hayley it was a customer. Then Roy spotted him with Sharon in Felpersham and started to play the big brother and warn John off. On top of it all, there was this poxy play that opened in the first week of September, and which he needed like a hole in the wellie.

'You haven't forgotten I'm coming?' Sharon asked him seductively when she rang on the opening night. 'Am I going to be able to see you?'

'It's all pretty hectic,' prevaricated John. He wasn't sure if it was a good idea. The whole of Ambridge would be there. Someone was bound to see them together.

'What about the interval?' Sharon was saying. 'There must be somewhere we could meet.'

'I'm thinking,' replied John. He was thinking about Sharon's arms round him, her hands untucking his shirt and how she tasted when he kissed her. He was thinking about an old potting shed in the walled garden, close to where Sean, the landlord of The Cat, had constructed the stage under Lynda's hawk-eyed supervision. He was thinking how much he wanted even a few minutes alone with her.

'Can't say I understand it all,' she remarked of the play when, in the interval, they'd creaked open the door of the shed and were sitting on some sacks, their arms twined round each other.

'I'm not sure I do,' admitted John.

Lynda had kept droning on at rehearsals about something called motivation. Supposedly he (or rather, Demetrius) had genuinely thought he'd loved Hayley (or rather, Hermia) but then, thanks to Puck, his eyes had been opened to Helena, who was the one who loved him truly and with whom he belonged. John felt dimly that there might be a message there for him in his present dilemma, if only he had the time to sit down and work it out.

'Anyway.' Sharon leaned closer and whispered in his ear. 'You look dead sexy in that outfit.'

'Sharon –' he began, but she leaned forward and pressed her mouth against his in a long, long kiss.

'How was that?' she queried when they broke apart. As if she needed to.

'Nice,' said John weakly. His head was spinning. He felt like a diver who'd come up too suddenly.

'It's made me go all tingly,' sighed Sharon wistfully. 'It brought it all back to me.'

John listened to the thud of his heart. He ran his hand up and down her bare arm. A line from the play kept running through his head. 'Lord! What fools these mortals be!'

'Perhaps I'd better be going,' he said. This was madness.

'What, now?' There was a long pause. He didn't move. 'You don't want to go, do you?'

John shook his head.

'No,' he whispered.

There was nothing he could do. He was due on stage in a minute but there was no point him trying to get up. He was simply incapable of walking away.

It was crazy, but it was exciting. His mum had always said that Sharon was dangerous but John had never believed her. Now he could see the truth of it, but he didn't care. For God's sake, he was only twenty-one and they'd practically got him married off – living in April Cottage with Hayley, with his Uncle Tom, who lived next door, dropping in for cocoa every night and bringing them vegetables. If

John wasn't careful, he'd be turning into Uncle Tom himself, wearing tartan slippers and wittering on about the old days.

Sharon might well want to take the blame for walking out on him, and it had crucified him at the time, but really he owed her a lot. She'd been the one who'd got him out of Bridge Farm, for a start, when he moved into her house. She'd made him grow up. She'd been not just his first girlfriend, but his first love.

The days were growing shorter, the shadows lengthening on the grass. Soon the field where he kept his pigs would be ankle deep in mud: he'd be going round breaking the ice on the drinkers and patching the arks that the wind had overturned. So surely, in the meantime, he deserved a bit of fun?

Somehow they managed it. Occasionally, they could meet up at Donna's in the day, when the kids were at school and Donna was out. Sometimes they met at The Cat, or The Griffin's Head in Penny Hassett. His mum and dad realized Sharon was back when she managed to wangle herself a job in the village shop, but nothing was said. This time round it wasn't his parents who were on his back, but Roy. He'd been in the shop one day when Hayley had come in, and he'd had to introduce her to Sharon.

'There's nothing in it, all right?' John insisted angrily when Roy challenged him about it. It was a brilliant day at the beginning of October. St Martin's little summer, this late sun was called, according to Uncle Tom, and John was feeding his pigs.

'I think you should tell her to sling her hook,' muttered Roy mutinously. 'I don't want to see anybody get hurt.'

John ripped open a paper sack of pig nuts impatiently. What the hell business was it of Roy's?

'Nobody's going to.'

Roy folded his arms across his Felpersham University sweatshirt. He was studying Accounts and Finance and John reckoned he was on the right course. He was turning into a proper geek.

'You really think you can handle it, do you?' Roy persisted.

'I know I can.' John heaved up the sack and tipped pig nuts into a trough with a clatter. 'If Sharon comes on to me, I'll just say no.'

It was all very well maintaining that he was in control, but he wasn't in control a month later when he'd again arranged to meet Sharon on the sly. Hayley was supposed to be babysitting somewhere, and Sharon had decided that a nice quiet night in at April Cottage was just the thing for a dark, wet, November evening. Why sit in the pub, she'd smiled, when what they both really wanted was a bit of privacy? Snuggled up on the sofa with a couple of cans, it wasn't long before they'd abandoned all pretence at conversation. He'd already let her peel off his T-shirt and was unbuttoning her top when he heard the front door open.

'Hi, honey! I'm home!'

'Hayley!' hissed John, leaping off Sharon as if he'd been stung. 'Quick!'

'Oh, John,' wailed Sharon, disappointed. Her hair was tousled and her bra was peeking out. John threw her her jumper.

'The babysitting was cancelled,' trilled Hayley. He could hear her taking her boots off in the hall. 'I wish I'd known, I nearly got soaked –'

John sank down and put his head in his hands as Hayley pushed open the door. He knew that the look on her face as she saw Sharon still sprawled on the sofa – she'd made no effort to get up – would stay with him for ever.

'Hello, Hayley,' said Sharon coolly.

'John?' There was no life, only disbelief, in Hayley's usually strident voice. 'John . . . what the hell's going on?'

He'd brought it all on himself and he deserved everything he got: the dismay of his parents and the lectures from Roy. None of it was as hard to put up with as the bollocking he had to give himself for being such a complete prat. Hayley had gone upstairs and packed her things that same night, then she'd called a taxi and gone back to her mum's in Birmingham. John had gone to see her there the next day, to try and explain.

Explain what? Hayley had quite reasonably asked him. Explain how he was sleeping with Sharon behind her back?

'It only happened a few times,' he pleaded pathetically. 'And that was the first time I'd brought her home –'

'Oh, forget it,' stormed Hayley. 'I don't want to hear your pathetic excuses. I just don't care any more.'

'I care,' implored John, as she started to close the door. She'd kept him standing on the step. 'I still love you. I don't want you to go.'

There was a pause and Hayley looked at him scornfully.

'Love?' she demanded. 'How dare you say that to me? You don't even know what it means. You think it's an excuse to get off with anyone you fancy!'

'I didn't want this to happen!' How could he make her see? 'I didn't want to hurt you!'

'Well,' she retorted, 'that was the last time you'll get the chance. I've got nothing more to say to you. I don't ever want to speak to you again. Go away and leave me alone!'

She'd slammed the door in his face then, and he'd stood looking at the paint, remembering that she'd told him her brother had chosen the colour – the claret of Aston Villa's claret and blue. He walked slowly away down the path between the winter pansies, which he knew she'd bought for her mum in the garden centre on the Borchester road. He marvelled at all the detail he knew about her, the trivia that she'd chattered on about and that he'd dismissed, but which had stuck in his head, her nan's funny old Birmingham sayings and her dad's jokes. And he thought about other things too: the way she'd said he had lovely cheekbones, and looked like Keanu Reeves, the way she'd curled round him, night after night, and the way she'd called him 'lover' and meant it. And because he was walking away, he didn't hear her burst into tears on the other side of the door and run upstairs to her room.

• • •

Christmas had come and gone and it was that peculiar limbo period between Boxing Day and New Year: you'd seen all the relatives, consumed your own body weight in mince pies, and there was no point in going to the sales till you'd lost the resulting half stone.

For Hayley it had been a miserable festive season. She'd run into Pat before Christmas and they'd agreed that they'd still remain friends. Pat had told her that John was truly sorry about what had happened, but it was no consolation at all. She'd already heard that from Roy – and that Sharon had turned up at April Cottage assuming she could move in, but that John had sent her packing. That wasn't the point. It didn't matter whether he was with Sharon or not: the point was, he wasn't with her. Hayley knew she still cared about him and, according to Roy, John meant it when he said still loved her – but what was she supposed to do? Pretend Sharon had never existed?

'The trouble is,' she said to Kate when she came to see her on a dank December afternoon, 'that Sharon will just always be there in our heads. Well, in mine anyway.'

Kate nodded vaguely. Hayley wondered if she'd been listening to a word she'd said. She seemed even more spaced out than usual, though Kate insisted that she didn't even smoke dope any more.

Still, Kate hadn't had a very easy autumn either. She and Roy had split up in October after a row about this bloke, Luther, who'd been staying at Kate's cottage while he was protesting about the widening of the Borchester bypass. Kate had insisted their relationship was just platonic but Roy didn't believe her, and it was true, she did seem a bit besotted with Luther, who had a wispy beard and long dreadlocks under a little embroidered cap. So Kate and Roy had had a row and she'd said Luther was worth a dozen of Roy and she didn't want to go out with him any more and Roy hadn't been able to get her to change her mind.

It was funny, really, thought Hayley. They'd all been in that play of Lynda's as couples, but within a few weeks of the last performance, none of them were together any more.

'More tea?' asked Kate.

Hayley nodded, though she wasn't all that keen on it. Apple and ginseng, apparently.

As Kate poured, Hayley looked at her closely. She hadn't seen much of her in the run-up to Christmas: what with Becky's playgroup parties and Christmas shopping and commuting from Birmingham, there hadn't been time. Kate was looking different. A bit fuller in the face, somehow, but tired and pale.

'You know what we need, don't you?' she said, taking the pottery mug that Kate passed her. 'A blooming good night out. Why don't you come up to Birmingham, stay over at mine and we'll go clubbing?'

Kate held her hands over the steam rising from her mug. Her mirrored velvet sleeve glinted in a sudden sunbeam that arched in through the window.

'I don't know,' she said. 'I don't really feel like it.'

'Neither do I,' sighed Hayley. 'But what else can we do? I've wasted enough time crying over John.'

'I don't honestly think I'll feel like it for a while.' Kate raised her eyes. 'You see, the thing is, Hayley, well . . . I'm pregnant.'

·19·

Throwing It All Away

The first person Kate had told had been Debbie. They hadn't always been close: sometimes Debbie could be a right pain, siding with her dad about the farm, and being the perfect daughter. Although, as Morwenna, one of Kate's wisest friends, always said, that was good because it gave Kate the space to be what she wanted to be. Anyway, at the end of November, when Kate was two weeks late and had got a test kit from the chemist's which confirmed that she was pregnant, it was Debbie who'd given her a cuddle and told her that everything would be OK.

'But I don't know what to do about it,' Kate had wailed damply into her sister's shoulder.

'Well . . .' hazarded Debbie, 'surely the first thing you must do is to tell Roy?'

Kate had gulped in a sniffy sob.

'Yeah, well . . .' she said in a muffled voice. 'That's another problem. I'm not actually sure that Roy's the father.'

It wasn't that she'd been sleeping around. When she'd told Roy that her relationship with Luther was platonic, it had been true at the time. But when he hadn't believed her and they'd finished, it had seemed only natural to turn to Luther for comfort, and he had been a comfort.

Luther was sorted. He told her that relationships were just another straitjacket that people talked themselves into, like jobs and mortgages: better, surely, to take what they needed from each other, enjoy it and move on. It hadn't taken Luther long to move on: when the bypass protest was finished, he'd packed up his dayglo VW Beetle one morning and told her he was heading off again – to the protest site at the Manchester Airport runway extension. When she'd expressed her disappointment and asked him to stay, he'd held her gently by the elbows and prised her away from his chest.

'Listen,' he'd said gently. 'No strings, right? No regrets. You'll always be beautiful to me, Katie. But in my head I'm out of here.'

Debbie had listened circumspectly as Kate explained how things had worked out with Luther.

'In the circumstances,' she asked delicately, 'have you, er . . .'

'Thought of having an AIDS test? Yeah, I have.'

Debbie looked relieved.

'That's good. It means you've started to be . . .'

'Please,' begged Kate. 'Don't say positive.' She didn't feel positive about the baby. She felt nothing but frightened and confused.

'I wasn't going to say that.' Debbie stopped to examine a patch of rabbit damage: they'd come out for a walk round the arable acreage. 'Practical. You've started to be practical.'

Maybe she had, but it was another couple of weeks before she could even think about telling her mum and dad. Kate knew instinctively that she should start with her mother: Jennifer had had the same thing happen to her, for God's sake, thirty years ago. If anyone should be sympathetic, it should be her.

But to Kate's disgust, Jennifer's first reaction was for herself. All she seemed concerned about was that Kate should see a doctor – but one well away from Ambridge and – and this really amazed Kate – that she felt too young to be a grandmother. And what hurt Kate most deeply was that her mother even suggested she consider an abortion – just when, after weeks of soul-searching, she'd decided she wanted to keep the baby.

'Why can't you get it into your head?' shouted Kate. 'This baby has nothing to do with you, it has no effect on you, the decisions are not yours to make!'

That had seemed to shock her mother into submission: an echo, perhaps, of the Kate who might take off at any moment and raise her baby on the streets. Jennifer had come over all contrite. They'd had a cuddle – one that Kate badly needed – and they'd both managed to smile together at the prospect of telling Brian.

Somehow it didn't seem the right moment to talk about the question mark over the baby's father: Kate didn't explain about the baby's doubtful paternity until an incandescent Brian, assuming the obvious, had told Mike Tucker in no uncertain terms that he should be ashamed of his son. Kate braced herself for another dose of opprobrium both from her father and from the Tucker camp. She'd already had a bemused Roy on her doorstep: he'd heard Kate was pregnant from Hayley who, not unreasonably, had also presumed he was the father.

Roy had started on in that slightly preachy way he sometimes had about how she should have told him, and how he had rights, and finally Kate had flipped. She hadn't meant to because Roy was a good bloke, and she hadn't exactly treated him well, but he'd begun to do her head in.

'My baby, Kate,' he'd said brokenly. 'Didn't I have a right to know?'

'It's not,' she replied coldly.

'What?'

'It's not your baby.'

'Not mine? But –'

He stood there with his mouth hanging open.

'That's what I said,' Kate continued relentlessly. How could she ever have fancied him? Hormones did funny things to you. 'So you don't have to worry about losing your precious rights. You haven't got any. So could you just get out, please? And leave me to get on with it.'

She didn't feel nearly as brave as she sounded, but Kate had had many years to perfect the art of putting a good face on things when they were completely dreadful. Anyway, she reasoned, as she lay in bed that night, stroking her swelling stomach, what did the baby need a father for anyway? It was her body and her baby. She knew people who'd had babies born in a bender, who lived half the year on the road and the other half in a squat. Their kids had turned out OK. Whereas Kate had a warm cottage to live in and her family close at hand. If they decided to go cold on her – not that she thought her mother would dare – she could always get some part-time waitressing work at The Bull or The Cat. Kate turned on her side and squashed her pillow under her head. Luther was gone. She might never see him again. And Roy Tucker could just butt out.

• • •

'So how was it for you?'

'Valentine's Day?' John took a melancholy sip of his pint. 'I stayed in and watched the telly. What about you?'

Roy was saved from replying straight away by a thunderous crashing of coins from the fruit machine. Stuart Horrobin had struck lucky for once in his life, though his good fortune didn't look set to last long from the way a couple of Neanderthals loomed out of a dark corner of The Cat, evidently expecting a cut, or at least a couple of pints. Still, the diversion gave Roy time to consider his answer, one he wasn't looking forward to giving.

'You're going to have to know sooner or later,' he confessed. 'I spent Valentine's night with Hayley.'

John's face was a pantomime of shock and disgust.

'Oh, well, thanks, Roy. You're a real mate.'

'Not like that,' said Roy impatiently. 'We were both as miserable as sin if you want to know.'

'I'm sure you managed to cheer her up.' John's tone was icy.

'I would have if I could. I like Hayley.' Roy shook a stream of peanuts into his mouth. 'But she spent the whole evening talking about you.'

'Did she?' John sat forward.

'Yeah. And when she wasn't going on about how she was missing you, I was going on about Kate and the baby. I've thought, you know. There's DNA tests, aren't there, they could do when it's born? I could prove I'm the father.'

'Yeah, probably.' John waved away the advances of modern science. 'So what did she say?'

'Kate? I haven't told her yet.'

'Not Kate, Hayley. What did she say about me?'

'Well, she thinks you treated her really badly –'

'Tell me something I don't know,' sighed John. 'And?'

'And she still misses you. You're a lucky beggar, you know.'

As the gregarious February sun made the dust motes jiggle over the pool table, John began to feel that he might just be. Sharon had gone for good: she hadn't turned out to be a serious bunny-boiler. And if he got together with Hayley again and they had a kid – well, of course he'd expect a say in how it was brought up. He suddenly felt bad about not paying more attention to Roy's predicament.

'Kate'll see sense,' he advised him. 'Wait till it's born and she wants help with the nappies.'

Roy shook his head sadly.

'Kate's not like other girls,' he reflected. 'That's why I love her.'

John wasn't sure how anyone could love Kate, with her spiky hair and spikier attitudes: the only conclusion he could come to was that Roy must like a hard time. Whereas Hayley – well, Hayley was worth making a fool of yourself for. She was one in a million. He knew that now.

'I owe her a pancake,' he said out loud.

'Eh?'

'Hayley,' explained John. 'I said I'd take her out for pancake night last year and I never did. I was supposed to take her out to Felpersham and I forgot. Perhaps she'd let me make it up to her this year.'

'Blimey, last of the big spenders. You're trying to get back with her and that's the best you can do?'

The sun was still shining brassily on the worn wooden floor and the chalked blackboard advertising The Cat's Happy Hour.

'Of course not, you great plank. I'm going to take her somewhere really special. But if I tell her that, she'll think I'm coming on too heavy and back off. Don't you know anything about women?'

'Obviously not,' said Roy gloomily. 'Time for another?'

He took her to the Mont Blanc. It was the poshest restaurant in Borsetshire – Uncle Brian had a table booked there practically permanently. He and Auntie Jen weren't there that night, thank God, though Shula was there with Alistair Lloyd, the vet, and Caroline Pemberton was there with Graham Ryder: it was a special Mardi Gras-themed evening. Hayley's face had been a picture when they'd pulled up outside, but it was nothing to her consternation when she saw the prices on the menu.

'John, when you said a pancake –' she began.

'I wanted it to be a surprise,' he explained, taking another slug of wine. 'Never mind the cost.' He'd never felt so nervous in his life. He lifted the bottle from the ice bucket: it was already half empty and they hadn't even ordered. 'Would you like another drink?'

'I'm only halfway through this one.' She looked gorgeous in a shiny purplish dress and a black net cardi. John gulped his wine.

'Don't be so nervous,' she chided. 'There's no need.'

'I want you to have a nice time, that's all.' He wanted to make her happy – not just this evening, but for the rest of her life. It had to be with him. He'd tried life without her and it was totally awful.

'It's not the first time we've been out together, after all,' she teased.

'Do you remember the first time we went out?' He could. He'd driven all the way to Birmingham to pick her up. He'd even been on time for once.

Hayley smiled and her cheeks dimpled in the way he loved so much.

'Of course,' she grinned. She leant forward and beckoned to him to do the same. 'I think I was ready about an hour before you called for me.'

'You never told me that!'

Hayley sat back with one of her all-knowing looks.

'It never does for a girl to look desperate,' she pronounced. She took a sip of her wine. 'Oh, John,' she said. 'I'm so glad we can be friends again.'

'So am I,' he replied, heartfelt.

'Better than that,' she added. She looked at him consideringly. 'I mean, I do love you.'

'Do you?' This was better than he'd dared hope.

'Of course I do,' she said in a tone that implied he should never have doubted it. 'But . . .'

But he couldn't wait any longer. He reached into his pocket. This had to be the right time.

'Hayley, look,' he began. 'I've got something for you.'

Her shoulders tensed and he heard her drawn-in breath.

'No, John,' she murmured.

He passed the small leather box across the table, opened her clenched fingers and closed them round it.

'This is for you,' he said simply. 'Just open the box. Please.'

Hayley looked at him gravely. She looked terrified. He watched her as she snapped the box open and the diamond he'd chosen winked at him cheerfully under the lights.

'It's lovely,' she said tightly.

'Marry me, Hayley?' he implored her. 'Please?'

She raised her eyes and he knew at once he'd blown it. For all his bravado to Roy, he'd been so desperate to get her back that he'd totally misjudged things.

He could see now that she'd need time to get used to him again: time to trust herself with him. He knew what she was going to say before she said it. She sounded heartbroken but it didn't soften the blow.

'Oh, no, John. I'm sorry. No.'

As the words swirled round in his head he tried to hear in them something else, something he could hang on to. Try as he might, he couldn't. He'd blown it. Totally.

'I'd rather trust a three-year-old than you!' Next day, Tony Archer faced his son over the stripped-down engine of the Bridge Farm tractor and let rip.

'Sor-ry!'

'If you weren't a member of my family,' blustered Tony, 'I'd sack you!'

'Feel free!'

As his dad ranted on, John looked stonily past him to the sodden fields and the muddy track. Fine, let him sack him. He couldn't have cared less. He'd lost everything else he valued in the world; what did his job and his family matter?

He felt a wreck and he knew he looked one. After he'd taken Hayley home, he'd lain awake for hours, listening to a vixen calling in the woods: he'd dozed off finally at about four and then, of course, he'd overslept. He hadn't bothered shaving and he'd clambered into the same clothes he'd thrown on the bedroom floor when he'd changed to go out with Hayley the night before. He tuned back in to Tony's tirade in time to hear his father raving on for the billionth time about a strip of fence that John had been promising to mend all week.

'I'm going, OK, I'm going,' he yelled. 'Only one problem.' He pointed to the heap of engine on the ground. 'The tractor's still in little bits.'

His dad had the grace to look sheepish: he'd been promising to mend that all week as well. Pat had gone off in the Land Rover to collect the yogurt money: that left only the old grey Ferguson tractor that Tony had renovated as a labour of love. John had wrong-footed him: Tony was on the defensive.

'Take the Fergie, anything,' he snapped irritably. 'Just get the job done!'

Great, thought John. The Fergie didn't even have a cab and it was already drizzling.

'By the way,' called Tony as John stormed off to start it up. 'How did it go last night?'

'I thought you wanted me to mend your stupid fence,' retorted John, not wanting to think about it. 'Not discuss my private life.'

'John!' pleaded Tony. 'I was just trying to show some concern.'

'Then just stop shouting at me!' barked John, at the end of his tether. 'The only thing you care about is your fence. Well, OK, I'm going to do it!'

'If you don't keep your promises, I've got a perfect right to shout at you!'

'Then perhaps this'll make you shut up!' The engine spluttered into life and John threw the Fergie into gear. 'OK? You've got what you wanted!'

Then, without looking back, he bumped away down the track.

What was it about birthdays? wondered Pat that afternoon. It was Tommy's seventeenth and all she'd wanted was for the family to have a nice day. She realized, of course, that he was well beyond the stage of even appearing grateful for the CD Walkman she and Tony had bought him: she hardly expected him to want jelly and ice cream. But still, irrationally, rather like Christmas, she expected birthdays to pass in an idyllic Oxo-cube family way, and she'd hoped that the four of them – Helen was back at Reaseheath – could have sat down to supper together before John took Tommy out for a birthday drink with Roy. She'd even made a cake.

Now, at half past six, she had Tony moaning that he was starving, Tommy complaining that there was no need to have cooked, they'd be having a curry when the pubs closed, and absolutely no sign of John.

'He's coming back, is he?' asked Tony.

'I don't think he's gone,' said Pat, puzzled. 'His van was still in the yard when I got back from Borchester.'

'Then where the hell is he?' Tony finished washing his hands and fished a towel from the floor. Of course, thought Pat, if he'd put her a hook up for it, she wouldn't need to hang it over the back of the chair and it wouldn't slip off all the time. She added a drop more stock to the casserole: the meat on top was already crusted and brown.

'He's not going to let me down on my birthday!' whined Tommy, slouching up from his chair to pour himself a Coke.

'Was the Fergie in the yard when you came in?' demanded his father.

Tommy shrugged.

'I don't remember.' He heaved a sigh of adolescent angst. 'He ought to be back by now! We're supposed to be meeting Roy in half an hour.'

Tony was at the back door, putting his boots on again.

'I'm going to go and look for him.'

Pat looked across at her husband. He sounded anxious.

'Wouldn't it be easier to ring him on his mobile?'

'I tried it,' sulked Tommy. 'It's switched off. I'll come with you, Dad.'

Pat prodded the potatoes which fell helplessly apart. Damn. She'd have to mash them now.

'Well, when you find him, tell him to get a move on,' she admonished. 'Or tea's going to be ruined.'

It had been damp and drizzly all day, but it had started raining properly at the end of the afternoon, and angry clouds, blue on black, were scudding past in the sky. Tommy had been to open a gate.

'Honestly,' he grumbled as he clambered back in and the Land Rover jolted off again, 'by the time John's had a shower and got changed, he's going to be seriously cutting into my party time.'

'Let's just find him, shall we?' worried Tony. 'He should have got it done by now.'

The row he'd had with John was weighing heavily on him. The fence wasn't in that bad a state: it couldn't have taken all day. He should have checked after lunch to see how things were going.

'You know the state he's been in,' replied Tommy. 'Probably took all the wrong stuff up with him.'

'Right.' Tony hadn't thought of that. That could have accounted for some of the delay.

'Mind you,' continued Tommy. 'You'd think he'd have been back for tea. He must have known the fuss Mum'd make about my cake –'

'Tommy, will you just shut up a minute!'

In the headlights, through the sheeting rain, Tony had seen something: a shape at the side of the field, in the ditch. Tommy leant forward and peered through the windscreen.

'It's the tractor!'

Tony jerked the Land Rover to a halt, managing to yank at the handbrake and scrabble at the door at the same time. He told Tommy to stay where he was, but as he stumbled towards the side-slanted

Fergie, he could hear his younger son panting behind him. Tony knew he was calling something: it was only when it came back to him on the wind that he realized it was John's name. When he was still twenty feet away, he could see what he'd dreaded: the tractor was on its side with John underneath it.

'Don't come any closer!' he shouted to Tommy. 'Go straight back to the house. Ring for an ambulance.'

'Is he hurt?'

Hurt? If they were lucky, he was hurt.

'Go and ring for an ambulance – now!'

For once Tommy didn't argue. He turned and ran. Tony could hear the wet swishing of grass under his wellingtons.

'And tell your mother to stay at home,' yelled Tony after him. 'Whatever you do, don't let her come up here. You can tell her there's been an accident but when the ambulance gets here everything's going to be fine. Do you hear me?'

Thinly, on the wind, he heard Tommy's assent.

Only then, on legs like lead, did Tony move forward, crouching low by the bulk of the tractor.

'Oh, John,' he whispered. 'John . . . ! My boy . . . ! What have you done?' In the cold and wet, in the mud and the brambles, he crept nearer and touched John's face. 'You're cold. You're so cold,' he said helplessly. And then, though he knew it could make no difference, he ripped off his own jacket and tucked it round his son. 'I'll stay and talk to you till someone comes,' he faltered, feeling tears mix with the cold rain on his cheeks. His voice cracked. 'Talk to you – what do I say?' A cry snagged in his throat. 'Oh, John! John!'

·20·

In Sickness and In Stealth

Shula leant her elbows on the fence and smiled. Every year since she was tiny she'd loved to watch this moment: the time when the cows were first let out after their winter confinement. Heifers and ten-year milkers alike, they trotted into the field, some of them almost breaking into a run: then, as David closed the gate behind them, elation got the better of them and they scattered into excited groups, scampering to the furthest corners of the pasture, revelling in the feel of the turf beneath their hooves.

'They're like puppies, aren't they?' called David as he moved off to see to the tanker driver. 'Didn't Daniel want to watch?'

'He's in the house with Mum,' Shula called back.

Daniel had a nasty sore throat and a runny nose, and was miserable with it: when she'd asked him to choose between a video versus the delights of the great outdoors, it had been no contest. He hadn't been well for weeks: it had been one thing after another. It was so difficult when he couldn't tell her where it hurt. Sometimes he complained that his arms and legs ached, but that was probably just another flu symptom. Richard said it was only to be expected now that he was mixing more with other children: gradually he'd build up his immunity, and by the time he went to school, he wouldn't be so susceptible. But still Shula worried. She couldn't help it.

She often thought about Pat when she was worrying about Daniel. Pat must have been through all this with John: the childhood ailments and the scraped knees: the bedtime stories and the tantrums and the clutching, dimpled hands in the fiercest of hugs. Had Pat been through all that, the hours of worry and the unprompted smiles, only to lose John in the mud and the rain, and on their own farm?

Shula didn't know how Pat was coping. Another death in the family had brought back Mark's death to Shula: it had happened at much the same time of year, and John had died on Tommy's birthday, just as Mark had died on Pip's. Shula remembered how pointless everything had seemed, even with the baby she'd been carrying: she'd lost a husband, but Pat had lost her child.

It was just as dreadful for Tony, of course, and for Tommy and Helen. Tony had sat with John, out in the field, in the dark and the cold, until the ambulance had come: he blamed himself for shouting at his son about neglecting his farm work, and for not mending the tractor so that John had had to drive the less reliable, and cableless, Fergie. Tony had loved that Fergie: he'd spent a whole summer restoring it, but after John's death he'd given it away to the Owners' Club. It wasn't the sort of reminder he and Pat wanted to have around.

John's pigs were a different matter. Fired by Hayley's determination to keep John's business going, Tommy was hoping to keep them on, so he was dropping out of his A-levels and taking a day-release course at Borchester Agricultural College. But even though the practical considerations were being sorted out, it would be months – years, even – before Pat and Tony could really grapple with the import of what had happened, before they could assimilate it into their lives in a way that made it make some sense. And, given the circumstances – a point-less accident, or an avoidable accident? – the Health and Safety people were still investigating – there was always the possibility that that day would never come.

The cows had calmed down a little now and were savouring their first mouthfuls of the juicy spring grass. Shula walked slowly back towards the house. The twin flower and leaf buds of the blackthorn were poised to open and the wild daffodils were breaking out in yellow frills. Spring was definitely here.

What a winter it had been. Nelson had left the country, apparently to live in Spain, abandoning the wine bar at its busiest time. By a stroke of good luck, though, Kenton had been home from Australia, where he'd finally settled, for one of his infrequent visits. He'd taken over the wine bar for the festive season, sporting a white tuxedo and even opening on Christmas Day. He and Shula had held an early joint fortieth birthday party there on New Year's Eve. Alistair Lloyd, the vet, had said he couldn't wait till midnight and had kissed Shula right in the middle of the party: Shula had felt guilty because Caroline fancied him like mad.

But when she'd confessed what had happened, Caroline had wished her luck and told her to go for it: after all, she'd smiled, they couldn't both be merry widows all their lives. Now Shula was going out with Alistair and Caroline was seeing Graham Ryder, who seemed to be a changed person, even taking riding lessons to give himself and Caroline something in common.

Shula was happy with Alistair. He was thoughtful and intelligent and he made her laugh. He had warm brown eyes and he tried really hard with Daniel. After Simon Pemberton, it was good to be with someone she knew she could trust and who, she sensed, would never hurt her: he'd been hurt himself, by his ex-wife's infidelity with his best friend, and already she knew he was serious about their relationship. There was something in her, though, a niggling doubt that she pushed down ever deeper, that told her there was, maybe, something missing – the extra spark that came from liking someone more than they liked you. Alistair had that devoted look; and though she found it flattering and in a way seductive, Shula knew it made him less of a challenge.

She'd reached the yard and wiped her boots on the scraper outside the back door. She must be mad, she reflected. She was a single mother, with all the responsibility that that entailed. Although she'd given up her job at Rodway's, she was working with her Auntie Chris at the stables on almost a full-time basis. She had a house and a garden to run, and relationships with her friends and family to maintain. And she wanted a man who was a challenge? Honestly, she smiled to herself as she lifted the latch to let herself into the kitchen and caught the first whiff of her mother's early batch of Easter biscuits, honestly, Shula Hebden, you must need your head testing. You ought to be grateful!

She eased off her boots by the door as Jill made the coffee. She and her mother had a lot to discuss. Ruth and David's little boy, Josh, had been born the preceding September and they were planning to hold his christening to coincide with Phil's seventieth birthday at the end of the month. Then there was the church rota for Easter, and the new cows that were still arriving as part of the herd expansion scheme that Ruth had finally managed to push through.

Although the price of milk had hit the floor, and farming, everyone agreed, was going through its worst slump since the 1930s, she and David were convinced that expansion was the only way forward. Phil hadn't been so sure, but he'd finally bowed to pressure. As he'd said to Jill, before too long Brookfield would be Ruth and David's to run: maybe it was time he let them do things their way.

Which, thought Shula, as she padded across to the table in her socks, brought her round full circle again to Pat and Tony. The assumption had always been that John would one day take over Bridge Farm, just as Shula had assumed she'd live happily ever after with Mark. It just showed, she reflected, as she sat down and took the mug her mother was holding out to her, that you couldn't make assumptions in life.

She suddenly remembered something that Richard Locke had said to her, rather irreverently, when she'd been so upset and he'd been so kind and had spent such a lot of time with her after Mark had died.

'How d'you make God laugh?' he'd asked her, and when she'd shrugged in reply, had answered: 'Tell him your plans.'

As Shula took her first sip of coffee, there was a grizzle from the sitting room.

'Mummy!' whined Daniel. 'I'm too hot!'

Jill tutted.

'He's not right, is he?' she said.

He wasn't right, and over the next ten days he didn't get any better. Richard gave Daniel penicillin for his throat, but beyond that, he said, there wasn't much he could do. It was that time of year: there was a lot of it about. Shula was to keep him warm, give him plenty of fluids, and the infection would run its course.

But on Good Friday Shula had to call Richard out again. Daniel was hot and whingy. He'd got what looked like the beginnings of a rash and his temperature was nearly forty. Shula had thought he'd had meningitis once before, when he was a baby, and she'd thought that had been bad enough: this time Daniel seemed even more unwell. Alistair was there when Richard came. He examined Daniel thoroughly while they watched.

'What is it?' Shula asked, agonized, as he felt Daniel's neck.

Richard turned to her, looking grave.

'I'm sorry, Shula,' he said in his abrupt Mancunian accent. 'I really don't know. He seems to have deteriorated a lot in a short time.' There was a pause and Alistair put his arm round Shula. It felt heavy and unnecessary and she wanted to shake it off. Daniel gave a pathetic little whimper. Richard stroked his chin reflectively. 'I think,' he concluded, 'I'd like to get him to hospital.'

'It's the best place for him,' Alistair reassured Shula as they sat in the back seat of Richard's car, Shula holding Daniel, on the way to Borchester General. 'At least when we get there, they can find out once and for all what it is.'

Shula smiled thinly. She knew he was trying to be comforting, but she didn't have the energy for conversation: she hardly had the energy to hold Daniel any more. It was almost a relief when they got to Casualty and Richard took him from her arms.

'It's all right,' he said. 'I'll take him.'

There might have been some comfort in Alistair's reassurances if they'd turned out to be true, but the worst of it was that the hospital didn't seem to be able to find out what was wrong with Daniel. They swiftly eliminated meningitis, but that still left the problem of the alternatives. First they talked ominously about 'a virus'; then they gave him an ESR test, which could show up some kind of blood disorder. Shula's mind immediately leapt to leukaemia.

'They need to do more tests,' Richard told her when the ESR

result came back slightly raised but inconclusive. Shula was staying at the hospital and Richard was popping in every day to check on Daniel and, he said, to keep an eye on her.

'Not knowing,' she whispered. 'It's awful, Richard.'

'I know.' He squeezed her arm just above the elbow. 'But they will get to the bottom of it.'

'Sorry to interrupt,' Alistair peeped round the door of the day-room. 'You said to let you know if Daniel woke up?'

Alistair was popping in every day, too. Shula had left him sitting with Daniel while she came out to talk to Richard.

'I must go back to him.' She moved towards the door. 'Thank you ever so much for dropping in, Richard.'

'I'll come again. Hang in there, eh, Shula?'

'I'll try.'

Alistair threw himself down in one of the squeaky plastic armchairs and let out a sigh.

'Exhausting, isn't it?' said Richard sympathetically.

Alistair nodded. 'And there's so little I can do.'

He and Richard were good mates. They played cricket together and, as village professionals, they shared a lot of the same principles and problems. Neither of them, they often joked, could go into the pub, for a start, without someone coming up to them with a question about bunions or blowfly.

'You've just got to be there for her,' advised Richard. 'That's all you can do.'

In the end, it was over two weeks before they had a diagnosis: for all her plans, Shula couldn't attend the Easter services at St Stephen's. She wasn't able to shop for her father's birthday present and she had to miss Josh's christening and the joint party. That was the day when the hospital finally concluded that Daniel had systemic junior rheumatoid arthritis. It sounded frightening, and the prognosis could be, but it seemed that Daniel had it in a mild form. It would flare up now and then, but it was treatable with drugs and it shouldn't interfere with his normal development. For Shula, the relief was palpable.

'Now we know what it is, at least they can start treating it!' she exclaimed to Richard when he told her that the diagnosis confirmed what he'd begun to suspect.

She'd given Alistair the day off: he'd spent so many hours sitting with her in the stuffy hospital atmosphere that she thought he deserved a break. Richard had brought apple blossom from the Brookfield orchard to put on Daniel's locker: as Josh's godfather, he'd come straight from the christening party.

Shula couldn't help smiling as he'd walked into the ward, stopping for a chat with another little lad from Loxley Barrett who'd come off his bike, flirting with the nurses and pinching their chocolates. He even persuaded the incredibly grumpy auxiliary to make him a cup of tea.

'I don't know how you get away with it!' she challenged him.

'Don't you?' he grinned. 'You're not affected, then, by my natural charm and magnetism?'

But when she finally took Daniel back to Glebe Cottage, Shula found that Richard did have the same powerful effect. Alistair had been trying for days to persuade her to go out: Jill would happily have had Daniel. It was Richard who understood that she still didn't want to leave him. It was Richard who managed to persuade Daniel to take his medicine by bringing him a special Teletubbies mug. It was Richard, too, who saw how drained she was, told her how brave she'd been, and told her she needed to look after herself. He also told her she needed to stop worrying quite so much about Daniel, but even as he said it, he held up his hands in submission.

'OK, I know, stupid thing to say. But you've got to loosen up a bit, Shula. You won't do him any favours if you become an over-protective mother. And you won't do yourself any favours either.'

'Thank you, doctor,' smiled Shula sarcastically. 'I'll bear it in mind.'

So she thought, not twice, but three times, about taking Daniel to see Richard when, in early June, he seemed off colour again. As far she could tell, there was no stiffness or soreness in his joints, but his temperature was up and he was waking in the night, crying. She went down at the end of morning surgery, hoping for an appointment that afternoon, but when she got there, she remembered it was Richard's half day. Just as she was dithering about whether to take Daniel home again, Richard came out of his room with a pile of notes and caught sight of them. He told her to come straight through, even though he said he'd got a busy afternoon: he was marking out the cricket pitch with Alistair.

Now Shula felt even more guilty: not only was she holding Richard up, but mention of Alistair reminded her of the row they'd had yesterday about her tendency to fuss over Daniel: just, in fact, what Richard had warned her against. Still, Richard didn't seem to think she was fussing. He examined Daniel's eyes, throat and then his ears, and those, apparently, were the cause of the trouble. Daniel had an ear infection, quite separate from his arthritis and nothing, really, to worry about. Richard said he could prescribe some antibiotics that would clear it up in no time.

'How's the patient?' he asked cheerily when he called round unannounced at Glebe Cottage that evening.

'Asleep,' said Shula with relief. She'd just got Daniel to bed and had been about to phone Alistair to apologize for yesterday. Still, it could probably wait. 'He's so much better already,' she added, leading Richard through into the kitchen.

'Happier now, are you?' he grinned, leaning against the stove while she fetched a bottle of wine from the fridge.

'Much!' replied Shula. 'Now all I need is to sit down and relax.'

'Me too.' Richard's reply sounded heartfelt.

It turned out that his restful afternoon at the cricket pitch hadn't been quite so restful after all. After waiting over an hour for Alistair, and searching the whole village for him, he'd ended up breaking a window to get into the shed, and doing the whole job himself. When Alistair had finally returned the message Richard had left on his mobile, it was to say that Bert Fry had changed the rota.

'They'd arranged to do it tomorrow instead!' Richard gulped his wine indignantly. 'But nobody thinks to inform me! And then, to top it all,' he continued, 'Jack Woolley rings to say I'll be charged for the pane of glass I broke in the shed window!' He looked at Shula, offended. 'You're trying not to laugh, aren't you?'

'No, of course not.' Shula controlled herself with difficulty. 'I think it's shameful.'

Richard shot her a look. 'I suppose I'll find it funny myself,' he admitted, 'in about five years' time.' He put his glass down on the table. It was then that she noticed the cut on his hand.

'I suppose you did that on the shed window,' she admonished. 'Shouldn't you put a plaster on it?'

'Eh?' Richard turned his hand to look at the cut. 'No, it's fine. I cleaned it up.'

'You doctors!' laughed Shula. 'Come here. Let me have a look.'

Richard eased forward on the settee. He obediently held his hand out to Shula and she took it.

'Ouch,' he winced as she twisted it round to get a closer look. 'Maybe I should have put a plaster on it.' He grimaced. 'Some doctor, eh?'

Shula could have given him his hand back, but she continued to hold it lightly in both of hers. Then she placed it gently back on his knee and edged forward in her chair.

'I think you're a wonderful doctor,' she said.

Richard gave an embarrassed laugh.

'And thank you,' she added. 'For everything.'

'Shula . . .' he began 'I . . .'

But there was nothing that needed to be said. He moved his head and kissed her.

It couldn't be, of course. Shula had Alistair, who, as David never stopped telling her, was a really great bloke, and Richard had Usha, who, to make things worse, was working really hard for her Higher Court Advocacy exams.

'That was really stupid,' Richard said as soon as their lips had parted. 'I shouldn't have done it.'

'It's all right,' Shula replied gently, thinking to herself that it had been much more than all right.

But Richard had jumped up, saying he thought he should go, and she had no choice but to let him. He said that it shouldn't have happened – she was his patient, Daniel was his patient – and that they had to forget it. But for Shula, that was a lot easier said than done.

·21·

A Scandalous Affair

Shula did the only thing she could and got on with her life. She continued to go out with Alistair, though she knew her heart wasn't in it any more, if it ever had been. She couldn't rationalize her feelings: after all, Richard wasn't exactly offering to give up everything to be with her, and it seemed mad for her to give up Alistair on the basis of one kiss which should never have happened in the first place. She made a half-hearted attempt at explaining things to Caroline, without mentioning names or specifics, of course. All she could boil it down to was an inarticulate sense that perhaps she shouldn't be involved with anyone at the moment if her feelings were so unpredictable.

She thought back over all the time she'd known Richard, from the moment he'd first come to the village. She thought about how good he'd been to her over her childlessness and how he'd supported her, encouraging her to carry on with the IVF treatment after Mark had died, even though it had been the last thing she'd wanted to think about. She felt, obscurely, that he knew her as no one else did, and she reflected that she'd never, ever in her life been out with someone whom she'd known for so long as a friend. From her teenage years, the pattern had always been fierce attraction, sexual fireworks and, all too often, disaster. As her gran had been known to remark, so innocently, yet so percipiently: 'Up like a rocket, down like a stick.' So Shula couldn't help wondering if things would be different with Richard, around whom she felt so comfortable – and yet now so unsettlingly aroused.

When they'd met at Grey Gables – he was there for a swim – on the Sunday after it had happened, he'd apologized again. Shula had said that there was no need, that there was nothing to apologize for – but then Usha had called him from the pool and he'd said he had to go.

Shula had watched him walk away. It had given her a shock to see him half-naked: she was desperate to touch the springy hairs on his body and to feel them brush against her fingers. She watched him dive in and swim over to where Usha was waiting, treading water. Then she turned away, unable to watch their closeness any more.

June bloomed abundantly all round the village, and Ambridge shook itself down into its summer routine. The first cut of silage was already clamped: now there was hay to be mown and baled. The potatoes needed spraying: lorryloads of lambs sped off to market. As England made a shamefaced exit from the World Cup, a new sporting attraction was planned for the village fête – a gut-barging competition. Kate gave birth to her baby – a girl – in a teepee at the Glastonbury Festival, and Roy Tucker determined to get the court to order blood tests to prove he was the father. Phil drove everyone at Brookfield mad, practising the *1812 Overture* which, as a birthday present, he was to conduct at an open-air concert at Lower Loxley. And, unbeknown to Shula, Richard and Usha's relationship began to come undone.

It was the middle of July. By mutual agreement, Shula hadn't seen much of Richard in the month since he'd so unexpectedly kissed her at Glebe Cottage. They'd both decided, with admirable restraint – two honourable people in a potentially dishonourable situation – that this was the only way.

But then, one morning, Shula had to call early at Blossom Hill Cottage. Usha was sorting out the contractual side of her partnership agreement with Auntie Chris at the stables and there was a detail that Shula had said she'd clarify. To her dismay, she walked in on a full-scale row.

'I knew things had been a bit rocky betweeen you and Usha,' she said on the phone to Richard. They'd agreed not to meet, but she couldn't stop herself from phoning him. 'But I hadn't realized it was quite so bad. I didn't want to believe it, I suppose,' she added.

'Why not?'

'I need to know,' said Shula haltingly, because it both was and wasn't what she wanted to know, 'that you two are still together. Having problems, maybe, but still together.'

'Why?'

All these open questions. No wonder he was such a good doctor.

'You know why,' replied Shula, all her defences down. 'Because if you're not – if you're free – it changes things. And it scares me to death.'

'Can we meet?' he asked abruptly.

It was what they'd both agreed they shouldn't do.

'Yes,' said Shula, reckless. 'Can you come round tonight?'

It was madness: they both should have known what would happen. And though they started off in the usual civilized manner with wine and pleasantries, the emotional temperature was too high for it to have turned out any other way.

Richard told her that a friend in Manchester was looking for a partner in an inner-city practice and that he was thinking of going. It was the only way, he said, to control what was between them. Shula heard him out, then she decided it was time she told him the truth.

'I've been lying to myself for weeks,' she said. 'Pretending we were friends. That I'd grown fond of you because of what you did for Daniel.'

'It happens,' shrugged Richard equivocally.

'I agree that's what threw us together in the first place,' Shula conceded. 'But when he was getting better, I was so relieved, of course I was. But it meant you wouldn't be coming to see me any more.' She glanced at him. He was looking at her intently. 'And I couldn't bear the thought of that.' She met his eyes. 'And you felt the same, didn't you?'

There was the minutest of pauses.

'Yes.'

'And yesterday,' she continued, 'when I came round to the cottage. I didn't just feel awkward because I'd barged in on a row. I wanted to comfort you.'

'Don't, Shula.' He could tell she was getting upset.

'It's all right,' she demurred. 'I've said it all. I was just tired of keeping all those feelings under control. I had to tell you.'

'I'm glad you did.'

'But,' she said brightly, 'I'm sure you're right about going to Manchester. It's the sensible thing to do.'

Obviously her voice didn't think so. It went all wavery and out of control.

'Shula . . .' he began.

'Yes?'

'Right now I don't want to go anywhere.'

'Then don't,' begged Shula, unsteady with relief and longing. 'Stay here with me.'

He left at six the next morning. Usha was away but he said he didn't fancy being spotted on his way out by Lynda Snell or Marjorie Antrobus walking their dogs.

For Shula, the night had been revelatory in more ways than one. As a lover, Richard was all she'd ever wanted, but, even in his arms, she'd had the curious sensation of standing outside herself, judging herself and being judged. This sort of behaviour didn't come naturally to her, and when he'd gone, she lay rigid in bed, thinking.

From childhood, she'd only ever done what was expected of her. Even her overland trip to Thailand at the age of twenty had been a predictable sort of rebellion. Now, widowed mother of one, pillar of the community, bell-ringer and ex-church warden, she was two-timing a thoroughly nice man who thought the world of her – and with the village doctor.

It simply couldn't happen. With dreadful clarity, she saw what the future would be like, the lies and the subterfuge. It wasn't just a question of not being able to get away with it under the eyes of all Ambridge, though they clearly wouldn't. It was a question of what she could get away with under the scrutiny of her own conscience.

In retrospect, all she could say was that she handled the situation exceptionally badly, but she hadn't been prepared for Richard to act quite so suddenly or so decisively. Just three days after he and Shula had spent their first night together, he abruptly told Usha that their relationship was over. He didn't tell her that there was anyone else involved, let alone who it was, but his decision to leave Blossom Hill Cottage and sleep at the surgery put Shula on the spot. He'd left Usha for her, even if he said he hadn't. Now she had no alternative but to finish with Alistair.

She was torn. On a sheer physical level, on the level of her gut instincts, she thought – *thought* – it was Richard she wanted to be with, but she hadn't expected to have to end things with Alistair so precipitately. There were still so many unanswered questions. How serious was Richard about Manchester? Did he expect her to move? If not, how did he propose conducting their relationship if he were there and she was in Ambridge? Maybe, if she finished with Alistair, she and Richard could observe a decent interval, then start to see each other openly. Then he needn't move at all. Wasn't that the most sensible course?

But there was no time for sensible thought now that Richard had set things in motion: there were too many other people's feelings to be considered. Having gone to see her one day about the partnership agreement, Shula was horrified when Usha, distraught, confided in her about Richard's departure. In agony, Shula had to sit there and pretend she knew nothing, while Usha, who never lost her cool, broke down in tears and berated herself for neglecting him through working too hard. As she mouthed platitudes, Shula knew that doing nothing was no longer an option. She would have to tell Alistair it was over. And there was no point in half measures. She would have to tell him everything.

But this was where Shula failed. When tested, she was found wanting. Richard found the courage to seek out Usha and confess that there was someone else and it was Shula, but when Shula tried to tell Alistair that the 'someone else' she'd admitted to seeing was Richard, she realized he was already so wounded that she couldn't bring herself to hurt him any more. In the end, a horrified Alistair had to hear it from David, whom Shula had told only in desperation, and whom she'd sworn to secrecy.

By the time Shula's fortieth birthday rolled around at the beginning of August, she was utterly despondent. She'd given up Alistair for Richard; she was supposed to be in love. So why did she feel wretched the whole time? She couldn't even pray any more: her attempts to confide in Janet had foundered when she couldn't even formulate the words to tell her what had been going on. Usha had coldly told Shula that she thought it best if one of her colleagues took over the remaining work on the stables' partnership agreement: David had berated Shula for making him keep secrets that put him in an invidious position with his wife and two of his best friends.

Although she and Richard had given up their other partners so that they could be together, that was the last thing they could be, and as Shula sat down to her dismal birthday dinner with her close family, she had never felt so alone. It was all Ruth could do to bring herself to be in the same room; not only was she one of Usha's closest friends, she was furious that David had kept Shula's secret from her. Under her mother's wary eye, Shula forked the delicious yet tasteless food into her mouth. To make it worse, a vast bouquet had arrived on her doorstep the night before. The card had read: 'To Shula on her birthday. I love you. Alistair.'

For all their efforts to make things right, to enable them to be together, Shula and Richard seemed to be living parallel lives. They saw each other covertly and infrequently until, attacked by Alistair both for his treachery to a friend and his unprofessional conduct, Richard revived the Manchester job offer. He told Shula that he didn't think Ambridge would forgive them lightly: the only solution was a fresh start.

At the end of August he arrived back from a speculative trip to Manchester full of enthusiasm. He wrapped Shula in his arms until she could hardly breathe.

'Come and sit down,' he urged her. 'Great news. I've got confirmation. I'm being offered the job.' When Shula didn't react, he added, 'You'll love it up there.'

'Richard,' she began. 'I've got to tell you something.'

While he'd been away, she'd been doing a lot of thinking.

'I'm going straight back to look at houses,' he enthused. 'Come with me.'

'I can't,' she said at once.

'Too short notice?' he sympathized. 'We'll go up next weekend instead.'

She'd made a mess of things once, with Alistair, through being unclear and trying to avoid unpleasantness. She mustn't do it again.

'I'm not going to Manchester with you,' she said. Her mouth was dry.

Richard's face creased as he tried to take this in.

'I've already said I'll take the job.'

'And I want you to.'

What she was saying began to register.

'That'd mean . . . You're not thinking straight, Shula. Look at me.' He took her by the shoulders. 'You love me, you know you do . . .'

She looked at him impotently.

'What's changed?' he demanded. Then: 'Is this about Alistair?'

'No.' Shula heaved a big sigh. 'I don't have an answer. Not one you'd understand.'

She didn't know how she could begin to explain to him the complexity of her feelings. She'd loved him, or thought she had, but when she put that in the balance against all the other things she held dear, it simply didn't seem to count for very much.

While Richard had been away, her father had taken up the belated seventieth birthday balloon flight the children had bought him. Pip and Daniel had spelt out 'Happy Birthday, Grandad' in fertilizer bags so that he could see it from the skies, and David had shown Shula Pip's drawings of the adventure. She'd been to place fresh flowers on Mark's grave, and she'd had to consider what the implications of leaving him behind in Ambridge would be for her and for Daniel. And then – it seemed such a little thing – she'd had a ride with Caroline along the Am, right up past the golf course. The beauty of the trees and the perfection of the way they tucked into the folds of the countryside, the glinting sun on the river and the beat of the horses' hooves on the ground had reinforced what she already knew. She could never leave Ambridge, her family and her friends.

She couldn't expect Richard to understand that – Richard, who admitted he'd come to Ambridge looking for a country idyll. She didn't know if he thought he'd found it with Usha, or if he could have found it with her, but he seemed perfectly at ease with the idea of living in a big city again, so it couldn't have meant that much to him.

Richard was looking at her, waiting for some kind of explanation. He was entitled to one, she knew, but she didn't think there was anything she could say that would satisfy him.

'I belong here, that's all,' she said quietly.

'And I'm not reason enough to leave?'

'I'm sorry.'

His fingers tightened on her shoulders.

'Do you understand,' he exclaimed, 'what I've given up for you? Do you have any idea?'

Shula nodded mutely.

'Everything!' he cried. 'Usha, the practice . . . I've turned my whole life upside-down! And now you just change your mind?'

'I'm sorry . . .' Shula sniffed and put the back of her hands to her eyes to stem the tears.

'Sorry?' He sounded incredulous. He dropped his hands to his sides. 'Is that it?'

There was nothing more to say. All the passion, all the purpose seemed to have gone from her feelings for him and there was nothing she could do to get them back, even if she'd wanted to. Word spread round the village that the doctor was leaving, and everyone conveniently assumed that it was due to his break-up with Usha. He'd been a popular doctor, a useful cricketer, a real team player, and there wasn't a soul in the village, except for Shula, who'd be glad to see him go. She sat at home, unable to confide in her family, talking only to Caroline, waiting for Richard to work out his notice.

'I did something dangerous and stupid and wrong,' she mourned to Caroline. 'I thought I could cope but I couldn't. I never could. And now I've lost them both, Richard and Alistair. I haven't even managed to keep their friendship.'

Caroline didn't insult her by pretending it was all right. She knew how badly Shula had handled things but, veteran of many a broken romance herself, she patted her hand soothingly.

'Yup, you well and truly blew it,' she told her. 'Well, sweetheart, join the club.'

'Thanks,' said Shula dejectedly.

'Any time,' Caroline confirmed.

Richard left and Shula went into purdah. She'd read somewhere that a woman in a true state of purdah was supposed to do nothing but look at the clouds, and she watched a lot of skies that autumn – the sky outside Glebe Cottage, the sky over Lakey Hill, early morning skies when she woke and wept, and dusky skies that drew the curtains on another unhappy day.

She'd tried to get things going again with Alistair, whom she felt she'd treated so badly, but in her awkwardness and guilt, she'd phrased her approach clumsily. She'd implied that, now Richard was gone, the coast would be clear, as it were, for them to resume their relationship. He'd given her a dusty answer and since then had preserved a cool distance between them. Shula berated herself daily. A bare month ago he'd been leaving her flowers and 'I love you' notes. Now, when the obstacle to their being together had been removed, she'd managed to alienate him so much that he thought of her not only as a hussy but a manipulator as well.

She didn't think things could get any worse one evening in early October when she dragged herself, under pressure from David, to attend a meeting in the village hall. There was a proposal that Ambridge Cricket Club, which had had a disastrous season, should merge with Darrington, their arch-rivals, and to say that village opinion was divided on the issue would have been an understatement.

David wanted Shula there both as the club's social secretary and a long-time supporter. After Mark's death, Shula had donated a trophy in his memory for an annual Single Wicket Competition, and David insisted that she was entitled to have her say.

She already felt ludicrously self-conscious about being in any gathering that would contain Alistair: all she wanted to do was to say her piece and leave. But the village hall was packed when she got there, and she had to squash in between the Snells and Mr Pullen, whom she knew would have to squeeze past her to get to the loo about seventeen times during the course of the evening. Sean, the team captain, couldn't be there, so Roy Tucker was chairing the meeting, and things had already become pretty heated when Shula got up to speak. She said more or less what she'd intended to say, about the club being part of the village, and so on, but she'd hardly sat down when some bickering broke out over the loss of good players, Richard Locke included. Then Bert had a go at Neil, who was in favour of the merger, and Susan rushed headlong to Neil's defence.

'Hang on,' she protested. 'You can't go round blaming Neil for the break-up of the team. We all know why Richard Locke left Ambridge and it certainly wasn't anything to do with cricket!'

The hubbub died down and there was an embarrassed silence.

'Susan!' hissed Neil.

'Well,' said Susan defiantly, staring at Shula, 'we do, don't we?'

Shula froze. If Susan knew, and Neil knew, then maybe everyone knew. It was the gossip of the surgery, the pub and the shop. Living with her guilt and folly had been bad enough when she'd thought it was private. Now, it appeared, the whole village had known all along.

'Excuse me . . .' she stood up shakily. 'Can I just get past?'

Alistair caught up with her as she was fumbling her car keys into the lock.

'It's all right,' he said, taking her into his arms.

'It's not all right, is it?' Shula broke down. 'They all know, Alistair, they all know.'

He hugged her close. He knew he'd never stopped caring about her, but seeing her so humiliated, her very public embarrassment, had made him realize just how much.

'All this week . . .' she stuttered, 'all this week, people have been

giving me looks or going quiet when I walked into a room . . .
I thought I was just being paranoid.'

'Maybe you were.' He sighed against her hair. 'No one cares.'

'I've ruined so many people's lives,' she burst out. 'Not only do
I have to live with Richard and Usha and you despising me, I've got
to live with the whole village despising me as well.'

'Shula, look at me.' He held her face in both his hands and tipped
it up so he could look at her properly. 'Just listen,' he said urgently. 'It
doesn't matter what anyone else thinks. It doesn't matter whether
they know what has or hasn't happened, OK? Because we have each
other.'

Hardly daring to hope, she looked at him directly for the first time.

'I'm sorry if I've hurt you over the last few weeks, Shula, but that's
finished now,' he assured her. 'We have each other, I promise you we
do. Look . . . Oh, I'm not being terribly articulate at the moment . . .
I'm sorry.'

'Don't be sorry,' she wept. 'You shouldn't be sorry.'

'I just love you, Shula, OK? I love you.'

·22·

Retribution

'Cup of tea?' Ruth hung her Barbour on the back of the kitchen door at the bungalow and kicked off her shoes. 'Or a hot chocolate?'

'Ugh, no thanks.' David yawned. Eleven thirty on a Sunday was a late night for him and Ruth but they'd had a surprise invitation to supper at Bridge Farm. 'Not after all that red wine Tony was plying me with.'

Ruth shot him an ironic look.

'Yeah, I saw him pouring it down your throat.' She lifted the kettle, found it half full and switched it on. 'Don't start moaning to me about your hangover when you have to get up at five for the milking.'

'All right, all right.' David moved to the sink and filled a pint mug with water. 'Happy now?'

Ruth cuddled in under his arm and gave him a hug.

'It's for your own good. It was a nice evening, though, wasn't it?'

'Yeah.' David gulped a couple of mouthfuls. 'And Tony was right. It did us good to get off the farm for a bit. Put things in perspective.'

It was only the middle of January – barely halfway through the winter – but sometimes it felt as if it was never going to end. The routine farm jobs themselves were bad enough at this time of year: unfreezing the drinkers, lugging concentrates out to the ewes, mucking out the cows, all done with your fingers smarting with the cold and your breath misting in front of you.

But at Brookfield, as on many farms this year, things were worse than usual. Farming was in the depths of a recession – the worst, it was agreed, anyone could remember. Thousands of small – and not

289

so small – farmers had already given up, selling their animals at knockdown prices before things got any worse. There were stories of farmers being offered derisory sums for stock: 10 pence a head for culled-out ewes, a few pounds for calves that had cost hundreds to rear. No wonder some farmers were resorting to extreme action, abandoning their animals at RSPCA centres and tying them up outside the Ministry of Agriculture. At market, in the pubs, everyone in the countryside agreed: they couldn't remember a time when things had been so bad.

The theory behind a mixed farm such as Brookfield was that when one sector of the industry was in trouble, profits would be buoyed up by the other farm enterprises. The exceptional thing about this farming downturn was that every branch of farming was affected. The milk price had tumbled, British beef was still banned in Europe, the lamb price was an insult, and the strength of the pound, together with a world glut of pigmeat, meant that the pig industry was in crisis too. The result, at Brookfield last week, had been a summit meeting of the directors – Ruth and David, Phil and Jill – at which Phil had announced that they'd all have to make economies. He'd cancelled an order for the fertilizer spreader David had had his eye on, and had told his son and daughter-in-law that they'd have to reduce their drawings on the farm by up to 40 per cent. But when they'd whinged about it to Pat and Tony this evening – they were laughing, of course, with the demand for organics increasing at a rate of knots – Pat had been circumspect.

'I don't think any of us can conceive what being hard up is like,' she'd said. 'Really hard up, I mean. Take poor old Clarrie. I've just had to sub her for a second-hand washing-machine. That poor woman is robbing Peter to pay Paul at every turn.'

David felt chastened. Eddie had come looking for work at Brookfield lately and he'd sent him away with a flea in his ear: if Brookfield employed anyone, it would be Neil Carter or Mike Tucker, who were chasing contract work too. Yet in his heart of hearts, David knew that there were ways in which he and Ruth could cut back, maybe not as much as his father wanted, but at least in the spirit of compromise.

It was just that whenever the subject came up for discussion, every-thing seemed to get heated. Ruth was still feeling oversensitive about the bought-in cows – the result of her herd expansion idea – bringing in another dose of TB from which Brookfield was still not clear. David felt that carrying on with clapped-out machinery was a false economy: his dad thought they should make do and mend. All it needed was for Jill to chuck in some comment about Ruth cutting back on the housekeeping and not buying so many ready-meals and . . . Krakatoa. But, David had to admit, when you put it in the scale against the Grundys' endless struggle to pay the bills and find the rent, it all sounded ridiculously petty.

'I'll have a word with Dad in the morning,' he suggested now, rins-ing his mug and putting it on the draining-board. 'Tell him we'll look at some ways of economizing.'

'OK.' Guiltily, Ruth knew she hadn't been very accommodating to Phil and Jill's proposals either. And she really wasn't looking for any other way to fall out with her in-laws.

Quite apart from the sorry state of farming, Brookfield had had a turbulent winter. In November, Uncle Tom and his wife Pru had died within days of each other: they were greatly missed in the village, as well as in the family. Then Shula and Alistair had announced that they were engaged and wanted to get married before Christmas, and Jill, usually so amenable, had felt they were rushing things. She'd come round in the end, of course, but Ruth still felt her loyalties were divided because of what Shula had done to Usha. More awkwardness was the last thing any of them needed and if it meant cutting back on the Chinese takeaways, so be it.

'David . . .' she began.

'Yup?'

'How did you think Pat looked?'

'Uh.' David scratched his head. 'Dunno. Why?'

'Well . . .' Ruth shrugged inarticulately. 'Their first Christmas without John, his birthday on New Year's Eve and now the anniver-sary of his death coming up. Her life isn't exactly a barrel of laughs at the moment, is it?'

Ruth was right. Pat didn't have much to be cheerful about that winter, and as the dismal weeks went on, even the odd day of sunshine couldn't lift her spirits.

In addition to the usual post-Christmas rush on yogurt (all those diets), Tommy and Hayley wanted to branch out into producing organic sausages and call them Ambridge Originals. They wanted Pat and Tony's backing, which they might well have got, had not Helen come back from Reaseheath with her head full of marketing-speak.

She'd started going on about branding and the right image and unifying all their production under one identifiable Bridge Farm label, and Pat could see that it made sense. So she and Tony had vetoed the sausage idea, but Tommy and Hayley had gone off and produced them anyway. And now Helen said Hayley was trying to worm her way into the Bridge Farm set-up and Tony had had to break it to Hayley that the so-called 'partnership agreement' that she and Tommy had worked out between them didn't count for anything. If Hayley wanted to be involved in Bridge Farm, he'd told her, it would have to be as an employee. More in sorrow than in anger, Hayley had withdrawn with dignity. Tommy had been livid, there'd been another row, and Pat . . . Pat had felt nothing.

That was the problem. She couldn't feel anything about anything these days. She loved Hayley like a daughter, and she was a precious link with John, but when she'd come and appealed to Pat to speak up for her against Helen, Pat had just felt tired by it all.

'I'm sorry, Hayley,' she'd said. 'I can't. I just can't.'

So now she felt she'd let Hayley down, and she'd let Helen down because she really was her daughter, and she'd let Tommy down spectacularly, by allowing his eighteenth birthday be overshadowed by the anniversary of John's death. She even felt she'd let John down. That was what she'd told Hayley on the day of the anniversary, when Hayley had found her at John's grave in the dark.

'I shouldn't have neglected John.'

'You didn't,' Hayley soothed her.

'I must have done,' Pat whispered. 'I lost him.'

'You loved him,' said Hayley fiercely, who'd loved him too. 'No one could have loved him more. He knew that.'

'It didn't help. Didn't keep him safe.' Pat scrubbed at her eyes, which were overflowing with tears. 'And I keep on loving him and he's not here any more.'

It was no good anyone pointing out that Tommy and Helen and Tony were still there, and that they cared about her. That didn't seem to matter, because Pat really didn't care very much about herself any more.

Things dragged on, as they do. Day after day Pat slogged on in the freezing dairy, churning ice cream and stirring yogurt and feeling utterly blank. Clarrie, her most loyal worker, would ask her a perfectly reasonable question and Pat would stare at her, puzzled, or sometimes, to her shame, snap at her. But there was nothing she could do about it. She was low, that was all. It was because of John, and it was because it was winter time.

In early March, she fell ill with the flu, but after a week or so in bed, she hauled herself up again and carried on as before. Tony wanted her to see the new doctor, Tim Hathaway, who, with his wife, Siobhan, had moved into Honeysuckle Cottage, Nelson's old place. Pat wouldn't hear of it. She was all right, she insisted irritably. Just a bit low.

It happened one day at the end of March. A Friday, the week before Easter. Pat had come in from the dairy and was making lunch. It was only soup, and not even home-made. It was ages since she'd had the energy to make soup, even with a barn full of vegetables just across the yard. Anyway, she was stirring the pan at the stove when Tommy and Tony had come in. Arguing, as usual. Something about another batch of sausages. Tony was needling Tommy about having a professional approach to things, and Tommy suddenly flipped.

'You're not very professional the way you manage people, are you?' he demanded.

'What do you mean, the way I manage people?'

'Hayley was happy here until you mucked things up for her,'

retorted Tommy, slamming cutlery on the table, which Pat had asked him to lay.

'I didn't muck things up!'

'Of course you did!' Tommy threw a stack of table-mats down with a crash. 'It was all going great until you had to interfere. You wrecked everything!'

'Tommy, that's not fair and you know it!'

'Stop it!' screamed Pat. Her hand flailed out and caught the handle of the soup pan, tipping it right over. It clattered to the floor, splattering soup all over the cooker and the cupboards. 'Stop it, both of you!'

'Pat? Are you all right?' Tony leapt up. 'Have you scalded yourself?' Pat ignored his concern.

'Will you stop rowing!' she cried shakily. 'I can't bear it!'

'I don't want to argue, Mum,' said Tommy defensively.

Pat was dimly aware of Tony crouching at her feet with a cloth, mopping up the spilt soup and picking up the pan. She stood there, rigid, soup dripping from the wooden spoon she was holding.

'Forget it, Tommy,' Tony ordered.

'But he's been on at me all week, non-stop!' complained Tommy.

'Not now.' His father straightened and went to the sink to wring out the cloth.

'He just goes on and on and on!' Tommy strode over to the kitchen door and flung it open. 'Sorry, Mum, but this is doing my head in. I can't stand it.'

The door banged behind him and Pat heard him start the tractor engine. A sick dread rose from her stomach to her throat. Tommy and Tony had argued and now Tommy was driving away, furious, on the tractor, just like John had done . . .

'Tony, stop him!' she cried. 'Don't let him go!'

'Oh, let him get the frustration out.'

'He shouldn't be driving that!'

'Pat, now, come on . . .'

'You've got him so wound up,' she panicked. 'And he's got on the tractor and he shouldn't be, he shouldn't be anywhere near a tractor, not now.'

'Look, this isn't . . .'

It was out before she could help herself.

'You're doing it again, Tony,' she accused him. 'It's like a nightmare starting all over again. You're driving Tommy away, like you did –'

'No!' Agonized, Tony cut her off. 'Pat, Pat. Don't. Don't blame me for John. You don't, do you?'

She had to say it. She couldn't keep it in any more.

'Yes.'

'Pat . . .'

Tony's face was tragic. She couldn't look at him. She moved away, through to the sitting room, just wanting to be on her own, but he followed her.

'Tell me you didn't say that, Pat. Tell me you don't think it. I'd give my own life to have John back. You know that.'

He looked at her pleadingly, but Pat couldn't reply. Her breath was coming in short gasps, her chest felt tight and there were pins and needles prickling down her arms. What was it? Was she having a heart attack? Was she going to die?

'Tony,' she panted. 'I can't breathe.'

'What's the matter, love?'

'I don't know.' Frightened, Pat struggled for breath. 'I think I'm . . .'

'Here, let's get you on the sofa.'

He caught her arm and forced her to sit down.

'I can't get any air,' she gasped.

'Try and calm down.' Tony snatched up the phone. 'I'll get help.'

'What's wrong with me?' Pat's chest was heaving. 'What's happening?'

Tony was punching numbers into the phone. The room was swimming in front of Pat's eyes, and Tony kept going in and out of focus.

'It's all right, love, it's all right. You're going to be OK.'

Pat let out a whimpering cry. The pain in her chest felt as if something was squeezing her heart.

'Tony,' she stuttered, terrified. 'Tony!'

'Hold on, darling,' urged Tony. He was waiting for the other end of the phone to be picked up. Pat leant her head against the back of the sofa. She must be bad: he hadn't called her darling for years. He squeezed her hand with his free one.

'Please, Pat,' he begged her. 'Just hold on.'

It was all rather humiliating really. Tim Hathaway came out straight away, but what Pat had thought was a heart attack he diagnosed as a panic attack. She'd obviously been overwrought, he said, and she'd begun to hyperventilate: once he'd helped her to get her breathing under control, she felt better – just totally washed out.

But when Tim came back to see her on the following Monday, he told her that what had happened on Friday couldn't have been the only reason for her exhaustion. So she found herself telling him about John, and about how everything lately had seemed such a monumental effort. How exhausted she'd been, and how tearful.

'It's a terrible thing you've been through, Pat,' he sympathized. 'You've been incredibly strong.'

'No . . .' she said weakly.

'You have, believe me. But you've got to recognize that you're at the end of your resources. You can't draw on your own strength any more. You need some help.'

He told her, in short, that she was depressed. That it wasn't surprising, given the year she'd had, and that it was nothing to be ashamed of. He wrote her a prescription for anti-depressants and said he'd arrange for her to have a visit from the local Community Psychiatric Nurse. He told her to take things easy, not to punish herself, and to give it time. The tablets themselves would take two or three weeks to work.

Everyone rallied round. Jill and Jennifer called with flowers and home-baked biscuits. Kathy came to keep her company and brought her all the latest gossip from the pub. Clarrie and Helen coped in the dairy: Peggy took on the domestic duties at Bridge Farm.

Pat had nothing to think about but herself. All her responsibilities were removed at a stroke, but somehow, even the removal of outside pressures didn't seem to help. In some ways it made things worse because she had nothing to think about all the long days except how wretched she was feeling.

It seemed as if it would go on for ever. Tony was huffing and puffing about a trial of genetically modified rape that Brian was growing on his land on behalf of a biotech company, Bealtech, and how it could cross-pollinate with weeds and contaminate Bridge Farm's crops, but Pat couldn't muster an interest. Years, even months before, she'd have been the first to castigate Brian: now she just couldn't be bothered. Mike Tucker found her one day, walking aimlessly outside the village, tears coursing down her face. He offered her a lift. Mike knew all about depression: after an accident in which he'd lost an eye, he'd sunk into gloom and had nearly lost Betty and the kids as a result.

'It does get better,' he told her.

'But how long does it take?' Pat asked him, anguished. 'I want to be better. I just can't see the way forward.'

But gradually, over the next few weeks, she did begin to feel a little more cheerful. It could have been any number of things – the tablets kicking in, the chat with Mike, who'd been through it and come out the other side, or a chance at last to talk to Hayley and to rebuild their friendship. One day Pat even felt strong enough to go back into the dairy and do a couple of hours' work. The next day she felt washed out again and had to stay in bed, but it was a start. And when, in early May, Janet Fisher, the vicar, gave her the name of a retreat that she thought might be useful, Pat found she had the energy to pick up the phone and book herself in for a week.

When she came back, she finally felt able to tell Tony what she knew he'd been aching for her to say for the past two months: that she didn't really hold him responsible for John's death – at least, no more responsible than she was, or Hayley was, or any of them were. In the end, she'd recognized, some of the responsibility even had to lie with John himself.

Tony's relief was palpable. It had been tough for him seeing her suffer, she knew, and it had been tough for him trying to cope with the farm and the children.

'I'm not promising that I'm better,' she told him. 'I know I'm not my old self, and perhaps I never will be, quite. But I'm getting better. I'm sure of it.'

'Oh, Pat.' Tony took her in his arms and she knew it was so that she shouldn't see his tears. 'That's all I wanted to hear.'

It was just as well that Pat was feeling better because the pulverizing that some punitive force had decided to mete out to Bridge Farm was far from over.

It was the first day of June. It had been a beautiful, iridescent dawn: Pat knew because she'd woken early and had lain watching the sky shimmer through a crack in the curtains. The farmers of Ambridge were counting on a good June: for the second year running, it had been a cold, wet spring. Silage-making had been accomplished scrappily, between showers: what everyone wanted now was an unbroken spell of dry weather so that the ground could warm up, the crops could prosper and the beasts in the field could put on condition.

Waking early no longer held the fear for Pat that it had done: she could lie comfortably with her thoughts. But to stop Tony from worrying, she still often pretended to be asleep when he rose to do the milking, affecting sleepy surprise when he brought her a cup of tea on his return. Then she'd get up, make his breakfast, and another day would begin: and if she ever thought that the tasks she carried out were pointless, they were pleasantly pointless, and a harmless enough way of passing the time. If she was to go on living, if this was to be her life – well, why not this than any other way?

So it was ten to nine on the first of June and Tony was helping her to stack the dishwasher. Tommy was still in bed. Yesterday – Bank Holiday Monday – had been the day of the annual Single Wicket Competition for the Mark Hebden Trophy – the trophy that John had won twice and which, ever since his death, Tommy had been desperate to win on his behalf. Yesterday he'd succeeded and had celebrated well into the night: why shouldn't he have a lie-in?

Pat was just screwing the lid back on the marmalade jar when there was a knock at the back door. When she went to open it, two policemen were standing there. They asked to see Tommy, and, despite Pat's frantic questions, they wouldn't say what it was about. Tony shouted for him to come down and when he appeared, dishevelled, the police said that they wanted to talk to him about the destruction of the rape crop at Home Farm.

Pat gaped. Back in May, before the rape had come into flower, a group of eco-activists had chopped down about a third of the trial plot before Ruth and David, on their way back from the cinema, had disturbed them, and David had been punched in the face for his trouble. There'd already been a lot of fuss in the village about Brian's GM rape, not least from Bridge Farm: Tony had challenged him openly about it at a public meeting in the village hall. But the idea of Tommy being involved in an act of vandalism – well, criminal damage, Brian called it – let alone violence, was unthinkable. Wasn't it?

The funny thing was, Tommy didn't seem all that thrown by the police's arrival. And then they produced a warrant and searched his room and found a black balaclava.

'Right,' said the policeman. 'Let's get you down to the station.'

Pat wanted to go with him, naturally, but Tony said he'd go. He left it to Pat to phone Usha. She was away, but she assured Pat that whoever was down as the duty solicitor would do just as good a job as she could, and that she'd take up Tommy's case when she got back. She told Pat to try not to worry. Great advice.

Little by little, to Pat and Tony's stupefaction, the facts emerged. The police had linked Tommy to a van at the scene – Ruth had given them the number. When traced, it emerged that it belonged to a mate of Tommy's, and that on the night of the trashing, Tommy had borrowed it, saying he needed it to move some furniture. But the police forensic team had done their stuff: they'd found traces of oilseed rape. What with that and the balaclava, Tommy was clearly implicated in the trashing, if not the violence against David.

At first, Tommy seemed only too willing to admit his involvement, though he refused to name the others in the gang. By the time Usha came back, however, he'd had a meeting with some eco-warrior friends of Kate's, who'd made him aware of the wider implications. They said that if he pleaded *not* guilty when formally charged, the case would have to go to court. Then all the issues about GMOs could be aired, there'd be huge publicity and, as Tommy put it to Pat and Tony, it would be GMOs that were on trial, not him. This was how he wanted to play it, and Tony supported him. He was genuinely worried about GM plots and their effect on organic crops; and, anyway, there had never been any love lost between himself and Brian.

Pat didn't think it was quite that simple: she knew Usha had warned Tommy that, even for a first offence, pleading guilty to criminal damage might land him with a custodial sentence: pleading not guilty carried a far greater risk. Tommy insisted he could take it: even when, after appearing at the Magistrates Court, he was placed on remand for a week because, the bench believed, there was a chance he might carry out further 'similar offences'.

A shocked Pat and Tony were allowed to see him in the visiting room after the hearing. There were cameras in every corner, scuffed lino, battered tables. Out of sight, keys rattled and doors banged. Someone was shouting obscenities.

'Don't worry, Mum,' Tommy assured Pat. 'It's only for a week. Usha says they're bound to grant bail next time. There won't be any reason not to. It's just down to who you get on the day.'

'You must change your plea,' Pat begged. 'Surely you can see that?'

'I can't,' said Tommy. He spread his hands. 'Otherwise none of this will have made any sense.' He leaned forward and touched her hand. 'You're talking like the whole case has been judged already. Usha says we've got a good defence. I didn't break the law, because I had a lawful excuse: not just the danger of cross-pollination with our crops, but the GM pollen being released into the wider environment. I was, like, acting in the public interest. Honestly, Mum, it's going to be OK.'

'You don't have to be this brave,' pleaded Pat. 'You don't have to take on the world by yourself.'

'But if we all just sit on our hands and do nothing, then nothing's ever going to change, is it?'

Pat bit her lip. She looked at her son – her only son, now. She knew Tommy had always felt overshadowed by John. She could see him so clearly, toddling round the yard after his older brother, trying to keep up. She knew he felt that John had always been encouraged more – with his pigs, his discos, even his passion for American football. Here was something Tommy felt passionate about, and that he was prepared to take a stand over. It was something for him, and for all of them. It was something admirable and unselfish. But it was also something very scary. She'd lost one son. If he went to prison, was she going to have to lose the other, maybe for years?

Pat realized that she hadn't truly thought about her children for ages. On Tommy's eighteenth, she'd tried to conjure up a picture of him as a baby, his first word, his first day at school. There'd been nothing. There'd been nothing about John, either, on that day – just a blank.

Now it all came rushing back: the very different feelings she'd had about all her babies. With John, it had been sheer, unadulterated delight: delight that she was pregnant, and delight in him when he arrived. Helen had been a much-wanted baby but her difficult birth had made bonding difficult: their relationship, Pat sometimes felt, had never really recovered. When she'd found out she was expecting Tommy, Pat had been, frankly, horrified. Another baby was the last thing she wanted. He'd slipped into the world easily, late – and he'd been the easiest of babies, placid and easy-going – except where John was concerned.

Though Pat had often reprimanded John for fighting with his brother, or leaving him out of games, Pat knew she'd also frequently been impatient with little Tommy, whose ambitions so outstretched his ability. She didn't know that she'd ever focused on him in isolation. As soon as they were able, she'd got the older ones to go through his word tin with him, and read his bedtime stories – and it was no good anyone saying to her that she'd had other things to think about, such as keeping her marriage together, or turning Bridge Farm organic. Nothing would ever be able to convince her that she hadn't neglected Tommy in some way – sins of omission rather than commission, but sins all the same.

Pat thought about it all the way home in the car. She knew Tony was worried that this business with Tommy would set her back, that she'd sink into depression again, but, surprisingly, Pat felt more energetic now than she had for months. Mike had said something to her about the turning point for him being when he'd begun to think about things outside himself for the first time. Tommy's problems were certainly that, and they might provide Pat with another opportunity as well. They might just give her the chance to show him that he really was as important to her as the others.

A week later, Tommy was up before the bench again. He'd endured his week on remand stoically. The only thing he'd complained about was the food – he was yearning, he said, for fresh fruit and salad. He was pale as he stood up in court, with panda-like circles under his eyes: not just from lack of sleep, but from lack of fresh air and exercise.

When the magistrates decided to grant bail, albeit with conditions attached, Pat squeezed Tony's hand so hard that her fingernails left tiny indented crescents in his palm, and when they met Tommy in the corridor outside, she hugged him so fiercely that she could feel her sinews stretching. Yielding to his protests, Pat finally pulled away and said, 'Can I ask you something?'

''Course you can.'

'You're really determined to go through with the "not guilty" plea?'

Tommy nodded.

'Yes, I am.'

'Right,' said Pat, 'I've decided.'

Tommy looked at her. Tony looked at her.

'I'll support you,' she said. 'You must believe in what you're doing or you wouldn't put yourself through all this. I'm going to back you all the way.'

'Oh, Mum!' Tommy flung his arms around her in an unprecedented hug.

Pat looked over her son's shoulder to see Tony beaming at her.

'Well done, Pat,' he whispered. 'Thanks.'

Pat knew that he wasn't just thanking her for her support of Tommy. He was thanking her for the glimmer of her old self: the old Pat, fighting-spirit Pat, the Pat who believed in causes and had supported a few herself. He was thanking her for taking charge, and telling them how it was going to be. He was thanking her for coming back to him.

·23·

Battle Lines

It was a fact universally acknowledged in farming circles that the weather for Royal Show week was always fine and dry. There'd been a couple of wash-outs, of course, but this year didn't look as if it was going to be one of them, and when Jack and Peggy, chauffeured by Higgs in the Bentley, set off for Stoneleigh, the sun was already bouncing off the windscreens of approaching cars and making the cornfields glimmer.

'The Dancing Diggers!' enthused Jack, referring to the choreographed routine performed by JCBs in the Grand Ring. 'I love that!'

Brian and Jennifer had been to the Royal the day before – Brian was a governor, of course – and had bequeathed them their Show Guide. Jack riffled through the pages. 'Cattle judging, Shetland ponies – oh, and the Flower Show, Peggy. We mustn't miss that.'

Peggy smiled and nodded. A trip to the Royal was always a treat, but she couldn't really spare the time at the moment. Jack would be eighty in a couple of weeks' time, and Peggy was organizing a party for him. She'd already had a few disappointments when trying to contact his schoolfriends from Stirchley – so many had passed away – but the person Jack most wanted to see there was his adopted daughter, Hazel. When Peggy had rung her, she'd been non-committal about the date, and Peggy had formed the distinct impression that she'd rather expected to hear that Jack himself had died, leaving her a share of his wealth. Hazel had, however, promised that she'd ring back, and when she did, Peggy had resolved to give her a good talking-to. If she couldn't be bothered to turn up, the least she would do, Peggy determined, was to send a card.

Still, it was one thing to moan about the complexities of Jack's relationship with his daughter when relationships on her own side of the family were hardly harmonious: Peggy didn't dare think about how she was going to stage-manage those for Jack's birthday do. Since Tommy's arrest for the GM crop-trashing, the battle lines had been drawn between the Aldridges and Bridge Farm. Peggy had spent Sunday with her daughter, and although Jennifer maintained she could feel some concern for Tommy, especially now he'd got this crazy idea about pleading not guilty, Brian was adamant that they should lock him up and throw away the key.

'Anything else is condoning vandalism!' he'd asserted, joining them on the terrace for tea and accepting a piece of Jennifer's glazed lemon cake. 'What are we going to do, lie down and show these eco-activists our bellies? It's just mob rule!'

Jennifer had managed to calm him down – she should have been a Vestal Virgin, Phil had once said, the amount of oil she had to pour at Home Farm – and Brian had stomped off to the tractor shed, where he was checking over the spares situation before harvest. Peggy had managed to steer the conversation round to Kate, who'd taken little Phoebe back to Glastonbury for her first birthday, and then to Debbie.

'I was hoping to be able to see her,' she'd commented.

'She's being a little bit secretive about her movements at the moment,' said Jennifer with a trace of smugness. 'You know, I could have sworn she was wearing mascara this morning.'

'Perhaps she just felt like it.'

'And,' added Jennifer with a note of triumph, 'she was wearing a dress. Pale blue,' she added. 'Short, sort of gypsy style.'

Peggy's eyebrows shot up. She hadn't seen Debbie out of jeans since last Christmas, and then she'd spent the entire day complaining how uncomfortable she was.

'Of course,' said Jennifer self-righteously, 'I pretended not to notice. I don't want to pry.'

'Of course not,' said Peggy drily. That'd be the day.

'Let's just say . . .' Jennifer cut herself another small sliver of cake. 'There's definitely a spring in her step these days.'

Jennifer's instincts were right. There was a new man in Debbie's life. Well, not a *new* man exactly . . .

Just last week, Debbie, too, had been sitting on the terrace at Home Farm, chatting to Elizabeth, when her mobile phone had rung. Mike Tucker had been there as well, asking about contract work, and Debbie had had to take the call under the scrutiny of two pairs of eyes. When she'd realized who it was on the phone, she'd got up and moved away, but she could feel Mike and Elizabeth eyeing her. When she'd finished the call, she came back to find them chatting about Mike's PYO strawberries, but she knew they'd both been straining to hear her conversation.

Had it been so obvious? She'd felt herself blushing, but they surely couldn't have heard her heart hammering against her ribs, or detected the quiver in her voice? She hoped he hadn't either because she knew she had to play it cool.

The phone call was from Simon Gerrard, her first love, her old lecturer, back in England from Canada. He was on contract to Felpersham University, of all places, and he'd arrived early to teach a summer school. He wanted, he said, to see her again. He'd missed her. He'd often wondered about her. He was the 'new kid on the block' as he transatlantically put it, and he was hoping she'd be able to spare some time to show him round.

'I was hoping,' he'd said on the phone, 'we could meet up.'

'Do you think that's a good idea?' Debbie was trying to rein in her racing pulse rate.

'I think it's a great idea,' Simon rejoindered. 'There's no reason why we can't at least be friends again, is there?'

Debbie could think of one or two, and when she met up with him – he talked her round, of course – she told him what they were. Had he forgotten how he'd messed her around with another woman all those years ago? Or how he'd then pursued her to Ambridge, saying he'd been a fool, wanting her to move to Canada with him?

'Of course I feel bad about it,' he admitted in the garden of the pub in Felpersham, topping up her glass from the jug of Pimms he'd ordered. Debbie had tried to tell him that it was stronger than it seemed, but he was in love with everything English. When the land-lord had assured him that it was what they drank at Wimbledon and Cowes, and that the Queen and Prince Philip were probably enjoying a glass this very minute, he'd been sold on the idea. 'But heck, Debbie, it was what – eight years ago? I'm a changed man. Different. You'll like the new me.'

Debbie refrained from saying that she'd liked the old one, actually, heartbreak and all, but Simon was going on to explain that he'd had a pretty bruising time in relationships himself in the meanwhile. He'd lived with someone in Canada for four years but it hadn't worked out – his fault, he said. And the reason? He'd never truly got over her.

Debbie looked into her glass and poked the damp sprig of mint down among the ice cubes. He didn't know – or did he? – how exciting and enticing it was to hear him say that. Her forays into rela-tionships since Simon, let's face it, had been pretty disastrous: a fling with Richard Locke which had never really got off the ground, Steve Oakley, who'd done contract work for her dad, and, of course, the odious Simon Pemberton. She'd never met anyone else like Simon Gerrard, with his sexy, appraising eyes and literate humour – and if she let him go this time, she probably never would again.

The timing wasn't perfect, but then when is it ever? Debbie reflected. She and Simon started to see each other – without, naturally, a word to her parents – but after only a couple of weeks, Debbie had to warn him that she wasn't going to be very available in the near future. Harvest, she explained, was about to start, and when she said she'd be working twenty-four hours a day, seven days a week, she meant it.

He bleated on about missing her, but she told him crisply he'd just jolly well have to put up with it: he could concentrate on titivating the rented flat she'd helped him find in the Old Wool Market. When she'd queried his decision to live in Borchester rather than Felpersham, he'd told her winningly that it was, after all, closer to Ambridge. As far as he was concerned, he said, he'd got his priorities right.

'When can I see you?' he pleaded pathetically at the beginning of August when he phoned her for the umpteenth time that morning. 'It's been a week now.'

'Simon, we have to combine when the weather's right,' she explained. 'I can't just slope off, much as I'd like to.'

'It was raining yesterday,' he pointed out.

'And I had grain going through the dryer, an oil filter to change . . .'

'I'm beginning to think you don't care.'

Debbie shook her head, exasperated.

'You know that's not true.'

She thought fast. She'd got barley to cut but there was no reason why he shouldn't join her on the combine. He was always claiming he couldn't understand a word she was talking about when she went on about the auger and the threshing drum. Now was his chance to find out. It was a risk, yes, inviting him on to the farm when Brian was around, but one she thought was worth taking. After all, she wanted to see him too. Very much.

Jennifer's pledge not to interfere in her daughter's love-life had lasted about as long as Debbie's determination to play it cool: when she'd found out that Debbie's new boyfriend was rather more of an old boyfriend, in both senses of the word – Simon was fifty – she'd been aghast. It wasn't so much that she didn't like the idea of Simon – if he made Debbie happy, as he patently did, she felt she should at least be open-minded. Her fear was that, when Brian found out, history would repeat itself: he'd drive Simon away – and this time, he might just drive Debbie away too.

So when Debbie told her that she'd invited Simon to go combining with her, Jennifer was understandably anxious, but Debbie was on a high. As she pointed out, she was hardly going to parade Simon in front of her father. But in the end, that wasn't what happened at all.

'You mean you *knew*?' Brian wrenched at the wheel of the Discovery, bouncing them out of one rut and into another. 'You knew it was that smarmy creep, Simon Gerrard?'

What Jennifer had feared had happened. Brian had been driving her up to the riding course when their route had taken them alongside the field that Debbie was cutting. And there, in front of them as they'd come down the track, had been Debbie in the combine cab – with Simon standing behind her, leaning over her shoulder, pointing to the controls. They'd been laughing – or at least they had until Debbie had spotted Brian.

'This mysterious new boyfriend of hers isn't so mysterious after all, and you don't even tell me!' Brian fulminated, changing down a gear, it seemed, in order to change straight up again.

'He's not her boyfriend!'

'What is he then, her lover?'

'No, nothing like that!' Jennifer tried to laugh it off. 'Honestly, Brian, you've got it all wrong. He's just come back as a friend. He's working over here, she's the only person he knows, so he got back in touch.'

'Hah!' sneered Brian, jolting them up and down what felt like a crevasse. 'That's what she told you, is it?'

'It's the truth,' pleaded Jennifer, though she really had no idea how far Debbie and Simon's relationship had got. 'Do be careful, Brian. You're throwing us all over the place.'

Thank goodness she'd been able to persuade him not to stop when they'd first seen them on the combine. The thought of Brian having a blazing row with Debbie – and with Simon, no doubt – on the edge of the field while the tractor driver stood by smoking and pretending not to listen was too ghastly to contemplate. Last time Simon had been involved with Debbie, Brian had manhandled him out of the house and Debbie had disappeared for days. Jennifer really didn't think she could go through that again – not after what Kate had put them through. And Brian wondered why she hadn't told him Simon was back!

'Anyway,' she pointed out, trying to sound reasonable, or as reasonable as she could with several compressed vertebrae, 'Debbie's sensible. She's older now, she's twenty-eight. She can see Simon whether we like it or not.'

'Really?' snarled Brian. 'Well, not on my farm, she can't.'

And he stuck to it, even though Jennifer warned him that the upshot might be to drive Debbie off the farm and into Simon's arms. Throughout the rest of harvest, he was sniffy when Debbie took a night off, even though she'd been working flat out all day, and he daily predicted some farming disaster, insisting that her mind wasn't on her work. High on adrenaline, inexhaustible, Debbie proved him wrong. The Home Farm harvest came in on time and with excellent bushel weights, but even then, Brian wasn't satisfied. He continued to needle Debbie, finding fault with her work and criticizing Simon, until, exasperated, Jennifer took matters into her own hands.

'This has gone on long enough,' she told him at the end of August. 'What happened before is all water under the bridge. I'm going to invite Simon and Debbie to dinner. Then you can meet him properly.' As Brian's face pantomimed disbelief, she added, 'And I expect you to be civil.'

As far as Jennifer was concerned, the dinner party was a success. Simon complimented her on her menu – the king prawns were, he said, the best he'd ever eaten – and she was able to have a fascinating conversation with him about Canadian literature while Brian glowered and Debbie looked edgy. Simon had, very sweetly, obviously mugged up on GMOs, and he was all too keen to understand Brian's point of view on the need at least to continue with crop trials, if not commercial plantings. He also quizzed Brian about every aspect of the farm – usually the subject closest to Brian's heart – and was rewarded with monosyllabic answers.

At the end of the evening, they all stood in the yard and he thanked Jennifer effusively for the meal.

'And it was so good to talk to you properly at last, Brian,' he added.

'Was it?' grunted Brian. 'I'm glad one of us thought so.'

'Brian!' Jennifer reprimanded him. 'You'll get used to his sense of humour in time, Simon,' she soothed.

'I intend to,' said Simon firmly.

Brian started moaning about being cold and went back to the

house: much to his disgust, Debbie was staying over at Simon's for the weekend. Jennifer watched as Simon escorted Debbie to the car: she noticed how he immediately linked his fingers with hers and how she momentarily laid her head on his shoulder. How sweet!

Pleased with the way the evening had gone, she went inside and began to stack the dishwasher. Brian poured himself a whisky and moved over to the window.

'It's disgusting!' he snorted. 'You'd think they could wait till they got home.'

Jennifer looked across. Outside, in the yard, Simon and Debbie were deep in an embrace.

'Will you come away from that window!' she hissed. 'I don't know about disgusting. You're behaving like a Peeping Tom.'

Brian turned contemptuously away.

'I suppose we should be thankful he just about stopped himself from pawing her while we were eating.'

'I don't know what's the matter with you,' retorted Jennifer, sorting cutlery. 'I thought he was charming.'

'All that rubbish about GMOs?' said Brian sarcastically. 'It was a transparent attempt to suck up to me. Can't you see what he's up to?'

'Trying to be pleasant to the family of the girl he loves?' hazarded Jennifer.

'He doesn't love Debbie,' sneered Brian. 'Surely you can see what he's after?'

When Jennifer looked blankly at him, he expounded.

'All those questions about the farm, those insinuations about how well I must be doing? It's obvious! He's a fortune hunter! He's after her money, Jenny.'

Jennifer didn't believe it for one moment and when, prompted by her initiative, Simon and Debbie were invited to Peggy and Jack's for tea, and to Kate's for supper, nor did they. Peggy's shrewd view was that Simon was charming, in the way that her GI boyfriend, Conn Kortchmar, had been charming. His charm was what the Americans called schmooze, but it was nothing sinister, it was just the way he was. Kate's candid assessment was that he didn't know the first thing about GMOs or the countryside, but that at least he was honest enough to admit he was a straw in the wind – added to which, he'd been brilliant with Phoebe, which counted for a lot with her.

But Brian wouldn't be convinced. Simon gave it another month and then, defensive of Debbie for the chilly way Brian was still treating her, he rang him and suggested they meet. He said he thought it would do them good to clear the air.

It was a Friday morning, and Debbie was working, but he rang her on her mobile before Brian arrived to tell her of the preparations he'd made.

'I've made the bed and done the dishes and the hoovering,' he announced proudly.

'Wow,' said Debbie ironically. 'Dad is going to be seriously impressed.'

'And,' added Simon, 'I bought some chocolate chip cookies to offer him with his tea.'

Debbie did a double-take.

'You really think he's going to sit down with you and drink tea and eat chocolate biscuits?'

Simon was irrepressible.

'Sure, why not?' There was a pause. Debbie didn't want to disillusion him. 'Do you love me?' he asked.

''Course I do.'

'I love you too. So everything's going to be fine.'

Simon's confidence, however, was in for a battering, and it was a different story when Debbie called in to see him later. She'd managed to organize it so that she had to go into Borchester to collect some drenches for the sheep: she'd been thinking about his meeting with Brian all day.

Simon looked crushed. Not only had Brian not relented, he told her, but he'd come out with his line about Simon being after Debbie's money – and he'd taken it a stage further.

'If I persist in seeing you,' Simon explained sadly, 'he's going to cut you off without a penny.'

Outraged, Debbie gasped. 'He never said that!'

'Those were his exact words,' confessed Simon. 'I was so stunned, I'm afraid I laughed.'

'Well,' prevaricated Debbie, hurting for him when he'd had such high hopes, 'best response, if you ask me.'

'That just made him even more mad.' Simon sighed. 'I thought I was going to make things better, talking to him. Instead I've just made everything ten times worse.'

'No, you haven't.' Debbie got up. 'At least we know where we stand.' She bent down and held his face in her hands. 'Simon, I love you, OK?'

'Do you?' The meeting with Brian really had knocked him. Usually she was the one needing reassurance.

'You know I do,' she asserted. 'Don't go away. I'll be back in about an hour.'

When she got back to Home Farm, Auntie Jill's car was in the yard. Debbie felt briefly guilty. Elizabeth was expecting twins in December, and she hadn't phoned her or been round to Lower Loxley for ages: juggling Simon and her father had taken up too much energy. It was Auntie Jill's birthday on Sunday, too, and she hadn't even got her a card – not that Auntie Jill said she'd got much to celebrate. She and Uncle Phil had been living in Ruth and David's bungalow all summer, where they'd moved after Jill had broken her knee in a fall. They'd finally moved back to Brookfield last weekend, but they were having to share it with Ruth, David and the children: they'd taken the decision to move Bert and Freda Fry into the bungalow when a lorry had gone into Woodbine Cottage. Still, thought Debbie, she could sort out a card and some nice perfume or something for Auntie Jill tomorrow – after all, Underwoods would be just round the corner.

Debbie wasn't an impulsive person: often in the past she felt she'd missed out through being too cautious, especially in her love life. And the thing she'd wondered about most of all had always been what would have happened if she'd had the guts to give up everything and move to Canada with Simon. She might not be a farmer, of course – Simon would be working at a university in Quebec or Toronto or somewhere. But they could always have lived out of town – there was plenty of countryside in Canada, after all. She thought she could have hacked it.

She slammed the car door and strode towards the house. She'd passed up one chance with Simon – she'd let Brian tell her what she wanted when she hadn't been sure, and she'd let him come between them. She wasn't that naïve twenty-year-old any more: as she'd spent all summer trying to tell Brian, she was a grown woman who knew her own mind. This time she was sure. She'd make the choice and stick to it. Her mum would be upset, naturally, but Debbie couldn't help that. Working alongside her dad would be a pain, but she'd just have to grit her teeth and get on with it: it hadn't exactly been a picnic these last few months anyway.

She braced her shoulders and reached for the door handle. She stepped into the warmth of the kitchen. They were all there, her mum, her dad and her aunt.

'Oh, hello, dear,' said Jill.

'Dad, what do you think you're playing at?' she demanded, moving towards Brian.

'What do you mean?'

In the background Debbie was aware of Jill, embarrassed, getting up and excusing herself, and of her mother saying goodbye.

'I don't know how you can behave like that!' she cried, infuriated by his protestations of innocence. 'Like you're in some Victorian melodrama!'

Jennifer was fluffing around beside them now, practically wringing her hands, and Debbie turned to her. 'He's going to disinherit me, Mum, did you know?'

'What?' squeaked Jennifer. 'Oh, Brian, you didn't say that, surely?'

'Now listen to me, Debbie,' said Brian silkily. 'I'm only trying to protect you.'

'Well, stop it,' Debbie retorted. 'I don't need your protection. And

I refuse to stay here and listen to any more of your stupid threats and your ludicrous prejudice.'

'Debbie,' called her mother anxiously, as Debbie stalked towards the door. 'Where are you going?'

Debbie turned and smiled sweetly at them.

'I'm going upstairs to pack some things,' she said calmly. 'And then I'm moving in with Simon.'

Jennifer watched her go, then she turned to Brian.

'Well, Brian,' she said. 'I presume you've got what you wanted. Debbie's leaving home. Well done.'

·24·

Trials and Tribulations

'Oh, Tommy! Tommy! You were fantastic!'

Pat clutched him to her as if she'd never let him go.

'When the foreman of the jury said "not guilty"!' As kindly as he could, Tom tried to loosen her grip. 'Careful, Mum, I can't breathe!'

'It's such a relief it's all over. Oh, Tony . . .'

'What can I say?' Tony clapped his son on the back. His eyes were shining and his lips were compressed: Tom knew it was so that the emotion didn't escape.

'We're both so proud of you!' Pat reached for Tommy again. 'We are going to have such a celebration!'

Tom's trial had taken over a week and, in the end, had become something of a test case.

In the six months since the trashing of the crop at Home Farm, the words 'genetic modification' had hardly been out of the news. It had started out as an issue that only a small and concerned minority knew anything about, but, over the summer, as successive crops around the country had been trashed and scare stories circulated, it had become fodder for the tabloid press as well as the broadsheets. Suddenly, everyone was checking the labels on tins and packets, and there were phone-in polls about 'Frankenstein foods', as well as serious debate on whether even trial plots should be allowed, let alone cultivation of the crops on a commercial basis. All this, as Usha had said, made Tom's trial even more high-profile.

From a position of relative ignorance, as she freely admitted, Usha had immersed herself in the science – and the politics – of genetic modification. Over the months, she'd lined up an impressive number of expert witnesses in Tom's defence. They'd all agreed to give their time for free, and their evidence had obviously impressed the jury.

She was pleased, too, with the barrister she'd appointed, Adrian Manderson. He'd made mincemeat of the man from Bealtech, the company that had planted the crop on Brian's land, forcing him to admit that the environmental monitoring they carried out was minimal. And when Adrian had cross-examined Professor Armstrong, a toxicologist called by the prosecution, about the so-called safety tests on GM foods, he'd managed to establish that there were no actual feeding trials in progress. Instead, a committee of experts was supposed to anticipate any likely risks.

There'd been some nervous moments as well, though, and Usha knew that Tom had been rattled. At the end of their fourth day in court, the barrister for the prosecution, Corinne Holford, had given a couple of the defence witnesses, a geneticist and a bloke from the Soil Association, a hard time, and Tom had admitted to her in the tea room that he was scared. Usha had been scared herself when, after the first day of discussion, the jury had failed to reach a verdict and the case had been adjourned overnight. After another day of deliberations, the foreman had reported that they still couldn't achieve unanimity and the judge had ruled that he'd accept a majority verdict.

The longer the jury was out, the less confident Usha became, but Adrian – good old Adrian – had buoyed her up, reminding her of the Hawk jet case, where the defendants had been found not guilty despite causing £1.7 million worth of damage to a fighter plane that they believed was going to be used against civilians in East Timor. Their defence of 'lawful excuse' had been believed.

This, in principle, was the same defence they'd put forward for Tom. Adrian had posited that he'd had reason to believe that the rape crop, once it came into flower, would cause untold damage to organic crops at Bridge Farm: he'd therefore had no alternative but to destroy it. Corinne Holford, on the other hand, had argued that Tom hadn't taken any legitimate measures to deal with the problem, such as writing to Bealtech, but had taken the law into his own hands, resulting in an act of wanton criminal damage, which had, in fact, turned violent. Nonetheless, the verdict had gone their way.

'It might have been a long wait,' Usha smiled as she approached, 'but I think it was worth it.'

'Usha!' Tony clasped her in a boisterous hug.

'Tony!' she squealed. 'I don't very often get hugged in here!'

'You have done the most fantastic job.' Pat had tears in her eyes.

'Brilliant,' confirmed Tommy. 'Absolutely brilliant.'

Pat beamed. All she could think about was what she'd been spared: the loss of her other son. If Tommy were found guilty, Usha had warned them, he could easily go to prison.

'I can't believe it's all over,' she marvelled. 'You're going to wake up tomorrow morning in your own bed! I can't remember the last time I felt like this.'

'That's one thing at least,' as Jill remarked to Phil a week or so later. They were in the kitchen at Brookfield and Jill was potting up her honey. 'Poor Peggy was so afraid that all the worry about Tommy would send Pat right back into her depression. But, if anything, it seems to have pulled her out of it.'

'That's often the way, isn't it?' Phil replied. 'Having something else to think about.' He was poring over the builder's estimates for the repairs to Woodbine Cottage: Jason, the builder, had promised he'd start work this week. 'Mind you, I still wonder about the judge accepting a majority verdict. I bet it was a close-run thing.'

Jill held a up pot of honey to the light. She'd met Brian outside the court-room on the final day of the trial and he'd been incandescent.

'They haven't even given him so much as a rap over the knuckles!' he'd fumed. 'Lawful excuse! Liberalism run riot if you ask me! If I'd taken my shotgun to them when they were destroying that rape, I bet I wouldn't have got off on "lawful excuse"!'

Brian wasn't the only one in the village who thought that Tommy had got off lightly: Mike Tucker had harangued him publicly, and Susan Carter felt that if she'd had to go to jail for her crime, then so should he. Jill, as usual, took the conciliatory view. Like Peggy, she hated the idea of a rift in the family, and with Pat and Tony's twenty-fifth wedding anniversary on the horizon, not to mention the Millennium, surely it was time for the Home Farm and Bridge Farm camps to declare a truce?

But Jill didn't really have time to get involved in anyone else's wrangles: things were quite complicated enough in her own immediate family.

Elizabeth and Nigel's twins were due on 28 December, and although they'd had to put up with any amount of teasing about trying to cash in on a 'Millennium baby' as a publicity stunt for Lower Loxley, Jill knew it was likely that Elizabeth wouldn't go to term. A so-called 'normal' mother carrying twins would probably deliver them at around thirty-eight weeks, and Elizabeth's pregnancy was far from normal.

As Jill lined up the glowing jars next to the Aga, she reflected what a good thing it was that she'd taken Elizabeth to her last appointment with the cardiologist who'd been monitoring her from the start. When Elizabeth had broken down and admitted to feeling exhausted all the time, her mother had been on hand to drive her straight back to Lower Loxley and tell Nigel that she'd been ordered to rest for the remainder of the pregnancy.

It was hardly surprising. Elizabeth had been born a 'blue' baby, and when she was five she'd had an operation to replace her faulty heart valve. Any pregnancy would have put a strain on her heart, but the added burden of carrying two babies was making the already leaky valve work much harder. The cardiologist obviously didn't want to take any chances.

Not that Elizabeth was proving a model patient. Lower Loxley was in the throes of a big change of emphasis, from conference venue to 'a fun day out for all the family', as Nigel put it. There was to be a shop in the converted stables and a café in the orangery. There would be new attractions – a tree-top walk and rare breeds, as well as falconry displays and a nature trail. On top of that, they'd just opened a new art gallery – very much Elizabeth's idea – and she was constantly on the mobile to Julia, checking up on how things were going. Jill had tried to keep her supplied with reading material to occupy her time, but Elizabeth had spurned the WI magazine in favour of piles of stuff she'd borrowed from her father about rare breeds. When she'd last phoned, she'd been displaying a dangerous knowledge of Derbyshire Redcaps and Cotswold sheep.

Children! Jill shook her head exasperatedly over her daughter as her granddaughter, bursting with the energy that had been contained all day in the classroom, catapulted through the door, jabbering at the top of her voice. Jill slid the tray of honey jars to the back of the work surface, away from curious little hands. She crouched down and helped Pip off with her rucksack, then propelled her over to the sink to wash her hands before letting her investigate the cake tin. Phil got up long-sufferingly.

'I'll just take this through to the office,' he said, gathering up his papers. Much as he loved his grandchildren, he'd never envisaged having to live under the same roof for any period of time. 'I can't see I'm going to get much more done in here.'

'Nearest and dearest' was all very well, thought Jill a few weeks later, as she stood in the village hall awaiting Lynda Snell's latest instructions on costumes for the village pantomime. Sometimes you could be just too near.

When she and Phil and Ruth and David had swapped houses in the summer, she'd never imagined that getting back into Brookfield would have taken so long or have been so difficult. And with setback after setback at Woodbine Cottage – Jason had now discovered woodworm in some of the beams – she was beginning to wonder if she and Phil would ever have their home to themselves again.

The problems had been apparent from the start: Ruth and David's lives were run at a totally different pace from Phil and Jill's. Inevitably, their routine, such as it was, was dictated by the children, but when Phil came in from a hard day hauling potatoes, he didn't want to learn that Pip had taped over an episode of *Inspector Morse* that he hadn't even watched – not that he'd have been able to anyway, since Josh had fed a biscuit into the video recorder. Nor did he want to find out that supper would be delayed as Pip had scribbled over the cooking rota they'd devised and everyone thought it was someone else's turn. That had resolved itself, finally, when Pip had been made to redo the rota, and had sweetly put Jill down to cook every meal. 'Except Fridays, Daddy,' as she'd explained to David, 'when you and me get a takeaway.'

Ruth, who always felt inadequate in the kitchen with Jill around – who wouldn't? – had given in gracefully: after all, as Jill had told her, she was working full-time on the farm. She was expecting too much of herself if she thought she could prepare a home-cooked meal every night, and Jill didn't expect her to, either.

Even so, Jill and Phil had found themselves guiltily looking forward to a quiet Christmas: Ruth and David were taking the children to her parents at Prudhoe on Christmas Eve. Shula and Alistair would come for the day, and Nigel and Elizabeth – well, who could say? Elizabeth was to be induced two weeks before Christmas. With two tiny babies to care for, Christmas at Lower Loxley was likely to be the noisiest that the great house had seen for a long, long time.

In the end, the twins' birth didn't go entirely according to plan. Elizabeth had been suffering more and more frequent heart palpitations, which had first confined her to bed at home, and then in Borchester General. Finally, feeling that she'd benefit from the facilities of a bigger hospital, her consultant transferred her to Felpersham, and there they'd decided to deliver the babies by Caesarean.

So on Sunday, 12 December, supported by an awed Nigel, Elizabeth, who was awake throughout, watched as Baby G – Lily Rosalind – and Baby B – Frederick Hugo – were born. Freddie spent a few days in an incubator before he was breathing properly on his own, but the good news was that neither baby had inherited Elizabeth's worrying heart condition.

Nonetheless, the birth exhausted Elizabeth. It took some days for her heart to settle down, and her consultant warned her that within a year she'd need an operation to replace the leaky valve. Although she did slowly improve, the hospital refused to let her out for Christmas.

It was the end of December before she was installed in her own bed at home, in a room that Julia had filled with lilies, fussed over by Nigel, both babies feeding well and with a future to look forward to for all four of them.

• • •

Everyone was looking to the future: with the twenty-first century just around the corner, the only topic of conversation, it seemed, was what everyone was doing for the Millennium. For most of Ambridge, the answer was the same. They'd be going to the bonfire and fireworks on the village green, fuelled by Sid's twenty-four-hour hog roast and drinks at The Bull, which was to be manned throughout the night by a team of volunteers.

There were some exceptions, of course. At the end of November, Kate had amazed everyone – as she had a habit of doing – by taking off for Morocco with Phoebe. There was nothing for her in Ambridge, she declared: it was claustrophobic, petty-minded, and it was 'doing her head in'. Poor Roy, naturally, hadn't wanted her to go: Kate couldn't give him a timescale for her return, and the Christmas and New Year he'd imagined with his baby daughter evaporated before his eyes.

But Kate had only been gone a few days when there was a frantic telephone call to Home Farm. Phoebe had fallen ill: she was vomiting, she had diarrhoea, she was dehydrating and Kate was terrified. Brian and Jennifer promptly wired her the money to fly home, and home she came, chastened.

Phoebe recovered quickly enough, but Kate, having seen an alternative, however briefly, found that Ambridge held even less appeal. Although she loved Phoebe to bits, as she explained to Roy, she was so miserable in the village that she couldn't possibly be the mother Phoebe deserved. She had to leave, but realizing now that she couldn't take Phoebe with her, she proposed leaving her with Roy.

Jennifer, who was committed to spending the Millennium in the Caribbean with Brian and Alice, had wavered about going: she worried about Kate trying to get in touch and finding no one at

Home Farm. But that problem was solved by Debbie and Simon moving in over the holiday – against Brian's wishes, of course – and Jennifer finally agreed to fly off to the sun. She also had to concede that Kate had gone for a good long while this time.

Jack and Peggy had gone off to Guernsey to stay with Lilian, and Pat and Tony, after their traumatic year, had elected to have a quiet night in with the children at Bridge Farm. But for everyone else, despite the light rain that was falling, the venue for Millennium Eve was the village green.

'Janet! Well done, I thought you wouldn't make it!'

Jill moved up to make room at the bar. It was half past eleven and Ambridge's vicar had just arrived hotfoot at The Bull from Penny Hassett, where she'd been leading their Millennium Eve service. Soon it would be time to go out into the cold for the big countdown, to hear the bells ring in the new year – and the new century – from the tower of St Stephen's, as they had for the past 700-odd years. But first, as Janet said, she wanted to warm up.

'What can I get you?' enquired Phil, hoping he could catch David's eye. He and Ruth were coming to the end of their stint as bar staff, although David had volunteered for another shift in the early hours – after which he'd have to go straight off and do the milking.

'It's all right, thanks,' smiled Janet. 'I'll wait for the champagne.' She turned to Clarrie, who was perched on a stool nearby. 'Nice to see you this side of the bar, Clarrie.'

'Yes, it makes a change.'

Jill shot her a look. Clarrie had seemed constrained, she thought, all evening, and though she'd seemed interested in Jill's stories of Elizabeth, Nigel and the twins, there was obviously something on her mind.

'Where are Joe and Eddie?' asked Janet blithely. 'And the boys? I'm sure they must be celebrating somewhere.'

There was a pause. Clarrie looked down into her empty glass, then thrust it back on the bar and slid down from her stool.

'Well, I – I mean they . . . Excuse me,' she blundered. 'I think I'll go outside.'

'Oh dear.' Janet watched her go. 'Is there anything . . . ?'

'It's all right.' Jill reached for her coat. 'I think I'll go and join her.'

She found her crying in a dark corner by the duckpond. Everyone else was gathered round the bonfire or the hog roast: over here, the only company Clarrie had were a few mallards and a pile of sodden leaves.

'Clarrie?' Jill put out a tentative hand. 'Oh, Clarrie, you poor thing.'

'I'm sorry!' Clarrie burst out. 'It's just . . . oh, Mrs Archer, it's so terrible! I don't know what we're going to do!'

Jill put her arms round her and Clarrie relaxed into them: it was what Jill's arms were for.

'There,' she soothed. 'Do you want to tell me about it?'

Clarrie told her what Jill had already half suspected, because of what David had said. Eddie had been doing some concreting at Brookfield yesterday when, as David told it, he'd had a visitor. The chap had obviously been serving some sort of writ or final demand because Eddie hadn't wanted to take it, and David, embarrassed, had had to stand by until he did. When David had asked if there was anything he could do to help, Eddie had said brusquely that it was too late for that, and now the full sorry story emerged.

'It was a Statutory Demand,' Clarrie explained between snuffles. 'From Borchester Mills. They want the money we owe them – over £8000 – and if we don't pay in three weeks, they'll make us bankrupt.'

'Oh, Clarrie.' Jill hugged her even tighter. She knew that whatever she said would sound pathetically inept. 'It may not turn out to be quite as bad as you think.'

'But we can't pay!' cried Clarrie. 'We haven't got the money!'

Jill racked her brains.

'Well . . . perhaps if you talked to Borchester Mills,' she suggested, suddenly inspired, 'you could come to some kind of arrangement.'

Clarrie replied that they'd already tried that: the answering machine had told them that the office was closed until after the holiday. All they could do was wait.

'And everyone's so happy and busy celebrating,' sobbed Clarrie. 'And I can't. I just feel so worried!'

Jill rubbed Clarrie's back as you would a child's, while Clarrie apologized and tried to pull herself together. She'd promised she'd be home, she said, to see the new year in with Eddie and Joe and the boys.

It was nearly midnight. Phil would be looking for her, Jill realized: Ruth and David and the children would be looking for them both. Clarrie was calmer now, and though Jill didn't want to leave her, she promised that she'd be all right. She was just going to have a few quiet minutes on her own, she said, and then she'd get off home.

As Jill made her way through the crowds to the welcome warmth of the bonfire, she couldn't help thinking how lucky she and Phil were. They had a roof over their heads, even if they were sharing it with Ruth and David, they had a close and happy family, just extended by two brand new grandchildren, and, above all, they had each other.

She waved at her husband as he came towards her from the pub.

'Anyone without champagne?' Sid materialized with a tray of glasses and she took one for herself and one for Phil.

'Just in time!' Phil commented, arriving to stand close to her. 'I think it's about –'

But he was drowned out by the church clock, which began its wheezing preamble towards chiming the hour.

'Here we go!' Jill was excited. 'A new century!'

The clock began to strike. The crowd fell silent, so silent that all you could hear close to was the bonfire crackling and the flurrying ducks. With just five seconds to go, the crowd began the countdown: five, they chanted together, four, three, two, one. Then on the first stroke of midnight, a general cheer went up, and everyone grabbed someone – their partner, their neighbour, their friend.

'Happy new year!' Jill gave Phil a smacking kiss. 'We're here – the new Millennium!'

'And after all these years, we're still together,' he joked.

'Of course!' smiled Jill.

He reached for her again.

'Welcome to the twenty-first century!'

Jill cuddled into Phil's protective arm and looked around her. Ruth and David were pulling apart from a long, warm kiss as David went off to light the fireworks: typically, Shula and Alistair had managed only a brief embrace before Daniel had wormed his way in between them. Sid and Kathy, she noted, were busy on different parts of the green – too busy making sure everyone's glasses were topped up, poor things, to snatch a moment together. George and Christine seemed to have taken Marjorie Antrobus under their wing: as Jill watched, they were accosted by Robert and Lynda Snell, and Jill smiled to herself as George tussled with the prospect of giving Lynda a celebratory kiss. Roy Tucker didn't seem to be having any such problem with Hayley: they'd hardly come up for air! Well, well, thought Jill: perhaps it was a good thing that Kate was 1000 miles away.

She looked vainly for Clarrie: she was nowhere to be seen. Jill hoped she'd made it home in time to see in the new year with her family, even if it did look as though it would get off to a bleak start for them.

It was on the tip of her tongue to say something to Phil. It was a quiet time of year, and they weren't exactly flush at Brookfield, but surely they could offer Eddie some work? There was fencing to do, and ditching: soon there'd be lambing. They could maybe even pay him up front. She'd talk to Phil about it. Not now, but in the next few days.

The first of the fireworks exploded overhead in a shimmer of stars: the crowd gasped and applauded. Jill wondered if the Grundys were watching them out in the yard at Grange Farm. Still, she consoled herself, somehow they'd bounce back: the Grundys always did. They'd have to. Grange Farm without the Grundys? It would be like Ambridge without the Archers. Unthinkable.

·25·

Dividing the Spoils

In a way, though later none of them would have been able to trace it back, nor would have wanted to, when things turned out as they did, it was something Pip said that started it all off.

It was the afternoon of her birthday in February, and she'd been promised a party after school. She was allowed to invite seven friends – one for each year of her age. David had collected them all from Loxley Barrett in the Land Rover, and had returned to Brookfield complaining that he'd had less trouble getting the sheep down for lambing and that he was sure he'd gone deaf in one ear. Jill and Ruth, busy putting pizza slices on to baking trays, had laughed, but then Pip had burst in demanding to play pass the parcel and they'd all got caught up in the high-pitched pandemonium that only eight small girls can create.

But when it was over, and the last few children had gone home clutching their party bags, Pip made her pronouncement.

'I wish Freddie and Lily could have come,' she reflected. 'I wanted to show them to Alexandra. Guess what she's having for her birthday,' she continued, managing to find room for another handful of crisps.

'An elephant?' hazarded David.

'David,' chided Ruth. 'Don't give her ideas.'

'A little brother or sister,' replied Pip, regarding her father with pity. 'I wish I could have a little brother or sister.'

'You've got a little brother,' smiled Jill.

'I want a sister,' said Pip simply.

And later, when Ruth and David were clearing up, the subject came up again.

329

'Remember how exciting it was when they were born?' mused Ruth, stuffing discarded paper hats into a black plastic sack.

'It's the cleverest thing I've ever done.' David stooped to retrieve a squashed fairy cake from under the settee.

'D'you mean that? Really?'

David nodded. Ruth stopped, the lip of the sack drooping ominously. She smiled at him tentatively.

'Maybe it's just seeing Lily and Freddie, or Pip getting to be such a big girl, but . . . David. What would you think about us having another baby?'

It obviously wasn't going to happen straight away – they were in the middle of lambing, for one thing, and when David got into bed at the end of the day, he was asleep before his head hit the pillow. But somehow it got mentioned to Jill, who was delighted, of course, and naturally it set her thinking.

They were all still living under the same roof at Brookfield, but the end of the rebuilding work was in sight at Woodbine Cottage, and the hope was that Bert and Freda would be able to move back there in a matter of weeks. Ruth and David, therefore, would be able to move back to the bungalow, and Phil and Jill could at last have their own home to themselves again. At least, that had been the plan. Now, though, things were different.

Jill broached it with Phil one night when he came in from a stint in the lambing shed. She'd been lying awake, all kinds of thoughts flitting through her mind. Alistair wanted to adopt Daniel, and Bunty and Reg, Mark's parents, feeling they'd be pushed out, hadn't been too receptive to the idea. Jill and Phil were going to have supper with them this week, in the hope of making them see that Shula would never let this happen, and Jill had been rehearsing what to say.

Then there was the problem of the Grundys. Things had gone from bad to worse at Grange Farm. Unable to pay off their debts, Joe and Eddie had been made bankrupt, swiftly followed by a farm sale in which they'd seen the accumulated possessions of a life in farming go under the hammer, including their much-loved Jersey herd. David had gone along, and Phil had been open-mouthed when he'd come home with an antiquated gas dehorner, but at the same time he understood the sentiment that had made David buy it. It was a sign of solidarity, of sympathy, something that said, 'There but for the grace of God go any of us.'

And thinking about the Grundys had made Jill start thinking about Brookfield again.

'We're very lucky here,' she reflected, as Phil took off his socks. 'The security we have . . . relative security, anyway.'

Phil dropped his socks into the washing basket.

'That's true enough. Although I still end up working all hours to achieve it.'

'Be honest though, Phil, you don't have to, do you?' Jill propped herself up on one elbow. 'I mean, really it's David and Ruth who're running things now. We've begun to take a back seat, haven't we?'

Intrigued, Phil gave her a sidelong glance.

'And you know . . .' she went on, 'if David and Ruth do have another baby – well, this has been such a wonderful house to bring up children in . . .'

Phil draped his worn quilted waistcoat over a chair and shook his head in wonder.

'If I didn't know you better, Jill, I'd wonder if you were thinking something you once would have said was unthinkable. That we might move aside to let David and Ruth take over the farmhouse – as well as taking over the farm.'

It was certainly a departure from Jill's previous position. In all the time that she and Phil had been at the bungalow, she'd been the one who'd most missed Brookfield. She'd been desperate to get back – to her kitchen, to the dip in the floorboards on the landing, to the strange thrumming in the pipes when you ran the cold water. But now, suddenly, it seemed selfish and hard-hearted – and entrenched. Brookfield was a family home. A home that cried out for a young family to crash its toys into the skirting boards and chip the paint, to slide on the rugs in the hall, and to race, laughing, from room to room.

Phil and Jill didn't decide anything that night, but by the end of the week, they'd decided to see their accountant.

They told David and Ruth the results of their deliberations one Friday evening in the middle of March, when they called a directors' meeting at Brookfield. They led up to it by saying that Phil was now virtually the same age that Dan had been when he'd retired and that the time had come to think about handing things on. The only difference was that, this time, there was no convenient Glebe Cottage equivalent for Phil and Jill to move in to. Although the bungalow had been built with Phil's retirement in mind, having tried it, neither he nor Jill could imagine living in it. Nor did they want to leave Bert and Freda there and move to Woodbine Cottage which was, for them, far too noisy and too overlooked. And Rickyard Cottage, though on the farm, was only suitable as a holiday let. They were obviously going to have to buy something else in the area.

'We've had a look at house prices,' Jill told a slightly shell-shocked Ruth and David, who hadn't been expecting anything like this to be discussed. 'We don't think we'll come up with anything for less than £200,000.'

David frowned.

'The only way you could release that much is by selling some land.'

Phil nodded. He'd realized that for himself, but Anthony, their accountant, had come up with a solution. The proposal was that Phil and Jill sold Ruth and David about 100 acres of Brookfield, but at less than the market rate – in fact at about 75 per cent of its value. They'd have to borrow the money to buy it, and Anthony had calculated that the interest on that sort of amount would, at current rates, work out at around £17,000 a year. In addition, Phil and Jill would need a pension of some £18,000 a year to live on. It didn't take David long to do the sums.

'That's 35 grand a year we've got to find before we start paying ourselves.'

'We do realize it's a big financial commitment for you,' put in Jill.

'We'd have to do some major streamlining,' brooded David, already turning things over in his mind.

Ruth said nothing. She was obviously still struggling to take it all in. This was what she and David had been looking forward to for years. But inevitably, there were conditions attached.

'Well,' said David finally, 'I just hope we can find a way of working it out. After all,' he smiled, 'we've got the next generation of Archers to think about, haven't we?'

Phil and Jill hardly thought that that would be the end of the debate, but neither of them could have predicted the extent of the animosity that one seemingly simple decision unleashed.

While Ruth and David scratched their heads and spent hours fiddling with figures on the computer, his parents told first Shula, then Elizabeth about *their* proposed share of the Brookfield legacy: half each of whatever property Phil and Jill subsequently bought. Shula was equable about it: she was more than comfortably off and had, of course, been left Glebe Cottage outright by her grandmother. Elizabeth was quite a different proposition.

Phil outlined what they were proposing to do, how Ruth and David would work the farm and how Kenton, who'd been phoned in Australia, was quite happy with the arrangement. After all, he'd already had, as it were, an advance on his inheritance to set himself up in business. Elizabeth went very quiet.

'What do you think?' prompted Jill.

'I'm sorry, Mum,' answered Elizabeth. 'It's a bit sudden.'

'You do think we're doing the right thing by leaving Brookfield?' probed Phil. Something in her face was making him feel unsettled.

'I suppose so,' she shrugged, 'if that's what you've decided.'

But by the time she got home to Lower Loxley, to Nigel and the babies, she was furious.

'I've been to see Mum and Dad,' she told Nigel, pouring herself an angry sherry. 'You'll never guess what they're going to do. Oh, Nigel, it's awful.'

It was like anything. It was like a job offer, it was like a bereavement or a divorce. The minute money came into the equation, the haggling had to start. And Elizabeth was not happy.

'A measly hundred thousand!' she fumed to poor, patient, non-confrontational Nigel a few days later. 'Brookfield's worth over a million! Well over.'

'So you keep saying. But that's all tied up in the farm. You could only get something out of it if the farm was sold up.'

'That's the last thing I want!' cried Elizabeth. 'Brookfield's part of me, and I want that to continue. But I want to have a share in it. I'm sure it's possible. And I owe it to Lily and Freddie, too.'

Being Elizabeth, she didn't just seethe in silence: she saw her own accountant, who, not surprisingly, backed up her claim. And to their dismay, Phil and Jill found themselves caught between the very real needs and the insistent demands of two of their children.

It seemed there was no sort of compromise that everyone could agree on. Phil mooted the idea of giving Elizabeth shares in the farm: David scoffed at the notion of having to pay her a cut of the profits before he and Ruth earned a living. Then Phil suggested making the farmhouse over jointly to Elizabeth and Shula: Ruth and David would pay them rent for living there. Elizabeth refused, still insisting on some sort of share in the farm as a whole, a sort of sleeping partnership.

As a weary Nigel told Shula a few weeks later, Elizabeth's attitude, which was hurting Phil and Jill and driving David to distraction, was painful for him, too. They'd had to meet secretly, in Underwoods restaurant: having found her mother in tears over it all, Shula had had a blazing row with Elizabeth.

'Lizzie keeps saying how perilous a proposition Lower Loxley is,' he confided. 'And I know we've had our tough times, but I really think all the new attractions we're putting in for visitors this summer are going to take off.'

'I'm sure they are,' said Shula warmly. She and Nigel were such old friends: she could see he was hating every minute of this squabbling.

'And I don't like being made to feel a failure all the time. As if I can't provide for her and Freddie and Lily.'

Dividing the Spoils

'Oh, Nigel.' Shula put a hand on his arm.

'She says she's doing it for them,' he sighed. 'Well, it's their baptism next week. Don't you think we could call a truce?'

Nigel got his truce in the end, though in the meantime, to make things worse, Ruth and Elizabeth had a stand-up row of their own. They'd met by chance on Good Friday, which also happened to be Elizabeth's birthday. In the hope that the inheritance issue would eventually be resolved, Ruth and David had drawn up rationalization plans for the farm, including the loss of the pig unit and thus the job that they'd promised Neil Carter. He'd been devastated and, catching Ruth at a bad moment after a diatribe from Susan, Elizabeth's stubborn insistence on what was 'fair' had riled Ruth beyond reason.

But everyone agreed that the baptism was the babies' day. Neither Ruth nor David felt like going, but everyone conceded that they should rise above their real feelings for a few hours.

They very nearly made it. The service in the church, just the immediate family gathered in a pool of light around the font, was achingly beautiful. Afterwards, they clustered outside St Stephen's in benevolent sunshine, with Simon and Debbie, who were godparents, shooting roll after roll of film as if practising for their wedding, which was to be in a fortnight.

Back in the elegance of Lower Loxley, where Elizabeth had arranged a buffet lunch, if the conversation was strained, it was at least polite. It was only when Ruth and David, who'd shown commendable restraint, got up to go that Julia, inevitably, had to open her mouth.

'Dear me,' she trilled brightly. 'The life of the yeoman farmer!'

'Oh, it's not so bad.' Phil smiled at David. He didn't smile back.

'No, I'm sure,' Julia backtracked. 'And Jill's made Brookfield a lovely home.'

'Thank you,' said Jill drily.

'Charming, of its kind – though not as large as Lower Loxley, of course. In fact,' Julia carried on blithely, 'I don't quite know what Elizabeth's making such a fuss about.'

There was a deathly pause.

'Nigel . . .' appealed Elizabeth, in distress.

Poor Nigel.

'Mummy . . .' he signalled.

'What did I say?' Innocently, Julia opened her eyes wide.

'Nothing,' said David tersely.

'Nothing!' echoed Elizabeth.

'I think it might be better, Julia,' Phil intervened, 'if we overlooked the fact that you'd said anything at all. It doesn't really concern you.'

Now it was Julia's turn to look affronted.

'Well, really!' she objected. 'Nigel . . .'

Poor, poor Nigel.

'Look, Phil,' he began awkwardly, 'that's a bit strong.'

There was a small sound from Elizabeth – exasperation mixed with offence.

'Julia's got a point, Dad,' said David curtly. He was already on his feet and he glowered down at his sister. 'Lower Loxley's a stately home; it's in all the guide books. Why would anyone who had a stake in it want to get their hands on anything else?'

'Exactly,' seconded Ruth. 'Julia's only said what we're all thinking.'

Elizabeth jumped up then, shouting something about knowing that Ruth and David would manage to spoil her day somehow – 'Your day, right,' mocked David – and, not surprisingly, the twins woke up and started to wail. Nigel dragged Julia off to see to them, and Jill got to her feet.

Never one to chastise, she was famed for her saintly patience. Her family would have to push her to the edge before she spoke out. They'd done it this time.

'Have you all quite finished?' she enquired coldly.

'Sorry, Mum,' said David quickly.

'Mum . . .' appealed a tearful Elizabeth.

'I have *never*,' Jill stressed the word, 'been so ashamed in all my life. Phil, I think we should go.'

It was hard to see how they could claw anything back from such disastrous and public bitterness on what should have been a joyful day. For Phil, however, there was only one way left – one that led straight back to where they'd started.

It was a Sunday afternoon at Brookfield and Phil and Jill were alone: Ruth and David had moved back to the bungalow in a futile gesture of protest against the continuing stalemate. Jill had put some calming Vaughan Williams on the stereo: she had a pile of mending to do.

'You know I've always tried to be fair with the children.' Phil placed a cup of coffee at her elbow.

Jill bit off a length of thread. She was turning the collar of Phil's favourite work shirt: the way things were going, he might be needing it a good while longer yet. 'I know you have, love.'

'And that's always proved the best way. Until now. So now, instead of trying to decide on the basis of what my children *want*, I'm going to have a look at what they *need*.'

'I see.' Jill took off her glasses and considered. 'That makes it fairly simple, doesn't it?'

Phil sat down heavily opposite her. All this quarrelling was putting years on him.

'The point is,' he said firmly, 'David's a farmer and he needs a farm.'

As Phil often said, however, if you could rely on your children for one thing, apart from their ability to cost you money, it was their capacity to surprise you, and when he put his decision to David, he was frankly astonished by his response.

'I don't want you to think I'm not grateful, Dad, because I am,' David told him. 'But I want to have one last go with Elizabeth.' Before Phil's eyebrows could take off into the stratosphere, he went on. 'I don't think she deserves it, but I can't not try. I've been think-ing and, well . . . I thought I could offer her a share of the profits, should Ruth and I ever decide to sell up. What do you think?'

But whatever Phil thought hardly mattered because, as with every other compromise that had been offered to her, Elizabeth turned it down flat.

'It's perfectly simple,' David told her when he went to Lower Loxley with his 'peace offering', as he put it. 'You get a share of what-

337

ever the place makes if Ruth and I sell up and move on. Or Lily and Freddie get it . . . whatever you want.'

Elizabeth looked at him for a moment. An intense memory of all those childhood humiliations flashed in front of her, of being excluded from games, of the others running away and hiding, leaving her standing there in her little ruched sun-dress until her mother came and rescued her, dried her tears and took her to help in the kitchen, podding peas or washing up.

'Oh,' she said. 'And are you planning on doing that? Moving on? I mean, you're suddenly going to stop being a farmer and – I don't know – join the civil service or something?'

'Well, no,' faltered David. 'But . . .'

'Then forgive me, David,' contested Elizabeth, 'but you seem to be offering me a percentage of a very big round zero!'

And that was where things were left, more or less, though Phil did manage to get Elizabeth to agree at least to think about David's offer. But, she said, with the big relaunch of Lower Loxley as 'a fun day out for all the family' just two weeks off, she hadn't got time to go and see her accountant until the beginning of June. They'd all have to wait.

It was unsatisfactory, it was incomplete, but it was all they could do. Phil and Jill, and David and Ruth, would have to put their plans on hold until she came back to them with her answer. If it was no, Phil still insisted, he would revert to his original idea and make the farm and the farmhouse over to David and Ruth.

But then something else happened. Something that none of them could have predicted.

·26·

Deliverance

Ruth had had a horrible week. Correction, another horrible week. Ever since Phil and Jill had announced, back in March, their intention to retire, every succeeding week had brought some new difficulty – another demand from Elizabeth or another painful decision about the future of the farm, like getting rid of the pigs, which had been Phil's life's work. But this week, for an entirely unconnected reason, had been the worst of all, and by Friday evening, when David came in, Ruth was at the end of her tether.

She hadn't seen him since mid-afternoon, when she'd taken over at the silage clamp so that he could go and do a few hours' spraying. It was a busy time at Brookfield – not that any time was quiet – but at least they'd managed to get most of the silage in while the weather had held. Next week they had the shearers coming, and they had to keep up-to-date with the spray programme on the emerging crops.

Nonetheless, May was usually one of Ruth's favourite times of the year. The countryside seemed to pulse with life. Leaves unfurled and blossoms emerged with such alacrity after a few sunny days that she sometimes felt as though she were living in one of those time-lapse nature films. This week, however, it had felt more like some grim, kitchen-sink drama. She was in the kitchen, in fact, when David came through the door. She was shouting at Pip at the time.

'I won't tell you again,' she scolded. 'Go and tidy your bedroom or you don't get any tea!'

Pip stared at her, then spat, 'I hate you!' before running off and slamming her bedroom door.

339

'I've tried asking nicely,' insisted Ruth defensively to David's raised eyebrows. 'If she won't do it when I ask nicely, then I'm going to shout at her, aren't I?'

She was wreathed in steam. She'd just drained the potatoes and she looked like some vision of vengeance. David sat down at the table and eased his boots off.

'Bedroom again?' he asked mildly.

'She's pulled all the soft toys out!' Ruth raged. 'They're all over the floor! If I wasn't here to make her clear them up, they'd stay there permanently!'

'OK . . .' David wiggled his toes.

'Well, she has to be made to realize.' Ruth clattered the lid off another vaporizing saucepan and stabbed a knife into the contents. 'I'm not her maid of all work!'

'Ruth,' protested David. 'Enough! It's not like I don't agree with you.'

Ruth merely sighed and took the saucepan to the sink.

'Look,' said David. 'What is the matter with you at the moment?'

Ruth turned to face him.

'What do you mean?' she asked dangerously.

'It's been going on for days,' he sighed. 'You've been distracted and moody. And you keep flying off the handle. Especially at the kids. Now what's going on?'

Ruth clenched her fists at her side.

'What,' she began, 'apart from Elizabeth being awful, and seeing your father's face as he watches half his life's work disappear, or having Neil Carter treat me like dirt . . . nothing's going on . . .'

So why was she crying?

'Look,' David got up, crossed to the sink and put his arms around her. 'Come on,' he said, smoothing her hair back. 'It's all right.'

Ruth sagged against him and sobbed. He could feel the weight of her sorrow.

'No, it isn't.'

'It's been a bad week,' he consoled her. 'You've had those before.'

She sobbed some more.

'Not like this, I haven't.'

'Why?'

She was crying like he'd never heard her cry before, but he was still completely at a loss.

'I've found a lump, David.'

Deafening alarm bells rang in his head. His heart plummeted.

'What? What do you mean?'

Ruth sobbed into his shoulder. She was clinging on to him desperately.

'There's a lump in my left breast. I've kept waking up in the morning, hoping it would be gone, but it hasn't. David, it won't go away and I don't know what to do any more!'

The truth was, she did know what to do, and being the sensible person that she was, she'd done exactly what you're meant to do in the circumstances. She'd already made an appointment to see the doctor the following Monday. So the doing wasn't that difficult. The hard part for them both was knowing what to think and what to feel. And as the weeks went on, that was a situation they would both get very used to.

What was evident from the very beginning, and which Ruth, as a healthy person, had never appreciated before, was that once you get involved with doctors and hospitals, things take on their own momentum and it can never be as fast as you would like.

Her first appointment with Tim Hathaway felt, frankly, like rather a waste of time. He was terribly nice and concerned and everything, but when he found out that Ruth was in the middle of her period, he told her that he couldn't say anything conclusive until after it was finished because the lump – which he could feel too – might just be part of the usual monthly change in her breasts. So Ruth had to go home to David, by now at least as worried as she was, and tell him that they would have to wait another week. And so another seven days ticked by – no, eight, because agonizingly, the following Monday was a bank holiday.

It was the day of the great Lower Loxley relaunch, which was somewhat dampened by a day of downpours – not that Ruth could

341

have cared less. All she knew was that, although her period had finished, the lump was definitely still there. To her at least, it was starting to feel harder, more tender and more invasive than ever. And there wasn't a moment when she wasn't aware of it.

At her second appointment, Tim examined her very carefully. When she'd got dressed, he told her that he was going to refer her to the Breast Unit at Felpersham for a triple assessment – a mammogram, an ultrasound scan and something that sounded really appealing, called a fine-needle biopsy. But he still couldn't answer her when she asked him if he thought it was cancer: that, he said, was why he was referring her. The appointment, he told her, would definitely be through within a fortnight.

One week had felt like an eternity: now she was going to have to wait another two before she was even seen, and no doubt there'd be another wait for the results. Although logically she knew it could still all be nothing – Tim had told her that 90 per cent of breast lumps were perfectly harmless – she couldn't help but imagine the worst.

David was brilliant. He hugged her, he let her cry and then he told her his plan. It was half term, and he suggested that she take a few days off to be with the children. She was certainly too distracted to be around farm machinery and he knew the anxiety was affecting her sleep. Reluctant at first, Ruth finally agreed – but she was adamant about one thing. She didn't want anyone to know anything until she'd had the results from Felpersham.

As the oncologist showed them into her office, it was impossible to tell from her face what the news was going to be. She must spend half her life doing this, thought Ruth, as she clutched David's hand. And the other half examining people so she can tell them.

She suddenly caught sight of a photograph on the desk: one of those posed school photographs in an oval cardboard frame. It was of two boys, about six and eight, both blond. The older one was standing, his hand on the little one's shoulder. The little one had glasses. Both were grinning toothily at the camera. So she didn't spend all her time dealing with sick people, thought Ruth. Somehow the thought cheered her.

'This is my husband, David,' she said hurriedly, coming to her senses.

The oncologist smiled.

'How do you do? Have a seat.'

They both sat down. The oncologist did too, and pulled a file towards her.

'Now,' she began. 'We've got the results of the tests we did on Monday.' She paused briefly. 'I'm afraid it's not good news.'

Ruth swallowed hard.

'The lump you found in your breast is cancerous.'

'I knew it,' breathed Ruth.

'And the tests,' the oncologist went on, 'have shown the presence of some other masses, which leads us to believe that the cancer is multi-focal.'

David gulped. 'What . . . what does that mean?'

'It means we can't just operate to remove the lump,' explained the doctor. 'In a case like this, we'd have to recommend a mastectomy.'

Ruth was staring fixedly at the desk in front of her. As the doctor said the word, the desk tipped frighteningly away from her, then rose up again. But in the split second that it had tilted, it had carried away from Ruth everything she held dear – her entire life as it was, or had been, up to this point. Tipped away down some giddying chute into nothingness went Pip and Josh, and David, and her parents, and his parents, and all their friends and family, and the farm . . . and Ruth was left on the edge, looking helplessly after them, but stranded, on her own.

'What . . . what chance do I have?' she heard herself asking. 'I mean . . .'

The oncologist smiled reassuringly, a practised smile, but one with some warmth.

'Survival rates are improving all the time. When we catch the disease early, when it's still operable, well over 70 per cent of people are alive and well after five years.'

'Seventy per cent,' echoed Ruth.

'That's good, isn't it?' David's voice sounded forced.

'Better than most people think, yes,' confirmed the oncologist.

'You really have a very good chance of going on to lead a perfectly normal life.'

If waiting for the various appointments and keeping it to themselves had been awful, telling everyone was even worse. Ruth rang her mum as soon as they got home, and Heather said she'd come down straight away. They told Phil and Jill on Father's Day, after Sunday lunch, and, if nothing else, their stunned and pained reaction made Ruth realize that she was going to have to find resources of strength from somewhere deep within her. Her own shock and disbelief were hard enough, and David's: now she would have to cope with everyone else's as well.

The oncologist had said that the operation would be in around three weeks, and, compared with the other weeks of waiting, the time passed relatively quickly.

In between the crying – and there was plenty of that for herself and David, together and alone, and with other people – there was a lot that Ruth felt she needed to organize. Everyone else, she knew, was focusing on the cancer. Shula gave her books on nutrition and diet. Jill took Pip and Josh off her hands as much as she wanted. Her own mum cooked and shopped and tutted about the dust under the children's beds. But for Ruth, the cancer was almost too big a concept to deal with. All she was thinking about was getting through the operation.

There were practical things she wanted to sort out. She felt an unusual compulsion to sort the kids' clothes and give away the ones they'd grown out of. Calmly she told David that she wanted to check their wills. Realizing that in hospital she couldn't wear what she usually wore in bed – nothing, or one of David's old shirts – she went shopping for nighties. When David wasn't around, she read the book she'd bought herself, imaginatively titled *Breast Cancer*, and learnt about secondaries, and even stages three and four. But most of all, she just sat and thought.

She was due to go into hospital on the Friday of Royal Show week. Disappointingly, the weather had turned dull and damp. No one from Brookfield had bothered to go this year, though Ruth knew that Brian was going, as usual, as were Pat and Tony, who wanted to check out suppliers for the organic shop they were opening in Borchester.

In fact, there were all sorts of things going on that Ruth couldn't take any interest in. Kathy and Sid were trying to make a go of their marriage after Eddie had blurted out in the pub the truth about Sid's affair with Jolene Rogers; Debbie and Simon had zipped off to Canada before harvest started to see his relations; and Joe Grundy, who'd gone missing from the grim council flat in which the Grundys had been rehoused, had been found delirious at Grange Farm, and was still in hospital. But all that mattered to Ruth was that she get through Friday's operation.

On the night before, they all had supper together at Brookfield. She and David had decided to tell the children as little as possible. All Pip knew – who could tell how much Josh understood? – was that Mummy wasn't very well at the moment and had to go into hospital. She was going to have an operation, but it would make her better. They wouldn't see her for a few days, but then they'd be able to go and say hello to her in the hospital. They would, however, David warned them, have to be very careful and not climb all over her like they usually did.

They'd also been told that, while Mummy was sick, they were going to have a little holiday and stay at Brookfield with Granny and Grandad. So, on the Thursday night, it was in the Brookfield bathroom that Ruth gave Josh his bath, patted his little bottom dry and eased his flailing arms into his pyjamas. Then she went and lay with him on his bed in the littlest bedroom, with the air outside the window heavy with the threat of rain. After he fell asleep, she lay and listened to his breathing. It was the dearest sound in the world.

After supper, she took Pip upstairs and tucked her in, too. She read her a story: they were part way through *Alice in Wonderland*.

'More . . .' said Pip sleepily when she closed the book.

'No,' said Ruth softly. 'You're tired. Daddy'll finish it tomorrow.'

'I want you to finish it.'

'Not tonight,' replied Ruth, her throat tight. 'Another day. When I'm back from hospital.'

David took her in the next day. He stayed with her through all the boring bits, the tests, the weighing and the same old questions. He stayed with her right till the anaesthetist arrived. Scared, and scared of being on her own, she gripped his hand.

'Just relax,' he told her. 'Remember, everything's going to be fine.'

'Yes . . .' said Ruth faintly. She could her the squeak of the anaesthetist's shoes as he walked down the ward.

'And just remember that I love you.'

Ruth did remember that: she kept reminding herself of it over the weeks that followed. She kept telling herself how fantastically lucky she was to have David, and to have her mum there to look after her, and to have Jill to take care of the children. She was grateful for the wider family, too, and for her best friend Usha, who came to see her almost daily, and to whom Ruth felt she could safely talk when things got on top of her.

The problem was, she realized, that while she'd been pacing herself for the operation, and for getting through it, she hadn't given a moment's thought to what would come after. She hadn't begun to imagine how chronically exhausted she'd feel, or how sore, or how weepy. Her mum told her over and over again that it was normal. It was partly the anaesthetic, partly the huge shock to her system, but Ruth hated feeling so debilitated.

As time went by and she found she still couldn't do the simplest thing, like reach a jar of coffee from the top shelf, she became more and more frustrated. For God's sake, she'd scream at herself silently, you've had the operation, you've come through it, they've told you they think they got it all! Yes, sure, you've got to have chemotherapy, but it's really only an insurance! You're probably one of the 70 per cent! So why couldn't she be a bit more grateful? And why, oh why, couldn't she open up more to David?

She couldn't really express it to anyone. She couldn't even really express it to herself. She did have a go with Usha, but as she struggled to articulate her feelings, it didn't sound as if she was making much sense.

'I find myself . . . tensing up with him,' she faltered. 'It's hard to understand why, really.'

'Has he said anything to make you?'

Ruth shook her head.

'He couldn't have been better. He only wants us to feel comfortable again. And that's what I want. But instead I keep pushing him away. I don't know why, Usha. I can't let him get close to me.'

But she did know why, really. She'd done nothing but think about it. The trouble was, she concluded, that though David thought he understood, it was more complicated than he knew. He thought that she thought he'd mind the way she now looked. He thought that if he reassured her that he loved her, that he'd love her whatever she looked like, that it would all be all right. What he just wasn't getting was that it wasn't about what he thought she looked like: it wasn't even about how she looked at all. It was about how she *felt* she looked. If she was so repulsed and saddened by the idea of herself so mutilated, how could he not be, whatever he thought he'd feel? That was why she was keeping him at arm's length. She didn't – couldn't – trust herself to trust him.

In truth, she'd let Usha see more of her, literally, in the past couple of weeks, than she had David. She'd even shown Usha the scar. And that was something Ruth hadn't yet been able to look at for herself.

'I'm sure David understands,' Usha reassured her the following week. Things were just as bad.

'How can he,' pleaded Ruth, 'if I don't tell him what I'm really thinking or feeling?'

'Well, perhaps that's your answer,' counselled Usha. 'Somehow, you have to find a way of opening up to him.'

'I know,' sighed Ruth. 'It's just that it's so difficult. It's like there's this big knot inside me and if I start to let someone else unravel it . . . I'm scared it's all going to fall apart.'

'You let me unravel a little bit of it,' Usha replied gently.

Ruth sighed. 'Yes, I did, didn't I?'

Earlier, and not for the first time, Usha had urged Ruth to look at the wound. Finally, together they'd stood with a mirror and looked at the scar – so tidy – which ran from her armpit to her breastbone. And Usha had hugged Ruth as she wept – for the breast she had lost and for everything else.

July passed into August. School had broken up, and Pip and Josh spent their daylight hours in the paddling pool or the sandpit in the bungalow garden. On the farm, they were starting to dry off the cows: the first barleys, thankfully, were almost harvested. In the village, inexorably, life went on. Kathy's attempt to patch things up with Sid hadn't worked and she'd left him, and The Bull, taking Jamie to stay at Bridge Farm. The Grundys had a new home, too: a dilapidated caravan that they'd fearlessly parked by the release pens on Estate land. Joe was in his element.

Another few days slipped by. David was working flat out finishing the last few acres of barley: when he wasn't out on a grain trailer he was out baling, or carting the big bales back to the yard. Ruth mooched about at home: the appointment had come through for her first chemotherapy session and she knew she ought to be making the most of feeling even this well. Most of all, though, before the chemotherapy laid her low, she wanted to mend things with David, and one night she got her chance.

He'd come in late, about nineish, after yet another evening lugging bales.

After he'd eaten, he'd padded through to the bedroom to take his boots off and he'd never reappeared. When Ruth had checked ten minutes later, he'd obviously lain down on the bed for a moment and had fallen asleep. Silently, she crept out again.

She went into the kitchen and poured herself a glass of wine, then wandered out into the garden, such as it was at the bungalow. Bert had tried to knock it into shape when he and Freda had been living there, but the ravages of Pip and Josh's games had soon made themselves felt again. Still, the sweet peas were looking good – even Ruth could get those to grow – and the lavender that Jill had given her was pungent when Ruth brushed past.

She stood at the bottom of the garden looking out over the Am at the cornfield on the other side. The wheat was packed tight, stiff, awaiting the combine. A flock of swallows swooped low over it, foraging for flies. It was the only activity to be seen.

It had been August, Ruth remembered, when she'd first come to work at Brookfield. She'd first met David in the yard. It was 6.30 in the morning and he'd been waiting for her to bring the cows in for milking. He'd told her off for being late. She smiled to herself. She hadn't dared answer him back too smartly, then – how things had changed!

She stood there a few moments longer. How, indeed. Then, her mind made up, Ruth took a big swig of her wine and marched back towards the house.

'I've locked up,' she smiled, when she'd woken David to tell him it was time for bed.

He sat up. She was already unzipping her jeans. She knew he'd assume she'd want him out of the way.

'I'll, erm, I'll go in the bathroom.'

'There's no need.'

'What?'

In her knickers and T-shirt, Ruth walked across to him where he sat on the side of the bed. 'You stay where you are.'

'Are you sure?'

She stood in front of him and painfully tugged her T-shirt over her head.

'Ruth –' he began, as she went to take off her bra.

'It's OK,' she told him. 'I've thought about it. I want to.'

Slowly, awkwardly, she unhooked her bra. She laid it, and the soft sponge breast that the hospital had given her, on the chair. She lowered her arms to her sides.

David looked at her. He looked at the scar.

'Oh, Ruth,' he whispered. He reached his hand out. 'Can I . . . ?'

Ruth nodded and she felt his fingers trace the line of the scar all across her chest, where her breast had used to be.

'Can you feel that?' he whispered.

'Yes,' she replied, half amazed. 'Yes, I can.'

'Oh, Ruth,' he repeated. 'Ruthie.'

It was his private, very private name for her. She felt the tears start.

'Come here,' he said and she could tell that he, too, was about to cry.

With a muffled, inarticulate sound, she flung herself against him and he hugged her tight.

'It's all right,' he said. 'It's all right. Oh, I love you. I love you so much.'

Sobbing now, all she could do was say his name. He rocked her like a baby.

'There, there,' he soothed. 'Shhh. I've got you, I've got you.'

Still she cried, weeks of pent-up emotion spilling out against his shoulder, wetting her hair.

'I love you, Ruth,' he kept saying. 'I love you, I love you, I love you.'

And they stayed like that, rocking and crying, until her sobs had shuddered to a natural, exhausted, but finally peaceful end.

'Phil! Coffee for you!'

Jill hailed him from the gate and Phil trudged across to meet her. He'd been checking the cows that were about to calve: there were sixteen of them in a small meadow near the farm, and it looked as though a couple were close enough to warrant being brought in to the buildings.

'Going blackberrying?' he asked as he drew near and saw her basket.

'I thought I might as well. There must be pounds of fruit still.'

'All that rain we had,' mused Phil, taking the mug of coffee from her. 'I thought summer was never going to get here.'

Luckily, things had improved in line with the new weather pattern that seemed to be establishing itself: mild winters, cold, wet springs and a late summer that extended into what had used to be thought of as the beginning of autumn. Now, in early September, the sun gave a poignant beauty to the turning trees. It filtered gently through the loosening leaves, throwing a gentle, more understanding sort of light on the fields and lanes.

Jill sighed.

'Do you remember something I said back in the winter?' she asked. 'When we were talking about your retiring, but we hadn't discussed it with the children? I said how much I was looking foward to our last summer at Brookfield. How we could enjoy it, just the two of us.' She shook her head. 'If only I'd known.'

'We never can know, can we?' replied Phil rhetorically, eyeing a cow that was struggling to get up. 'If we did, we'd never start anything.'

'I know, but . . .'

'Come on, Jill,' he tried to rally her. 'Things aren't going too badly at the moment. Ruth's nearly halfway through her chemotherapy . . .'

Jill nodded. 'I'm getting quite used to her hair.'

'There's a load of birthdays to look forward to – Josh's, David's, your seventieth . . .'

'Thanks for reminding me!'

'Well, we've been through worse,' he said softly. 'We haven't lost Ruth.'

Jill knew that seeing David suffer had dredged up for Phil all the buried memories of Grace, just as Shula had relived the loss of Mark and Jill had felt again the sick terror she'd experienced when she'd thought they might lose Elizabeth as a baby.

'It'll be Elizabeth's heart operation next,' she reminded him.

'Yes, but we'll get through that too. And don't forget you're going to be a grandma again.'

Kenton had rung to say that his wife Mel was pregnant. The baby was due in the spring.

'We'll have to go and see them,' Phil continued.

'Oh, Phil, how can we!'

'I am still supposed to be retiring!' chided Phil. 'Of course we've had to put the inheritance business to one side over the summer, but it's got to be resolved eventually.'

'Do you think we really can sort something out?'

'Of course we can!' he assured her.

'What's made you so cheerful?' Taking his empty mug and stowing it in her basket, Jill smiled at his optimism.

Phil shrugged.

'Oh, I don't know. I feel the same every year after harvest. Seeing the stubbles cleaned, and the next lot of crops going in. It's endless, Jill. And it's satisfying.' He put his hand over hers on the warm metal of the gate. 'Come on, life's not so bad really, is it?'

'I suppose not.'

'It's been tough, I agree, but I guarantee that by this time next year we'll have something else to worry about.'

'Oh, now you really are cheering me up!'

Phil released her hand and moved to open the gate.

'Come on,' he said. 'I'll walk up the lane with you. I might even pick a few blackberries. Let's practise being retired.'

'Go on, then.'

She waited while he latched the gate.

'But I can tell you one thing,' he continued, taking her hand again. 'Whatever happens, even when we've gone, there'll always be Archers at Brookfield. And there'll always be Archers in Ambridge.'

Jill smiled and squeezed his hand. She knew just how important that was to him. Together they walked up the lane under the slanting rays of the sun.